BOOKS BY JAMES T. FARRELL

Novels

STUDS LONIGAN

A trilogy comprising "Young Lonigan," "The Young Manhood of Studs Lonigan," and "Judgment Day"

The Danny O'Neill Tetralogy:

A WORLD I NEVER MADE

NO STAR IS LOST

FATHER AND SON

MY DAYS OF ANGER

BERNARD CLARE

GAS-HOUSE MCGINTY

ELLEN ROGERS

Short Stories

THE SHORT STORIES OF JAMES T. FARRELL

Comprising "Calico Shoes and Other Stories," "Guillotine Party and Other Stories," and "Can All This Grandeur Perish and Other Stories"

WHEN BOYHOOD DREAMS COME TRUE

TO WHOM IT MAY CONCERN

$1,000 A WEEK

Criticism

A NOTE ON LITERARY CRITICISM

THE LEAGUE OF FRIGHTENED PHILISTINES

Novelette

TOMMY GALLAGHER'S CRUSADE

JAMES T. FARRELL

My
Days of Anger

WITH A NEW INTRODUCTION WRITTEN
BY THE AUTHOR FOR THIS EDITION

THE WORLD PUBLISHING COMPANY

CLEVELAND AND NEW YORK

Published by THE WORLD PUBLISHING COMPANY

2231 WEST 110TH STREET · CLEVELAND 2 · OHIO

By arrangement with The Vanguard Press, Inc.

World Reprint Edition

First Printing May 1947

FOR KEVIN—MY SON

"Nevertheless, I will let these pages stand—since I wish to record my days of anger."

The Intimate Journals of CHARLES BAUDELAIRE

"Ah star of evil! star of pain!
Highhearted youth comes not again.

Nor old heart's wisdom yet to know
The signs that mock me as I go."

JAMES JOYCE

Bahnhofstrasse, Zurich, 1918

Introduction

M*y Days of Anger* concludes the tetralogy dealing with the life history of the O'Neill and O'Flaherty families. This novel differs in method of presentation from its three predecessors, *A World I Never Made*, *No Star Is Lost*, and *Father and Son*. Here, the story is told with auctorial concentration on one central character, Danny O'Neill. This reveals one of the central motifs of my tetralogy. In telling the story of Danny O'Neill, I have tried to present the way in which the disposition of an American artist is forged.

When Danny O'Neill was last seen, in *Father and Son*, he was ready to wage his own war with his destiny. In *My Days of Anger*, the reader can discover how he arms himself for that war. Danny, as a young man with artistic ambitions, differs from many of his predecessors in fiction. When he is first met with at the age of seven, in 1911, he is not superior to others. He does not stand out as one with special gifts, on a special sensibility. The pattern of his life, of his contacts with his own generation, is similar to that of other boys of his *milieu*. However, there is a social abnormality in the circumstances of his life. He does not live with his parents and brothers and sisters. As a little stranger, who is afraid in a world that he never made, Danny is forced to have divided loyalties. He has, in reality, two homes: that of his parents, and that of his grandmother and uncle.

As he grows up, his life story becomes one of preparation. He is, however, being prepared without really being aware of what his future will be like. His disposition as an artist is forged in bewilderment and anxiety, in confusion and insecurity. But as he grows from boyhood to young manhood, he makes small decisions, resolves again and again to do things. These small decisions and resolutions suggest a tension within him, a tension which is symptomatic of his need for change, for escape from the circumstances of his life. He must learn how to depend on himself, and how to hew out the course that he will take in life. And here, in *My Days of Anger*, we see him making his final preparatory decisions.

From the little stranger who is afraid, Danny changes into the young man who wants, by struggle, to help make a different world. He is last seen in these pages as he leaves home to go to New York. His mood is one of determination. He asks no quarter. He looks forward to struggle. In this sense, *My Days of Anger* is an optimistic book. When the reader first meets Danny, he is a rather passive little boy; when last seen, Danny is no longer passive. His feelings are active and determined. This dialectics of his feelings is central in the story of how the disposition of Danny O'Neill as an artist has been forged. At the same time he rejects the values of his past, but he does not completely destroy his sense of identification with his own people. He feels that he is going forth to fight not only war but their war. His conception of art, of writing, is a militant one. From childhood on, he has not been spared from direct contact with the realities of life and death. He goes forth to meet and to deal with the realities of life and death, and to write about them. He emerges from an American background which is common rather than special; it is the background known to millions of Americans. Here, in short, I feel, is a detailed story of the American Way of Life. And I am happy to present it, as such, to that body of readers which makes up the public for the reprint editions of books.

JAMES T. FARRELL
New York City

SECTION ONE

1924-1925

Calm and blue, Lake George stretched to the mountains which humped their backs toward the sun. Al O'Flaherty chewed on a cigar as he leaned against the rail of the chugging excursion steamer. He stared at the mountains, wondering how high they were; he would have to look that fact up in an almanac when he returned to Chicago. He was lonely. He hadn't been able to find anyone on the boat worth conversing with. They were lowbrows. It was more gratifying to drink in the beauties of nature than to participate in petty converse with such people.

His vacation was over. He had rested and enjoyed himself at the camp on Lake Champlain. The people there had been refined, well-mannered, cultured. The swimming and fishing had been good, and he had enjoyed some long tramps in the woods. He had feared he wouldn't be able to afford this vacation, but he had managed it. Business was good—for the other fellow. The big factories were manufacturing a cheap and standardized brand of women's shoes, and he was losing sales as a result. His shoes were the class, but they were too expensive for a lot of pikers. The big factories could copy his styles and put out imitations of them. Cheapness, not style and quality, was the order of the day. And this was an election year. Election years affected business. He wondered whom he should vote for, Davis or Coolidge? He ought to vote Democratic, but perhaps it would be better to vote for Coolidge. Maybe the Republicans would bring better business.

Now he was going back to worries and troubles. Well, his head was still above water, but he didn't like the trend. Still, he would be able to keep comfortably afloat.

The boat passed an enchanting group of small islands. He saw low, rambling red houses and pavilions half visible through the tall trees. A few men and women in bathing suits were lolling on a pier. He waved, and a woman waved back. He smiled with gratification, thinking that this casual act of recognition truly warmed the cockles of a man's heart. Some day, when he was rich, he would own a place like that.

But, golly, the mountains were beautiful. Majestic cathedrals of nature created by the hand of God. Chef d'oeuvres of the Supreme Artist. If he knew enough Latin, he would be able to write letters to his friends describing this beautiful scene in the great dead language. His ignorance of Latin saddened him. If he had only had the chance to get a college education, he'd now be able to converse in Latin like a scholar.

A stranger joined him at the rail. Al talked to him, and soon they were engaged in an argument about the height of the mountains.

The excursion boat chugged on through the even blue waters, heading for the town of Lake George.

Chapter One

I

The long elevated train smashed along the center track, bound for the Loop.

Wedged in by fellow passengers, Danny O'Neill clung to a strap. In his free hand he read the Dred Scott Decision from an opened copy of Beard's *Readings in American Government and Politics*; his briefcase was standing between his legs. The train swerved, and he felt the body of a girl jolted against his back. He kept his eyes on his book. He was aware of a man maneuvering behind him in order to press his body against that of the girl. He flipped a page. Another lurch of the train almost catapulted him into the lap of a young cake-eater. It was a struggle to study on a crowded elevated train, but he had to utilize every possible minute of his time. Even though it was a strain on his eyes, he had to take the risk. His eye doctor had told him that he shouldn't study so much. But what could he do? He had no other alternative. Another jolt. The man was still pressing against the girl. Men and women yawned and coughed; they stood or sat, half asleep, a stoical patience expressed in their tired, bored, vacant faces. A few passengers tried to read morning newspapers. One man, turning the pages of *The Chicago Questioner*, jammed a sharp elbow into Danny's back.

"Something ought to be done about the traffic problem," a man complained loudly.

"Chicago needs a subway," someone else said.

His mind was lost in American history. In order to understand the politics of the present, you had to know American history. He was reading famous documents in American history

5

for the first time. The thrill of study walled him off from people whose stale breaths blew in his face.

The train curved onto the outer track and slowed down. Danny flipped a page. The train stopped at Roosevelt Road. Passengers shoved and elbowed their way out of the car, past Danny, jabbing him as they passed. He stopped reading. The train rolled on. His station was next. He couldn't finish this selection now. Disappointed, he closed the book and put it in his briefcase. He clutched his strap and stared, sleepy-eyed, out of the window.

Danny shoved his way out at Congress Street. A burly man stepped on his heels.

"Let 'em out," a woman cried shrilly.

"Take it easy! Easy, lady!"

He stepped out of the car. It was four minutes to eight by the station clock. He bounded down the station stairs and set out lickety-split along Wabash Avenue. He had to punch the clock on time. He swerved out of the road of people, using his hips and shifting the way he had learned to run when he was a high-school football player. He thrilled with pride and power because of the way he ran and wished someone who knew football were looking at him.

II

Sociology Notes

Tastes, ambitions, approvals, prejudices, hatreds and loyalties are transferred by sympathetic radiation and suggestion.

The minute hand on the clock in the Wagon Call Department was stretching from eleven to twelve o'clock. The noise and shouting rose to a deafening roar. Cigarette smoke fogged the rectangular room. The air was stale. The clerks hunched over the long table with the sunken keyboards, shouting into their telephones, taking one call after another. Gas-House McGinty sat in a corner, wearing a head phone. He barked orders and moved varicolored numbered pegs in and out of the little holes of his large black tractor board, which was mapped into squares by horizontal and vertical white lines. Route Inspectors drifted in and out of the office, quarreling, wise-cracking, shouting.

Danny had had two ham sandwiches and coffee for lunch. He sat at a small table next to Chief Dispatcher Willie Collins' end of the telephone table, absorbed in a textbook. He made notes as he studied.

Suggestion, the transference of ideas to others. It required little exercise of the reasoning faculties. It took the place of a real exchange of ideas. Was most of the talk in the office here suggestion? How much of it was sympathetic radiation? He puzzled, trying to grasp and make concrete the sentences he was studying.

Heinie Mueller got up from his place at the other end of the table and went to the pencil sharpener just behind Collins. He stood for a moment watching Danny. He squeezed past Collins' chair and glanced over Danny's shoulder.

Imitation! That was an important conception. There was imitation in the office here. If one fellow made a good wise-crack, then others would pick it up and use it. Imitation was a causal relationship between—

"*Introduction to Sociology?* What the hell is that?" Heinie asked.

Heinie's voice dragged Danny out of his intense concentration. He jerked back in his chair. He stared up at Heinie, his expression vacuous.

"What?" he asked.

"What does it all mean?" Heinie asked, pointing to the textbook.

"Sociology? It's the study of social phenomena."

"For Christ sake!" Heinie exclaimed.

"Heinie, what's she doing?" asked Needles Moylan, a Route Inspector, pointing at Danny.

"Studying—sociology. Know what that is?"

"No, and I don't give a damn what it is, either, unless it's something to drink."

"It's the study of social . . ." Heinie scratched his head quizzically. "Hell, I forget the rest of it. Anyway, it's the study of some kind of social jawbreaker."

"Let me alone. I got to study," Danny snapped.

"I wouldn't disturb you," Heinie said, going back to his place.

He bent over his book again. Why subject himself to this on his lunch hour? He could go out, eat in peace, and take a walk in the sun. But he needed this time for study. Imitation, a causal relationship . . .

At five minutes to twelve, Danny put his book and note-book in his briefcase. His eyes ached: strain. He'd have to take two more aspirin tablets in order to get through the afternoon. He faced five slow, boring, nerve-racking hours answering telephone calls.

Casey burst into the office.

"Hello, Clarence Darrow," he called to Danny.

"Calling him Darrow? Casey, that punk is so dumb he thinks he can get an education," Mike Mulroney sneered.

"Listen, brother, Bones O'Neill there is smart. I wish I knew what he does. Why, the day before yesterday I was workin' a crossword puzzle and I was stumped for a six-letter word for a Roman general. So I turns to him and I says: 'Bones, give me a six-letter word for a Roman general.' And goddamn it, quicker than I could let out a fart, he tells me, 'Caesar.' You can't convince me he ain't smart," Casey answered.

"Come here, O'Neill. I want to talk to you," Willie Collins said.

Danny moved over to Collins' chair.

"You know, I knew your old man. I always liked him, you know. I'm always glad to give a break to one of his kids. My boy, I'm glad to see you goin' to school, studyin', tryin' to make something out of yourself."

"Yes, Mr. Collins."

"Now, my boy, if you want to make the extra money, I'll fix it for you to work every Sunday on the wagon sheets. Do you want the extra dough?"

It meant a seven-day week, with night school. But he could get some studying done on Sundays. He needed the money.

"Why, sure, Mr. Collins. Thanks very much. I need the extra money for books and tuition."

"I thought you would. Well, you're all set for Sunday work."

"I'm very grateful."

"And one more thing. I got three bellyaches here, you know, from them goddamned lamp-shade people about service. Them bastards think that the only thing I have to do is to feed them gascars the minute they call for them. They wrote to the Old Man, and I got to answer his letter. Here it is. You check up on the back calls and sheets—you know, the time I got the calls from them bastards, the time I sent them cars, and you answer this squawk. You can dictate it to one of the girls in the front office. You know what to say. Use a lot of big words. I don't want the Old Man to think I'm a dumbbell like McGinty and them goddamned Route Inspectors. Use big words like you did when you answered that squawk from the Main Office for me last week."

"Do you want me to do it right away?" Danny asked, taking the letters.

"Yes, go to it, my boy."

This task would free him for a little while from the boredom of the telephones. Christ, how he hated the telephones!

III

She walked with grace and beauty and she was a hash-slinger. Sitting at the marble-top horseshoe-shaped counter of Marcel's Restaurant, his eyes followed her. She passed him and set a combination blue-plate supper before a crusty-look-ing fellow who was dressed like a racetrack tout. Tall, stately Elizabeth, she was one of the most beautiful girls he had ever

seen. She was modeled on the lines of a noble statue. Her
blonde hair was luxurious. Her blue eyes were so bright, so
merry, so sparkling. She wasn't cut out to be a waitress. What
bitter fate had forced her into this work? Didn't she feel resentful, sad?

The crusty-looking fellow leaned over the counter, covered
the right side of his mouth with a hairy hand, and told her a
joke in half whispers. She laughed spontaneously. Danny
frowned. The crusty-looking bum could ruin the life of a girl
like Elizabeth. Could she see anything in a man so crude and
coarse? He—he was prepared to adore her, to love her as a
tender flower. But he couldn't tell her dirty jokes to make her
laugh. If she only knew how sympathetic he was to her in her
plight.

Danny's heart beat faster as she approached him. What wonderful teeth she showed when she smiled. Was there any personal feeling in her smile, or was it merely professional?

"Ham sandwich, coffee, apple pie," he ordered, masking his
confusion in a matter-of-fact manner.

"You don't eat much," she said.

Her voice was refined; it was like music. How utterly happy
he would be to hear words of love addressed to him in her
gentle voice. If she loved him, he would look in her eyes as she
spoke and then he would kiss her.

"If I eat too much supper, I'll fall asleep at night school,"
he said flatly.

Did she admire him because of his ambition? Or did he bore
her, telling her how hard he worked?

"Yes," he went on monotonously, "I have a hard night
ahead of me. I got to study, pay attention to what goes on.
It's no use paying money to go to school and then falling
asleep there."

"I guess not," she answered without interest.

Elizabeth swung on her heels and went back to the cubby hole
connected with the kitchen. She gave the cook his order for a

sandwich. Most waitresses bawled out the orders. She never did. This proved he wasn't wrong in believing she possessed innate refinement. Given a chance in life, she would be a cultured lady.

"Say, Lizz, I heard a good one," the crusty-looking fellow shouted.

That monkey ought to be poked for assuming such a tone of familiarity and possessiveness with her. Calling her *Lizz!* She swept past Danny, leaned her elbow on the counter, and listened while the crusty fellow told her another joke.

Yes, the monkey must be telling her dirty jokes. He was disillusioned. Well, she would never know how he had dreamed her into loveliness. He had been a damned fool again. Now he must be very casual. He must act as if she couldn't possibly mean anything to him. He was confused. In order to do something that would mask his confusion, he took off his gold-rimmed glasses and cleaned them with meticulous care.

He took *Pickwick Papers* out of his briefcase. He could get in a few minutes' reading during supper time. She laughed again as the crusty-looking fellow talked to her. Would she notice him reading? It ought to impress her. He couldn't concentrate. He was posing for her, and she was an unappreciative audience. He was a damned fool. But she didn't know he was. She might be impressed by his seriousness. If she only knew how he felt toward her, how he dreamed of her standing by him during the tough years of struggle and then enjoying with him all of the fruits of wealth and success! A poor clerk and a poor waitress struggling together. He would lift her with him up each rung of the ladder. She would encourage him at each step.

"So you liked it Saturday night?" the crusty-looking fellow said in a leering voice.

"Oh, it was grand. It was simply grand."

She was just another hash-slinger with feet of clay. The hell with her! His sandwich was ready, and instead of serving him she gassed with a loud-mouth monkey. No, she wasn't the girl he wanted as the future Mrs. Danny O'Neill. She wasn't as interesting to know as was Dickens, one of the greatest writers who had ever lived. What characters Dickens created: Pickwick, who was like a gentleman in a silk hat forever falling on a banana peel, and Sam Weller, a true diamond in the rough. He laughed affectedly as he read. Would she notice his laugh?

"Just a minute," Elizabeth told the crusty-looking monkey.

He was aware of her sliding by him. In a moment she was back with his order. He looked up with simulated astonishment, as if he hadn't known that she had come with his order.

"You like to read?" she asked.

"Yes. I don't like to waste time, so I read while I eat."

"It sure takes a lot of different kind of people to make up the world, doesn't it? Some people like books and some people don't."

"Do you like books?" he asked.

"Don't make me laugh."

She turned from him and went to resume her conversation with the monkey.

Danny ate and read, smoldering with jealous resentment. She preferred that cheap clown to him. Let her! She'd see where it would land her soon enough. Beauty was skin deep, and golden girls grew old quickly. He didn't have any cheap racetrack, hotel-lobby *savoir faire*. Ergo, he wasn't the answer to the prayers of a waitress. Listen to her laugh at another bum joke. Well, he was traveling a different road from all such people. And he had no complaints. He had found out in time that he had been ready to make a sentimental ass out of himself over a good-looking rag, a bone, and a hank of hair. That was a lesson well learned.

"Can I have another coffee?" he ordered curtly.

If he didn't drink a couple of cups of coffee, he'd fall asleep in school. But he had to hurry now or he'd be late for classes at Saint Vincent's.

IV

Sixty freshmen students in pre-law school were crowded in the long, narrow room. Mr. Donovan, a gawky young man, faced the class.

"Speaking of Thomas Henry Huxley," Mr. Donovan said in a nasal voice, "reminds me of a story. One day in the classroom, Huxley went to the blackboard to illustrate a point in a lecture. As he drew the figure, he talked on. A student called out for him to stand aside so that the class could see what he was drawing. Huxley turned around and told his students: 'I can be clear, but it is impossible for me to be transparent.' "

Corcoran, the little insurance clerk who was always trying to shine up to the professor, laughed loudly. Only a few of the students enjoyed the joke.

"Now," Mr. Donovan went on with good humor, "I trust that none of you will fall asleep. But if any of you must doze, please do it as quietly as you can."

This joke was appreciated more, Corcoran leading the laughter.

"Mr. O'Neill, what do you think about the essays of Matthew Arnold and Thomas Henry Huxley on the idea of a liberal education?"

"Well," Danny answered, rising, "I don't think that there was a real dispute between them. They were both right."

"It seems to me that there was a clearly defined issue between them, Mr. O'Neill."

"Yes, that's what I think," Corcoran called out.

"I thought that Matthew Arnold didn't really mean to discredit science; he wanted to point out the value of classical literature, *belles lettres*." Danny mispronounced the French phrase. "Huxley, he thought that science was most important, but he didn't dismiss the classics completely. They seemed to me to agree on the fundamental issue, but to make different emphases."

Three students raised their hands.

"Mr. O'Mara, have you something to say?"

O'Mara, a nervously energetic student, rose. He talked in whirlwind fashion. Danny considered him the most brilliant student in class.

"Huxley's idea is that you should go to school and get a practical education so that you'll learn how not to get knocked down by an automobile when you cross the street. To him, education was mere practicality. He thought that all a student needed to learn was petty facts, and to prove them by the authority of verification. He was wrong. Unless we see life as a whole, science will merely teach us that little facts are correct. Huxley saw only the little spokes and parts of the whole. Matthew Arnold saw life as a whole. So did Cardinal Newman. Arnold and Newman were sound. They merely asked of science that it be humble, accept its place in the scheme of things. Of course, technical training is important. I'm a certified public accountant. I have received a necessary and valuable technical training. But will that be enough to make me a better citizen, a more interesting person in cultivated society? If I can only converse about public accounting in a meeting of good minds, won't I be a boor? Specialized training is not enough. We must gain a general culture, a total philosophy of life. That is why I agree with Newman and Arnold, and not with Huxley."

"You raise a good point, Mr. O'Mara. An educated man must have general culture, general ideas. He must, as Matthew Arnold said, know the best that has been thought and said in the world."

"Yes, Mr. Corcoran," Mr. Donovan said when Corcoran raised his hand.

"I was going to say, isn't that why we're all here, to become educated men?"

"I think so," Mr. Donovan answered curtly.

Farranaci jumped to his feet. He was an undersized shipping clerk who always wore a spotted, shiny, unpressed blue suit and a stringy black tie. Danny was unable to make up his mind whether Farranaci was a loud-mouth or a brilliant student. Many students looked at Farranaci with contempt and resentment.

"To Arnold and Newman an education was merely thinking about thinking. It wasn't even that, it was polite talking about thinking. Arnold said, for instance, that the critic need not apply his ideas. It was enough that he develop them on Mount Olympus. Such ideas are all right for anyone who wants to be a gentleman and doesn't have to take the world too seriously."

"Then you object to people being gentlemen, Mr. Farranaci?" Mr. Donovan asked.

"No, not if you can afford it and haven't anything better to do," Farranaci replied scornfully. "But in that case, why go to night school? You ought to go to a big university that's run like a country club. We haven't got the time to be gentlemen and to waste our time talking about thinking from the viewpoint of eternity. That isn't going to butter our bread. We have to gain knowledge so that we can do something for humanity."

"Now I think Mr. Pearn has something to say," Mr. Donovan announced.

"I'm not finished," Farranaci said.

"Are you ever finished?" boomed a voice from the back of the room.

It was Kilpatrick, a husky bully who had kept the Jews and Italians from being elected to any of the offices during class elections. Danny didn't like the dumb Irishman.

"If the essays you people are reading don't teach you manners, you might as well quit this class," Mr. Donovan declared sharply. "I'll tolerate no more ill-mannered interruptions in this discussion."

"I wasn't interrupting. I had the floor," Farranaci said. "To continue, Huxley makes scientific verification the real authority in education. What's wrong with that?" Farranaci rose to the pitch of an orator. "I ask—what's wrong with that?"

"Do you claim that science is superior to all authority?" Mr. Donovan questioned.

"If it is, then God has no authority," O'Mara called out.

"That's the point I was leading to," Mr. Donovan said.

"I wanted to make that point. I'm glad you raised it, Mr. Donovan," Corcoran interrupted.

"I don't know what God has got to do with this," Farranaci went on heatedly. "Does the authority of God make the world flat? Would we know that the earth is a globe if we didn't verify it? That's Huxley's point. He proposed a system of education that would teach us how to gain knowledge and mastery over nature. I agree that much with him, but no more."

"You find it difficult to agree fully with anyone, don't you, Mr. Farranaci?" Mr. Donovan asked.

"Huxley was too conservative," Farranaci continued, ignoring the teacher's sarcasm. "He feared the power of the masses. I reject his social conservatism."

"Now you are getting off the point. This is a class in English literature, not in politics," Mr. Donovan reproved.

"Doesn't Arnold write in praise of the politics of Edmund Burke? Wasn't Burke a reactionary politician who opposed the French Revolution? Then why can't we discuss what these men wrote?" Farranaci replied triumphantly.

"I pay money to learn something here, not to hear people talk because they like the sound of their own voices," Kilpatrick shouted.

"I pay my tuition, too. I'm talking because I have something to say," Farranaci snapped back.

"Well, we have heard your views, Mr. Farranaci, and now Mr. Pearn is anxious to get the floor," Mr. Donovan said, nodding to a bald-headed businessman who wore pince-nez glasses.

Mr. Pearn rose, adjusted his glasses, and cleared his throat. Danny thought him a man of brains and experience. He turned his eyes toward Mr. Pearn. The discussion had puzzled him. His mind had swayed back and forth from one view to the other. He hoped Mr. Pearn would help him to clarify his own mind. If he had anything to say, he'd join in the debate, but he had nothing to say because he didn't know his own mind.

"I'm a practical man," Mr. Pearn began. "This is a practical world. I've had much practical experience. So I ask what will Greek and Latin do to help me in practical affairs? The answer is nothing. We people here, we don't have the time for frills. We have to learn practical things. Education should be practical, teaching trades and practical science. I agree with Huxley that far. But let me add, let me make it unmistakably clear, that I don't agree with Huxley's agnosticism. He had no place for religion in his system. Religion is practical, and belongs in a curriculum along with trades and other useful knowledge."

"Why do we have to read Huxley? Isn't this a Catholic school?" Kilpatrick asked.

"Because he was a fine essayist, Mr. Kilpatrick," Mr. Donovan hastened to state. "And, after all, do you think that Huxley was powerful enough to destroy our religion, our faith in God?"

"But then it's wasting our time," Kilpatrick said.

"Some people waste their time no matter what they read," Farranaci called out bitterly.

"That's enough, Mr. Farranaci," Mr. Donovan said emphatically.

Farranaci shot a look of silent contempt at the teacher.

"Hey, O'Neill, the Wop always disturbs my sleep," whispered Hayes, the happy-go-lucky law clerk who sat in back of Danny.

Mr. Donovan gave O'Mara the floor with a nod.

"Matthew Arnold," O'Mara explained, "clearly stated that he was not opposed to practical training. But he pointed out that in the case of a necessary choice, classical training should be given preference. He was correct. As he wrote, nature does teach us something about her laws. She thrusts knowledge of herself upon us. But we can only learn the classics, philosophy, general ideas by serious and diligent application."

"That's fairly sound," Mr. Donovan commented unsurely.

"I just wanted to add to what Mr. O'Mara said by saying that this is an age of science, and we can't help but imbibe some science whether we study it or not, and that's all the more reason for seeing the value of Matthew Arnold's balanced suggestions," Corcoran cut in.

"But isn't science awfully dull?" asked Hilda Day, the only female in the class.

Danny thought she was too fat. And she was dumb.

"What do you mean, Miss Day?" asked Mr. Donovan.

"Oh, in high school, chemistry was always dull. You know, test tubes, bad smells—that isn't interesting, is it?"

"I wouldn't say that, Miss Day. It's not dull for some people. But I think that we've had enough discussion for this session." Mr. Donovan ignored Farranaci's nervous, waving hand. "Matthew Arnold wrote that for some men, for instance, Darwin, science was an all-embracing interest. He didn't criticize or object to men of this temperament. He admitted that they added to the store of human knowledge. But he did demonstrate that science alone does not minister to what is most important in human nature. He pointed out that men have various needs, needs that are derived from our sense of beauty and our sense of conduct. We can't administer to the human sense of beauty merely by classifying skulls and bones, by naming prehistoric animals or by listing the chemical elements. Similarly, we can't administer to the sense of beauty if we merely learn all that there is to be learned of Law. For you people, the words of Arnold and Cardinal Newman should be pondered deeply. Especially Cardinal Newman, who was the greatest mind of nineteenth-century England. . . ."

Danny listened attentively, struggling to make up his mind. Suppose that Arnold and Newman were right? How could he get the kind of education they proposed? Would he have the time and the money? He didn't want to be narrow, just a lawyer. All he could do was wonder, ponder, try to learn as much as he could, reach out at every kind of knowledge that could be assimilated. He wanted to achieve Huxley's program, and also Arnold's. He wanted everything, every kind of education. And look at what he was getting—one year of catch-as-catch-can pre-legal work, and then the long, plodding study of law. He despaired of ever becoming truly educated.

Mr. Donovan went on lecturing. Most members of the class were bored.

Margaret O'Flaherty sat at the cashier's desk in a corner of the crowded, noisy, glittering Crystal Room of the Shrifton Hotel. She had a splitting headache. Her eyes ached. Waiters swarmed around her, babbling, yelling, complaining about the change she gave them and demanding that she take care of their checks more speedily. All evening the waiters had been nasty to her; she had quarreled with one after another. They were mean, uneducated and ungrateful men, foreigners. Her nerves were like pricking needles.

In rare moments of respite she looked out at the scene of gaiety. She was almost thirty-nine. Her life was over. Here she was slaving, watching others enjoy themselves. The beautiful young girls in their lovely dresses were so fresh, so pretty; she had once been young and stunning. She hugged memories of the past, recalling many scenes like this one. Remembering Lorry Robinson, she cried. She told a waiter that she had strained her eyes. Yes, she had known more than one gay New Year's Eve. But now her life was over. She would grow old, slaving like this, quarreling with mean and ungrateful waiters —she, Margaret O'Flaherty, who deserved so much from life and who had gotten so little.

Oh, God! She could scream! She could run to one of the windows, jump out, and end it all.

The noise, the terrible din and racket, would drive her crazy. Drunken men in swallow tails blowing horns, ringing bells, beating toy drums like little children. Girls getting disgustingly drunk. Near her, a man in formal clothes vomited on a clean white tablecloth. A lovely girl passed out cold. And the music brayed until she thought she would go out of her head. The sight was enough to make her vow she would never touch another drop of liquor as long as she lived.

Happy New Year! Happy New Year! What happiness could she expect in 1925?

Marty Mulligan and Mike Flood staggered past her. They didn't recognize her as Danny O'Neill's aunt.

"Mike, this is costing me fifty bucks, but it's worth it. Everybody in town is here. I just had a drink with two judges and three aldermen in the crapper."

What fools people were!

Happy New Year!

Chapter Two

I

"Little Brother, I'm so proud of you. Last night when I saw all these people drinking and dancing at the Crystal Room, I thought of you. There wasn't one young man who could hold a candle to you, and they were all rich—my goodness, the sons of judges and lawyers and all kinds of successful people," Aunt Margaret told Danny at the supper table.

"I don't understand people who want to go out on New Year's Eve and blow all their money getting drunk and yelling like wild Indians. And they call that a good time. Cripes, the damned fools," Uncle Ned said, fingering his coffee cup.

"Ah, I'd fix them, I'd tan them if they were mine—that I would," Mrs. O'Flaherty said.

"Well, we had a lovely holiday season. Let's give thanks to the Lord for that," Ned said.

Margaret glanced aside, sad.

Danny yawned. He was tired, but he didn't want to stay in. He hadn't had one day off now in over a month, not even Christmas or today. He wanted to do something. What was there to do? He couldn't get a date. He didn't feel like seeing a movie or hanging around the poolroom, hearing the boys tell each other how drunk they'd been last night.

"It looks like this will be a fine, happy year," Uncle Al said.

"I hope so," Ned said.

"Ah, when you get to be my age, sure, and what is the New Year?" Mrs. O'Flaherty asked in a deep melancholy.

"Last night when I saw all these people drinking, I won-

22

dered what is life? What is a New Year, after all, but just another year, the same as the last one?"

"Don't be blue, Peg."

"I'm not blue, Al. I was just philosophical. Isn't that the word to use, Little Brother?"

"Yes, I guess so," Danny answered, absorbed in his own thoughts.

"Where's your sister?" Ned asked Danny.

"She went over to Mama's for supper."

"She's sulking. She wanted to go out last night and Al wouldn't let her," Ned said.

"She'll have time enough for that," Mrs. O'Flaherty commented.

"Oh, it was just a harmless party, Al. I would have let her go. Poor kid, let her have her fun when she has a chance," Margaret said.

"There's all kinds of fun in the world, but I can't see what fun there is in all this hell-raising," Ned said.

Danny was depressed. Perhaps it was merely because of his fatigue. He didn't know, but he kept imagining that something like an insidious and paralyzing sorrow was floating through the very room. Theirs was a sad home. And now another year was starting. Would Mother live through this year? What would happen to them all? How could they face her death? Couldn't she just live until he became a success? He could drive her to church in his car. Perhaps he would even have a chauffeur in uniform to take her wherever she wanted to go. Why should he feel sad? Why should he feel that death was coming here? He felt in the dumps because he was so tired. That was all there was to it. He ought to go out and relax, rest his mind.

"Dan, throw out good wishes that things will be better this year. And then maybe I can afford to send you to Notre Dame or the University of Chicago," Uncle Al said.

If that were only possible! An idle dream. He finished his coffee, folded his napkin, and got up.

"Where you going, Dan?"

"Oh, I thought I'd go out. Maybe I'll see a movie."

"Why don't you stay in and we'll have a nice quiet talk," Uncle Al said.

"I want to get some air. I never get any air any more."

"I tell you, he's working too hard. When you work like that, and him just a boy, too, you can go into the consumption," Mrs. O'Flaherty said.

Danny was utterly frightened. Must he ruin his health in order to satisfy his ambitions? He tried to shake off this fear.

"Son, don't you dare be out late," Mrs. O'Flaherty ordered.

Danny put on his coat and left. Outside, he stood for a moment on South Park Avenue, breathing deeply. A fine night, not too cold. He looked at the sky yearningly.

He was proud of himself. He'd gone to bed early on New Year's Eve while others were out raising hell. He'd worked today, earning extra money. And at work he'd been able to study. He'd studied every night of the Christmas vacation and was all caught up in his school work. He'd get good marks this first semester. He had a real right to feel proud of himself.

He wandered over to Fifty-eighth Street, running into Dick Buckford, Ralph Borax, and Fat Landsdale. They invited him to go along with them in Fat's car on a parlor date at Natalie O'Reedy's. What luck! Here was something to do. And Roslyn Hayes was going to be there.

II

This was a happy home! He was certain it was. The O'Reedys owned their home, and the furniture was all new and attractive, not like the old sticks they had at home. Old man O'Reedy was an undertaker. The undertaking business ought always to be good—somebody died every minute. It always made him sad and envious to come to a happy home. Roslyn Hayes hadn't even greeted him when they'd all arrived. He wasn't sure about her looks. From some angles he thought she was pretty, and then again her face would seem to be too thin, too angular. She was tall and slender now, with a nice figure. Natalie was as beautiful as ever, but he'd never realized before how small she was; she was almost tiny. Dark eyes, black curly hair. Still, Natalie didn't really interest him. His feeling for her back in the fourth year at high school hadn't been love; it had been infatuation. Roslyn's kid sister, Harriet. She must be seventeen, and she was blonde like her sister. Terribly good-looking. Plump and buttery, just beginning to bloom. She was so lovely.

Once their cousin, Glenn, had given a party. None of the girls would have him as a partner. They'd given him Harriet. He had been ashamed. Now look at her. Who wouldn't want to date her?

But was the girl sitting opposite him in a black dress the same Roslyn Hayes who used to walk to school on Sixty-first Street wearing a green sweater, the girl he had kissed in post office at parties? Was he the same Danny O'Neill who used to wake up every morning with her name on his lips like a prayer? He was and he wasn't; she was and she wasn't. Would she care about him now? Her family was rich. They owned a Lincoln. She went away to an expensive convent school. He was a poor clerk, working his way through night school. She hadn't even said hello when he'd arrived. All the way out here in Fat Landsdale's car he'd thought of her nostalgically, trying to recapture his old feeling for her, wanting to love her now with all the feeling he had poured into the very thought of her when he was a boy. How he had been hoping that he'd dance with her, win her admiration and love. She wasn't even looking at him.

Her sister was damned pretty.

Was Roslyn silently observing him, criticizing him? Was her indifference real or feigned?

The others were talking, and here he was mooning, stewing away like a dope. Why didn't someone start dancing? The carpet had been rolled up. Why didn't he start the ball rolling? He waited, concealing his inner anxiety.

"Doesn't it seem like it was only yesterday when we were all in grammar school together? Remember the parties we had, and how we'd go to movies on Sunday afternoons and the nuns didn't like that?" Natalie reminisced.

The wound of an old insult rankled. He'd never been invited to go to the movies with the bunch on Sunday. Did the girls remember that now?

"It's not so awfully long ago," Danny said, facing Roslyn. She avoided his gaze.

"I heard you're going to school, Danny," Natalie said.

"Yes, I'm going to night school," he said defensively, burning with shame inwardly. "I stayed home every night during Christmas week studying."

Would that win Roslyn's admiration? Saying he went to night school meant telling them that he was too poor to go to college in the daytime.

"Next year I'm going to the University of Chicago."

Another of his wild, impossible dreams.

When would they start dancing?

"I go back to school in Dubuque this week. There's no comparison between going to school at home and going away to school. And I'm doing a lot of writing for the school paper," Landsdale said boastfully.

"I like going away to school better. It's so much fun when you come home, especially around Christmas time," Roslyn said.

Yes, she had dates, a good time. And he had to study all through Christmas week.

"I had a swell time this vacation," Landsdale said.

Landsdale wanted to write. And Fat was getting a chance to on his school paper. Would he ever really be able to write, to have something published with his name signed to it? Would he ever be good enough to write books that Roslyn Hayes would read? He didn't dare admit in public that he nursed this ambition. Was this still another of his impossible dreams?

"Oh, say, Natalie, I saw Ellen Rogers at the Drake last night.

Remember, she was in your class. She was smoking, too, in public. No girl with any pride or self-respect would do that. And she a Saint Paul girl. I was ashamed," Roslyn said.

"I don't see anything wrong with a girl smoking. It isn't a sin," Danny said, hoping to talk with Roslyn by provoking her into a discussion.

She ignored him.

"Oh, let's dance. Why mope around," Ralph Borax said, going to the electric victrola to put on a dance record.

"Would you like to dance?" Danny asked Harriet.

She was a fine dancer. The size of the parlor cramped his style, but he could twirl her around and prove to her sister that he was a good dancer. He led Harriet to the small hallway off the parlor and whirled her around until she was almost dizzy.

"You're a good dancer."

"So are you," she said with a shy smile.

To feel this body so close to his, to have it in his arms, this beautiful and mysterious body of a girl of seventeen! He wanted to hug her, kiss her, pet her. The words of the song, *My Wonderful One*, ran through his head.

"You go to Saint Paul's now?"

"Yes, I do."

"Well, me, I quituated from Saint Stanislaus," he said flippantly, dancing her back into the parlor.

She laughed. He glanced at Roslyn out of the corner of his eye. Dancing with Fat Landsdale, she wasn't even looking at him.

He led Harriet back into the hallway.

"Yes, I like the way you dance," he said.

She giggled.

"Did you make any New Year's resolutions?"

She giggled.

"Don't tell me that you think New Year's resolutions are a joke," he said, his voice going flat. "Me, now, I make them wholesale. The more I make, the more I have to break. That's arithmetic. I add to my fun in life."

"I want to keep mine."

"What was it?"

"If I told you, you'd think I was silly."

"Nothing could be silly about a girl as pretty as you."

She giggled.

"Tell me your New Year's resolution," he coaxed, smiling broadly.

"Well, I've been saying my prayers in bed at night because the floor is so cold. I thought I ought to kneel down, even if it's cold, so I made a resolution to say my prayers on my knees before I get into bed at night. Now you'll think that's silly, won't you?" she said, blushing.

"Not at all. That's sweet."

"We'd better not dance so much in the hallway," she said, embarrassed.

"Why?" Danny asked.

"My sister might notice."

"What if she does?"

"Oh, she's my older sister, and she might notice."

Did Harriet have any idea about Roslyn and him? She must.

"Is your sister your keeper?" he asked.

"Why, no, but . . ."

He spun her around dizzily. He lowered his cheek to allow her hair to brush it.

Roslyn Hayes belonged to the past.

"Eats! Eats!" Fat Landsdale called.

They crowded out to the dining room, where the table was spread with cakes and sandwiches. Danny sat next to Harriet.

III

Lorry Robinson strolled along Flagler Avenue, bored. He was plump from good food and easy living, and he had just been barbered and manicured. His fine Panama hat was set back on his head, exposing his graying temples. He wore a white palm-beach suit, a white silk shirt, and a black knit tie with a diamond pin flashing from it. He had intended to go to the races this afternoon, but the barber and manicure girl had taken too long, and he just hadn't gone. The enervating Florida climate and his idle life were gradually robbing him of all power to make decisions. He was drifting through the last good days of his life, rudderless. What could he do with himself? He was retired, living on a good income. He had no taste for any business other than the lumber industry. And he was out of that. And what was income, money, without power?

He strolled along, bored.

Bigger fellows than himself had squeezed him out. He'd been lucky to have escaped with money. Men he knew, some of them fellows whom he once could have bought and sold, were now men of power in this country. He had once dreamed of being such a man. And here he was, a retired gentleman of leisure. His children patronizingly called him Governor and cared as little for him as he did for them. The less he thought of his wife, the better. The final good days of his life were being burned out by Miami sunshine.

Brophy, the Chicago lumber man, had licked him. After he had testified against Brophy before a Senatorial Committee in the Graham scandal, Brophy had fought him relentlessly. And

29

Brophy had won. There was no use in crying over milk that had been spilled so long ago.

He walked on, Lorry Robinson, the man who might have been the lumber king of America. A girl ahead of him brought back memories of Peg O'Flaherty when Peg had been young. Poor Peg! What had happened to her? He'd had to drop her. She should have married some decent fellow. But she had been a fine girl once. Old lecheries stirred in him. He quickened his pace in pursuit of the girl who reminded him of Peg. He lost her in the traffic.

He went to a branch office of a New York brokerage house and sat like other bored men, reading the tape which told the story of the day on Wall Street. He wondered what he would do to pass the evening.

Chapter Three

I

His heart palpitated from fright. Tense, anxious, he sat up and waited for Dr. O'Donnell to talk. He had had pains in the abdomen at work today and had felt nauseated. Around three o'clock he had almost fallen asleep over the telephone.

"It's your appendix, Dan," Dr. O'Donnell said, licking his lips and playing with his mustache. Danny felt himself growing weak. He might faint. Was he a coward? "Don't worry, don't worry," the doctor said. He revived Danny with smelling salts.

"Will . . . will I have to have an operation?"

"Relax, Dan. Don't worry."

He was limp, exhausted.

"I don't know yet, but I don't think we'll have to operate. I don't think so. Perhaps an operation can be averted."

"What can I do—not to have to have an operation?"

"Well, that's what I'm going to tell you. You'll have to take it easy, Dan. Now I want you to apply ice packs on your abdomen in the region of the appendix."

Dr. O'Donnell placed his hand on the region of Danny's abdomen he meant.

"And then you will have to go on a soft diet. No meats. Eat vegetables, but no meats. And nothing like peanuts. You have to go on a soft diet so you'll have no gastric upsets. You must do nothing to cause trouble with your inflamed appendix. You try this, get plenty of rest, don't strain yourself, and we'll see how things turn out. I'm inclined to think that we can avoid an operation."

"I hope so, Doctor."

Danny dressed. Dr. O'Donnell wrote out the diet he wanted Danny to follow, listed other directions, and handed him the note.

"I think you'll be all right, Dan."

"Thank you, Doctor."

"How's the knee?"

"I haven't had any trouble with it since last fall," Danny said, reassured now.

"Those semi-lunar cartilages are a nasty business. If they get worse and your knee starts locking on you, we'll have to get it out. But if it doesn't lock, then there's no cause for worry. Your knee doesn't lock on you, does it?"

"What's that?"

"Catch up, stiffen on you."

"I can walk and dance. I only have trouble if I strain it with a sudden wrench to either side," Danny said, dressing.

"Well, that's all right.

"I'm going to college next year, though."

"That's good if you can afford it. But I'd be wary of going to the University. It's not on our side of the fence, Dan."

Danny didn't answer. His only chance of going to a first-class college was to get to the U. of C. He'd never be able to afford Notre Dame.

"If I go to college, do you think I can go out for athletics?"

"I can't say. I'm afraid your knee will give you trouble. If you want to play football or basketball again, the cartilage might have to come out. If that is done, of course there is a small chance of your getting a stiff knee, but the percentages favor one in such operations.

"I'd like to play more football."

"You kids are all alike," the doctor said genially.

Danny finished dressing.

"Dan, you're working too hard. You'd better take it a little easy. If you don't, you might have a nervous breakdown."

But what other alternative had he?

"Yes, you better take it easy. You're run down. Working

too hard. There's no color in your cheeks. Dan, it won't do you any good to get ahead in this world if you ruin your health doing it."

Danny nodded.

"Otherwise are you behaving yourself, Dan?"

Danny shook his head affirmatively. He blushed.

"Good, I'm glad to hear it. Always remember, Dan, you can't fool with your body. You can't take chances. A lad your age meets with temptations, but you have to become the master of yourself."

Yes, he had learned that in his short time at school. In order to study conscientiously, he had to sacrifice other inclinations and pleasures. He had to be the master of himself—master of all his desires.

"You follow the instructions I've written out for you, rest a lot, and I think this will clear up."

"Yes, Doctor, I will. And thank you."

"If you have any trouble, call me. Come back and see me in about two weeks, in any case."

There was a chance that he wouldn't have to be operated on. But if he did? Would he tell intimate embarrassing secrets under the ether? Would he never come out of it?

"And, Doctor, you think I mightn't have to have an operation?"

"I don't think it'll be necessary—if you follow my instructions."

"I will, and thank you. . . . And, Doctor, what is the bill?"

"Two dollars."

Danny handed him the money.

"Remember me to the folks, Dan."

"Yes, and thank you, Doctor," Danny answered, putting on his coat.

Riding home in a cab, he felt his ambition was hopeless. Besides the trouble he had with his eyes, must he also endanger his health? He ought to be proud of himself for having worked so hard that he had put his health in jeopardy. If he wrecked his health and wore out his eyes, he would do it because of a worthy aim. But, no, his dreams were vain. Hopeless Danny O'Neill!

II

The piercing ring of the doorbell jarred Danny out of a troubled, restless sleep. He lay disorientated in the darkened front bedroom, feeling the agony of the dreams that had already been blotted out of his mind. He heard his grandmother answering the door just outside the room.

Drunken voices. He guessed that it must be one of Aunt Peg's girl friends, Dora Hilton or Cynthia Gray. Sometimes they came around late at night, stewed to the gills.

"Grandmother O'Flaherty, we were dancing at the Bourbon Palace, and we found out that we both knew you."

He recognized Tommy Doyle's voice, but who was the girl? They both were telling Mother that she was a wonderful woman.

"Yes, Grandmother O'Flaherty, we were at the Bourbon Palace . . ." Tommy repeated.

"Sure, and what place is that?" he heard his grandmother asking Tommy.

"Yes, we were dancing at the Bourbon Palace, and I met Anna Hamilton, and so we came right up here to see you, Grandmother O'Flaherty," Tommy said in a thick voice.

Anna Hamilton! A plump, sweet little blonde girl who had played with Little Margaret years ago around Fifty-first and Prairie. And then at Fifty-seventh and Indiana Aunt Margaret had brought the Hamiltons to live with them and they'd stayed the whole summer. The apartment had been overcrowded and Mother had always been on the warpath about the strangers in her son's house.

"My, but didn't you become the pretty thing!" Mother said to her.

Anna's mother was a big, wild, divorced blonde. She and Aunt Peg used to go out with men on dates.

"Mrs. O'Flaherty, you haven't changed a bit," Anna Hamilton said drunkenly.

In the summer of 1916, Johnny O'Brien had asked her to screw him in front of a bunch of them in the bushes behind the Washington Park tennis courts. She'd said no. She was outside his door now, drunk with Tommy Doyle.

It must be after twelve. He had reached the age of twenty-one.

"Sure, and the two of you sit in the parlor and wait until me daughter gets home from the hotel."

"Where's Danny?" Anna asked.

"And where would you expect him to be? He's asleep. He's a decent boy, not the likes of some that I know."

"I'm not asleep," Danny called out.

"Hello, Dan," Tommy called to him.

He heard Mother going out to her room in the back. Tommy and Anna whispered in the parlor. Why didn't they come in and talk to him?

Anna came in. She looked filled out. She wore a red dress. He couldn't make out her face clearly in the darkness.

"Hello, Danny."

"Hello, Anna, you came to see me on my twenty-first birthday," he said.

"That calls for congratulations."

She bent down and kissed him. She ran her hands through his hair. She gave him a long French kiss.

"Isn't that a nice present?" she asked coquettishly.

"Kiss me again!" Danny said.

She bent down and opened her mouth to his. Her hand slid under the covers.

He jumped out of bed and embraced her awkwardly. She was soft, obedient in his arms.

"Come on," he said huskily.

"I got to ask him," she answered, slipping out of his arms and leaving the room.

Danny waited, gasping for breath.

"He says it's all right," Anna said, returning, and sliding into his arms.

"We got to hurry," he said.

"Kiss me, darling."

"We got to be careful because of my grandmother. We don't want her to catch us," he said huskily.

He fumbled at her clothes.

"But we can't do it standing up, darling," she said, smothering his lips with her own.

III

The front door closed. He heard their drunken voices in the hallway. He ran to the bathroom. She might have given him a disease. He used iodine. He hurried back to bed. The iodine burned him.

He was no longer a virgin.

He was ashamed of himself. She might tell Tommy Doyle how dumb and innocent he'd been. Then Tommy might spread the story all over Fifty-eighth Street. Whenever he passed the poolroom, someone might ask him if he knew what it's for, and then everyone would laugh at him. He'd been so dumb that he'd wanted to do it standing up.

It was done.

He wanted to undo his act with Anna. He wished he could erase it from his life. But he had crossed the Rubicon of sex on his twenty-first birthday.

For years it had been on his mind. It had filled his thoughts. Time after time, hadn't he gone to confession and told the priest how he had sinned by thoughts of desire? Now he had sinned by action. And after the worry, the agony, the yearning —was that all that it was? So clumsy! So ugly!

He'd sinned just when he most needed the grace of God.

Oh, my God, I am heartily sorry . . .

He struggled with himself to make his *Act of Contrition* good. To wash this sin from his mind, he had really to be sorry.

His mind wandered. Anna. He wanted her back for more. No, he didn't. He didn't!

He said the *Act of Contrition* automatically.

The iodine still burned him.

He had broken the ice. The future opened up to him as a vista of girls and girls. If he had had one, he could have many others.

God might punish him for his sin. Suppose he had to be operated on? God might take his life. He was in the palm of God's hand. Were God to strike him dead this minute, he would be doomed beyond hope. He had committed the one sin which was blackest in the eyes of God. And he had then lain here and hoped he could commit it again, many times.

He wanted to feel real contrition. The image of Anna drove it from his mind.

The window curtain flapped. He lay in bed, with fear of the wrath of Almighty God robbing him of sleep.

"Hello, Mrs. O'Flaherty. Hello, how are you today? Isn't it a fine day," said Mr. Herschfield, the grocer.

"Good day, good day to yourself."

"Your sister was in here just a few minutes ago."

"Glory be to God, and who's that?"

"Why, Mrs. O'Neill!"

"Ah, she's me daughter."

"Now, who would have thought that? Mrs. O'Flaherty, how do you keep so young?"

"I'm eighty-four years old. Have you any nice carrots for me son and me grandson?"

"Yes, I've got some baby carrots, Mrs. O'Flaherty."

"So you have, give me a peck of potatoes."

She nosed around the store while Mr. Herschfield weighed the potatoes and then she came back to the counter.

"How is your wife?" she asked.

"She's fine, very well indeed, thank you, Mrs. O'Flaherty."

"Do you have lettuce?" she asked.

"Yes, here, come and pick a head out yourself, Mrs. O'Flaherty."

"I don't want it. Give me a loaf of bread."

He put the bread on the counter.

"So, Mrs. O'Neill is your daughter? I never thought it."

"How in the name of God did you lose your hair, a fine man the likes of you. Ah, and why don't you wear a wig? Give me a half a dozen eggs."

"Yes, Mrs. O'Flaherty. The best eggs?"

"And what else is fit for me son and me grandson?"

"Your son is a fine man, a fine man."

"And don't I know it?"

"Don't you want some of our new baby carrots, Mrs. O'Flaherty?"

"Who in the name of the Lord talked about carrots? Give me a bar of Ivory soap."

Chapter Four

I

Marty Mulligan had a good job pumping gas for Nation Oil. Marty had told him that if you wanted to land with one of the oil companies, you had to talk big. Tell them how good you were.

Five other applicants sat with him on the benches in the bare anteroom on the first floor of the Upton Oil and Refining Company office, waiting to be interviewed. He'd already waited about a half hour. But his turn was next.

Suppose he landed a job? How did he know that he could hold it? He had security at the express company. Patsy McLaughlin wouldn't fire one of Jim O'Neill's sons. Here he might fail, and then where would he be?

He had to think success, not failure. He had to go on.

The white-haired chap opposite him was fidgety. The others were placid. Did they feel as he did? When you looked for a job, you were ashamed. You were nothing, dirt, and you had to come asking for something. If you amounted to anything, you didn't have to go hunting work with your hat in your hand. Well, he was somebody, a clerk in the Wagon Call Department, Continental Express Company; somebody who was nobody. If you amounted to anything, you had drag, an old man, friends, uncles, someone to get you in on pull.

He couldn't go on at the express company. He'd stewed for two weeks before making up his mind to try. But he had tried now. The other oil companies had cold-shouldered him. Nothing doing. He knew that they needed attendants for the spring and summer business. He'd failed. This was his last hope.

Think success, not failure, he advised himself.

40

"Mr. O'Neill," the office boy called.

Danny rose. Anxiously he followed the office boy into the presence of Mr. David Gallagher, Supervisor of Service Stations for the Upton Oil and Refining Company.

Mr. Gallagher, a tall, well-built, youthful man, sat at a littered desk, speaking on the telephone.

"What did you say his name was?" Mr. Gallagher asked.

Danny stood. How could he sell himself to this man? He had come here in vain.

Danny tried to size up Mr. Gallagher.

"Yes? Well, send him around. We're always looking for a good man," Mr. Gallagher said; then he hung up.

Mr. Gallagher glanced at Danny. He seemed like a frank, decent, regular fellow.

"Well, here I am," Danny said boldly.

Mr. Gallagher popped with surprise.

Danny was astounded by his own words. They had come without any exercise of will.

"Yes, here I am," Danny repeated in a self-assured manner.

"What do you mean?"

"You just said you were looking for a good man. Well, here I am."

"That's interesting news. Would you mind sitting down?"

Danny took a chair facing Mr. Gallagher. Now that he'd started talking big, he had to carry through.

"What's your name?"

"O'Neill, Daniel O'Neill."

"What's on your mind, Mr. O'Neill?"

"My ultimate plan is to be a lawyer, a corporation lawyer, working in the Legal Department of the Upton Oil and Refining Company."

"But this is the Service Station Department."

"I know. You see, I want to work my way up from the bottom. I want to work my way through school."

"If you do that, how can you work for me?"

"I've thought a lot about this and about my plans." Danny

continued to be amazed by his own words. But sensing that he was making a good impression, his self-confidence mounted. "While I'm working my way through college, I want to kill two birds with one stone. I want to locate now with the concern that I hope to stick with. Then, while I'm getting my education, I'll also be getting practical experience in all phases of the business to which I want to devote my life." Danny paused briefly. "That way I'll be putting theory and practice together. I'll be using my time advantageously while I'm going to college to get my formal education."

"You make sense, all right," Mr. Gallagher commented with interest.

"Yes, what I did was to consider the possibilities before me. I asked myself, 'What company would I like to be connected with?' I decided I wanted to get in the oil business because it's a coming industry. There's a future in it. And that's why I'm here now, applying for work."

"Are you in school now?"

"I'm registered at the University of Chicago. My credits have been accepted, and I'll be admitted there next fall without having to take any entrance examinations."

"How old are you?"

"Twenty-one."

"You don't look it."

"But I am. I can prove it. I've been out of high school almost two years."

"What have you been doing since you graduated from high school?"

"I've been working in the Wagon Call Department of the Continental Express Company. I'm still working there."

"Why do you want to change jobs?"

"Mr. Gallagher, I don't want to sound presumptuous."

"Go ahead—I'm interested."

"As I said, I don't want to sound presumptuous, but I want to make a future for myself. There's no future in the express company. There is one with the Upton Oil and Refining Company."

"How do you know there isn't at Continental?"

"I've worked there now for almost two years. The very way the company is organized militates against a young man having a future in the express business. The company organization is —it's stratified." He hoped that the word *stratified* would impress Mr. Gallagher. Now he realized he had to keep on talking fast. "Yes, if I may say so, I've thought a great deal about my plans and my problems. I know what I want to do, and I believe in myself."

"Perhaps you're right," Mr. Gallagher said in a noncommittal tone.

Danny wondered if he were overshooting the mark.

"You say you have a high-school education?"

"Yes, and I've also done a half year's pre-legal work at night school, at Saint Vincent's. My general average for this work at Saint Vincent's was 92. I'm going on with pre-legal work at the University of Chicago."

"Are you still going to night school?"

"I quit."

"Why?"

"At Saint Vincent's, the pre-legal course in night school is not thorough enough. You only have to take one year of pre-legal work. Then you go into law. At the University of Chicago, you have to take three years of pre-legal work before going into the law school. It's harder this way, but then it's more thorough. I'm willing to take the harder course, if I can get a more solid foundation."

Mr. Gallagher leaned forward, riveting an expressionless face on Danny.

"And all that I ask is a chance. If you give me the chance, I know I'll make good."

"How do you know?"

"I have confidence. I think I'm the kind of man you want."

"Can you sell oil?"

"Yes. Yes, sir."

"Have you ever sold?"

"No, sir."

"Then how do you know you can sell?"

"Give me the chance and I'll prove it."

Mr. Gallagher glanced down at some papers on his desk. If this man only knew what this job meant. There he was, calmly fingering papers, and he held a destiny, a future in the palm of his hand. These seconds were endless.

Mr. Gallagher pulled out more papers.

"Mr. O'Neill, here's our application form. I'd like you to go home and fill it out. And here's an application from the bonding company. We pay the costs of bonding you—that is, if I decide to employ you."

Danny took the applications from Mr. Gallagher. He smiled. Mr. Gallagher returned the smile. Danny liked this man. His confidence grew stronger. Now his dreams of the University might be realized.

"I'm glad to have met you, Mr. O'Neill," Mr. Gallagher said cursorily.

He rose and shook Danny's hand firmly. Then he pushed a button. An office boy appeared.

"Send in the next man," Mr. Gallagher said, sitting down.

"Good-by," Danny said, now wanting to get out of the office, lest he reveal his anxiety.

"So long, O'Neill."

II

"Well, well, well, look who's payin' us a visit," Heinie Mueller said.

Smiling, Danny looked around the office. Collins wasn't at his place.

"Come on, O'Neill, quit grinning like an idiot! Get your clothes off and get to work!" Heinie Mueller barked at him.

Danny went to the other office to hang up his clothes and

then he stopped off in the lavatory. Casey came out to talk to him.

"Kid, you act like you fell into the bucks or something," Casey said quizzically.

Danny smiled more genially.

"Listen, kid, I want to talk to you." Casey paused. "Barney Googles is sore as hell at you because you laid off work three days this week. You better watch your step."

"Collins' greatest gratification in life is the sound of his own voice!"

"Well, kid, forgettin' the dictionary, he's really sore. He's ridin' his high-horse like a jockey. It makes me look like a heel." Danny listened impatiently. "He said I got to take over the extra Sunday work you've been doin'. Bones, you know me. I want you to know I didn't have nothin' to do with it. What Collins says goes. I only work here like you do."

"Don't worry, Casey, I don't want it any more," Danny said generously.

"Say, kid, you got something up your sleeve. Tell me—you know you can trust me."

"No, nothing. I just feel good. But we'd better get to work."

"Take a tip from me, Barney's got crabs in his ass. Watch your step."

"Thanks."

"You're my pal," Casey said as they went back to the office.

"Hey, O'Neill, come here! I wanta talk to you," Collins commanded.

Danny took his time obeying Collins.

"What the hell's the matter with you?" Collins asked, looking up from his chair.

"Nothing."

"Listen, my boy, this is a business office. It ain't no fraternity or playground or whatever the hell—you know this is a business office. We've got to have clerks here that we can rely on. You've been layin' off goddamned often, givin' me cock-and-bull stories. I can't depend on you. Casey here is doin' your Sunday work, startin' tomorrow."

"That's all right."

"I was just in talkin' to Mr. Norris about you. I'm not foolin' around with you any more. If you keep knockin' off work the way you've been doin', you're going to come down here some mornin' and find out that there's no place here for you. If you want your job, you got to buckle down."

"Listen, Mr. Collins, I want to tell you something."

"Get down on them lights," Collins said, swinging away from Danny.

"I just wanted to say, *Willie* . . ." Danny continued, pronouncing Collins' Christian name with insolence.

"Answer them telephones."

"I'm quitting. This is my last day," Danny announced loudly enough for everyone to hear.

Everyone looked at him, neglecting the telephones. He'd really set off a bombshell.

Triumph was sweet.

III

"How much dough did you say you were going to make at your new job, Bones?" Casey called down to him.

"At the end of three months I'll make a hundred and forty a month and commissions on all the oil I sell."

He saw envy in Casey's eyes.

"Well, don't piss it away," Heinie Mueller warned him.

A dull Saturday afternoon in the Wagon Call Department. He had an hour and fifteen minutes to go.

He pulled a light and answered a call.

His life since his graduation from Saint Stanislaus now fitted into a pattern, took on meaning and direction. He had lost all bitterness about his fate, about this office and what he'd had to put up with here. His life here had been a series of days, one day crawling into the next, and the next still into the next, until these days had swollen into twenty-two months. Time that could not be regained, days that had fallen into a waste-basket of eternity. But he had learned from this very waste. Wasn't it because he'd come to see that he was a nobody that he had developed his ambition, his determination to make something of himself?

"Bones, what you gonna do if you don't make the grade at your new job?" Casey asked him.

"That question doesn't concern me."

It did, but why admit it to them here?

"Anyway, Bones, I'll be rootin' for you. I will, I will, old boy, old boy, and that's straight," Casey said.

Danny grinned.

If Collins were decent, Collins would O.K. his time card for a full day and tell him to go home now. Just as Shylock had demanded his pound of flesh, so was Collins requiring him to give his time to Johnny Continental to the last second. Shylock Collins! No, the idea of letting him off early just didn't enter Collins' head. Collins really wasn't a bad fellow. If he asked to go now, Collins would probably say go ahead. He wouldn't ask. I am too proud to ask. That wasn't the truth. He wanted to be out of this place, and yet he wanted to stay and savor his last day here to the final minute. Papa had had a last day working for the express company, and then he'd gone home to die. The irony of the difference between his last day with this company and Papa's. A last day, a last minute for everything in life.

"You say the Doc says your appendix is clearing up, Bones?" Casey asked.

"I saw him last night. He says I can eat meat now," Danny answered.

Casey was trying to be friendly. He knew why. While he was off, Casey had double-crossed him on the Sunday work. Casey had stuck a knife in him. The knife had turned out to be rubber.

The last hour dragged. At one minute to six, while the night shift was taking over, Danny pulled another light.

"Hello, Wagon Department."

A female voice.

"What is the name, please?"

He wrote.

"Yes, ma'am. And the address?"

He wrote.

"And what are you shipping?"

He wrote.

"Where to? Where's it going?"

He wrote.

"How much does it weigh?"

He wrote.

"Well, we'll get it on Monday . . . between two and five in the afternoon."

He flung the call across the table to be sorted properly.

WE. It was no more *we.* He was no longer a part of the *we* which made up the Continental Express Company. His hour of liberation had come. Shaken with nervous emotions, he went out to wash. Heinie Mueller followed him.

"Good luck, O'Neill. Stay out of trouble and be a good kid. And don't forget that no matter what happens, you always want to take care of your mother," Heinie Mueller said, clasping his hand. "I'm glad you're trying to make something out of yourself."

"Thanks, Dutch."

Now, farewell, and he was off.

IV

"Dan, that priest certainly raised the cost of the Devil's coal bill tonight, didn't he?" Jim Gogarty said, walking along Sixty-first Street with Danny after Sunday-night Lenten services at Saint Patrick's.

"Did you watch some of the people in church? He had them quaking."

"He didn't make me too happy."

He'd gone to confession last night, and received Holy Communion this morning, offering it for Papa and as a request to God that he be a success at his new job. Father Doneggan had been easy. Father, I broke the Sixth Commandment with another. A girl? Yes, father. For penance, ten Our Fathers and ten Hail Marys. How he had feared kneeling in the dark confessional box and admitting this sin! How light, how relieved he'd felt when he'd got it off his chest! And after mass this morning he'd seen Father Doneggan in back of the church and handed him five dollars for masses for Papa. Don't bother, Dan, I'll say the masses. You need your money. Danny had insisted. Father Doneggan was a swell fellow.

Nasty out. The mean end to a depressing March Sunday. But he hadn't been glum today because of the weather. Tonight was the eve of a future in his life. It was still hard for him to believe that it was now really going to be possible for him to be a student at the University of Chicago. Gallagher had said it could be arranged. He could work afternoon shifts when he started to school.

"Well, Dan, I hope you get a real break in your new job."

"I ought to. Hell, Jim, if other guys can make the grade as filling-station attendants, why can't I?"

"Them are words of wisdom," Jim said semi-humorously.

Pumping yourself up with hopes and words of confidence— that proved nothing. Effort, struggle told the tale.

"It's great, Dan, that you're going to be able to go to the University now."

"Yes, I want to go."

They turned onto South Park Avenue.

Would something happen to prevent his going to the U.? Would he lack the character and will power to carry through with this intention? He was impatient for next fall so that he would actually get started back to school. To wish that meant to wish that five unlived months of your life were gone; it meant that you were wishing yourself nearer to the last day. The priest tonight had warned: *Tremble in your boots.* From now on he had to live a clean life. Freud? You couldn't dodge your own nature. But you couldn't dodge the fundamental problems of conscience, either. Protestants were lucky. No, they weren't. The Catholic Church was like a safe, luxurious ocean liner, and the Protestant churches were like leaky old rowboats. Who would want to cross the Atlantic Ocean in a rowboat when he could take an ocean liner? But why did God select some souls to be infused in the bodies of Catholics and others into the bodies of those who would be Protestants? Jews, Mohammedans, cannibals? This couldn't be an accident, could it? He had many questions to answer. Well, from now on he must study and learn the answers to all the questions that troubled or perplexed him.

"We'll be able to walk to school every morning, Dan."

"Uh huh."

Just think. He could actually plan about going to the University.

"Won't it be swell, Dan, some day to have our law partnership?"

"Uh huh."

"We'll need to have a Jew in the firm, too. Gogarty, O'Neill and—what—Levinsky—Ginsburg—Cohen? Some name like that. Or would it be better to call it—Cohen, O'Neill and Gogarty, lawyers?"

"It'll sound good, no matter which order the names are in."

He'd been walking home the way that was forever associated in his mind with Roslyn Hayes. He wanted her to know that he would soon be going to the U. He'd been meaning to telephone Harriet for a date, but hadn't. He would this week. He'd be able to afford dates more easily now that he would earn more money.

"Dan, we ought to lay out our plans carefully for our careers, and for our law firm."

He and Jim saw eye to eye. They could talk frankly about their common dreams. He'd been acquainted with Jim for years, but had really gotten to know him only in the last few months. Jim had gone to Carter School. He'd worked and saved for a whole year after graduating from Park High in order to go to the University. They were both starting out together to achieve something in the same way.

"Dan, if we're going to develop a successful law business, we'll have to go into politics."

"I want to."

The March wind was mournful in the trees across the street.

"We'll have to build and plan a political career carefully, day by day. We ought to start now. You and I, Dan, have a golden opportunity. We were born and raised on the South Side of Chicago in Irish neighborhoods, and we are getting to know more and more people in this neighborhood. If we play our cards right, all these people will be our capital—our constituency."

Hopes of the future made him so impatient with the present. He must prepare himself.

"It'll be great, won't it, when we've passed the Bar and are really able to hang out our shingles," Danny said enthusiastically.

"If we want to do it, we've got to plan now."

Could he ever succeed? Jim had more personality than he had. If he'd never been too popular in small groups, how could he hope to become popular in large ones? How could Danny O'Neill ever learn to sway people? Think of Al Smith! He couldn't ever be an Al Smith.

They walked on, suddenly silent, each absorbed in his dream of the future. Danny glanced across the street at the darkness shrouding Washington Park. Beyond the park stood the University of Chicago, now dark and quiet, its very stones the symbol of what he wanted. Tomorrow morning the University would come to life, and its life was what he longed for. Jim would go to classes. Jim would be part of that life, learning, getting ahead. And he would report to the gas station on Michigan Boulevard. Well, Jim had had to work for a year before he had been able to go to school. He, Danny O'Neill, was now definitely going there to be a student at the University.

"What do you have to do now, Dan?"

"I was going to read and go to bed early."

"How about going over to the poolroom and shooting a game of pool? We can hang around, and laugh and kid with the boys, and it all helps. After all, Studs Lonigan and the boys are future votes, and we might just as well begin working on them now as later."

"I'd like to, but I think I'd better get a good night's sleep. I have to report to work at seven tomorrow."

"Well, then, I'll do the prospecting tonight for the firm of O'Neill, Gogarty and an unnamed *sky*. Health is important, too."

"So long, Jim."

"So long, Dan. Good luck on your new job."

Climbing the steps to the second floor, Danny was disturbed by Jim's proposal about playing up to the boys in the poolroom. He put it out of his mind. They had to plan, take advantage of every opportunity, didn't they?

The green and white sign in the window of the small Upton filling station at Roosevelt Road and Racine read:

SERVICE STATION ATTENDANT
DANIEL O'NEILL
ON DUTY

Danny had been assigned to relief duty, and this was the dullest of the three stations at which he worked. But he considered it a good break to be placed in a slow station until he became more sure of himself at this job. He had just finished reading a volume of collected editorials by Arthur Brisbane, drawing new confidence and inspiration from this book. Brisbane suggested that everyone ought to keep a Thought Diary. He had always wanted to keep a diary, and decided to start one immediately. He wrote haltingly, pausing from time to time to formulate his thoughts.

THOUGHT DIARY

April 6, 1925

I begin my Thought Diary. This is my third week as an employee of the Upton Oil and Refining Company. My first week was spent being broken in by an old crank named Sperling. But I learned nothing. I was kept busy cleaning up the station, and when I came to this station last week, I was lost and confused. I made mistakes. I drained out the grease on a car, thinking I was draining the crankcase. But now I am learning. I am going to learn.

I begin my Thought Diary with the feeling that I am em-

barking on the hard battle of life. I write in this diary, knowing little of my business, and devoid of many of the things
that I must know for my battle. But my ambitions fly as high
into the empyrean as my feet are kept, by my lack of knowledge, rooted in the mud of prosaic "Mother Earth." My ambitions will teach me how to clean and lift my muddy feet.

I consider myself a child of success in an age of success. I am
prepared to offer myself no excuses if I do not succeed.

Now I have a customer.

Chapter Five

I

About two hundred service-station attendants, employed by the Upton Oil and Refining Company, sat packed together on camp chairs in a large, bare room on an upper floor of a Loop office building. At four o'clock sharp the meeting was opened by Mr. Gallagher, Supervisor of Service Stations. He introduced Mr. North, his successor who had just come to Chicago to take over and pep up the Service Station Department.

"You fellows may wonder why I called this meeting," Mr. North began in a deep voice of confidence and authority. "Well, I want to get to know all of you better. I want to achieve a better spirit of service, co-operation, go-getting in our stations. I want to put my cards down on the table before all of you, to let you know what I expect from you, what I want done, and also to let you know where I stand with you, and where you stand with me. I want to talk man to man with you. That's clear.

"Now, I'm going to have more to say to you later. But before that, some of the officials of our company have something to tell you. First of all, Mr. Stretchley, our General Sales Manager, will have a word or two. Here is Mr. Stretchley, fellows. Give him a hand."

The audience obediently clapped.

II

"I'm glad to meet you, boys. I'm glad you're here. I'm glad that Mr. North has invited me to talk to you," Mr. Stretchley said in a husky voice.

"Now, I'm going to talk to you about sales. Sales is all im-

55

portant. Sales is business. Without sales, no business. No business, no salary, no wages, and where are we? Any man, any corporation is in business for something else besides the fun of it. Of course, there's fun in it. Business is the greatest fun in the world. That's all true. But we're not in business for fun. We're in business to sell something that the public wants and needs. Sales keep the wheels of industry turning. Sales keep the oil coming up out of our wells, keep it flowing through the pipelines and straight on into every tin lizzie in the country." Some of the attendants laughed. "We're all salesmen. And we ought to be proud of it. I tell you, if I had my life to live over again, I wouldn't want to be anything else than what I am—a salesman. Today, in this country, we are climbing the high road of progress and prosperity. This is the greatest country in the entire history of the world. Why?" He paused for effect. "Because it is the country of the greatest salesmen in all history. What was Nero's Rome compared to America? Nothing! Alexander the Great conquered the world with a sword. But there are things greater than the sword. The pen is mightier than the sword. We Americans are going to conquer the world with the fountain pen and the order blank."

Mr. Stretchley ran a stubby hand over a bald dome.

"Yes, boys, without sales Upton wouldn't be the great corporation it is today. And it is one of the biggest in the industry, one of the biggest and the best, the very best. It has the most superfine products to sell. I've been in the oil game for years. I've sold oils, all kinds of it—in cans, in barrels, in tank cars. I've sold more products of refineries than Heinz's has varieties of beans." Laughs. Mr. Stretchley jutted a bull-dog face forward. "But I have never sold oil and gas to match those produced by our company. I tell you, it's a pleasure to sell Upton products. Why, when I sell a customer on our products, do you know, I feel that I am doing him a service. That's what I think of our products. And that's what I want you fellows to think.

"Before you can make someone else believe in something,

you got to believe in it yourself. You got to have faith in the product you sell. Without faith, you can't be a salesman. Now, my job here today is to make this sink right square down to the bottom of your hearts."

Mr. Stretchley pounded his right fist into his left hand, looked forward, with his shoulders hunched, and turned sharp cold eyes on the first row.

"The first crucial point is—faith. You got to have faith. If you don't have faith in what you sell, how are you going to sell it? Without faith, you go to see a prospect, and what do you do? You talk off the top of your head. You don't talk up from the heart, but down from the skull. Talking down from the skull— skull talk I always call it—well, that doesn't sell any barrels of oil. No, sir, skull talk doesn't sell any oil. And it doesn't permit you to buy shoes for the baby, either."

Laughs.

"But have you got a right to have faith? Well, if not, the thing to do is to quit. Quit right now. Upton Oil doesn't want anyone selling its products unless he's got faith in those products. Those of us who have been in this game a little while, we know, we know damned well that we got the best petroleum products on the market. Nothing that science can do has been left undone in the refining of our products. Nothing, absolutely nothing. The man who puts our gas in his car gets more mileage and less carbon as a result. The man who uses our oil gets smoother performance. Yes, sir, there is no least doubt that we got something to sell, something better than any of our competitors have on the market, something that the public wants and needs.

"But the good Lord Himself, Who was the Greatest Salesman of all time, told us that you can't live by faith alone. You got to have faith and works. Works means selling. It means being on your toes. It means being a live wire. It means having your sales arguments at the tips of your fingers. It means never losing a prospect. It means going out and getting the business. Faith is the motor, but it isn't the whole automobile. It's not the steering wheel and the tires, it's not the oil and the gas and grease. Yes, you got to believe, and then because you believe you go out and bring home the bacon. You got to get out there and pitch. You pitch arguments, the facts, and pitch them right down the groove. I say this because I know what I'm talking about from experience. If you do that, you can't help but sell our products.

"Just as a general marshals his troops for battle, so must a salesman marshal his arguments. Napoleon said that God is on the side of the most cannon. Sales is on the side of most arguments and the best products. That's one of the basic principles of good salesmanship, and never forget that principle. I know I never do. Now, let me tell you. . . ."

Mr. Stretchley continued for twenty-five minutes.

III

"Now, fellows, after the stimulating discourse you've heard from Mr. Stretchley, I want you to listen to our Public Relations Director, Mr. Dickinson," Mr. North announced.

Mr. Dickinson, a tall man in a conservative blue suit, stepped forward.

"Everything that Mr. Stretchley said to you boys is the God's one-hundred-per-cent truth. Now, what I want to say follows logically from what he has said to you. He told you how to sell. That's his function in our company. Mine is to tell you how to deal with the public—the principles of dealing with the public. This is also part of the general principles of salesmanship, just as salesmanship and public relations are part of the general principles of personnel work, that is, dealing with people. Both of these belong to the study of psychology. And the study of psychology is, after all, just a tall set of words for something very simple—human nature.

"To deal with the public, you have got to know human nature. What is human nature? It is people. Yourself, myself, the man who drives a Ford and the man who drives a Cadillac, they, everyone is human, and human nature has to do with everyone.

"Now, let me begin this way. Modern business has been built up on the great principle that the customer is always right. This is a simple little sentence. But it states a great and important principle, and it hits at the heart of old human nature. I'll put it this way. If you please a man, he is going to like you more than if you displease him. If you flatter him, he is going to be more receptive than if you antagonize him. That's horse sense. That's human nature. That's psychology. That's one of the primary laws of service—*Never antagonize the customer*. If a customer says something that gets under your skin, let it go in one ear and out the other. If he says it's raining out, and the sun is shining, tell him it's pouring cats and dogs. Let the weather man take care of the weather, and you sell the goods. If a customer is a Democrat, don't talk about the Republicans. If he is a son of Abraham, don't talk about kosher meat."

Mr. Dickinson spoke for twenty-eight minutes.

IV

"Fellows," boomed Mr. Schofield, Assistant General Manager of the Chicago District, "you get out of life what you put into it. You only get that, nothing more, and nothing less. Let me tell you again that you get out of life what you put into it. If you put a lot into life, you'll get a lot out of life. If you don't, you won't. This is the key to success and failure. And in this day and age, any man who fails, he fails because he hasn't put enough into life. If he put more into what he did, he wouldn't fail. America has seen its last depression and has no room for failures. Look at all of the men in this world who haven't failed. Look at all of the successful men! Take our own company. Most of the men in it didn't start at the top. Many of them started just where you fellows are starting. But they put something into life, and they put that into their work. Now they are some place. They are something.

"My message to you fellows is this . . . the world is your oyster. . . ."

After booming for thirty-two minutes, Mr. Schofield concluded: "You have to keep in mind, always, waking and sleeping, morning, noon and night, the unforgettable practical motto—you get out of life what you put into it."

At six minutes to eight Mr. North said.

"Fellows, I know it's been a long meeting, longer than I calculated. I wouldn't have kept you here if I didn't think it important for you to hear all that we've had to say. Now, let me say a very few last words. Our company has your interest at heart. You must pay it back by having its interest at heart. You can take my word for that. And so, let me see you all go out and get the sales. Go out and knock them dead. Go out and sell the oil! Good luck, and I know that all of us in the service station end of this game are going to work together like a well-knit team. That's all."

Danny O'Neill left the meeting wearied from sitting so long on an uncomfortable camp chair, but re-enforced in his determination to succeed. He pondered the words of Mr. Schofield. Yes, he was going to get more out of life than most of his generation because he was going to put more into life.

SECTION TWO

1925

VI

"Ned, do you think you'll get that job with this outfit in Springfield?" Al asked, sitting with him in the darkened parlor while Washington Park across the street was in twilight.

"I'm seeing the fellow tomorrow. But he's a dumbbell."

"What the hell, don't tell him that."

"Listen, I don't need advice on how to handle dumbbells in the shoe business."

"I was only making a suggestion."

"Well, I think I'll land something with him."

"God, I hope so."

"What's the latest news concerning your factory?"

"I don't know. Lovejoy wants to retire. He's not well. If he retires, the factory might go to pot. The owners are old New England highbrows who think that they mustn't soil their hands. They can't run a shoe factory. Business would soil their hands."

"What's the matter with Lovejoy?"

"His heart."

"Hell, he ought to have faith."

"I went to Holy Communion Sunday and offered it up that he would pick up, and that he wouldn't retire. I invested nearly all my savings in the factory. Golly, if it's left to these heirs, I'm afraid that they can't handle the business. Competition is getting stiffer all of the time. More and more of these cheap Jews are stealing our styles and selling imitations of them for four and five dollars. I ran into that Jew stuff all over the Middle West this spring."

"Leave it to the kikes to do that," Ned said.

Al looked off, worried.

"Hope for the best, Al. Auto-suggest yourself into faith that the best is going to happen."

"Yes," Al said, worried.

Chapter Six

I

This was his first date in months.

Should he take her arm now? He better wait until they crossed Sixty-fifth Street and then do it.

"Tomorrow morning I'm going to register at the University. I'm going to start there this summer."

"I wish my brother would do something like that," Beatrice Carberry answered.

"He ought to. He's smart. He can make something out of himself if he tries and perseveres," Danny said monotonously.

It would be wonderful to run his hands through her black curls. He liked her eyes, too. She was lithesome, and seventeen. Was she a beautiful girl? Her sensuous lips were a little too thick, but they invited kisses. She walked pigeon-toed; it was a cute walk. Beatrice was his type, a black-haired, dark-eyed Wild Irish Rose type.

Crossing Sixty-fifth and Woodlawn, Danny took her arm.

A pot-bellied, bald-headed man let a hose play on a neat lawn in front of a two-story, gray brick building. Danny was sorry for that man. He was fat; his youth was over. He could only look back on youth as a wonderful period of life that was gone forever. Did the man with the hose look at him with envy?

Women were entering Saint Kevin's church at Sixty-fourth Street to attend services in honor of the Sacred Rose of Jesus Christ.

"Are you very religious?" Danny asked her.

"I'm afraid I'm not."

"Neither am I. We ought to be, but we aren't."

Father Robert Geraghty would probably preach a sermon

65

there tonight. He'd done a wonderful job, organizing the Society of the Sacred Rose of Jesus Christ all over America. He'd given Shanley a good job as his assistant. Mama had been over yesterday and she'd told Mother that the Sacred Rose had come to her in her sleep. The Sacred Rose had told Mama that Papa was happy in Heaven. Mama was always dreaming of saints and the Blessed Virgin.

Papa had once walked along a street in June with Mama on his arm, dreaming of love and the future. It was hard to imagine Papa young, courting Mama.

"It's a swell night for a beach party, isn't it?" Danny said as they turned onto Sixty-fourth Street.

"Yes. I was surprised when you called me up and asked me to go," she said in a soft, lazy voice.

"Was it an unpleasant surprise?"

She laughed. The laughter of a girl of seventeen—lovelier than sunshine.

"Is Ed Lanson going to be there tonight?"

"No."

"I thought he was."

Danny suspected a note of disappointment in her voice. He was glad that Ed wasn't going to be at the party. Beatrice might compare him with Ed, unfavorably.

"Ed's going with Ellen Rogers," he said.

"Yes, my sister told me. The minute I got home from the convent, Kate sat down and told me all the dirt."

"You girls love to hear the dirt, don't you?"

She smiled.

"I suppose you're glad to be home from school?" he asked.

"Who wouldn't be? At school there's nothing to do, and you get to feeling silly. You count the days until you'll be going home."

A couple ahead of him. How different you felt, seeing couples on the street when you were out with a beautiful girl yourself.

"What did you do, count the days on your fingers?" he asked, merely to make conversation.

On a fine night like this, Chicago was lazy, so charming. He saw it through rose-colored glasses. Its streets were full of poetry. People strolling. Lovers. The bald-headed man with the hose. Kids playing. The poetry of life.

"I used to be in jail there," he said as they passed the new Mary Our Mother high-school building; when the new school building had been completed, the priests had changed the name from Saint Stanislaus.

"Yes, you were the star athlete of the high school."

"That was only a rumor," he said, beaming.

"I remember hearing all about the parties you had in those days. I was just a kid then."

"And now you're a big girl."

"That's a rumor."

"Sometimes I believe rumors."

II

Everyone was gathered in a group around a fire close to the water and just outside the wire fence of the Jackson Park beach.

Danny watched the fire. How soon ought he to ask Beatrice to take a walk?

"So you've got a regular station now, Dan?" Marty Mulligan asked.

"Yes, on Michigan Avenue. That's why I can go to school now instead of waiting until fall."

"How many gallons a day do you pump?"

"Can't you two big-shot oil men forget the oil business?" Dopey razzed.

How soon should he take her off for a walk?

"It's fascinating to watch a fire, isn't it, Bea? It makes you philosophical," Danny told her.

"Sometimes," she replied, pensive.

The lake was calm tonight. It was too bad that he and Beatrice hadn't worn bathing suits so they could go in swimming.

"Are you glad to be home from school?" Lillian, Marty's ball-and-chain, asked across the fire.

The moon shimmered on the lake. Small waves softly collapsed on the sand.

Dopey Carberry handed Marty a bottle of gin with an air of mystery. Lillian turned icy eyes on Dopey. Danny thought that he'd better not drink; Beatrice might not like it.

Ike Dugan and Mike Flood wandered off with their girls. The beach, the lake, the sky, the moon, the stars, the balmy June night, all invited love.

But he couldn't sit here all night like a log, could he? Why so pale and wan, fond lover?

He watched Beatrice out of the corner of his eye. What words could he use to describe her? Ineffable! She was more than real. She was a creature wearing a dress, living in a frame of flesh and bones, who breathed all the poetry that had ever been written. Was he getting romantic? Well, why shouldn't he?

"Let's take a walk," he whispered.

"Let's," she answered, rising.

They wandered off, their feet sinking in the sand. Had the others noticed them go? He hoped so. They'd see that he was in love with a wonderful girl who wanted to be alone with him.

The lake murmured. They heard shouts and cries from different parts of the beach. A girl laughed.

It's a long, long trail a-winding. . . .

At some other party, a group was singing to a banjo.

"Oh, Jake, come on in, the water's fine," a girl called.

"Are you fine?"

"You'd never know," the girl called insinuatingly.

Small fires danced here and there on the beach.

"This is nice," he said, putting his arm around her.

She muttered something, as if in agreement, but he didn't catch what she said. They sat down on an isolated bench, about three feet from the edge of the water.

He put his arm around her. He kissed her. She opened her lips and clung to him. He felt her thigh through her dress, and then he laid his hand over her breast. He wanted to do more, but he was timid. She was breathless. He kissed and caressed her. She ran her fingers through his hair. They seemed to tell him that, yes, she cared for him. He sat with her for a long time, kissing and looking out at the still lake. Beatrice continued to run her fingers through his hair. Shouldn't he try to go farther? He was afraid to try. She was a decent girl, the sister of his friend. But he vaguely sensed that he was making a mistake. He embraced her again, kissed her, and stroked her left thigh. They sank back, facing the lake. She rested her head on his shoulder.

"Beatrice," he said.

"Yes?"

"It's nice."

"Yes."

Remembering Shelley's poem, *To* ————, he wanted to quote it to her. He didn't.

"Isn't it wonderful here? There're stars out, a full moon. . . ."

"Oh, I never pay much attention to that," she said.

"To what?"

"Oh, the stars, and songs about love and the moon. It's silly."

Her words made him feel childish, sentimental.

"I really feel the same. All I meant is that it is a keen night, the air and the weather, and I-I- . . ." he didn't finish his sentence. He looked at her unsure.

He put his arms around her and kissed her again. He knew that he should go farther than he had. He was too shy.

III

They strolled back to the party. Alone with her, he had lost all sense of time. He had wanted to stay there on the bench, but he'd thought that perhaps they had been away long enough. He'd suggested that they go back and see how the party was getting on. Now he regretted his suggestion, but said nothing.

They'd walk home alone through the park arm-in-arm. Never in his life had he walked arm-in-arm in a park with a girl like Beatrice.

"Well, it's going to be a long summer," he said, as a preliminary to asking for another date.

"Yes."

"What are you doing next Tuesday night, Beatrice?"

He hung on her answer.

"Nothing."

"Want to go out and dance some place?"

"Yes."

The whole summer spread before him now with promises of pleasure and excitement. There would be school, and when he had the time there would be dates with Beatrice, swimming, dancing, parties, making love to her. 1925 was his year. So many things had happened to him already this year. He had changed so. His whole course of life had been drastically altered. And at last he had found the right girl.

He stopped and kissed her again.

"We're too near the party now."

"What do we care?"

"Yes, but then my brother—he's an awful teaser."

He took her hand and they slowly walked on back toward the fire.

"Well, did you explore the beach?" Marty asked knowingly, holding a hot dog.

"Yes, we explored the beach," Danny answered.

They sat down by the fire. Marty handed them hot dogs. Dopey flopped down on Danny's right.

"Dopey, why don't you get a job in a gas station and go to the U with me?" he asked, and then he glanced sidewise at Beatrice to note how his remarks had registered on her.

"Say, what are you—a boy scout?" Dopey answered.

"I thought it would be good for you."

"O'Neill, we know you're Horatio Alger."

Danny turned to Beatrice to gain approval. Her face was expressionless.

"Let's sing," Mike Flood said, tuning his banjo.

Whisper and say that you believe me . . .

"Mike, don't you know any other song besides *Whispering*?" Al Herbert asked.

"It's my classic," Mike answered.

Danny watched Beatrice avidly. He held her hand.

VII

Mr. North finished reading an article in The Chicago Questioner which reported the sentencing of Mr. Upton, Chairman of the Board of Directors of the Upton Oil and Refining Company, to a three months' term in jail for having given false testimony before a Senatorial Investigation Committee. He reflected that the trouble with the government was that there was too much politics in business, and not enough business in politics. Mr. Upton had merely wanted to develop the natural resources of America in the only sound way they could be developed. These politicians were interfering where they had no right to interfere. If they kept on, America would be in danger of socialism, and someone like that Trotsky fellow would light the fires of anarchy from coast to coast.

Mr. Gallagher entered the office.

"I've got a lot of bad reports here," Mr. North said, taking a stack of papers from a basket on his desk.

"Whenever you have people handling money, you run into headaches. It always was that way, and it always will be," Mr. Gallagher said.

"I'm discouraged. Now, here's a report on Station Six. They put three hundred gallons of water in one of the gasoline tanks. Five customers bought gas there and their cars wouldn't move. They got water. I questioned the men and they denied it. I had to let them go."

"That's Inmans and Shaughnessy. They always were trouble-makers!"

"And here's a letter from Brown at Number Eighteen on the

72

North Side. Brown's a promising chap. He tells me that his partner cut the bulk oil with kerosene."

"That's Johnson. He's got a good record."

"Will you go out and check up there today and give me a report? I'll have a spotter watch Johnson," Mr. North said, making a note of it.

"Yes, sir."

"Read this. The attendant on duty at Fifty-eight on the night of May twenty-eighth had some woman in his lavatory with him for a half hour. We can't let that kind of monkey business go on. Find out who the man was and have him come in and see me on Monday."

"Yes, sir."

"And look at this. The City Sealers caught Ingersoll at One Hundred and Four dead cold, giving short measure."

"Ingersoll? That's hard to believe. He's a crackerjack salesman."

Mr. North looked up.

"I can't understand the human race. I can't. Can you?"

"No, I guess I can't, either."

"I was thinking about it last night and I kept asking myself, why can't men be honest? I confess, I don't know the answer," said Mr. North, shaking his head wearily from side to side in bewilderment.

Chapter Seven

I

Today, I have symbolically grasped aloft the Torch of Learning. I will hold it Proudly on High all the . . .

A customer nervously punched on the horn of a Buick sedan. Danny shoved into the back pocket of his overalls the sheet of paper on which he had been writing and rushed out to the front pump island.

"I ain't got all day, Bud."

"I'm sorry, sir. I was writing out a report. Fill her up, sir?"

He'd been instructed always to say *fill her up* instead of *how many*. This was psychology. You suggested that a customer have a full tank.

"Five gallons."

Psychology, suggestion, hadn't worked this time.

Danny inserted the hose nozzle into the tank at the rear of the car. Lefthanded, he turned the handle of the red-painted Wayne pump, and gasoline gurgled into the tank. This job would put him in condition. Pumping so much gas, he'd harden his muscles. He was using his left hand a lot because it needed more development than the right. The pump bar hit the top, signifying that five gallons had been pumped. He drained the hose carefully, making sure no dripping spilled onto the outside of the tank. When he'd first started working for the company he'd spilled drippings when he drained the hose. How quickly he had gained self-assurance in this work. He must not forget to put the cap back on. In his first days as a gas pumper he'd had trouble because of his carelessness about this.

He screwed the cap on the tank.

74

"Check your oil, sir?" he asked, going around to the side of the car.

Every customer was a prospect for oil sales. Quarts of oil sold added up to gallons. Every little bit counted. It was more important for him to sell oil now than to write in his *Thought Diary* about how he'd felt registering at the U this morning.

"No, I don't need any."

"When's the last time you had a crankcase, sir?"

"Hell, I can't remember."

"Have you driven more than five hundred miles since your last drain, sir?"

This was the regular sales argument. But how did he really know that five hundred miles was the exact number after which a motorist should get new motor oil?

"I guess so—why?"

"You ought to have your motor drained every five hundred miles, sir."

He hated having to say *sir* so much. Servility. But the customer is always right, and politeness pays. Politeness drains the oil. Was that a good slogan?

"Who says so?"

He'd try to write good slogans and submit them to the company. Get the right one and it would reward him.

"You ought to. It's better for your motor."

Words—that was all he could give a customer. His ignorance of motors, oil, gas, of all the technical details of this business was profound.

"If you have a drain every five hundred miles, you get better, smoother performance from your car. Your motor will last longer if you do that. You know the old saying, sir, about an ounce of prevention . . ."

"I get all the performance I need from this buggy. When I don't, I'll buy a new one."

A shiny blue Lincoln waited behind the Buick. Roslyn Hayes' father owned a Lincoln. Why think of Roslyn or of

Harriet now? He had Beatrice. He must keep his mind on business.

"You see, sir, when you drive a car a long time without changing your oil, more than five hundred miles, you get dirt, grit in your motor, and it cuts the oil, makes it dirty. That means the oil is weaker. Your piston action isn't as good, and you might even wear your pistons out."

He hoped he'd said nothing he could be tripped up on.

"I've been driving my own cars for years. I never had any trouble, and I always got more than five hundred miles out of my oil."

A luscious mulatto passing. Creamy, light-brown skin. Was she a whore? He had his Beatrice.

"But if you get a drain every five hundred miles, sir, you'd get better performance. In our laboratories, scientists have made tests . . ."

"I'm in a hurry."

Don't give up. But don't antagonize him, either.

The gray-haired man at the wheel of the Lincoln jabbed his horn.

"Perhaps then, sir, you might come back here later this afternoon, and then I can give you a quick drain, sir . . ."

"For Christ's sake, shut up! You goddamn gas men talk too goddamn much. Here, give me my change!" the motorist said, handing Danny a dollar bill.

The customer is always right! He was only doing what he'd been told to do—trying to sell oil, hadn't he?

"I'm sorry, sir. We only aim to give service, to convince the public of the value of our products and of the results of the experiments which scientists . . ."

"Gimme my change, you four-eyed bastard!"

Danny pressed five cents out of the money changer on his belt and handed it to the customer. His lips drawn tight, his face pale, he said nothing.

The Buick drew out.

You dirty sonofa . . .

Failed on that customer. Try the next one.

The Lincoln stopped alongside of the low-test Wayne pump. Behind it there were five cars lined up.

"Fill her up, sir?" Danny asked.

The Saturday afternoon rush had really started. He wouldn't get the entry written for his *Thought Diary* until tonight.

II

Awake! . . .

Flies buzzed about the cake and ham sandwiches lying on the flat-topped desk in the center of the service station. Danny filled one side of his face with a bite of a sandwich and then he drank lukewarm coffee from a pint-size milk bottle. He glued his eyes on the little blue book.

Automobiles hummed by continuously, their tires crunching on the paving. Twilight was slowly coming on.

> *"Awake, my Little ones, and fill the Cup*
> *Before Life's Liquor in its Cup be Dry."*

Next week, on his date with Beatrice, he'd pass off a good wisecrack about how he wouldn't let the drugstore gin in his Cup of Life run dry. But it was cheap to read a great poem just to get remarks to use for a line. And he didn't want to impress her by springing a line of gab. He was too serious about her for that. He had walked home alone with her last night after the beach party, and they had stopped again and again in Jackson Park for long kisses. He felt as if he could still taste her lips this very minute. He had picked her up and carried her under an arch of trees which deepened the blackness of night.

Beatrice was going to be his girl.

> *The Bird of Time has but a little way*
> *To Fly—and Lo! the Bird is on the Wing.*

Her kisses were already drowned in the Sea of Time. They were past. And yet he held the illusion that last night could never be wholly past, wholly gone. Part of it seemed lodged in his mind forever.

The Bird of Time . . .

Yes, it was only an illusion that he had thwarted this Bird last night. But then, this summer there would be many more such nights, many more kisses from her lips. Her fate was going to be linked with his for life. She would be proud of him —a student at the University of Chicago. Standing in line this morning, he had imagined her present beside him, sharing in his seething, excited thoughts.

But no, not even love could stay the swiftness of time.

Time would one day rob Beatrice of her beauty, her wonderful girlhood. Look at how swiftly this afternoon had passed. The days were brief, fleeting. But before they were robbed of their youth, they would drink of the Cup of Life.

. . . Lo! the Bird is on the Wing.

A customer. Dreamy-eyed, he went outside and pumped five gallons of high-test gasoline into a battered Chevrolet.

Soon it would be dark. He'd had another rush around six o'clock, and he'd had to postpone supper until now. He went back to the desk. He finished his sandwiches and drank the cold coffee. He looked up from the little blue book before him. Tomorrow he'd reread that remarkable quotation from the Venerable Bede in one of his history books. How did it go? The life of man is short if it is seen against the darkness of all time. When the king sits in his banquet hall, feasting with his ministers and warriors, enjoying the warm fire while the elements rage outside, imagine a little sparrow that flies in one door of the banquet hall, flutters, and passes out the other door. That is the life of man, a short evening of warmth before the terrible winter morning of eternity. The sparrow comes and goes, and so does man.

Who was right? Omar? Venerable Bede and the Church?

The Church was right.

Another customer. Irritated, he hurriedly serviced a motorist in a newly washed Oldsmobile.

He stood on the driveway, watching the sun sink just above the buildings on Wabash Avenue, one block away. Another day gone! The sun setting on one of the most important days of his life.

He'd awakened this morning with memories of Beatrice burning in his mind brighter than any sun could. And he'd matriculated at the University of Chicago. How indifferent most of the people in line had seemed, as if it were a routine experience to register at the university. Today his great dreams were realities.

Yes, the sun would soon fall behind the buildings on Wabash Avenue. Time. You must remember its awful meaning, even in the brightest moments of your youth. Time and Death, these were the enemies of man. There seemed to be a meaning hidden in the sinking sun. That meaning was what? Death. And Death was a function of Time.

He went back inside the station to finish his meal and read.

Could any poetry be more seductive, more persuasive than this was? But there was more to life than a loaf of bread, a jug of wine, and a Beautiful Thou in the Wilderness. Beatrice was his Thou. Last night in the moonlight her lips had given him a taste of Paradise.

He could be proud of himself. She was a decent girl. He had respected her. He hadn't tried to go too far. Omar wouldn't have advised doing that. Against his will, in spite of his pride of virtue, he regretted not having gone farther with her.

> *Tomorrow?—Why, Tomorrow I may be*
> *Myself with Yesterday's Sev'n Thousand Years.*

Omar himself was now with Yesterday's Sev'n Thousand Years.

He hastened outside to service a Ford.

"Five gallons."

He casually inserted the hose nozzle in the tank under the seat.

This poem is a sweet-tasting poison that will destroy my faith. He pumped five gallons and absent-mindedly drained the hose. He started back to the station.

"Hey, don't you want to get paid?" the driver called.

"Oh, yes, thank you. I've been so busy I'm just finishing my supper. I was hurrying to get it over with before I get another drove of cars in on my neck."

"No profit in giving something away. Here's your money."

"Thank you, sir."

He couldn't daydream on duty. Suppose that fellow had been a spotter. But a spotter would have driven out without paying and then reported him.

He must resist this poem.

He finished his supper. Outside, an automobile backfired, barking like a machine gun.

Fools! your Reward is neither Here nor There.

Pagan philosophy. Some men accepted it. Ed Lanson did. How barren, how terrible the world must seem if one would be rewarded neither Here nor There.

He'd have to turn the station lights on soon. He wanted to read more while he had a chance.

The Flower that once has blown for ever dies

He repeated the line over and over again. Beatrice was a flower. His flower. Yesterday's Sev'n Thousand Years were strewn with dead flowers, limp, withered poppies, roses.

Omar was wrong. Men weren't flung into this universe not knowing why, nor whence they came. Nor were they flung out of it as wind along the waste. Our lives were not like water, flowing willy-nilly.

In quatrain after quatrain the poem expressed this same false idea. But the words sung in his mind as if they possessed a separate existence in themselves.

Willy-nilly blowing. . . .

What greater happiness could one have than of being able to use words beautifully? But beauty was no justification of false doctrine. And Omar was a false prophet.

'Tis all a Chequer-board of Nights and Days
Where Destiny with Men for Pieces plays:
Hither and thither moves, and mates, and slays,
And one by one back in the Closet lays.

Men were pawns. Even if he didn't believe in God, he couldn't accept this philosophy. He couldn't think of himself as a pawn. Hadn't he registered at the U in order to work and strive so he wouldn't be a pawn? The idea revolted him. Assume it true; would it be less revolting? No—it would be still more revolting.

Despair crawled through his consciousness like a snake. He read the final stanza and put the book in his pocket. Turn down an empty glass. He'd do that when his time came.

He pulled on switches in the closet, lighting up the station.

Yes, he'd turn down an empty glass. But it would be a different kind of glass than Omar's. A burning eagerness seized him. Today, of all days, he didn't feel futile. Nor was he a pawn. He remembered Pater, whom he had read for his English course at Saint Vincent's. To give the highest quality of your moments. That was an ideal. It was his aim. He would give the highest quality of each moment to Beatrice, to study, to work.

He dashed out to meet a customer. He pumped five gallons. He watched the car drive away. He stood on the pump island, thoughtful. He felt a slight wind in his hair. It reminded him of Beatrice's fingers last night. They had been softer than the wind.

III

The hands of the battered alarm clock on the desk pointed to nine-fifteen. After several rushes of cars, business had suddenly dropped off. In odd free moments for the last hour he'd been holding imaginary telephone conversations with Beatrice. He went to the phone by the window, inserted a nickel, and waited for the operator. He hung up. He wouldn't call her. She had given him a steady date on his night off all summer. He mustn't be too anxious and show his hand. He turned away from the phone, thinking regretfully that even in love tricks and concealments were necessary. He stood in the center of the lighted station and recited Shelley's poem *To ———*, with the image of Beatrice in his mind.

> *One word is too often profaned*
> *   For me to profane it,*
> *One feeling too falsely disdained*
> *   For thee to disdain it.*
> *One hope is too like despair*
> *   For prudence to smother,*
> *And Pity from thee more dear*
> *   Than that from another.*
>
> *I can give not what men call love;*
> *   But wilt thou accept not*
> *The worship the heart lifts above*
> *   And the Heavens reject not:*
> *The desire of the moth for the star,*
> *   Of the night for the morrow,*
> *The devotion to something afar*
> *   From the sphere of our sorrow?*

He looked out at the automobiles passing on Michigan Avenue. Couples out on dates had stopped in the station for gas and oil. Tonight was like last night. It was made for a date, for love, not for pumping gas. Well, he had had last night. Others were ahead of him.

He couldn't moon now. He sat down at the desk, drew out a new Upton leaflet advertising gasoline, and started to read it, prepared to take notes. It was dull. But if you wanted to be a success, you had to become the master of even dull subjects.

Upton High Test gasoline is the product of five decades of refining experiment. The result of this scientific endeavor is a gasoline which gives one the fullest power in internal combustion engines.

A sedan stopped by the doorway. Danny went out.

"Hello, Bud," said a middle-aged man with a pockmarked face.

"Hello," Danny said, remembering having drained this customer's car on Thursday afternoon.

"Business good?"

"Can't complain."

"Well, on a Saturday people like to fill up their tanks and have a good time. We all like a good time, don't we? Say, you like it around here?"

"It's a job. Of course, the neighborhood is run down. The whores go by here all night."

"Don't you like 'em?" the man asked, scrutinizing Danny closely.

Danny tried to grin knowingly, but he resented the question.

"Listen, Bud, I run a nice respectable little house on the third floor here," he said, pointing to the building north of the station.

Danny tried to be casual, to conceal that he was ashamed of the very facts of sex.

"Listen, if you get anyone asking for a place, send them up, and I'll fix it up with you. You can have whatever the fellows you send up takes. A three-dollar job and you get it; five bucks, and you get that. Take it out in trade. I've got some fine girls, too. And you needn't be afraid about recommending my house. I have the girls examined every week. You'll get complete satisfaction at my place."

Danny nodded as if he agreed with the man and would send business. Here was his chance. He could go there, pay his money, and get a girl for anything he wanted. Why not do it, tonight, after work?

"If you don't forget me, Bud, I won't forget you."

Danny nodded again. He didn't want even to discuss the proposition. His sense of shame deepened, warring within him with his desire.

"Did you want any gas tonight?"

"Nope, I've got to go and attend to business. But don't forget. You know—one good turn deserves another—that's the truest philosophy of life that any man ever spoke."

He wanted this pockmarked procurer out of his station. With relief, he watched the sedan roll away.

Back inside, he told himself that he had been asked to be a pimp. A pimp! Lurid fancies rose in his mind. Why not drain the Cup—follow Omar's advice. Right next door there was a young whore who would lie naked for him, ready to give him everything a woman could give a man.

He had to fight these desires. Blot them out of his mind! Destroy them! He had to be worthy of Beatrice.

This moment, he was sinning in thought. A sin of thought could be a mortal sin. Others went to can houses, Catholics, married men, and it didn't seem to cause them any distress of conscience. Why must even the thought of sin send crashing bolts of conscience down upon him?

No!

He wanted to.

No!

He wished there were customers so he could forget all this in dull activity.

He wouldn't go with a whore, and he wouldn't solicit.

I've a neater, sweeter maiden in a cleaner, greener land!

With an effort of will he sat down to resume his study of the leaflet.

At one time, when the demand for kerosene was greater. . . .

Suddenly he was aware that someone had just entered the station. He looked up, his face clouded in concentration.

"Oh, how do you do, Mr. Gallagher."

"O'Neill, I'm surprised to come in and find you dreaming. You know, we don't want our attendants to be sitting on their can, reading, dreaming while on duty. I'm surprised to find you doing this."

"Oh, I'm sorry, Mr. Gallagher. Business just fell off, and so I was studying the new leaflet on our gasoline. I thought that during this lull I'd use my time to study a little. The more I know about our products, the better I can sell them."

Mr. Gallagher picked up the leaflet and glanced at it. He smiled genially, dropping it on the desk.

"Do you like it here?"

"Yes, sir. Yes, I'm glad to have a regular station. I arranged with Mr. Sperling to work a straight afternoon shift and so I decided not to wait until the fall for school. I start classes on Monday."

"Good, good stuff, O'Neill."

Danny looked solemn and serious.

"I had seven crankcase drains today, and I sold about two and a half gallons of flushing oil, and one five-gallon can."

"That's the ticket."

Gallagher sat on the desk and gazed about the station; it was spick and span.

"Mr. Gallagher, I wanted to ask you a favor."

"What's on your mind?"

"Is it all right, if when all the work is done, at nights here— you see I'm on duty until twelve—if I did a little studying, too, while I'm on the job?"

Gallagher thought for a moment. Danny anxiously waited for his answer.

"You know, we have a rule—no reading while an attendant is on the job."

Danny's hopes sank.

"But I think I can make an exception. I know you're the kind of a man who won't abuse a privilege. I'll tell Mr. North about it, too. Yes, but understand, the station has to be kept as clean as it is now. You have to keep on your toes."

"I will. And thank you very much, Mr. Gallagher. I appreciate it very much."

A car drove in. Danny dashed outside and serviced the customer efficiently. He returned to the station.

"Well, O'Neill, go along now and do your work and sell oil, and you'll have no worries, no trouble."

"I will, and, Mr. Gallagher, I can't begin to tell you how much I appreciate it."

"Don't mention it, old man. So long."

IV

He lugged in the cans displayed on the pump island and waited for the clock to inch on to twelve.

A Hudson stopped near the doorway. Danny swung around, and seeing three young men in the car, was shocked into terror. The driver honked. A holdup? The driver honked loudly. He recited the number of the combination for the safe to be sure that he wouldn't forget it, in case he was ordered to open it with a gun at his back. To be slugged, killed now, over Upton money that was insured against robbery! He sauntered to the car, feigning utter composure.

"Say, lad, where's there a whorehouse?" the swarthy driver asked.

Danny was relieved.

"Gee, I'm sorry, but I don't know. I'm new at this station. But the girls have been parading by the station all night. You can find one, or else ask a cab driver."

"Thanks."

The car drove out.

Time to close up. He picked up the big monkey wrench, went outside, climbed on the lowered lid of the pump cover, and unscrewed the hose on the low-test pump of the front island. He unscrewed the other hose. He dragged them inside. He switched off the outside lights and locked the station doors from the inside. He opened the safe and put away his money changer and bills. He turned the knob to lock it.

The end of a perfect day. Tired, he glowed with the confidence of having accomplished something. He thought of Dopey Carberry, Ike Dugan, and other friends. He wasn't like them. He wasn't a child of the moment. He was a child of tomorrow.

A motor horn outside. He looked out. A car waited by the island. He signaled that he had closed up. The driver honked again. Danny signaled more demonstratively. The horn sounded in jerky impatience.

"Sorry, closed up," Danny said, going out to the driver.

"Can't you give me five gallons?"

"I'm closed up. It's after twelve. We close at twelve."

"What the hell kind of business is that? Don't you want business?"

"Yes, sir, but I'm sorry, I'm closed. It'll take me twenty minutes to open up again. I can't do that."

"Why, you goddamn flunkey!"

"What did you say?" Danny asked, clenching his fists and taking a step forward.

The motorist slammed the car door shut and stepped on the starter. Danny was glad nothing had happened. He might have been cleaned up. Even though he could have knocked hell out of the bastard, a fight would have meant a black mark on his record.

He washed up, changed his clothes, and left.

At thirteen minutes after twelve he turned the time lock on the station door and sauntered off toward Forty-third and Michigan.

Red lights peeped from behind the drawn curtains of a stone building. Was it a can house? Had he locked the safe? Yes, he remembered clearly turning the combination. No worry. But suppose he hadn't. If someone busted into the station, he'd be responsible for all that dough—more than a hundred dollars. It might mean his job. He had turned the combination. But suppose that he was accepting an *ignus fatuus*, a will-o'-the-wisp of fake memory for what he'd really done? He retraced his steps, let himself in the station, and in the darkness found the safe locked. He left, again putting his key in the time lock.

"All right, stick 'em up! Stand where you are! Don't move!" sounded a voice about ten feet behind him.

Danny's hands went up, and he swung around. He felt no fear, no terror; he felt nothing. A blue-uniformed policeman came across the drive toward him, gun in hand. Danny recognized Studs Lonigan beside the cop. Danny trembled, realizing how close he had come to being shot dead.

"I told you it was young O'Neill," Studs Lonigan said, pleased with himself.

Danny had no power of speech.

"You workin' here now?" Studs asked.

"Yes. I was afraid I hadn't locked the safe. I wanted to be sure, and so I came back to see for a certainty," Danny answered nervously as he dropped his hands to his side.

"You're lucky, O'Neill. I was going to plug you, thinking you was a stick-up man. But Studs here, he says, 'Hell, that's young O'Neill. I guess he must work there because I know he works in a gas station.'"

"Yeh, O'Neill, you don't know how lucky you are," Studs said.

"I was gonna shoot first and ask questions afterward. If it hadn't been that I was showin' Studs the neighborhood, you'd be a stiff now. We always keep our eye open for stick-up men bustin' into gas stations," the cop said, putting his gun away.

"You know Nolan here from Fifty-eighth Street?" Studs asked.

"Yes, sure I do," Danny answered, now recalling that he'd seen Nolan several times in George's poolroom.

"Well, so long, O'Neill. I'll see you around here." Nolan said.

"So long, and thanks."

"So long, kid," Studs said cordially.

Danny turned toward Forty-third Street.

Such a wonderful night. The moon really began to seem beautiful to you when you were in love with a girl.

"Hello, dearie, want some love?" asked a light-brown whore.

No, he wouldn't. It was sin. It meant damning his soul. It was a vile thing to do to Beatrice when he loved her.

Devoid of will, Danny rushed by the girl, fearful she might even pursue him. He passed a store at the corner of Forty-third and Michigan and turned eastward toward the elevated station. He ought to have gone with the whore. After Anna Hamilton, he'd felt degraded, defrauded. Still, the same desire came back again and again. But suppose he had? Besides the sin, he might have gotten a disease. He had done what was right, what was moral. But if he ever admitted or boasted about this moral action of his in public, he'd be laughed at. Wouldn't he, in a group, laugh at anyone admitting having acted as he had tonight? If he hadn't been afraid, he'd have gone with the whore. He'd shown cowardice, not moral courage. Self-contempt destroyed all feeling of pride in his righteousness. In a perverse way he was really turning upside down the preachments of the Church. He'd been plain yellow, afraid to do what he wanted to do.

He wanted to get home quickly now and go to bed. In sleep he could forget the self-contempt with which he scourged himself. It would be years before he'd be able to marry Beatrice—provided she'd have him. Would he have to go through all those years of struggle, fighting the sinful desires of sex in his own body, condemning himself because he refused to give in to them? What was wrong with him?

He brushed through the swinging doors of the Forty-third Street elevated station.

VIII

Daniel O'Neill

THOUGHT DIARY

July 1st, 1925

    Thinking of love, I am unable to write how I feel on that subject. I am in several kinds of a quandary, and have not even attempted to analyze my emotions. Beatrice is a "darn sweet kid" at times, and on other occasions I seem too preoccupied to notice what she is. However, that is perhaps the final struggle of one who has steadfastly maintained that he was, is, and always will be, above love, of one who has been a cynic, a mocker, a Schopenhauer if you will. I have always held the position that the emotions are secondary and naturally that position does not easily relinquish itself. When I registered at the University, I only thought that I was in love. Since then I have held various opinions. Whatever may be the result of my present mania, I must and willingly admit that already I have had two memorable dates with Beatrice, dates that I will not easily forget. Now world, laugh that off. Damn you, laugh.

Chapter Eight

I

Beatrice looked lovely in her fluffy organdy dress, and her black hair glistened.

He pressed her warm body against his own. Coming out of a series of spins and fast whirls, he took long, slow steps, and laid his cheek against hers. He whiffed her perfume pleasantly. She clung to him.

"Keen music."

"Yes," she muttered noncommittally.

"I'm glad the dance floor isn't too crowded."

"Yes, there's room to move around in. You don't get mauled around."

Marty Mulligan and Lillian veered toward them. Danny removed his hand from her back and warded off a collision. This was a neat trick he'd picked up at Louisa Nolan's.

"There's all the difference in the world dancing inside and dancing outdoors—isn't there, Bea?"

"It isn't so stuffy dancing outside some place."

"On a night like this, you can imagine that you're anywhere, in the romantic East."

"But after all, we're still in Chicago," she said.

Her answer made him feel foolish.

"I was only talking. What I said classifies as Line Number 1 A, Form X 4695 Z," he said with affected flippancy.

She didn't laugh. He mustn't give her the impression that he was moony and sentimental.

"And what if we are only in Chicago. Wherever you are, that is sufficient."

"What form number is that?"

91

He laughed. Taking side steps, he shimmied with her along the edge of the damn floor.

"It's keen dancing with you, Bea."

Not wanting his shimmying to become noticeable on the half-filled dance floor, he reluctantly relaxed his grip on her. They glided around and around.

The dance floor was surrounded by tables. Japanese lanterns hung over them. The murmur of the lake nearby was low, a dimmed song persisting like an overtone to the dance music.

"Don't dance so fast—you take my breath away."

He slowed down.

The music ended.

"Yes, this is a keen place," he said, politely applauding the orchestra. "But then any place is keen which a certain Miss Carberry graces."

"You just told me that a minute ago."

"I thought you'd forgotten the Form Number, that's all."

Wouldn't the orchestra play another tune? She had punctured him. He wasn't sure of her. If she only knew the contrast between his dull and affected words and his deep feelings underlying these words! The air was so soft. The moon was lucent. The stars were thick. All these seemed to be a part of her. If only he could tell her tonight, convince her. His long arms hung awkwardly at his side.

The orchestra played *Frivolous Sal*.

They slid over the floor. He hoped his dancing was being observed and admired. Beatrice and he were dancing as gracefully as any couple on the floor.

With a heart that was mellow, an all-round good fellow . . .

"I like the way you sing, Bea."

II

"What did you do today?" Danny asked.

"Oh, nothing much."

Love meant talking about all the little things you did—sharing everything. When you were in love, you imagined that all your thoughts and actions were reflected in a mirror which she alone could see.

"I tried to teach Dugan how to play golf today. He's hopeless," Mike Flood announced across the table.

"It's a sissy game," Ike Dugan yelled down from the foot of the table.

"Sour grapes," Mike Flood razzed back.

Some of the girls smiled with propriety.

"I was studying history in the library today. It had tough competition from the thought of a girl named Beatrice," Danny told her quietly.

She was listening to the raillery between Mike Flood and Ike Dugan.

"Hey, O'Neill, can't you stop cooing and be sociable?" Marty Mulligan ribbed him.

"I was discussing history."

He bit nervously into a chicken sandwich. He gulped ginger ale.

"I was at Fraternity Row last night," boasted raven-haired Mary Catherine Boyle.

"Ike must be holding," Mike Doyle remarked.

"I went with Mike Mooney," she said.

Marty Mulligan clucked his lips at Ike.

"Mary Catherine and me are just friends," Ike said.

"Say, I saw Mike Mooney on campus today," Danny said casually.

"He's taking courses this summer so that he can be eligible for football in the fall," Mary Catherine said.

Danny O'Neill might become an All-American end at the U. of C. He turned his eyes on Beatrice. She'd be proud of him then.

"Do you know what I want to do? I want to find out if there's anything to Kipling's poems. I want to go to the East and become a beachcomber," Dopey Carberry remarked.

Danny summoned up a vision of Mandalay, imagining a white pagoda resembling a classic Greek temple, its marble brilliant in sunlight. He embraced Beatrice on the shady steps of the temple. She was beautifully bronzed. Arm-in-arm, they stared out, watching the elephants piling teak. He kissed her again. They stood at the bank of the sludgy creek. He was a famous man, taking her around the world on a honeymoon.

"How will you ever get to the East?" Al Herbert asked.

"I might clean up on the races. I've just worked out a new system," Dopey answered.

Al jeered.

"Well, I'm glad that Marty doesn't play the races," Lillian said smugly.

"I went to the races at Washington Park once. It was so thrilling. I simply couldn't understand a thing about the betting, but I won six dollars," Mary Catherine Boyle said.

"Neither does Dopey understand anything about it—but he never wins six dollars," Al Herbert added.

"Herbert, you don't faze me," Dopey laughed.

"Carberry can lose money according to eight different systems," Danny said.

"Dopey, you'll never get anywhere with that kid talk of yours," Marty Mulligan said.

"I don't want to get anywhere. What's the use?"

"I can't understand why Carberry wants to go to the East and live with the niggers," Mike Doyle remarked, puzzled.

"They aren't niggers. They're Mongolians. And the Hindus are Caucasians," Danny corrected him.

"What difference does it make? They aren't white," Mike Doyle answered.

"I wouldn't want my brother or any good friend of mine to talk that way," Lillian said, looking at Marty possessively. "I don't know why a young man always wants to be off somewhere all of the time instead of settling down and sticking at something so that he'll get ahead in life."

"I'm going to get ahead playing my new system and then you'll hear from me somewhere east of Suez," Dopey said.

"You're going to sit yourself right down in front of the old Moulmein pagoda and smoke a cigar, aren't you?" Al Herbert asked.

"I'll get 'em off, doing just that."

"Maybe I'll trot along with you."

"It's a go, Al. You and I will loll on the beach out there, watching the time go by while poor black Fuzzy Wuzzies work for us. We'll get 'em off just thinking of Mulligan and O'Neill pumping gas on a hot day."

"Such talk!" Lillian exclaimed.

"I'll be a big-time salesman in Nation Oil by the time you get there, if you ever do. Brother, I'll be riding around in a company car with a fat cigar in my mouth. I won't envy you none," Marty said, laughing.

"Mike, I hope I never hear you talk that way," blonde Katherine Slavin warned Mike Flood.

"Don't worry, Kitty, there's nobody ever going to find any air in my head," he assured her.

She patted his cheek affectionately. Danny wished Beatrice would show as much demonstrativeness toward him in public.

"What else will you do?" Beatrice asked her brother, her face lighting up with interest.

"Plenty," Dopey said insinuatingly.

"What'll you do when you get old? What'll happen to you? Where'll you be then?" Marty asked.

"The Burma girls will keep me feeling like sweet sixteen."

"The Burma girls don't get a chance at two Chicago hot shots like us every day in the week, do they, Carberry?" Al Herbert kidded.

"I'd like to travel. I will some day. Maybe next winter I'll be sittin' pretty enough to take a trip to Palm Beach. But not the way Dopey wants to go, on the cuff. You don't meet anybody worth meeting that way," Marty said, lighting a cigarette.

"Chicago's plenty good enough for me," Mike Doyle cut in. "I used to have a job on a railroad and I went to Washington and Baltimore every week. That was enough traveling for me for a long time. There was nothing in Baltimore or Washington I can't get just as good right here in Chi."

"Will you send us postcards from the old Moulmein pagoda?" Beatrice asked.

"He'll write 'Having a wonderful liquid time. Wish you were floating with me,'" Danny said.

"Al, we'll get batmen and servants for nix. Every time I want to lift my arm, I'll call my batman, and I'll tell him, 'Gunga Din, lift my arm for me.' I'll be so busy doing nothing that I won't have time to write postcards. I'll have my batman write them in Hindustan."

"You know, I don't know where the time goes to. Why, it just flies," Mary Catherine Boyle said to Katherine Slavin. "I seem to have all day on my hands, and I'm always so busy I don't get a chance to do anything. There's so many things a girl has to do to take care of herself. You have to fix your hair, and tend to your manicure, and take a tub every day. And then, there's your clothes and shopping and, my goodness, what isn't there to do? A thousand and one things. I never get a minute to myself to sit down and just think."

"Neither do I, Mary Catherine," Katherine Slavin replied.

"The trials and tribulations of a home girl," Danny commented.

"That's not clever, O'Neill," Mary Catherine said coldly.

"O'Neill, was that the remark of a gentleman?" Ike asked.

He felt critical eyes on him, telling him that he was *gauche*. But it was a good crack. And Mary Catherine Boyle deserved it. She was a Saint Paul snob. If he had Beatrice, what difference did it make what he said to a Saint Paul snob.

"Has anybody seen the new Patsy Gilbride picture?" Katherine Slavin asked.

"Oh, I just adore him," Beatrice said.

"He's so handsome, he petrifies me," Mary Catherine Boyle said.

"Let's go see it," Danny whispered to Beatrice.

"I saw it."

The orchestra tuned up. It played *My Wonderful One*, and Danny led Beatrice onto the dance floor.

"Some day I might be sending you a postcard from somewhere east of Suez. That would be the life," he told her.

She didn't answer. He glanced down at her. Her face was lifeless.

Was she slipping through his fingers?

"The East couldn't be any nicer than this," he said, pressing her to him.

"Maybe it could."

She danced this way with him. She let him kiss her. But still, she showed no real interest in him. She hadn't even bothered to ask him how he was getting on at school. Wasn't that proof she didn't give a damn for him? Why didn't he read the handwriting on the wall?

The dance ended. They drifted back to the table. He glanced off at a Japanese lantern. To him it symbolized romance, adventure. He had hoped for love tonight, planning and dreaming of it all week. How many imaginary dialogues hadn't he had with her? Now the evening was drawing to its end. It had turned out to be so flat—so stale.

He had to take things in his own hands. He must drop her before she dropped him, jilted, humiliated him. He knew that he had to jump the gun on her. And he know that he never could do it.

"Al, let's shove out to the East right now," Dopey said.

"I'm game."

"You can't do that," Beatrice anxiously told her brother.

"Don't worry, he won't," Marty said to her.

"So you think! Don't be surprised some day if you hear from me from Mandalay," Dopey said.

"I'll settle for Shanghai," Al Herbert said.

"*By the old Moulmein pagoda, looking eastward to the sea . . .*"

Danny began reciting; he had associated this poem in his mind with Beatrice.

"Hey, O'Neill, this isn't amateur night," Al Herbert said, squelching Danny.

Yes, she was slipping through his fingers. He was frantic. Feeling he must say something, he talked, his words and pronunciation becoming sloppy and careless:

"Say, I had a lug in to see me at my station yesterday. Some guy who was off his nut who was sellin' pencils. He kept tellin' me that he had stock in the company and he did this just to get a chance to meet people. I thought I'd never get rid of him. He was a lug, all right."

No one commented on his story.

III

Danny sat crowded in the back seat of Mike Doyle's Ford with Beatrice on his lap. Dopey was beside them. Because her brother was so close, he didn't try to kiss her. No one spoke. Why hadn't Dopey gone home in another car? Brooding, he stared out the window at the deserted streets. All the romance of the summer evening seemed to have gone up like steam. He slunk in his seat. He squeezed her hand. She didn't press back.

IX

"*Danny O'Neill is sweet on you, isn't he, kid?*" *Dopey said, lounging in the parlor with his sister in the late afternoon.*

"*He's a nice boy.*"

"*Maybe you're gone on him, huh?*"

"*Gosh, no, what do you think I am?*"

"*He doesn't have the measles, does he?*"

"*He's awful serious.*"

"*He's not proposing, is he?*"

"*No, he's just serious.*"

"*I've seen him stewed when he isn't so serious.*"

"*I guess every boy drinks. But I couldn't really think he meant it if I did see him drunk. He doesn't know how to go out on a date and just have fun. He might be dancing with me and suddenly he'll talk about a poem or something, and then he'll shut up and dance and hardly say a word. When I go out on a date, I want to have a good time, and he just doesn't know how to show a girl a good time.*"

"*I've often thought he ought to be a priest.*"

"*Maybe he should be. Other fellows go to college, but they don't punish you for it.*"

"*I see that he's a real high-pressure Romeo!*"

Beatrice smiled.

Chapter Nine

I

He waited in the parlor while Beatrice primped up. Some young girls were singing outside the window; their voices were sweet and fresh.

I'll take you back, Kathleen.

An Irish song. So many Irish songs were sad, about partings and death. He was Irish. Not a drop of any other blood in him for generations. The past of his race was dark.

And when the fields are fresh and green.

The voices of the girls floated in. They must be going off. He no longer heard the song. The street was quiet.

He wished Beatrice would hurry. He'd have to leave soon in order to get to work on time. It had been a good morning. Right after classes he'd rushed here in a yellow cab and they'd played tennis in Jackson Park. Usually it was boring to play tennis with a girl. They were so awkward, there was no sport in the game. But when you loved the girl, the story was different.

It was a joy merely to see girls of Beatrice's age. You could spend hours watching a girl like her. You saw her small breasts bounce and the moving imprint of her thighs under her light dress. You stole glimpses of her legs with fascination. You gazed into her dark eyes—*wild eyes like the roe.* He'd never seen a roe. You looked at her red lips. You studied the changing expressions on her face. How could it be boring playing tennis with her, seeing her body in motion? He had been enrapt, excited, so enthralled that he'd played badly without deliberation. She'd scampered over the court, missing shots, her dresses flying, revealing bare thighs just above her rolled stockings. And whenever she'd missed a shot she had laughed so gaily. His hopes had risen on wings. The memory of his disappointing date with her last week at the Chicago Beach Hotel had faded. Yes, he had misinterpreted her attitude toward him because of overanxiety, that was all. She wasn't slipping through his fingers. She liked him. She was beginning to fall in love with him.

He closed his eyes, trying to recapture and fix in his mind an image of Beatrice on the tennis court. He longed to have her forever. He wanted more than dates, dances, kisses. Was it that he just wanted to make her? *Make! Lay!* Those were ugly words when applied to his desire for her. *The desire of the moth for the stars.* She was a thing of beauty. Yes, she walked in sun and shower. When he was with her he felt as one must always feel in the presence of an object of beauty. And there was nothing in the world as beautiful as a beautiful girl. He wanted to own her as he sometimes ached to absorb the stars when he would suddenly stare up at them on a brilliant night, seeing them as if for the first time in his life. In such moods he seemed to be possessed of a craving thirst that could not be slaked, a hunger that could not be satisfied. He wanted to grasp, press into himself, take in the mystery and wonder of life as one breathed in air. He almost wished he were God so that he might penetrate into the essence of objects and creatures. God had made the world. God owned the world. The beauty of Beatrice made him envy God. He wanted to be in God's place in order to own Beatrice.

"I hope I didn't tire you out and make you fall asleep waiting for me."

He opened his eyes in surprise. He became embarrassed, as if she knew what he had been thinking of. How could he tell her?

"Oh, no, I was just thinking."

"Thinking is a good occupation—if you like it."

"There's nothing goofy, nothing to apologize for about thinking, is there?"

His choice of words was often slovenly. Why had he said *goofy*? It didn't express what he meant. What did he mean? Forget it!

"Of course not. I wish I weren't so dumb and that I could think."

"You're not dumb."

His words rang fatuously in his own ears.

She sat down.

"Sit with me on the couch. You don't have to be so far away," he said, approaching her.

"Oh, this chair is so comfortable."

A rebuff. He mustn't show disappointment. Had he just been deluding himself? He turned around and sprawled gracelessly on the couch. He sat up erect, stiffening immediately. He was so damned awkward anyway—why should he advertise his defects this way? He hoped she had not observed his ungainliness.

"Bea, what do you think of the Middle Ages?" he asked after a short period of silence.

She looked at him, nonplused.

"What a question! I never give them a thought."

"Studying them now at school, I find them very interesting. Yes, they fascinate me."

If he could only establish an intellectual rapport with her.

"Well." He halted. "Well, as I said, it was a very interesting period. Sometimes I think it would have been better to have lived then than now."

"Why?"

"Life was more adventurous, more romantic. Think of what a thrill it must have been to go on a Crusade with Richard *Coeur de Lion*, that is, the Lion-Hearted."

"But it's silly to wish for something that's impossible."

"Doesn't the imagination make life free? You can roam the ages in your imagination. That's why I like history."

She gazed off, bored. A band of suspense tightened about him. He must do something. What? He tapped his toe on the rug. He went over to her, took her limp hand, and clumsily drew her to her feet. He kissed her ardently.

"We shouldn't do this," she said quietly, freeing herself from his embrace.

"Why not?"

"It's daylight."

"That means that I can look into your eyes like pools, Beatrice."

"My aunt might come in and catch us."

"Sit down on the couch with me." He took her hand. "Don't act like a stranger to me."

Listless, she sat down with him.

"Let's go some place beside the Palm Tree Inn this week on our date."

"All right, if you want to."

His blood surged. Grimly, he unscrewed his high-school fraternity pin from his shirt and offered it to her.

"What's this?"

"My fraternity pin. Take it. Take it in exchange for your class ring."

If she did, it would be tantamount to acknowledging an engagement to him. He wanted to be engaged, even though he couldn't think of marrying her for years.

"Here," he said, gasping out the word while she faced him in bewilderment.

She sat immobile. He saw himself as foolish with his pin lying unaccepted in his outstretched palm.

"You know, Bea, I'm pretty keen on you."

He knew he was making a fool of himself. And what dull words to use in a confession of his love.

"Yes, I'm pretty keen on you."

"I like you."

"Then take this pin. Please?"

"Oh, I couldn't."

"Why, why can't you?"

"I can't. I just can't."

It was clear, clear that everything was all over now. Why had he done this? He'd acted without intention or plan.

"But, Bea, is that a reason? Why can't you?"

"It's too serious a thing to do."

"Why?"

She cast eyes on the clean white window curtains. He studied her in profile, waiting to perceive the least sign of emotion on her immobile countenance. Her lips were too thick. She smiled meaninglessly. He pulled her roughly into his arms and ran his hand along her thigh. She was inert.

"Don't be silly!"

He ought to give up hope and leave now.

"Is there some other fellow?" he asked impulsively.

"No."

"Are you telling me the truth?"

"Of course I am," she answered, annoyed.

"There's no other fellow then?"

"There isn't."

"And still you won't?"

"Won't what?"

"Won't exchange your class ring for my pin?"

"No, it would be silly."

"Is that final? Absolute? Won't you change your mind?"

His heart palpitated. His head was light. He was weak. His physical sensations robbed him of all control.

Angry, he wanted to hit her.

"Bea, are you telling me the truth?"

"Of course I am."

"Then why won't you wear my pin?" he said, trying to force it into her hand.

She drew away from him. He saw contempt unmistakably in her eyes.

He tried to smile sardonically. He couldn't. He was too tense.

"I have to go," he uttered in a low voice full of intensity as he got up.

She looked toward the door in the hallway.

"You know this is serious now?" he asked gravely.

"Is it?" she sighed with boredom.

"I make this offer again. What do you say to me?"

"No," wearily.

His shoulders sagged. Her amused eyes played on him remorselessly.

"Well, I suppose there's nothing more to say." He consulted his watch. "I have to go and get to work on time."

She followed him to the door. He picked up his briefcase and tennis racket. He dallied with his hand on the doorknob.

"Good-by, Beatrice."

"Good-by," she said with indifference.

He left, desolate.

II

Danny waited a moment in the outer hallway before ringing the bell. How should he act tonight to regain the ground lost by his blunders with her? It was too late to decide. He regretted having asked her to accept his pin. He realized he had made a mistake in telephoning her after that fiasco. She ought to be able to see through his explanation—telling her he had offered the pin to her as a test of her character and that he was proud of her for having shown such will power in refusing to take it. The excuse was so damned transparent. And he shouldn't have asked her for another date. She'd see through that, too. Well, it was too late now for regrets. He rang the bell. The buzzer sounded. He pushed the inner hall door and slowly mounted the flight of stairs. Her aunt was at the door.

"Oh, Dan, didn't you get Beatrice's message. She had her brother telephone your home to say she couldn't see you tonight," the aunt said.

Danny stared, momentarily failing to grasp the meaning of her aunt's words.

"Yes, Beatrice had to go out . . . oh, she had to go out and she said she was very sorry."

"I wasn't home. Since today was my day off, I stayed over on campus all day studying and so I didn't get the message."

"She was so sorry. But she had to go out."

She had two-timed him. This was the irrevocable end.

"What time will she be home? I can wait for her."

"No, she won't be home early, and we're all going out."

"Oh, well, just say I came. I'm sorry I didn't get the message."

"She was so sorry. She felt very badly."

"Well . . ." Danny began.

What was there for him to say? He tried to put on a brave front before the aunt.

"She said you could call her up sometime tomorrow."

"Yes, I will."

"All right, Dan, and I'm very sorry this misunderstanding happened."

"Oh, that's all right," he said feebly.

"Beatrice was so sorry. But you call her up tomorrow, Dan."

"Yes, I will," he answered without spirit, turning to leave.

He walked back along Sixty-third Street, crushed.

I'm a no-dough, he told himself over and over again.

III

Anxious, Danny sat in the hall holding the receiver at his ear waiting for an answer at the other end of the line. He was frantic for a date tonight.

"Hello."

Danny recognized the voice of Harriet Hayes' cousin, Glenn. If he were refused a date, with Glenn and Roslyn there to learn of it immediately, he would feel doubly humiliated. They could talk about him, laugh at him behind his back. That would be too gratifying a victory for Roslyn. There was no time to think now.

"Hello."

"May I speak with Harriet, please?"

"Oh, you want her? All right, I'll get her," Glenn said flippantly.

"Hey, Harriet, some kid fellow of yours wants you on the phone," he heard Glenn calling.

Glenn hadn't recognized his voice.

"Just a minute, she's coming," Glenn said condescendingly.

He felt like hanging up. He tightened his grip on the phone, overcome by an inexplicable anger. He heard her voice, sweet, girlish.

"Hello, who is this?" she repeated.

He was speechless for a few seconds. He lost all control over his tongue.

"Hello, Harriet, this is Danny O'Neill. I called you up to make a date with you, but I changed my mind."

He banged down the receiver and strode into the parlor, manfully thrilled with a sense of self-justification. A clever stunt. He had paid Harriet back for all the humiliations he had been subjected to by girls. He smiled sardonically, thinking of how he had gotten the jump on a girl, beaten her to the punch, won the battle by one quick knockout wallop.

He flopped into the rocking chair.

He might have gotten a date with her. Last New Year's she had been very friendly. He should have courted her instead of Beatrice.

Why had he done this? What if other girls had scorned him? She hadn't. His trick wasn't clever. He'd been boorish.

He paced the floor nervously. He sat down again.

He had pulled this stunt out of fear that she would say she couldn't go out with him tonight. And what was this fear? He was afraid of what others thought of him. All his life he had been the slave of what he wanted others to think of him. But yet he dreamed he would amount to something some day. Christ, he was a joke.

He had to get a date. He had set in motion his plan of revenge on Beatrice. He had suggested that Mike Doyle date her tonight, and Mike had done it. Then he had telephoned her and flippantly asked for a date, and when she had refused, he'd carelessly said he'd see her soon. Now he had to get a date and then he could run into Mike and Beatrice casually, as if by accident, at the Palm Tree Inn. That would show her that she wasn't the only grain of sand on the beach.

He had to get a date, and it was six o'clock. Eight girls had turned him down.

He paced the floor, ransacking his brain for the name of a girl to telephone. He took out his watch. It was six o'clock. On an impulse he rushed to the telephone and called up his cousin, Anna O'Reilley.

IV

Heavy chairs and a large couch squatted like fortresses in the O'Reilley parlor. Danny glanced covertly at the new and massive furniture. Was it beautiful? Was it in good taste? How could he tell? He had no way of knowing in matters of taste. He always envied families whose furniture wasn't shabby, because at home their furniture was.

He was uneasy about this date and the success of his plan. He was sorry he had arranged it and wished he had merely forgotten all about Beatrice.

"If your poor father was alive, I know he'd be proud of you for what you are doing, Daniel," Mrs. O'Reilley said.

Your poor father! Wasn't she telling him that the O'Neills were poor relations?

"Aren't you going out this evening, Tommy?" she asked her son.

"No, I've got to look up something on torts for Uncle Joe."

"Daniel, Tommy works so hard. He's at his books until all hours."

"I don't work too much, Mother. There's no need to exaggerate."

Would Anna be ready soon?

He felt uncomfortable, waiting. And he didn't like Tommy.

"I believe in studying hard, but then, if you don't have

any fun when you're young, you'll have no memories later on
and you'll regret that. I try to mix fun and work in the right
proportion," Danny said.

"Try that, and later on you won't have anything but memories," Tommy answered.

"I believe in the golden mean," Danny told him, wondering
why Anna had even accepted a date with her poor relation.

"But when you talk that way, fun always wins out and you
don't get anywhere."

"I'll have my harmless fun in life and I'll still work hard,"
Danny said.

"I thought about going to day school, but it seemed a waste
of time to me. I can get all the law I need to know in school at
nights, and law is law. I'm glad I got started before a year of
pre-legal was made a requirement for night-school students,"
Tommy said.

"I think that in this age a lawyer ought to know about
sociology, politics, history, many things. That's why I quit
night school and registered at the University."

"Of course, Tommy, Daniel doesn't have the opportunity
you have—being in the office with Uncle Joe. Uncle Joe, Daniel, is a great man. Why, Uncle Joe is worth more than a college education to a young lawyer," Mrs. O'Reilley said.

She was rubbing it in about the superiority of the O'Reilleys
over the O'Neills. Her son had an uncle. He had a poor dead
father. Ironically, he reflected that here was the merit system
in reverse. He was exposing himself to the laughter of the
O'Reilleys. Wouldn't he ever learn anything from life?

Why had he made this date? He was a goddamned fool.
He'd known that he shouldn't call her. And he'd done it.

"One of the things I meant by saying that I think you
get a better preparation for law if you take a solid pre-legal
course is the course in medieval history I'm taking. My professor pointed out the role of law in the Middle Ages, and how
the monks had to study about property and property rights
because of the property owned by the Church. Well, that is

just one of the historical facts in the background of the history of laws about property. That's what I mean."

"Sounds to me as if they are trying to run down the Church at the University of Chicago," Tommy pronounced with finality.

Anna O'Reilley entered the parlor, wearing a shimmery blue dress. She was nicely dressed, and she wasn't homely. At least he needn't be ashamed of being seen with her on a date.

But if Beatrice learned that she was his cousin, his whole plan would collapse. What a fool he was!

Stripped of confidence, he left the O'Reilley home with Anna.

v

The orchestra played *Valencia*, one of his favorites. Gay couples danced by on the Palm Tree Inn dance floor. Beatrice sat across the table from him, prettier than she had ever been. Mike Doyle and Anna O'Reilley danced by.

"Would you like to dance?" he asked her, self-conscious.

"I'm awfully sorry, but my feet are so tired."

He had only asked out of politeness, but she'd misinterpreted it.

"It's just as well. I've lost interest in dancing anyway," he said flippantly.

She didn't answer. All evening she had ignored him. His plan had had no effect. He wished the evening were over.

"I like your cousin," she said, her eyes twinkling with amusement.

He had no answer. Anna had betrayed him, and Beatrice saw through his childish, transparent effort to revenge himself. He was a bigger fool in her eyes than he had ever been. It had been a dirty trick of Anna's. What amusement it would give the O'Reilleys, too. Now he was reduced to the status of a fool in Beatrice's eyes. She could never respect him again.

Wouldn't he ever learn?

"Yes, she's a nice girl," he said, choking out his words.

She fixed her eyes on him knowingly. Unable to bear her gaze, he turned to watch the dancers, assuming an objective interest in them.

She saw through him.

"Yes, I have lots of studying to do, so much work ahead of me that I'm not going to be having any more time for dancing. This is my last dance for a long time, and it's just as well," he remarked idly.

"What's just as well?"

"That I don't have dates. I haven't the time for that. A girl wants too much attention, and I'm too busy."

"Are you disillusioned?" she asked ironically.

"No, not at all. What have I got to be disillusioned about? I'm doing what I want, getting along in school, and that's what counts. Other fellows can have their fun now. I have a different idea."

"And what's that?" she asked, still ironic.

"Some fellows and girls my age want only good times now, so that, later on, they'll have memories. I want more than memories. I'm shooting big in this world."

Shut up, Danny! Shut your trap and keep your dreams to yourself! She doesn't care about them. Don't be a complete damned fool!

"I want to do many things, study law, study science, politics, literature, and I want to write."

Futilely, he was warning himself again not to go on.

The saxophone, dominating the dance music, gripped him. He yearned to take her in his arms on the dance floor.

"Some day I'm going to be a writer," he asserted, jutting his chin out belligerently.

"But if somebody wants to write, doesn't he have to have experience?"

"I'll have experience."

Let her laugh at him. He wanted to get drunk and tell the world to laugh and then, in the teeth of the world that was laughing at him, fling out an assertion of his ambitions. He tapped his feet to the music.

Both of them stared at the dancers, silent for several minutes.

"I like to sit like this, watch the world go by, watch people dance, and philosophize," he said.

"Yes?"

"Yes, I look at their faces and think about them. I wonder what they are like, what they do, and I speculate. I'll write about them some day."

"I never knew you wanted to be a writer."

"Yes, now, look at the guy with the brown suit, the way he lifts his nose. He's vain."

"Oh, I think he's cute," Beatrice said, glancing at a foppish-looking lad of about eighteen, whose partner was almost a foot shorter than he was.

"I didn't say he wasn't. If a fellow likes to be thought cute, I should worry."

"You wouldn't like to be called cute, would you?" she asked mischievously.

He was grateful that Mike Doyle and Anna O'Reilley rejoined them. He slouched in his chair, impatient for this humiliating evening to end.

X

"*At night when I get back to my hotel I try to forget the knit goods business. Often, instead of a card game or a show, I stretch out in bed and I read a book of philosophy,*" the bald-headed man said.

"*You have to have a high-horsepower mind to understand that stuff,*" the other salesman said.

Al puffed on his cigar and looked out the window as the train sped him home from a good vacation in Maine.

"*Yes, for reading, give me philosophy any time,*" the bald-headed man said.

"*Pardon me, there, but I overheard your conversation. I enjoy a book on philosophy myself now and then—the queen of the sciences,*" *Al said.*

"*I was telling my friend here how I read 'em all and take what good there is in all of 'em. Yes, my friend, I learned that there's some good in all philosophers if you take them right.*"

"*Tell me, who is your favorite philosopher?*" *Al asked.*

"*Well, it's just like I said. There's some good in all of them. I don't have any particular favorite.*"

"*What do you think of Gilligin?*" *Al asked.*

"*Who?*"

"*Gilligin. Didn't you ever hear of Dr. Gilligin, of Trinity College, Dublin—the greatest living philosopher according to the consensus of experts on the subject?*"

"*Oh, yes, yes, yes—Gilligin. Of course, sure, I read his books. Yes, yes, a brainy man. I was just trying to remember that book of his I read last winter in Pittsburgh. I haven't a good head for remembering titles. Just a minute, let me think . . .*"

"*His classic is* The Catogrammatic and the Syncogrammatic," *Al said with the assurance of knowledge.*

"*Of course, yes, yes,*" *the bald-headed man said.*

"*Well, good day, gentlemen,*" *Al said, leaving.*

He didn't know a great deal about philosophy himself, but he knew enough to spot a fourflusher. He walked to the dining car. He'd have to spring this one about Gilligin again, the next time he met some half-baked talker. When he saw Ned at home next week, he'd tell the story to him. He smiled. That fourflusher didn't even know that he'd made up the name Gilligin. Their eyes had popped out of their heads when he pulled such jaw breakers on them. It was a hot sketch, no mistaking that.

Chapter Ten

I

Inflamed nerves burned a path of pain from his aching, bloodshot eyes to his brain centers. And he had a sour stomach. Last night he'd slept only an hour or two toward dawn because of the intense pains in his eyes. This morning he'd dosed himself with aspirin, but it hadn't done much good. He'd had to force himself by sheer will power to listen to the history lectures and to make notes.

Danny left home early, carrying his briefcase stuffed with books and his lunch, wrapped neatly by his grandmother in a sheet of newspaper. Walking to the corner of Fifty-eighth and South Park Avenue, he wished these next two weeks were over. Until then he'd have to use his eyes more than ever in preparing for the final exams. He'd taken full notes on every lecture in both of his history courses, and he'd made notes on all he'd read. He was reviewing these thoroughly and memorizing all the salient points in the lecture notes. The lighting at the station was bad for reading, and he'd probably have a succession of eyestrains until this ordeal was over with. But then September would come. He would have a month's vacation. He could sleep late every morning, have a few good times, take it easy and rest himself for the long grind of school that would last from October to June.

He crossed over into the park, pausing a moment to watch a fast game of tennis on one of the end courts. He no longer had time for athletics. He missed them.

Why was he poor? Why was nine hours' work a day the price he must pay for an education? He had carried on this summer sleeping only five to six hours most nights. He couldn't go on like this forever. He feared he was breaking under the strain. He couldn't afford to let himself break. It was inadmissible. But he was so damned washed out. It seemed to him that he had sunk into the worst doldrums of his life.

He bent down to drink at the fountain near the park entrance. If the cool water could only assuage the pain in his eyes. The sensible course to take would be to go back and see his oculist. He turned from the fountain. Why had he been born with weak eyes? Earlier this year his doctor had advised him to read less. If he saw the oculist he'd be given the same advice again. What good would it be? He was an ignoramus. He had to read or else he would never know enough. What would there be in life for him if he had to sacrifice his ambitions and his study?

He found a shady spot of grass near the shrubbery close by the Fifty-eighth Street entrance.

He was clamped by fear. If he continued on at the same pace he had set this summer, he might lose his sight. He saw himself, blind, helpless, incapable of supporting himself. But if he were blind, there was the Braille system. And he might learn to be a writer. No, he would be a pauper, unloved, unwanted. Then he would never again see spring come over the world. The snow would fall silently without his eyes to behold it. Pretty girls would walk in Washington Park in the summertime, and he would not see them. He'd become a casualty of life with all his fine ambitions turned to ashes.

Pain shot through his head.

He might end a pauper, as tragic a figure as Papa had been.

He tried to pray that God might preserve his sight. His prayers froze on his lips.

He'd had eyestrains before and they had passed. He might not go blind. He lay on his back and closed his eyes. After class this morning, he'd sat on the grass on campus. The chimes had tolled *Nearer, My God, to Thee*. Drowsy, he had imagined he was hearing the Angelus bells ring out from a medieval monastery. He'd visioned brown-robed, barefooted monks pausing from their labors in the fields to kneel and pray to Mary. He'd lost his sense of time and place and for a few moments he had believed, as in a dream, that he was actually watching, hearing the monks pray in the fields. He'd recited the *Ave Maria* in Latin. Then the illusion had snapped. An intense longing had overcome him, a longing that had been almost unbearable. He had yearned to be living in the Middle Ages. The medieval centuries had risen in his mind, timeless, peaceful, sunny. He had thought of those dead years rolling slowly over the world while men had dedicated themselves to prayer, to the aim of achieving bliss in another world, to God. Men must not have lived in the same state of tension as he now did from day to day, sometimes from minute to minute. Questions had floated through his mind. What had the day-by-day life of the Middle Ages been like? What had students thought of, talked about in the medieval universities? He'd remembered fragments he'd read as supplementary readings, and he'd hungered for more knowledge of the Middle Ages. Professor Cotton, who was teaching History 121, had loomed up in his imagination as a man to be regarded with awe and envied. Although he was a Protestant or an agnostic, and often spoke against the Church, he had mastered so much knowledge of the history of those times. With Professor Cotton's knowledge you could live in your mind and imagination in the Middle Ages. The mind and the imagination made life bearable. Freedom was an attribute of thought and imagination. No matter what your actual situation was, no matter what problems you faced, your mind was free to roam the ages, to live ever gloriously in the past.

A girl had passed and he had glanced after her. The chimes had faded out in the summer morning. All had been still. Then he had heard the tapping of feet on the sidewalk near him. He'd looked around and seen Professor Cotton, a medium-sized man with a lined face and a red mustache, approaching. He'd wanted to talk to him, but had merely nodded. Professor Cot-

ton had returned the nod and gone on, perhaps to study still
more about the Middle Ages.

Danny opened his eyes. The park was green and sunny. In
the distance he saw the lagoon, blue, cool. An old man hobbled
along the path near him on worn-out legs.

He wanted to recapture his mood of the morning. It was
gone, as dreams always go. He thought of a lecture in which
Professor Cotton had pointed out that the men of the Middle
Ages had held a dramatic idea of the world. To them the world
had been a stage, created by an all-powerful, omnipresent God.
On this stage every human being was an actor, playing a role
in the great drama which involved the fate of his or her im-
mortal soul. And the dénouement of this drama had been either
the bliss and joy of Heaven, or else the misery and pains of
Hell. Today the world was that same stage. Automobiles, sky-
scrapers, steam engines, all the benefits, inventions, develop-
ments that followed the Industrial Revolution, these were but
new pieces of stage furniture and stage setting. It must have
been so much easier to have saved your soul in the Middle
Ages than it was today. Hundreds of saints had lived then,
offering examples of piety to the multitude. All of Christen-
dom had been Catholic. Men's minds had been turned devoutly
to an other-worldly ideal.

What was he doing to save his soul? Ambition could be the
vanity of vanities. Knowledge couldn't assure salvation.

In the distance he saw the sheep which were kept in the park.
He remembered how, when he'd been a kid, his airedale, Liberty, used to come over to the park and round the sheep up,
and then the park cops would come flatfooting it after the dog,
and Liberty would tear off. That was the past. The Middle Ages
were the past. The Middle Ages were part of Yesterday's Sev'n
Thousand Years. He couldn't live in the past. He had to go on.
His struggle was a hopeless one.

Here he was, wasting time. Across the grass he saw Long
Nose Jerry Rooney, Fat Mulloy, and Tommy Doyle wandering
about aimlessly. They didn't feel that they were wasting time.

He was different from them. He must always have been different. Perhaps that was a reason why, as a kid, he'd often been treated as a goof. Perhaps that was the reason why girls always gave him the cold-shoulder. Yes, he must be different. He'd tried to be like others, but he'd always failed.

What was Beatrice doing now? She might be at the beach, standing bronzed by the edge of the waters. Some fellows might be with her. Now she, too, belonged with Yesterday's Sev'n Thousand Years. He couldn't really have been in love with her. It must have been infatuation all over again. If it had been love, why had he gotten over her so quickly? Why had she faded into a nostalgic image in his memory? Two days after that final fiasco at Palm Tree Inn he'd been able to concentrate fully on study. She didn't know that.

He was wasting time. Eyestrain or not, he couldn't afford to.

He took a small leather-bound book from his briefcase and, lying on his stomach, he read:

> *Here, where the world is quiet,*

This spoke his mood. The world was quiet this minute. If the peace of the park, if the quiet lines of a poem could enter him, quiet him.

> *I am tired of tears and laughter,*

Yes, tired, tired, tired of tears and laughter. They passed like straws in the spent winds of life. Even the laughter of girls, golden girls, this passed.

> *I am weary of days and hours,*

He was weary, weary of the days and hours of this summer. Had the Torch of Learning he'd dreamed of holding last June when he'd registered for the U—had this burned out already? Where was the eagerness, the excitement, the hope, the zest for work and study of that morning—where was that now? The sun of that Saturday morning had seemed to burn with energy. The sun today was old and tired. Already he had grown weary of days and hours of study. He was tired of

> *. . . everything but sleep.*

Life had death for neighbor. And when you felt as he did now, what terror could there be in death? Man was a weak ship, a very weak ship, safe only in the last harbor.

His mind strayed from the little book. Yes, perhaps he hadn't loved Beatrice. Perhaps he had. If he only had her with him now. He could sink his head in her lap, close his eyes, feel her fingers on his eyelids, feel them in his hair as he had the night of the beach party. She would gently touch his aching eyes, softly nurse the pain out of them. But there was no Beatrice for him. He had been a chump in her eyes. That had happened in June and July. Now it was August. Beatrice seemed to belong to the July of another summer. *Where are the snows of yesteryear?* Where is the sun of last July? She had not known, and she never would know, how much he had wanted to love her, how much he had wanted her to love him.

The hell with Beatrice!

She'd never know of the terrible fits of depression, the moods of despair he had to go through, the days when his confidence was in shreds and he was ready to throw up the sponge. And if she did know, she wouldn't care. What did it matter to her if it cost him so much to lift his head high in confidence, to do something better and different from what Marty Mulligan and the whole gang wanted to do?

He turned back to his book.

> *Pale, without name or number,*
> *In fruitless fields of corn,*
> *They bow themselves and slumber*
> *All night till light is born;*

The words sang sensuously in his mind, calling him to life and joy. He read them over, caressing them with his voice. He was beginning to love words. Often they detached themselves from their meaning and ran in his head as if they were objects in themselves, sounds full of hidden mystery and emotion. *Willy-nilly. Drowsy. Fruitless fields of corn.* Swinburne used words as if he owned them. If he could only learn to use words that way some day.

> *She waits for each and other,*
> *She waits for all men born;*

He took off his glasses, closed his eyes, and sank his head in the grass. Small sounds, the summer wind high in the trees, the chattering of the birds, far-off voices, all blurred against his ears. *She waits.* Yes, she waited for all men. Somewhere, across dead green fields where flowers bloomed without purpose, a tall and beautiful majestic lady was waiting for him. Patiently, she was waiting for Danny O'Neill. Some day she would bestow a kiss on his lips, a kiss so different from that of Beatrice, from that of all the girls he had ever kissed. Her bitter kiss would be sweet, and it would say to him:

> *Sleep, sleep forever, Danny O'Neill.*

Death was the most beautiful, the loveliest lady in all the world, the only woman who would ever kiss Danny O'Neill with true sincerity. Why should he fear this beautiful lady? She had golden hair like the corn, and she wore a flowing white robe like a Greek goddess, and her lips were red. She walked slowly, with regal strides, with slow grace, slowly across the dead and dying years, past all of the barren flowers of the world, and she stopped here in the dreary green fields and she kissed this man, and then she walked on and stopped there to kiss that girl, and she walked slowly, slowly over the barren fields, this beautiful, majestic queen of the world. She was walking on, walking every minute of the day and night, walking on, slowly across the barren years, and in her mind she held the thought that some day she had an engagement with Danny O'Neill. When the time for that arrived she would find him somewhere across the green fields and she would approach him, and his lips would feel that bitter, lovely kiss from her red lips, and then never, never again, never again, would he be tired.

He opened his watery eyes. He saw waving blades of grass. Ants were crawling and working near him. He put on his glasses.

He read.

> *From too much love of living,*
> > *From hope and fear set free,*
> *We thank with brief thanksgiving*
> > *Whatever gods may be,*
> *That no life lives forever;*
> *That dead men rise up never;*
> *That even the weariest river*
> > *Winds somewhere safe to sea.*

He reread these lines, and then he read them again. He recited the two last lines aloud. They described the real end of all that he hoped for—and dreamed and loved and wanted. He was glad, suddenly glad, resigned that it was so, that the end of life was merely the end of weariness. And when the weary river of his own miserable life wound somewhere safe to sea,

> *Then star nor sun shall waken,*
> > *Nor any change of light:*
> *Nor sound of waters shaken,*
> > *Nor any sound or sight:*
> *Nor wintry leaves nor vernal,*
> *Nor days nor things diurnal;*
> *Only the sleep eternal*
> > *In an eternal night.*

Death! He wanted death. Swinburne had washed all fear of it from his mind.

Washington Park became dreamlike. People strolling on the path and over the grass seemed strange, unfamiliar. The world was unreal. It was quiet.

Suddenly he sat up. He had been seduced by the words of a pagan poet. *The Garden of Proserpine* was false philosophy. Death was not the end. There was no end. This world was only the stage on which he, on which every human being, acted out the drama of salvation. There was no consolation in the hope of a peaceful nothingness after life. He had been lulled into dreaming Swinburne's dream because of his fatigue. But he knew better. The purpose of life was death. And on the day of death, the soul faced God to learn its eternal fate. His task now was not that of being great in this world. It was to save his soul. He was failing to do that. Every day he sinned, sinned in desire. He'd sinned in desire with Beatrice. When the mulatto prostitutes passed his station at night, he sinned in desire with them. When he saw men going to the whorehouse next door to the station, he sinned with them in imagination. He was weak. One day he would face the unbending justice of Almighty God. Then, he could offer no excuses. It would be too late. Why didn't he try to save his soul now? He should practice spiritual exercises. He should pray for grace. He should receive the Sacraments regularly. Instead, he read pagan writers, Swinburne, Omar, the last chapter of Pater's *The Renaissance*. But he read other books also. Wasn't he reading *The Confessions of Saint Augustine*? Saint Augustine frightened him. Augustine pointed a way that was too hard. He responded spontaneously to Omar and Swinburne, but not to Augustine. Yes, he was sliding into Hell like one who helplessly slips down an icy precipice, unable to save himself. No, he was slipping willy-nilly into Hell. He could save himself if he had will, character. He didn't fight his sinful nature. In the eyes of God, he was no good.

The soft green of the park rested his eyes. Two lovers wandered by, hand in hand. The scene could have been laid in Arcadia. He told himself that death was impossible. Washington Park became an oasis, a Paradise set on the path of one's life as one journeyed toward the terrible storms, the winter rages, the fierce fires of eternity. He wanted to arrest this moment in the park and hold it as it was forever. He wanted to lie here forever. But his heart was beating. He felt his pulse. These were the signs that life was going on, that time was rolling inexorably onward to the horrors of eternity. The life of man was endless. The pains of this world were nothing as compared with those in Hell. They offered only a perspective of eternal hopelessness. *World without end.* The phrase came back to him from a prayer, licking his being with flames of terror. Momentarily, he cowered. He closed his eyes, and a red vision of Hell lit up his mind.

Another pain shot back through his head from his eyes.

Again he was unable to pray.

This Saturday he must go to confession. He must mend his ways.

How often had he not made that resolution?

He watched a weary old woman pass. His sadness deepened. She would die soon, perhaps sooner than he. Did she fear death? Did she fear the fires of Hell? He thought of Mother. She was old. She might die soon. Was she afraid? If she would only live a long time.

Reluctantly, he left the park. Why couldn't he be another Saint Augustine, abandoning the world to devote himself to God? Saint Augustine had lived a full life, had drunk his Cup dry before he'd gone to Africa. He hadn't lived yet. What was he to do? What could he do?

"Hi, O'Neill," Wils Gillen said, stopping to shake hands while Danny waited for a bus at Fifty-eighth and South Park Avenue.

"Working?" Danny asked.

"No, but I'm getting a swell jobber. Soft hours, big pay. I'm going to be the nuts."

"What doing?"

"I'm going to be a hot shot. Sellin'. Real estate."

"Good, congratulations."

"Where you bound for?"

"Work."

"That's tough tiddy, Dan. Too bad you can't come along with me and kodak on the beach. O'Neill, these days the beaches are full of ass that you'd give your life to kiss." Gillen blew a kiss to complete the meaning of his remark.

"Here's my bus."

"Well, I'll soon lay my head where it belongs."

Danny boarded the bus. With watery eyes he read Saint Augustine's description of the attributes of God. The bus shook and rattled, carrying him to another nine hours of work in the service station.

XI

"Well, Ned, what happened on that job with the outfit in Springfield?" Al asked.

"It isn't a job—it's a connection. Cripes, the way you are always reading and digging your nose in a dictionary, I should think you could speak better English. I wasn't looking for a job. I was interviewing a man about a position, a connection," Ned answered.

"Well, what happened?"

"He wants me to sell cheap shoes in jerkwater towns. I can't do that."

"Show it can be done, and you'll land something much better."

"Listen, I have a reputation to maintain in the shoe game. Suppose I go downtown to the Potter Hotel and tell some of my friends I have a job like that? They'll think I'm a has-been. I have my reputation to maintain. I can't sell cheap junk in jerkwater towns."

"It's better than nothing."

"Listen, I know what's good for me and my future."

Al turned back to his book. He breathed asthmatically, and fought with himself to control his temper. Ned read about New Thought in the Nautilus Magazine.

Chapter Eleven

I

His off day had drifted by pleasantly. The mild September weather had reminded him of afternoons of football practice in high school. He'd planned to go over to Jackson Park and watch the Mary Our Mother boys work out. He hadn't gone because he had been so absorbed reading a novel titled *Babbitt* that he couldn't put it down. Uncle Al had brought it home. Around four o'clock he'd soaked himself in the bathtub. He'd taken his time shaving and had dressed carefully, putting on clean B.V.D.'s, a fresh white shirt, and his newly pressed blue herringbone suit. He was only seeing Marty and the bunch, but he had felt quietly anxious all day, believing that tonight something exciting and wonderful would happen to him.

He left home at eight o'clock with the conviction that he was bound for an adventurous good time. He was rested and in tiptop condition. It was a shame he couldn't go out for freshman football, even though he only weighed a hundred and forty-five. Working in a gas station had certainly put him in condition.

The smell of autumn floated out of Washington Park. It was going to be a swell night.

All work and no play! He could play tonight. The mail this morning had brought him his marks from last quarter—two A's. That was cause for celebration.

He turned to the corner of Fifty-eighth Street and South Park Avenue, headed for the el station.

> For we'll always be together
> On a Chinese honeymoon.

127

Tim Doolan always sang this song in the old high-school days. The words had come to his mind. Singing them to himself, he believed he was really able to carry a tune.

They might all go dancing at the Bourbon Palace. He'd spring a line on the Lizzie Glutzes there about how he was a University student out slumming. He might get a pickup and take her over to the wooded island at Washington Park.

For we'll always be together . . .

Memories, old songs, words sometimes streaming willy-nilly into his consciousness without his knowing why nor where nor whence. Was Saint Augustine's theory of memory correct? He wasn't sure he had understood it fully. Was memory a receptacle, a roomy chamber or attic in which all experiences were laid away? Freud held that memories were suppressed in the unconscious, and that there was a reason for everything you remembered or forgot. He would learn the truth about memory when he took a course in psychology.

Sometimes the words of Latin songs would come to him, and he'd silently sing them over and over again. *Tantum Ergo, Pange Linguam, Adeste Fidelis.* The song, *Tantum Ergo,* rolled through his mind.

"You look like you got something good lined up," Phil Rolfe said, stopping Danny near the drugstore at Fifty-eighth and Calumet.

"Oh, hello," Danny answered, grinning as if to imply that Phil's guess was correct.

"That's the stuff, kid," Phil said.

"See you soon," Danny said blandly, walking on.

That's the stuff, kid! Rolfe had patronized him. It tickled him. Next quarter he might be bid for a frat, and then he'd live a social life Rolfe couldn't attain.

He brushed through the station doors. He sized up the people on the platform, his eye peeled for young girls. There were none. A pregnant woman of about thirty stood near the scales. Women must feel ashamed when they have to go around letting the world see that they were knocked up. They looked ugly, too, with their bellies swollen out of shape, announcing to one and all that they slept with their husbands. But didn't that make the world go around?

He bounded a Jackson Park train. He was riding the same old route he'd taken morning after morning to go to high school. How so many things changed, routes you took, buildings, streets, when you yourself changed.

Well, he'd have a big night with the boys.

II

"Hi, Scholar," Ike Dugan greeted him in front of the restaurant near Sixty-third and Stony Island.

He shook hands with everyone.

"Now that we're all here, let's get a bottle," Marty Mulligan suggested, grinning broadly and rubbing his hands together.

"Now you're talking," Al Herbert said, and they all assented to the proposal.

They contributed their shares of the cost and went with Marty to a drugstore on Sixty-third Street. They waited mysteriously outside while Marty went inside with an equal air of mystery. He came out grinning with a sense of accomplishment.

They walked over to the Sixty-fourth Street entrance to Jackson Park. Marty pulled the bottle of gin out of his pocket with ritualistic gestures. Danny recalled that on a sunny day in May, 1923, he and Marty had sat in this very spot with their classmates, talking about the future. Smilga had said that O'Neill would do something. Well, O'Neill was on the way toward fulfilling Smilga's prediction. What had happened to little Smilga?

For we'll always be together . . .

The words returned hauntingly. He wished he were back with the boys on the eve of graduation, talking about the future. He was happier now than he'd been then. He was developing. Was tonight a sign of development? A few drinks of gin wouldn't hurt him. He needed a couple of shots, but he wouldn't get drunk.

"Hey, you guys, don't drink it all," he jested while they kidded and bragged as the bottle was passed around.

"Up yours, O'Neill," Al Herbert said, taking a drink.

"He wants it down his. You got your tenses mixed, my hearty," Dopey said.

"Don't gag there," Danny razzed Al.

Danny took the bottle.

"Hey, one of youse guys keep your eye out for the Law. We don't want to be run in," Ike Dugan warned.

Danny gagged, and as he bent down Red Keene grabbed the bottle from him. His eyes watered and his throat burned. He hated the taste of gin.

"Gettin' yellow, Ike, worrying about the law?" Dopey asked as Danny gagged.

"Who's yellow?" Ike asked with braggadocio.

"O'Neill, I remember when you used to have cast-iron guts," Marty said.

"I drank it too fast. I got too much in my throat," Danny apologized when he was able to speak.

"Here, Dugan, you louse, drink now or get off the pot," Red said, handing Ike the bottle.

"Anybody comin'?" Ike asked, glancing at the path nervously.

"Yeh, the Chief of Police," Al remarked.

"Be careful, Ike, the archangel Gabriel is watching you," Danny said.

"Yeh, he's wishing he could have a shot with us," Dopey added.

"Say, I'm reading a dandy book, *Babbitt*," Danny said enthusiastically. "It's so funny and true to life. You guys ought to read it."

"Well, here I swill again, my lads," Marty said, accepting the bottle from Ike.

"Let's go to Twenty-two," Dopey suggested.

"Carberry, don't you ever get your mind out of the well-known mire?" Al asked.

"No, I never lift my mind above the well-known mire," Dopey shot back.

"Have you got the two bucks?" Marty asked.

"I thought someone would shell out for me. I'll pay it back tomorrow. I put all the jack I had on a tip on Jumping Jupiter. He'll jump me into the bucks."

They jeered.

"Let's go to the Bourbon Palace and dance," Danny said.

"Hell, I don't want to go and belly dance with Polacks," Ike said.

"Ike, don't admit you're ashamed of your country women," Red sneered.

"I'm as Irish as Paddy's pig, you red-headed monkey," Ike retorted.

"Another reason why you ought to go. Dance with the pigs," Red retorted.

"Pigs of a feather flock together," Danny said.

"O'Neill, come on, let's go to Twenty-two," Dopey whispered.

"Let's stick with the guys and see what they want to do," Danny said to shelve the idea of going to a whorehouse.

He took another drink. The gin went down more easily this time, warming his stomach.

They killed the bottle, and Danny flung the empty bottle in the bushes. His shoulder ached. An old football injury.

For we'll always be together . . .

Why did the song come back like a ghost of memory?

"Let's go to Twenty-two," Dopey said.

Without answering him, they trooped out of the park to get more gin.

"Jiggers, fellows, let's dash back to the park. There's Geraghty," Marty said as they were halfway across Stony Island Avenue.

They ran back to the park and Father Robert Geraghty turned the corner at Sixty-fourth Street.

"That was a narrow one. Wouldn't want him to see us pie-eyed and maggoty, even if we ain't in school any more," Marty said, puffing.

"A close shave," Ike said.

"Boy, he should know what some of his old students do, huh?" Marty asked.

They adventured out of the park again to buy more gin.

III

"O'Neill, you're maggoty," Marty said as Danny wavered, bleary-eyed, before the boys lined up on a park bench.

"I earned this drink. I worked like hell all summer studying. I got two A's, and this is my vacation. I earned a few drinks."

"What the hell do you have to earn a drink for? A guy gets drunk because he wants to," Marty said, puzzled by Danny's remarks.

"Do you want to know what I say?" Danny said.

"What?"

"To hell with the goddamned world!"

"Now that you said it, what else have you got to communicate to posterity?" Red Keene asked.

"To hell with the goddamned world!" Danny shouted in drunken defiance.

Al rose, staggered over to Danny, and laid a hand on his shoulder.

"Ladies and gentlemen, Professor O'Neill will now deliver an oration explaining his well-known views on the well-known world," Al proclaimed like a circus barker.

"All right, listen!"

"O'Neill, my ears are tired. Let's go to Twenty-two and get laid," Dopey said.

"Dopey, you're too drunk to get 'em off," Marty said.

"What you bet?"

"Demonstrate," Ike said.

"I will, on a black-eyed Bohunk at Twenty-second and Wabash," Dopey answered.

"Carberry thinks he's a C-man. O'Neill thinks he's an intellectual. What the hell do I think I am? I say, what the hell do I think I am?" Al yelled.

"I was talking when I was rudely interrupted," Danny declared.

"O'Neill, you're drunken Irish," Red said.

"And what are you—a sober Celt?" Danny asked.

"We N.D. boys hold our liquor," Red boasted; he jumped up and started to sing.

> *Beer, beer for old Notre Dame . . .*

"To continue again after I was rudely interrupted by a red-headed souse who goes to school in South Bend, I got something to say."

"Well, don't say it," Al said.

"Listen!" Danny said, straightening up in dignity. "Listen!" He tottered. "Are you listening?"

"I can't. I got to go to the bushes and take a liquid Carberry," Marty said, rising and staggering off to the bushes.

"Some day I'm going to lick the goddamn world."

They cheered him ironically.

"Do you want to see how I'm going to lick the goddamn world?" he asked, his voice thick.

He crouched, imitating Jack Dempsey. He swayed forward, ripping the air with a left, following up with a lunging right. He flailed the air.

"Well, now that I took my liquid Carberry, I feel better," Marty said, returning. "Say, is he seeing 'em already?" he asked, pointing at Danny.

Ike Dugan suddenly zigzagged to the bushes.

"Ike's passin' out," Dopey said.

Red Keene ran after him and held his head while he retched.

"Nobody can say that that gin isn't potent," Marty said.

"I won't pass out," Danny said, floundering back to the bench.

"I seen you pass out," Marty said.

"I won't pass out and I'm gonna lick the world. I suppose you don't believe that I'm gonna lick the goddamned world," Danny said.

"If you screw the world, you'll have more fun," Dopey said.

"I want a drink," Danny said.

"All right, divvy up. One more bottle and we'll all be swimming the crawl stroke in the gutters of Sixty-third Street," Marty said, getting up on unsteady legs.

Danny didn't care. He wanted a drink. Drink. He wanted to drink and tell the world and he didn't give six good goddamns. His head whirled. He saw a tree. It was two trees. It was three trees.

He dug into his pocket with an effort and handed Marty a dollar. Tears streamed down his face.

They staggered off. Danny's legs bent. He stumbled, and then he sprawled out on the grass. Marty and Red picked him up and dragged him along.

"Gonna lick the goddamned world," he mumbled.

"He better learn how to lick a bottle of gin first," Red said.

Al Herbert let out a war whoop and started running off like a madman.

"Al's pie-eyed, too. Hold on to O'Neill, Red, while I catch Herbert," Marty said.

Red supported Danny. Marty went after Al.

He staggered back with him. They straggled out of the Sixty-third Street entrance to the park.

"We're all pissy-assed," Marty said.

"And getting more pissy-assed," Red said.

"Oh, let's go to Twenty-second Street," Dopey wailed.

"Wahoooooo!" Al Herbert screamed.

SECTION THREE
1925-1926

XII

THOUGHT DIARY

October 10, 1925

My contribution to the Upton Coupon Book Sales Suggestion Contest was runner up for the five-dollar cash prize. I copy it into My Thought Diary.

Napoleon Bonaparte, the greatest man in history, devoted twenty minutes a day to his breakfast and dinner. How much should you devote to procuring energy and lubrication for your motor?

A need in our service stations today is facility for payments. Too much time is lost in making change, and the money becomes soiled so easily that it is disagreeably handled. What, then, is to be done? The answer is simple. BUY AN UPTON COUPON BOOK and save time. These books eliminate all handling of cash, and what could be more desirable?

These books will often save a minute when a minute counts. It is often that we lose out at work because of an avoidable delay at a gasoline station, or perhaps we see a competitor get a big sale simply because we had to change a twenty-dollar bill when buying oil where the attendant was out of change.

By the very logic of the fact itself, a coupon book is a decided benefit. It is easily kept; can be made nontransferrable, thereby releasing the danger of theft; serves as a ready budget for expenses, assures one of always securing peerless lubricants, superior gasoline, and efficient service, but why continue? The man who sees clearly, thinks clearly, and acts clearly, realizes these facts, and that is why he buys a coupon book.

Why not join the band wagon and be a happy member of our growing family of satisfied customers?

Chapter Twelve

I

"Who can tell me what Lyman Abbott has to say about the evils of the concentration of wealth?" Mr. Smithers asked.

Danny raised his hand and, receiving a nod from the youthful, bespectacled instructor, spoke.

"It concentrates the power of wealth in the hands of the few, causing depressions and a fall in the business cycle, and it leads to corruption and graft and a political oligarchy."

The loud noises of construction work on the Billings Memorial Hospital across the street jarred through the closed, leaded windows.

"Now, Mr. O'Neill, what conclusions do you draw from that?" Mr. Smithers asked.

"It's an evil."

"Would you say that it's a fundamental evil or an abuse?"

"I guess it's an abuse. You can't destroy all wealth, naturally. But too much concentration of wealth causes poverty, and that's where the evil comes in."

A student on the opposite side of the room from Danny raised his hand.

"Mr. Bernstein."

"I think a more fundamental statement can be made. The concentration of wealth is an effect of the profit system, capitalism. Under capitalism the concentration of wealth cannot be avoided. We have reached the point of development where machinery has supplanted the factory system of the early age of capitalism. We have reached the stage of monopoly. Instead of asking—'What are the effects of the concentration of wealth?', the question ought to be this—'How is it possible for there to be this concentration of wealth causing misery and corruption and injustice and other social evils?' "

"Of course, I was speaking without benefit of Karl Marx," Danny said.

"That's nothing to brag about. That doesn't answer anything at all. It seems to me we ought to ask the important questions and not lose ourselves in what's not important," Bernstein said, unruffled and without anger.

Realizing that he had made a cheap wisecrack, Danny felt he had earned Bernstein's rebuke. Bernstein was serious. Most of the students in the class weren't. They sat bored from one class hour to the next, and would have slept if they dared to. They read few of the assignments in supplementary reading, were irritated by discussions, and merely wanted to get by with a passing grade. And hadn't he been appealing to this laziness against Bernstein, who was a brilliant student?

"Isn't it open to dispute as to what are the primary and what are the secondary questions, Mr. Bernstein?"

"That's why we should try to apply critical intelligence. If we don't frame questions properly, how can we discuss them? If you ask the question—'What are the effects of the concentration of wealth?' you leave room for asking the question, is it an abuse of something good, or is it a fundamental evil, and then you can say it's just an abuse. That apologizes for capitalism. I don't think that's the real problem. The real problem is how, under what conditions, do we find the concentration of wealth in such a degree that we see these evils which follow from it?"

Capitalism? The very word raised more questions in Danny's mind than he could begin to try to answer.

"It's a matter of opinion, though, what are the right questions," Mr. Smithers replied.

The class stirred restlessly. A co-ed near Danny looked contemptuously at Bernstein.

"Opinions aren't all equally valid."

"How do you decide, then, which are more valid than others?" the instructor asked Bernstein.

"That's what we accept the principles of logic and science for. We offer our reasons and offer an alternative explanation to that which we find objectionable. When I objected to the question, I gave my reasons for it."

"Yes, but I'm afraid we're beginning to split hairs now."

"That doesn't refute my reason. Rather, it avoids answering what I said by making an invidious characterization."

Bernstein was his own age or younger. How could he know so much? How had Bernstein learned to talk so well, so brilliantly, never even pausing to reflect in an argument, never hemming and hawing? Here he had been priding himself on outdistancing so many of his own generation in the race of life, and now he was decisively put to shame by Bernstein. He compared himself with Marty Mulligan and Dopey and the bunch and thought he was really developing. But when he listened to Bernstein talk in class, he lost all his pride. He wasn't developing as fast as he had begun to believe.

"What do we mean when we say that there is hair-splitting? Do we mean that we are asking trivial questions? Or do we mean that we are being too precise? There is a difference between triviality and precision in the formulation of ideas."

"I grant that, but it seems to me, Mr. Bernstein, that your special bias dictates your objection."

"A Jew," Danny heard a nearby student say in a half-whisper.

"Did Darwin have a special bias in favor of science? And was this on the same plane as the special bias of the theologians of England?"

"I don't know what that has to do with a class in economics, Mr. Bernstein."

"I said that in answer to your assertion that I had a special bias, as if my views were not to be considered as objective but as prejudiced, biased."

"Well, I have the impression that they are. In the remarks

you make here, I see that there is always a bias against capitalism. You can't abandon the whole profit system, and do it
against the experience of years of history and economic thought,
Mr. Bernstein. Even Soviet Russia found that out. Isn't the New
Economic Policy, the so-called Nep, a concession to the profit
system?"

"Besides being a temporary measure, it isn't fundamental.
The fundamental property relationships there are not capitalist.
The means of production are not privately owned."

"But doesn't that contradict the gospel of Marx?"

He would have to read Marx. In history, Mr. Dorfman had
said that one of Marx's errors was his belief in the iron law of
wages. That seemed correct. Take his own case. He wasn't paid
according to any iron law of wages which permitted him merely
to subsist. Neither were the wagon men at the express company.
Millions in America received more than subsistence-level wages,
didn't they?

"Karl Marx made a mistake in accepting the iron law of
wages," Danny said after raising his hand to speak.

"That's wrong. It was Ferdinand Lassalle who defended the
theory of the iron law of wages, not Marx."

Danny looked as blank and bewildered as did Mr. Smithers.

A. Lincoln Jones got the floor. A dapper, undersized student,
he rose, casually running his hand through his wavy brown hair.

"I don't know anything about economics in Russia . . ."

"Then what's the point of talking about it?" Bernstein interrupted, speaking with ardor but with no trace of sarcasm in
his voice.

"Mr. Jones has the floor, Mr. Bernstein," Mr. Smithers cautioned.

"I'm sorry," Bernstein apologized.

"I don't care to talk about it, except to say I agree with Mr.
Smithers. Human nature has shown that socialism can't work.
Mr. Bernstein doesn't seem to understand that the ideas he is
presenting to us here are foreign importations." A. Lincoln
Jones waxed oratorical. "They aren't native to our Anglo-

Saxon American system of ideas of self-government and initiative. And we can prove he is wrong objectively, to use one of his own pet words. Look at the two richest and greatest nations, England and America. They are Anglo-Saxon. And it's because of the native Anglo-Saxon ideas and system of these two great nations that they are the richest and most powerful, allowing everyone to use his own initiative."

Danny laughed loudly. A. Lincoln Jones lifted his eyebrows in disapproval.

"I was wondering where I fit in in what he says. After all, I'm not Anglo-Saxon. I'm Irish," Danny said.

Some of the bored students were stirred to mild laughter. Mr. Smithers smiled with restraint.

"The facts prove my contention," A. Lincoln Jones proclaimed.

"What facts?" Bernstein asked.

"The facts. Look at our prosperity. Look at the money we loan to Latin America, Europe, the whole world. England and America are the bankers of the whole world."

"The Indians look on England with eyes that don't quite see what you see. They have no respect for imperialism, and neither do the Latin Americans."

Imperialism. He was getting some idea of it from Dorfman's course.

Mr. Smithers appeared embarrassed.

"What's imperialism? What's wrong with it? Isn't it the duty of the more civilized people to help those who are less civilized? What would the backward people do without the white man, the Anglo-Saxon?" A. Lincoln Jones declaimed.

"They'd be free," Bernstein said.

"It's a known fact of history that before the English colonized India, the people lived in dirt and filth. Now there's sanitation, public roads, schools, modern cities and . . ."

"And millions of peasants, illiterate, in rags, underfed, and owning no Ford automobiles to drive along mythical roads," Bernstein interjected.

"I think we're getting a little off our subject. And time is getting short, so I'll take over for these last few minutes," Mr. Smithers announced. "There are advantages and disadvantages, growing out of the concentration of wealth. The concentration of wealth and power into fewer hands is a disadvantage. It has led in the past, more than now, to corruption, graft, the venal purchase of special privilege and similar evils."

What about the present? Teapot Dome? Danny asked himself.

"Of course, nowadays there is still bribery and corruption, but it is not as flagrant as it was in the past. And every problem of this nature that arises in the process of social and economic evolution also points the way toward finding a solution. Take, for instance, the corporation—while it is true that because the corporation is treated as a legal person, unscrupulous businessmen, who do not play the game according to the rules and the law, do take advantage of this legal fiction. But while the corporation makes monopoly possible, it also suggests to us the way that the evils of monopoly can be cured.

"Just a minute, Mr. Bernstein. I want to finish first, and then if there is time, we'll have more questions and discussion.

"Through the corporation wealth is concentrated. Larger blocks of wealth function as a unit. This makes lower prices and higher wages economically feasible. It puts idle money to work, producing more goods, raising the general standard of living. And there is a counter-tendency now at work and gaining momentum. Through the issuance of stocks in a corporation, we are discovering a means of democratization. Thousands of persons can buy the stock of a corporation. These thousands of stockholders are among the owners of business. One of the trends in the corporation today is to sell stock to employees, and thereby to take the employees into a kind of partnership in the business. Of course, this trend is only in its infancy. The big stockholders still dominate a corporation. But the trend is becoming more general, more pronounced. It is a sign of the direction that economic forces are taking."

The bell interrupted him.

"I'll continue this analysis tomorrow."

Who was right, Bernstein or Mr. Smithers? They both knew a lot. Danny left the classroom puzzling over the question.

II

The morning was drab, gray. Students clustered in front of the entrance to Cobb Hall, talking, laughing, smoking cigarettes during the short interval between class hours. Danny's classes were over for the day. It was only ten o'clock. He was master of his own time until he reported to the station at three.

What should he do? He couldn't make up his mind whether to read in Harper's, or to go home and read and write in his *Thought Diary*. He stood on the edge of the crowd, indecisive, his eyes darting about anxiously in search of a familiar face.

He saw a girl with splendid legs. He gazed at her as if by his glances he could coax or induce her into speaking. She didn't notice him. A husky athlete, sporting a C on his maroon sweater, approached her, said something, and the girl's face answered excitedly. The incident made him feel even more lonely.

Every day after Professor Dorfman's class he experienced this same feeling of letdown. In class, he lived in history and ideas. Then he came outside to a scene like this, and he became an unimportant atom on the edge of campus life. Lost in the crowd of students, he felt like an interloper. The club girls, the frat men, the athletes, all seemed to belong here, and they acted as if students like himself were intruding on their rights.

He was more let down this morning than usual because of Professor Dorfman's brilliant lecture on Napoleon. His mind had been swept by the drama and tragedy of Napoleon's life. The Napoleonic period had been one of glory.

La gloire!

In the Napoleonic period every soldier had carried a marshal's baton in his knapsack. The poor young man had had a chance to rise in the world. Adventure had awaited anyone with talent, spirits, energy. How commonplace the present now seemed by contrast. He might have had more chance to be somebody then than he had now.

What should he do? Why hadn't he made any new friends on campus?

The crowd broke up. Students pushed into Cobb Hall. Others drifted away. The girl with the splendid legs disappeared. He stood as if rooted to the stones. A. Lincoln Jones, wearing a green pledge card from a fraternity, passed with a co-ed on his arm. He saw Danny but didn't nod. Every day he was cut this way by students who were in his classes.

He went over to Harper's to read.

III

The large reading room of Harper's was almost deserted. The light was dim. Sitting alone at one of the tables, Danny opened a blue-covered book in eager anticipation, rereading the title several times: *The Corsican: A Diary of Napoleon's Life in His Words.* An image of Napoleon, wearing a cocked hat, rose up in his mind. From Napoleon's own words he could gain a sense of intimacy with Bonaparte. Think of it. By the time he was thirty, Napoleon had just about been master of France. He himself was twenty-one; he was nothing, a plodding, grinding student, constantly at war with himself to preserve his self-confidence, his faith in himself.

He read. In school it had been said that Napoleon was no good in geometry, and that he had been "dry as parchment." Napoleon had not been recognized in school. He hadn't been popular like the campus heroes of his age. Others had seemed more promising and had been more popular. And compare what he accomplished and what his schoolmates did later in life. Shouldn't this give him some hope? Danny read more, eagerly, now and then taking notes, losing all sense of where he was; he didn't hear the occasional noises that disrupted the quiet of the library, books slammed, whispers, footsteps, giggles.

. . . *I can forgive, but forget—that is another matter.*

Was he really a Christian, and could he forgive and forget? He ought to, and already he knew that there was much in his life that he couldn't forget.

How had Napoleon gained such self-confidence? He had used the pronoun *I* with no qualms of modesty, and he had given commands so briskly, with such decisiveness. Hadn't Napoleon Bonaparte ever doubted and hesitated? Were some born to command and others to be commanded? He didn't know how to command, how to win loyalty. Whenever he had to make a decision, he stewed, worried, was afraid to make up his mind, and when he finally did make the decision, he acted as if it were a great achievement.

In his early twenties Napoleon had given confident commands as naturally as most people breathed. Yes, he was so far short of being like Napoleon. He could never hope to achieve such greatness. But he had no chance. Who had a chance to be like that in this day and age?

> *. . . but the man who fears for his reputation is certain to lose it.*

Danny pondered. Reputation was something that always worried him. He was always troubled in making decisions lest other people look on him with contempt. He was living and thinking in chains, in the fetters of what somebody would think, or whether or not somebody would approve of his thoughts and actions. He must change. But did he have the character to break these chains of social fear?

Seeking to escape from his own thoughts, he read and laboriously copied out notes.

He hadn't been aware that two girls had taken seats opposite him. They whispered. One of them giggled. He looked up. They bent over their books. He read. Again whispers, and then a giggle. He couldn't concentrate; he tried to hear what they were saying. They might be talking about him, laughing and giggling at him. How could he begin a flirtation with them? What should he say? They seemed to think that a library was

a social center. Reading was impossible. The words registered
on his mind, and then blew away like so many puffs of smoke.
They looked to him like popular club girls. They were damned
good-looking.

The blonde giggled again. Unwittingly, he looked up and
stared at them. They met his gaze impersonally.

He moved to another table, hearing more giggles.

Why should he have been singled out this way to have been
annoyed? Well, if they were laughing at him, let them! He
would show them that one had ways of revealing one's scorn.
His would be to let them know that a book was far more interesting than they were. They were empty-headed, scatter-
brained flappers. If they watched him, they'd see that he was
studying as if unaware of their very existence.

Imagine Napoleon in his place here in the library. Could they
even realize the scorn Napoleon would have had for them?
. . . But Danny O'Neill was no Napoleon.

*Great events hang by a thread. The able man turns every-
thing to profit, neglects nothing that may give him one chance;
the man of less ability, by overlooking just one thing, spoils
the whole.*

Here was a very good motto. Here was something that stated
what he had often realized but had never been able to express
clearly. Here was what he was struggling to do. This described
what he felt about wasting time, about getting an education.

He read on, stirred by the same sense of excitement, gripped
by the same feeling of discovery he had felt a little while ago in
Dorfman's class.

IV

Danny left at eleven-thirty and was stopped in front of the
bookstore at Fifty-seventh and Ellis by a pimply-faced student
wearing a red pledge cap.

"You're O'Neill, you went to Saint Stanislaus, didn't you?"

"Yes," Danny replied, pleased to have been recognized by someone.

The fellow probably knew that he'd been a Catholic high school athletic star, and this gave Danny a sudden and added self-assurance.

"I'm McGann. I went to Saint Augustine's."

"Oh, I knew some fellows there. Ike Dugan went there last year. I played against Saint Augustine."

"Sure, I know it. I know Ike. He's a swell guy. Say, you here now?"

Wasn't it self-evident? Danny asked himself as he shook his head affirmatively.

"I'm a freshman. Say, have you been pledged to any frat yet? I'm pledged to Psi Kap. I'd like to take you around to our house for dinner some day. Want to come?"

"Huh, I'll come," Danny said, affecting lack of interest in order not to show any eagerness.

"Suppose I meet you tomorrow in front of Cobb Hall after the ten o'clock class and then we can set a date for some day next week?"

"Yeh, that's all right."

"Well, I got to mosey off now. I'll see you. I'm glad to know you're here. Most of them here aren't on our side of the fence."

Danny watched him go off. His eyes trailed after the legs of a co-ed. This meant he'd be bid to a good frat. After all, he had more to recommend him by way of a high-school record than McGann had. He went on home. His period of loneliness on campus would end. Yes, he'd be a frat man. Co-eds, parties, the right contacts would be possible. The great man turns everything to profit. He'd turn Psi Kap to profit.

v

Danny repeated a syllogism to himself on the elevated train.
The great man takes advantage of every small event.
Sperling took advantage of small events.
Sperling was a great man.

To himself, he was ironical about Sperling. But he didn't stand up to the old codger. He had let Sperling get the Indian sign on him, and hadn't that been a type of cowardice? But then, didn't this put Sperling in the position of being responsible for the station? The old man did most of the cleaning at the station and that gave him more time for study. He could use Sperling.

He sometimes acted like a little schemer. He guessed that everybody did. Hadn't Napoleon? Yes, but on a grand scale. To be a schemer on a small scale or on a grand scale didn't really change the fact that you were scheming.

How was he ever going to stand on his own feet in big things if he didn't start standing on them now in little things, from day to day? Without character, he'd be nothing but a grandiose *reductio ad absurdum*!

He got off the train at Forty-third Street and turned reluctant footsteps toward work.

He had to have a showdown with Sperling.

A slight rain began to fall as he approached the tile brick, odd-shaped service station on Michigan Avenue.

Sperling stood frowning in the station doorway; he was a chunky, gray-haired man with strong brown arms, and a composed face.

"Well, wasn't this a change in the weather?"

"Yes, it's raining. How did it go today?" Danny asked.

"Everything goes tiptop when I'm on duty," Sperling said.

Without answering, Danny went into the small closet to put on his overalls.

"I cleaned up in here today. You couldn't even find a speck of dust if you used a magnifying glass. I was leaving the crankcase for you. I guess it won't be any use," Sperling said sourly, as if Danny were responsible for the rain.

"Well, let's check up," Danny said.

"You were a dollar short this morning again," Sperling complained.

"That's funny."

The old man handed Danny a scratch pad and pencil. He and Danny went outside. Sperling slid a long ruler into each tank pipe and, drawing it up, Sperling called out the number of inches wetted by the gasoline and Danny jotted down the figures on the pad. They went outside. Sperling measured the oil tanks with a smaller ruler. They checked their figures by the tank charts which listed the gallons according to a scale of inches. Sperling counted out the money and then made up the audit. Danny watched, bored. As soon as Sperling went home, he could study.

"Everything is straight now. See that you keep it that way," Sperling said with authority.

"I will," Danny answered sulkily.

"There's no use in sulking there. I only tell you the truth."

Why didn't he tell this old bastard to go to hell?

"You're lucky you've got me for a partner. You're damned careless and might as well realize that you are."

"I'm not careless," Danny snapped angrily.

"I didn't tell you, but I will now—you forgot to lock the safe two nights ago."

"How could that have happened?"

"I'm telling you you did. I suppose that's not carelessness?"

"I can't understand it."

"I'm telling you this for your own good. I can't be watching the station when I'm off duty. From now on, boy, watch your step. Mr. North is a strict man. He won't stand for any carelessness. And Mr. Gallagher is going to another oil company. He was easier than Mr. North will ever be."

"When did all this happen?"

"Gallagher was in this morning to say good-by. North is going to change the system of supervision, I guess. And he's going to watch the men himself more carefully. Gallagher told me that. I'm giving you warning."

He understood Sperling now—the old fool was a frustrated straw boss. He was giving warning. Who did he think he was anyway?

Sperling washed up, and Danny, growing angry, watched the cars stream by on Michigan Avenue. Yes, he had to have a showdown and check Sperling's authoritativeness.

Sperling came out of the lavatory ready to leave. Danny observed that Sperling was just about the size of Napoleon Bonaparte. He determined to have the showdown now.

"Oh, I meant to ask you, can you get here an hour earlier tomorrow? I have to take my daughter to the clinic. You can come at four the day after."

"Sure," Danny answered, his anger melting into sympathy.

"Well, I have to do the shopping and go home now. So long, boy."

"So long."

Danny watched Sperling drive off in a rickety old Ford. There was something very sad about the old man. His bossiness and crankiness were mere foibles. There was no meanness in the old codger. Danny felt like a sonofabitch for his mean thoughts about the old man. Sperling was over sixty. He had no future. He was ending his days supporting his wife and crippled daughter on a hundred and forty-odd dollars a month. He had a hard burden to bear, and he never complained. And above all else, wasn't Sperling square? He could leave at night without checking up and know that Sperling wouldn't gyp him. If he had another partner, he might have to watch him like a hawk.

A Chrysler interrupted his thoughts.

"Five," the driver said.

He pumped the gasoline.

"Check your oil, sir?"

"Nope, Bud, I only use Pennsylvania oils."

"It's never too late to change to the best motor oil on the market, sir."

"How do I know it is? Pennsylvania oils give me satisfaction."

"It's been proven by hundreds of tests. These tests show that an oil should have a viscosity of a hundred and fifty to two hundred."

"What's that mean?"

"Viscosity means the power of the oil to resist internal friction. It's the power of a lubricant to reduce the friction of the pistons, for instance."

"What's the meaning of a hundred and fifty to two hundred?"

"That's the unit of measurement. Making tests, it was found that various lubricants resist friction, more or less. They measure the difference in the tests. And Upton oils meet the requirements of a lubricant perfectly."

"All right, I'll try a quart of your heavy oil."

Danny serviced the customer with the oil, gratified at his success. It began to rain heavily. He studied for tomorrow's class in Pol. Econ.

VI

Danny was inwardly anxious, sitting face to face with Mr. North in his office. Who wasn't somewhat afraid of his boss?

"What did the doctor say about your knee, O'Neill?" Mr. North asked sympathetically.

Danny warmed, felt more at ease because of Mr. North's friendliness.

"It's a detached semi-lunar cartilage, just a slight wrench. I'll be back in shape for work in a couple of days."

"It's a shame. You say you slipped on the pump island in the rain."

"Yes, sir."

If he admitted that it was an old football injury, Mr. North might decide he was physically unfit for service-station work.

"I'm sorry to hear about it. And what else was it you wanted to see me about, O'Neill?"

"You said that attendants should come and put things to you, and that's what I want to do," Danny began.

"The door of my office is always open to you boys."

"I wanted to ask if I could be transferred."

"Is there anything wrong at your station? Sperling is a crackerjack man. I thought everything was going smoothly at your station."

"It is. There's no trouble between Sperling and myself. In fact, I'm very reluctant to ask you for a transfer."

Mr. North waited for Danny to continue. Danny looked him in the eyes, frankly.

"My problem is this. I work until eleven now at nights, and I have to get up at six-thirty or a quarter to seven in order to make my first class at eight o'clock. I honestly feel that I could do better work for you, and in school, if I got more sleep. I was thinking that it would be better if I could be transferred to one of the stations with a seven-hour-a-day shift. I don't mind the seven-day week if I get through at nine every night. Of course, if you decide not to transfer me, I'll give you my word that I'll hold up my end where I am. I understand that when I'm on duty business comes first."

Mr. North leaned back in his swivel chair, wrinkled his brow, and gazed thoughtfully at the ceiling. Danny hoped he hadn't made a mistake.

"Of course, I like to have a man like you, O'Neill, in a busy station." Mr. North paused.

Danny waited in mounting suspense.

"Let me think. If I can find one of our stations where I think you can improve the business, you'll still be doing a lot. I'll look the situation over and let you know in a day or two. How's that?"

"Thank you very much. I am very grateful, Mr. North, because this means a lot to me," Danny said, relieved.

Mr. North made a note on a scratch pad.

"In the meantime I think you'd better rest your knee a couple of days."

"Yes, sir."

"I want to be sure, Mr. North, that I've made myself clear to you. If you don't deem it advisable to transfer me, I can go on

at Station Forty-nine. I place my work above my studies. I'm
not at all dissatisfied."

Mr. North drew a chart from a drawer and studied it.

"O'Neill, I can put you at Twenty-fifth and Wabash. That's
a seven-day-week station."

"That'll be all right, sir."

"Good," Mr. North said, making another note. "As soon as
your knee is in shape, let me know, and you can start there.
It does about four hundred gallons a day. There's a Nation Oil
station two blocks away. Now see what you can do about bringing us some of their business."

"I'll do my best. And, Mr. North, I can't tell you how grateful I am . . ."

"Don't mention it."

"I won't forget, and thank you, Mr. North."

They shook hands.

"Now, take care of the leg. And I want you to know, O'Neill,
that we thought your essay for our Coupon Book Sales Suggestion Contest was dandy. We were sorry we couldn't give
you the prize. But we liked it."

"I'm grateful, Mr. North . . ."

"Keep up the good work," Mr. North said, going back to
a stack of papers on his desk.

Danny limped out of the office and caught an eastbound
Twenty-second Street car. He stared out of the window of the
streetcar. Twenty-second Street was dirty: cluttered stores,
vacant lots, factories, cross streets where poverty stared at one
like an accusation. He had seen poverty and dirt in Papa's
home. Papa ought to be proud of him now. Papa knew. The
souls of the dead knew what went on in this world. Papa would
know even his most intimate thoughts if Papa were in Heaven
now. But knowing that, Papa couldn't be proud of him. Papa
had been dead going on three years. He couldn't have gone
from Purgatory in such a short time; three years was hardly a
small fraction of a second in eternity. The temporal punishment due even for a venial sin was incalculably long. Prayers,

masses, Communions, good works had to be offered up endlessly in order to free one suffering soul from Purgatory. But
Mama prayed all of the time for Papa's soul. She had sent offer-
ings for Papa to the Society of the Sacred Rose of Jesus Christ.
Mightn't that be enough to have freed his father.

He'd have Father Doneggan say another mass for Papa's soul
this week.

Could he afford it? He'd have to. He bragged about how
much he made. But he gave Mama seventy dollars a month out
of his salary, and ten more went to Mother for his board. Out
of the rest he had to save for the installment payments on his
tuition. And he'd spent eighty-five bucks of his savings for a
new overcoat. It was worth it. He looked as well dressed as any
of the campus hot shots. If he didn't gyp a little on the pumps
for supper money, telephone calls, and odds and ends, he
wouldn't be able to make ends meet. That was stealing, stealing
from Peter to pay Paul, from Upton and the public to have a
mass said for his father's soul. What a good deed that would
be!

Dirty kids fighting in front of a candy store.

If he stole money and used it for a mass, would that mass
bring remission of punishment of his father's soul in Purgatory? Yes, it had to. You didn't buy the mass, or the remission
of punishment due to sin. You merely made an offering. And
the source of that offering couldn't taint the mass. But it piled
up years of pain for yourself in Purgatory. According to
Saint Augustine, even infants sinned. If he lived to be eighty,
he would have to burn in Purgatory for centuries and centuries,
provided he escaped Hell. In fact, the longer you lived, the
longer you would burn in Purgatory. Last night he'd dreamed
that his conscience was a State's Attorney grilling him in a
criminal court. Conscience was the State's Attorney of God.

He deliberately forced these thoughts out of his mind.

He could take pride in the way he'd ingratiated himself with
Mr. North. Even in his thoughts it was always Mr. North, not
North. His conduct in the office had been almost craven. He

shouldn't complain. He was getting all the breaks he needed from North and Upton. But he had to become almost an ass-kisser to receive this consideration. America was the land of opportunity. But was this the only way one could get an opportunity in America? He should be grateful. He wasn't properly grateful. Yesterday he had written an essay for his *Thought Diary* on the inevitability of socialism. North should only know that, then he wouldn't be getting breaks in order to go to school. He had gone to the U to learn, and college had completely unsettled his mind in less than two quarters. He didn't know what to think and believe any more. His eyes were opening. Every day now he would ask himself, again and again, wasn't the oil business full of Babbitts? Couldn't the speeches he'd heard at the pep meeting last summer be put into that novel? Hadn't the executives talked like George Babbitt? Did he want to be a Babbitt?

He had to keep a sharp eye on himself. He couldn't let doubts become excuses for giving up his struggle. He had to be a conscientious attendant. He had to be a good student. He had to preserve his dreams. They were precious. But did a good worker, a conscientious attendant, pull the pumps on customers for pennies and nickels? Hell, Mr. Upton, head of the corporation, had gone to jail himself. The company couldn't throw bricks at his glass house. He was avoiding this problem like an artful moral dodger. But then others did the same thing. No man was perfect.

Danny glanced across the aisle at an unshaven, coal black Negro in soiled work clothes. In front of the Negro sat a corpulent Slavic woman in a brown coat. By her side he saw a young girl with a pimply face and a pointed chin. What were the thoughts of these people? Could they hope or dream for anything in this life? How could they have any goal, any future? He understood how removed he was from so many others, how much better off he was. He pitied the others. The march to success generated in you pity for your fellow man. He looked out the window. Poor people were walking along.

The world was full of unfortunate people who had no future. He hadn't pointed out in his *Thought Diary* that this fact was one of the real reasons why he sometimes told himself that socialism was inevitable.

He alighted from the car at the Twenty-second Street elevated. He passed three men in expensive suits with padded shoulders. Gangsters. He limped upstairs and boarded an elevated train.

He read about Bismarck in his history textbook. His doubts, questions, and moral problems slid quietly out of his mind.

"I'm a mother," Lizz proclaimed loudly in self-defense.

"Ma," Bill answered, "all we're asking is where the hell our money goes to. We bring home our pay envelopes unopened, and Dan brings you half of his pay. You get over three hundred dollars to run the house, and yet Dennis and I have to keep borrowing money at work for our lunches. Tonight all we had to eat was tea and buns."

"How do you expect us to work, eating that?" Dennis asked.

"You try running this shebang yourself and see how you like it. I raised you. I'm your mother."

"I don't know why we're three months behind in the rent, either," Dennis added.

"Say, you, you shut your trap. You're still a minor. The Law will take care of you if you get smart with me. You'll be said by me or I'll see Joe O'Reilley and have you in court."

"Goddamn it, we never have a nickel. The rent isn't paid. I'm tired of this," Bill said.

"The Church is richer than we are. You don't have to give so much money to the Church," Dennis said.

"Begrudging their poor old mother a penny for the collection box," Lizz said.

"And where did Pa's insurance money go to?" Bill asked.

"I suppose I didn't spend it on my children. I suppose you didn't get a suit of clothes."

"That was only thirty dollars."

"You'll see the money, Bill. It's going to be a window in the new Saint Patrick's Church."

"Say, you, if your father was here, you wouldn't talk that

159

*way to me. Wait until you get wives, then you'll sing a different
song. Oh, no, you'll never talk to your wives the way you do
to your mother."*

"Mama, I'm tellin' you for the last time, you got to show
something for the money that comes here," Bill exploded.

Bob strolled into the parlor.

"Get the hell out of here," Bill said.

"What did I do?"

"I said get out, or I'll kick your ass."

Bob strolled back to the kitchen.

"I'm going to start a delicatessen store and not be bidden by
ungrateful children," Lizz said, and then she blessed herself and
said a Hail Mary aloud.

Chapter Thirteen

I

"Dan, it's a shame that the Weather Man has treated us this way," Uncle Al remarked, sitting with Danny in the crowded hotel grill at Champaign, Illinois.

A sense of the pre-game excitement enlivened the room. It was decorated with pennants and banners, the gold and blue of Illinois and the maroon of Chicago. Every table was taken. Waiters hurried to and fro. Conversation mounted almost to a roar. Students, old grads, sporting people, milled in and out. A gray-haired drunk tried to lead cheers for Illinois, and he was laughed at. He staggered away.

Danny did not answer Uncle Al for a moment. His mind was lost in vague revery, and he didn't grasp his uncle's words until about a half minute after they had been spoken.

"Yes, it's a disappointment," he then added.

The trip down this morning had been dull. He had boarded the train in Chicago full of hopes and anticipations. After having read about special football trains in the sporting pages for years, at last he was able to ride on one. But he had had no one to talk to. He tried to strike up a conversation with the students occupying the same seat with him. They had cut him dead cold. The scenery had been dreary in the rain. He had sat nervously, now and then reading, now and then daydreaming of meeting a co-ed by chance and having a date with her after the game, and restlessly wishing during all the trip that it would end. It had ended. And here he was, having lunch with Uncle Al.

He glanced out the window. The rain beat down. A group

of students wearing yellow slickers and turned-up hats dashed across the street.

He ought to talk with his uncle instead of thinking and mooning.

"It promises to be a slow game. Punting will count today, and Chicago hasn't a man who can come near to Britton as a punter, either."

"You never can tell. Grange might break loose, even in the mud. I hope he doesn't. I always like to see the underdog get a break. And then I have to root for your team, too, Sport."

When he thought of Chicago as his team, he sensed a falseness in his emotions. The words and songs of school spirit seemed hollow and empty.

"Grange couldn't shine Paddy Driscoll's shoes," a bald-headed man at the next table announced oracularly.

"Dad, you always say that the old-timers are best."

"Even though we've been given such bad weather, Sport, the game's worth seeing. It's one of the big games of the season."

Danny nodded absent-mindedly.

"There's compensation in everything. You ought to read Emerson on the law of compensation. He ought to be read for style as well as for his pearls of wisdom. He says that everything that happens has its compensation."

"Yes, I know it."

"Yes, Emerson tells us that if something bad happens, some good always accompanies it. He was the philosopher of the silver-lining. Now, take this game to prove it. The rain will make it a slower game. But then I was able to get you a seat more easily and it didn't cost as much."

"If I'd known sooner that I was coming, I'd have gotten one at school."

"I've seen them all, and I tell you none of them could touch Paddy Driscoll," the bald-headed man loudly reiterated.

"Say, pardon me, friend," Uncle Al called to him.

The man looked at Uncle Al, annoyed.

"I overheard what you said. Grange can't touch the old-timers. I've seen them all," Uncle Al told the man.

"That must be a Chicago man, Dad," the bald-headed man's son said.

"Not on your life. I'm a Harvard man. In my day our teams were the real class."

The father and son turned their backs on Uncle Al.

"Sport, when you meet a fourflusher, that's the way to handle him," Uncle Al whispered, leaning across the table.

Reddening with humiliation, Danny didn't answer.

"Hell, the world is full of fellows who don't want to give a new man a break. Grange must be good or he couldn't be where he is. Well, Grange has the laugh on them. Everybody's talking about him. It reminds me of the time I met a Bostonian on a train going east. All he talked about was his ancestors. Know what I told him, Sport?"

Danny couldn't remember precisely how many times he'd heard this story. He imagined himself dancing with a college queen in a frat house.

"I told him, 'The real live-wire doesn't think of having ancestors. He becomes an ancestor.' Dan, that put the Yale Lock on our Bostonian. After that he was cold as a clam."

"Anybody that believes this publicity about Grange should have seen Dolly Gray. Now, there was a halfback," the bald-headed man said.

"I'd rather have paid more money for your ticket and be able to see a fast game on a hard field," Uncle Al said.

"Yes."

"But we aren't the choosers, are we, Sport? We can be glad that we have the opportunity to see the game."

"Yes, I guess we can."

"Here, take your ticket now. I couldn't get you one near me, but it's a good seat. Put it in your inside coat pocket so that you won't lose it. Always do that, Dan."

"I do," Danny answered, taking the ticket and putting it away.

The talk rose to such a pitch that Danny couldn't make out the individual words that spattered all around him. With lonely, envious eyes he saw assured, composed students talking and eating.

"Dan, is everything at home shipshape?" Uncle Al asked, to break the silence which hung like a wall between them.

Danny nodded affirmatively.

"Fine, fine, and don't forget to jolly your aunt along."

They ate. There often was so little to say with Uncle Al. He felt unduly shy with him.

"I got an A in a history quiz last week," he said, to make talk, and wanting to please his uncle.

"Good, very good. But watch the lingo there, Dan. A real guy doesn't say got."

For how many years had he been hearing this? He drove critical thoughts about his uncle from his mind. After all, Uncle Al was very lonely and wanted to talk to him.

"How were you able to get off work to come down to the game, Dan? You didn't mention it when I phoned you last night."

"I've been off a few days because I slipped and wrenched my bad knee. But it's better now."

"Take care of it. Is Mother well?"

"Yes, she seems all right."

"She seems to have been aging of late, Dan. Be very good to her. We won't have her with us always. Pray, say a prayer that God will keep her with us for a long, long time."

"I always do."

Winter was coming on. Every winter he feared it might be Mother's last.

"It's a fine thing to be a student at a good university. Dan, I always regretted that I couldn't get a degree. But I couldn't. I had to go to work. Your grandfather was getting old, and I had to help take care of Mother. And Ned went off and was married. I never could go to college, but I've tried to make up for it. I've always tried to read the best."

"I'm getting something out of school, I think."

"Dan, be more positive. None of these mental qualifications. That doesn't make the right impression. Don't say, 'I think I'm gaining knowledge from it.' Say, 'I am acquiring knowledge.' Remember that Frenchman Coué who was over here? He had the right idea. He was psychologically smart."

He'd once thought that you could achieve things, attain your ends, realize your wishes by merely wishing them. Yes, he'd tried Couéism. Now he knew better.

"Is business good?" he asked.

"Yes, it is. But say a prayer that it gets better."

It was clear that Uncle Al didn't want to talk about business.

They finished lunch. Uncle Al leaned back in his chair, lit a cigar, puffed on it with contentment, watching the smoke rings rise. Danny observed that each ring retained its own form when two came together, and then saw how the rings were lost in the general nicotine haze. His eyes watered because of the smoke.

He looked out the window. It was still raining.

He wished it were time for the game.

II

Down on the muddy gridiron the twenty-two mud-caked players took their positions. The ball was shot to a blue-jerseyed halfback. The crowd roared. The halfback ran into his own interference and fell. There was a pile on. The crowd yelled. Red Grange had lost three yards.

The referee, his white clothes streaked with mud, handed a towel to the Illinois center. A whistle announced a time-out period. The two teams grouped themselves together. The ball lay in the rain.

Danny shivered. He sat all alone, bored. It seemed silly to him to have come all this way to see this dull game. It was silly that it should have been written about in the sporting pages of the Chicago press all week. What difference did it make which team won?

Mike Mooney, wearing a clean, fresh, maroon jersey, trotted

across the field, reported to the referee, and then stood alone in the rain, adjusting his headgear. There was a lackadaisical cheer from the Chicago rooting section near him. Mike pranced up and down. It was all silly.

Once he would have thought that he had attained his greatest chance in life if he could be doing what Mike was doing at this moment. Imagine him getting into position at right end in a minute, ready to break his neck to stop Red Grange from carrying a football a few yards forward in the mud.

The time-out ended. The teams lined up. The crowd, miserable in the beating rain, cheered without enthusiasm.

Why were all these damned fools sitting here watching this game, welcoming pneumonia? Why was he a damned fool like other damned fools? A football crowd was a herd.

Britton, the Illinois fullback, gained three yards on a plunge inside of Mooney, earning a siss-boom-ah! from the Illinois students.

Danny shivered again. He was bored. He wished the damned game were over.

III

In the picture on the wall of the hotel room a hoop-skirted belle of the Civil War South gazed at a garden of red and pink roses. Question: did flaming youth flame after the Civil War as it was supposed to be flaming now?

Danny folded his hands in his lap. He heard Uncle Al flush the toilet in the bathroom. He heard the water running in the sink. Dimly, from some place outside of the hotel, he heard a band playing the Chicago song, *Ever Shall Her Sons Be Victors*. Chicago had lost. Who cared? He was glad his own football career was over. Was this sour grapes? No, it was a change of values.

Uncle Al came out of the bathroom and sat on the bed. The hotel room was small, friendless. When he'd been a kid, he used to peer into restaurant windows, wishing he could eat all the meals of his life at their marble counters. Now hotel rooms seemed as romantic as restaurants had then. But there was nothing romantic in this room.

Danny took out his watch.

"You have plenty of time before the train leaves."

"I know it. I was just looking at the time," Danny said, putting back his watch; he'd already forgotten what time it was although he had just looked to find out.

"Dan, change your mind and stay over."

"I'd like to, but I can't."

"It's stopped raining now. Tomorrow ought to be a fine, crisp, autumn day. After mass we'll take a brisk walk in the country, and then I'll show you around the Illinois campus. We'll have a dandy fried chicken dinner and you can catch a train in the afternoon."

"I wish I could, but I have to get back. I'll have to study all day tomorrow. I have two quizzes on Monday."

"You haven't your books with you. Otherwise you could study here tonight, and I'd get a good book and sit here and read."

"I haven't them with me."

It was little enough to do for Uncle Al after all Uncle Al had done for him. Just give him one night when he was lonely. Sit here, too shy to talk about anything, knowing that at frat house parties and dances others were having the good times that were denied him. Well, next week Psi Kap ought to bid him.

"Tomorrow might be a beautiful day. You could see the last of autumn in the country."

"If only I didn't have these quizzes, I could do it."

"It's always the wise policy, Sport, to keep ahead of the game in your studies. Then, when occasions like this one arise, you can be free to knock off a day. It's not a good policy to leave everything to the last minute this way."

"I try to do that, but I have so much work to do that I can't always manage it."

"You're getting good marks at school, profiting from your study?" Uncle Al asked, lighting a cigar.

"Yes, I am."

"Of all the palaces in the world, there is none as consoling as the Palace of Intellect."

Uncle Al wistfully watched a smoke ring drift to the ceiling. Gay voices floated in from the corridor.

"Too bad you fellows didn't win. But when you lose, you have to be a good sport. One of the earmarks of a man of breeding is that he is a good loser. Sport, always be a good loser."

You fellows! He had neither won nor lost. Should one be a good loser if one were to be defeated in life? Take a case like Papa's. If the poor were always good losers, progress toward social justice would be slower, wouldn't it?

Was he a loser because he wasn't one of those going to parties tonight?

"Did you ever read William James, Dan?" Uncle Al asked.

Uncle Al wanted to talk, wanted to have a confidential talk that would bring them closer together. He wanted to avoid it. Why? Danny couldn't understand himself.

"I met a Jesuit, a smart priest, last week in Toledo. The cream of the intellect in the Church is the Jesuit. We discussed books. He said that William James is very dangerous to the Church. He has an elegant style. He writes with such style that he soothes and convinces with honey. I asked him about James' psychology, and he told me to read a book by a Jesuit named Father Maher. Ever hear of him?"

"No, I didn't."

"Some time when you're in the library, read him. But you ought to read William James for style. Style makes the man, Dan, in all walks of life."

The ride home would be long and dull. But he'd read, and that would make the time pass more quickly.

Did Uncle Al suspect that he was out of the social side of college life, a failure at it? He mightn't be after next week.

"Yes, it's too bad your time isn't free so that you could stay over."

He felt deep sympathy for his uncle. They'd hardly talked

all day, and their conversation had been nothing but common-places, words to fill up a vacuum of time. But he had gained a new sense of his uncle, seen him with a sharp clarity that he'd never had before. Uncle Al was a lonely and disappointed man. There was no romance and adventure in his life. It was dull. He traveled from one hotel room like this to another. He did it to make a home for all of them. And they were never happy in their home.

The past came choking up on him—fights, his aunt drunk, endless worries about money. This was all part of the home that Uncle Al had kept going for years, living in rooms like this, spending nights as lonely as this in hotel rooms all over the Middle West.

He wanted something different from such a life.

He ought to stay over. He didn't have any necessary studying to do. He could stay. He was a louse.

He looked at his watch, anxious for the time to pass so that he'd be on the train.

"Anyway, Sport, you had a good time today."

"Yes, I did."

"Fine, fine, I'm glad to know it."

Uncle Al's great frustration was that he'd never been a college man. Now he himself was a college man, and he, too, felt thwarted, frustrated. It was ironical. Life was ironical. But today he had learned and felt something he knew he would never forget. It was a clearer knowledge of the sadness, the fundamental sadness, of all life. It was of a sadness so pervasive that it could never be eradicated from the world. Wrapped up in himself, thinking of Uncle Al and of home, seeing carefree students out for fun, he had come to this realization. As a kid he'd looked forward to manhood. He had grown into young manhood. Young men could be sad and unhappy. He was. He was looking forward to the future. Then he would be older. One day he would be as old as Uncle Al. Uncle Al was sad and unhappy. Must the future always disappoint one? This day seemed like the epitome of all life. All day he had been anxious for what was coming, never enjoying the moment at hand. On the train he'd been anxious for the ride to end. At lunch he'd kept wishing the game would start. During the game he'd wanted it over with. Now he wanted to be on the train. On the train he'd want to be home.

"What's the matter, Dan? You're so quiet. Is there anything on your mind?" Uncle Al looked at him apprehensively. "You're not in any trouble, are you?"

"Oh, no, not at all. I was just thinking."

"Dan, if you ever get in any trouble, you want to let me know," Uncle Al said, embarrassed.

"I'm not in any trouble. Everything's going fine with me," Danny answered, equally embarrassed.

Uncle Al puffed on his cigar. From outside, he heard jazz music.

"When you get home now, Dan, don't forget to forward my mail regularly. You have my itinerary, haven't you?"

"Yes, I will."

"Jesus Christ!" Uncle Al said, consulting his watch. "You better hurry. You always ought to make it a rule to be fifteen or twenty minutes ahead of time traveling. Come on, I'll walk down to the station with you."

IV

The coach was almost empty. Danny put his book beside him. He thought of Uncle Al's life as a lonely vista of nights like this one. He remembered the drunken students he'd seen in the lobby leaving the hotel for the station. He was leaving a scene of fun where he'd been a stranger. He wanted this dreary train ride to end. An inconsolable misery took hold of him. He forced his attention back on his book. He heard the whistle of the engine as the train plowed on toward Chicago. He asked himself, would people look out of windows or stand on the streets of small towns and look at this train pass, enviously wishing they could be those who were traveling on it?

He wanted the train ride to end.

V

Danny sat at one end of the long, rectangular table in the Psi Kap dining room. Twelve brothers and pledges were having lunch, and he was the thirteenth person present. But no one seemed to notice this. And he had no superstition about the number thirteen. A white-coated student waiter set his plate before him. He cut up the roast beef immediately into small pieces and then he reached across the table for a bottle of catsup and used it to douse his meat and potatoes. A fat boy, wearing a polka-dot bow tie, watched him from the other end of the table. He caught the eye of a handsome brother with wavy hair, who wore a major C on his maroon sweater; the fat boy nodded toward Danny and then shook his head negatively. The handsome athlete silently signaled agreement.

"You like it here at school, Mr. Nolan?" the handsome athlete asked him.

He was Koll, the popular halfback who had played a bang-up game against Illinois last Saturday. When Danny had been introduced to him by McGann, Koll had repeated his name correctly. Danny felt he was being insulted.

"Yes, I do. But my name is O'Neill."

"Oh, I'm so sorry," Koll said blandly. "I confused you with a chap named Nolan who came to lunch here yesterday."

"Yes, how do you like it here, Mr. . . . ah?" asked a skinny brother with big ears.

"Yes, I like it," Danny said, perplexed, wondering why he should be treated to this insolence when they didn't even know him.

"Oh, it's a good school," the lad with the big ears commented meaningfully.

What ought he do to correct the bad impression he seemed to be making?

"What time are your classes?" the big-eared one asked.

Was this sparring before they asked him the important questions on which to decide about pledging him? Or was this merely a means of politely making talk because he bored them?

"Eight and nine o'clock."

"I couldn't get up for classes that early if my graduation depended on it," said Big Ears.

"Well, I work in the afternoon," Danny replied.

"Oh, you do?" a skinny brother asked snottily.

Koll shook his head profoundly. Many fraternity men from Chicago and elsewhere worked during vacation periods.

"How did you happen to become interested in us, Mr. O'Neill?" asked a languid, overdressed brother who was built like a bean pole.

"Yes, how did you happen to pick us?" asked Koll.

"What?" Danny asked, stalling for time because he could think of no ready reply.

"I invited O'Neill. I knew him in high school," McGann interrupted.

Had McGann told them about his high-school athletic record? If they knew that, they wouldn't treat him this way. Why were they doing it?

"Where did you go to high school?" asked Koll.

Now the conversation was becoming more promising.

"Saint Stanislaus. It's now Mary Our Mother," Danny answered, pleased that since his high-school days the old school had developed better teams and gotten lots of publicity in the sport pages.

"Where is it?" asked Koll.

"South Side," McGann answered.

"I know that and I didn't ask you. You're not to speak until you're spoken to," Koll told McGann in a surly voice.

"I'm sorry," McGann said obsequiously.

Danny was indignant. He knew he couldn't take this. He couldn't be a pledge and be spoken to that way.

Danny concentrated on the food as if it were a problem. The potatoes were cold and lumpy; the roast beef was fibrous, tough. None of the advantages of belonging to this fraternity was to be found in the food they served. That much was definite.

No one spoke to Danny for a while. He heard cross currents of conversation about co-eds whom he didn't know, fraternities that were mere names to him, and the editor of the campus paper, *The Daily Maroon*. He didn't read it. Perhaps he ought to. Why had they bothered to invite him here? He remembered how, when he had belonged to the frat in high school, he'd felt superior to those who weren't members. One used to become almost bloated with a sense of one's worth when a possible pledge was brought to a meeting to be looked over. They were probably regarding him now as he had used to regard others. What cheap snobbery it was! And he had ambitiously looked forward to this lunch. The fat boy grew almost poetical as he described a week-end date. He might as well not be present. Here they were, like a jury of his betters, judging him, alternately ignoring and insulting him. Why? Because they had old men with jack, and he didn't.

"Who do you know on campus, Mr. O'Neill?" Koll asked with a sudden revived interest in him.

"Well . . . Mike Mooney, but not very well, and I know Jim Gogarty—he's out for track."

"Mooney and you saved us last Saturday," Big Ears told Koll with flattery.

"Everybody played his best," Koll answered with a gesture of deprecation, almost of stage-like modesty.

"I thought Mike played a good game," Danny said.

Koll was uninterested in his comments about football.

"Gogarty—what fraternity does he belong to, Al? Do you know?" Koll asked the fat boy at the end of the table.

"I know him. He's not a fraternity man," the fat boy answered.

The student waiters removed the dinner plates. With embarrassment, Danny saw that he had spilled gravy on the tablecloth. He planted his elbows on the table and leaned forward to conceal the grease spot. They were served coffee and dessert.

More cross-currents of talk about campus affairs and personalities passed up and down the table. This was humiliating. He had to get out of here as quickly as possible.

After lunch they drifted into the front of the house. Several of the brothers flopped into chairs. The scene reminded Danny of magazine advertisements for collegiate clothes. The bean pole ordered McGann to go upstairs and get him a pipe. Danny stood near the fireplace, awkward, ill at ease.

"Do you play bridge?" Koll asked him.

"No, I don't . . . pardon me, but I forgot your name," Danny replied in a sudden fit of proud insolence.

"I'm just a fellow named Koll," the halfback answered while his fraternity brothers cut Danny with glances of sharp disapprobation.

"Koll, Koll, I'll remember it now."

McGann returned with the wrong pipe, was bawled out and sent back upstairs.

"I have to go to work now," Danny said.

"I'm so sorry. We might have had a good chat," the bean pole said.

"Well, it's been nice meeting you, Mr. O'Neill," the fat boy said.

"Yes, thank you for dropping around," Big Ears said.

They shook hands with him, each one offering him a limp paw and pumping his hand as if it were a ritual.

Danny left without thanking them for the lunch. He hastened off and across the campus thinking of insults he might have hurled at them. Without his willing it, his anger turned into a cold contempt. He realized that he had had the makings of a first-class snob in himself, and he could thank Phi Kappa Epsilon for the lesson in snobbery it had taught him. He would go through this University without benefit of a fraternity. He could make his own way here and in life without one. His lips were drawn into a tight, thin line. He jutted out his jaw as if to express his own resolution. He boarded a Cottage Grove Avenue car to go to work.

XIV

"Any good news, Al?" Ned asked after Al had unpacked his suitcases.

"Lovejoy is sticking. His doctor says he can do it, if he watches himself."

"I told you that this would happen. I poured good-health thoughts into him—now see—I was right."

Al assented.

"If he stays, the firm will go on, and I'll have nothing to worry about."

"Al, the biggest evil of this world is worry."

"I have my fingers crossed that now everything is going to be for the good."

"You can forget crossing them, Al. Everything is for the good."

"You know, I think that business will pick up, and we're going to have a lot. In a few years I think we can have a big house of our own, everything we want."

"Of course we can."

"Some day we'll be able to own a yacht. Think of it, we'll sail it any place we want to. We'll be admirals on our own yacht, Ned."

"There's no reason in God's world why we shouldn't."

Ned had a sudden coughing fit. His face reddened, and he rushed out to the kitchen for a glass of water. He returned to the back parlor wiping his watery eyes.

"Ned, you'd better watch that cough. Why don't you see a doctor?"

"I don't need those butchers. I'm all right. If I can cure Lovejoy, I'm sure I can do better by myself than these butchers they call doctors."

Chapter Fourteen

I

Bob O'Neill, dressed as an altar boy, struck the bell.

Saint Patrick's Church was lit up with candles and electricity. Father Gilhooley officiated at high mass. There was not a vacant pew, and people were banked several deep in the narrow space at the rear. The school children singing in the choir seemed to be sending words directly into Danny's heart as he bowed his head and softly beat his breast with a closed right fist. For he was not worthy. He had not gone to confession last night when he had had time after closing the station. This was the first Christmas since he had made his first Holy Communion that he was not receiving. He heard scraping feet and rustling clothes as many began leaving their pews to march to the altar rail. An old man and an old lady crushed by him. He watched them join the crowd parading forward. He was not worthy. He had not gone to confession last night because he hadn't wanted to go. Wasn't this willfully scorning the grace and Sacraments of God? He always dreaded confession, kneeling in the dark box, pouring out the catalogue of his sins, ashamed of them. But after confessing he would always step out of the confessional, feeling free, light, filled with joy. He could be feeling this way right now if he had really wanted to. There was no obligation to receive Holy Communion on Christmas Day. Failure to receive was no sin. But it proved to God that he was rejecting grace, that he was more than a negligent Catholic.

The bell sounded through the church. Unworthy for the Lord to enter him. His lips were dry. He wanted to feel the taste of the dry Host on his tongue, to feel it melt in his

176

mouth. How much more he always enjoyed breakfast after receiving Holy Communion. It whetted the appetite. You ate with such a clear conscience, such pleasure.

There would be a long wait now. Over half of those at mass were receiving Communion. Already people were crowded about five deep at the altar and others were leaving their pews. Father Gilhooley and Father Doneggan moved back and forth at the altar rail, mumbling Latin and laying the Host on one tongue after another. Oh, why had he been too weak to go to confession last night?

Life eternal was lodged in the wafer of unleavened bread. *In vitam aeternam,* the words sang in his mind. The greatest of all mysteries had taken place before him, and he was unworthy. Father Gilhooley had changed the wafers of unleavened bread into the very body and blood of Jesus Christ. Now he was placing God on the tongue of one person after another, on the tongues of Mrs. Doyle, Loretta Lonigan, Fat Mulloy, Natalie O'Reedy, her father and mother, Red McCarthy, and all the others at the altar rail. They were all worthier than he.

He had been afraid to admit in confession the venial sin of appropriating little sums of nickels and dimes and quarters. He had been afraid to admit he'd sinned against the sixth commandment by immoral dancing and by sins of desires. He'd not wanted to admit that he hadn't gone to confession since last March. And after all his luck and progress this year, he wouldn't do this much to give thanks to God.

Five o'clock mass this year wasn't the same. He had not come to church with the same eagerness and hope as he had in other years. In his mind he had already begun to leave the parish, the neighborhood.

Communion was taking a long time because of the crowd. And this was a high mass. He wouldn't be able to wait until the end. He had to open the station on time. But then, he hadn't missed the important parts of the mass, so this wasn't a sin. He dreaded leaving the warm, brightly lit church to go home.

He watched Jim Clayburn march up to the altar. All around
him he saw faces, some familiar, others unfamiliar, frozen in
piety. The moment people entered church their faces changed.
Yes, *frozen in piety* was a good description of this change.
They took their hearts out and put them on their faces; they
put their hearts on display in honor of God. The women seemed
almost to swoon in prayer.

Corpus Domini.

The body of God, the flesh, bones, heart, blood of Jesus
Christ was in all of those little wafers. Jesus Christ had been
God and man..God could punish him for his inexcusable laxity.
Did God really take such revenge on people? Fathers often
forgave children. Wouldn't the Heavenly Father of All be
forbearing? After all, human nature was weak and corrupt.
The ways of God were mysterious. Why had the omnipotent
God sent His only Begotten Son onto this earth to be scorned,
maltreated, murdered by a mob? No earthly king had ever
willingly suffered to redeem his disloyal subject. Why had God
had to do it? God couldn't be God and be subject to laws of
necessity. Couldn't He have changed man's nature instead of
sending Jesus down to be crucified? And suppose God had
been disappointed in Lucifer? Then why hadn't he swept
Lucifer and all of his fallen followers from the universe? If
God could make something out of nothing, why couldn't He
also make nothing out of something? And why had He pun-
ished all the children of Adam and Eve for their sin of pride?
Most men didn't enjoy seeing even a dog suffer. God surely
couldn't enjoy the spectacle of human suffering. Adam and
Eve had bit into an apple, and here he was, thousands of years
later, suffering problems of conscience, sinning, suffering, fear-
ing eternal doom as a consequence because they had done this.
Fallible reason asked questions because it couldn't understand
the infallible ways of God.

The school children, seated in the two center aisles, left their
pews in order and approached the altar directed by eighth-
grade children. The little ones went first. After they received,

the mass would go on and end quickly. He used to march up like that and receive.

God knew everything that was going to happen in the whole future of the world. He knew every thought that every human being would ever have. Because of God's foreknowledge, what was the use of praying to Him for grace? God must know that when he endowed some sinners with grace it would be a useless gift, like giving money to wastrels. He knew that the grace wouldn't soften their hardened hearts. If He didn't know that, He didn't know everything. But He did know everything. He knew who would receive the last Sacraments, dying and unconscious, and thus be assured of Heaven without a last confession, and He knew what unholy sinners would die in sin and be doomed. He decided on the hour of everyone's death. He could prolong a life until the dying person had a chance to receive the Sacraments, whenever He wanted to. This was a knotty question. Predestination was a Protestant idea, and yet Saint Augustine seemed to have accepted it. Saint Augustine's *Confessions* didn't contain satisfactory answers to these questions. Yes, fallible minds were bewildered by God's infallibility.

You prayed to God for favors. That meant, didn't it, that God intervened in this world. He restored health to some but not to others. He granted favors as He wished. What was the principle on which He acted? It was a mystery. A mystery was something that couldn't be comprehended by man. No man on this earth could ever comprehend the mystery of God. So— why try? Why risk damnation by doubting? His questions would not be stilled. He wanted to know their answers. And who could explain these answers? Not even Saint Augustine could. Saint Augustine contradicted himself on predestination and free will.

Yes, God acted differently from earthly fathers. Earthly parents shielded their children from temptation. God didn't. God tested his children by exposing them. And if God created everything, He created evil. But God was incorruptible. The

Incorruptible couldn't create anything corruptible. God couldn't create evil or sin. Man did. Man had free will. This brought him all the way around the circumference of a circle of mystery.

He ought to pray instead of thinking in this vein. He bent his head to pray. Trying to keep his mind attentively on God, he asked himself what was God? He'd always imagined God as a stately old man, dressed in ecclesiastical robes and a tall golden hat, a kind of super-Pope. But God could not be like a man with flesh and bones that were corruptible. Saint Augustine had written that God was not a corporeal substance. Mother said God was a good man. Meister Eckhart had said that God was neither this nor that. Neither this nor that, how could that mean anything? What was God really like? If he went on thinking like this, he would sin in pride, doubt. He would risk losing his faith. Others had doubted, and then they had settled their doubts. Francis Thompson had.

> *I fled him down the night,*
> *I fled him down the days,*
> *I fled him down the labyrinthine ways of mine own mind.*

The children were parading to and from the altar. Around him everyone seemed to be getting restless. He was restless himself.

> *I fled him . . .*

He looked at his watch. It was time to leave. Danny squeezed out of the pew and left the church. He walked home in the cold as the dawn of Christmas slowly broke.

II

Mama had moved to a better apartment across the street, and there was some new furniture bought on the installment plan, and Dinny Gorman's wife had given Mama a good couch and a big chair. This apartment looked much better than the old one.

Danny sat on the couch, talking to Bill. Papa now seemed to be fading into the past, far away. In the old apartment he had always sensed Papa's presence like a tragic ghost.

"So you had a good Christmas dinner, huh, Dan?" Bill asked lazily.

"Yes, I ate too much."

The day was passing. Outside it was growing dark. This had been a happy Christmas Day, a good one. He had worked until one, reading in the station with almost nothing to do, and then he'd closed up and arrived home just as they were putting dinner on the table. Everybody had eaten his fill. Mother had had a good appetite. She had looked so cute, eating and talking away, wearing the new lace night cap he'd given her for a Christmas present. There had been no bickering or squabbling. And Peg had been in a wonderful mood, proud of the dinner she had cooked, especially of the chocolate cake she'd baked. Home had seemed good, precious to him, a fortress set in the center of a harsh and unfriendly world. And yet he had been uneasy. The calmness, the happiness of their dinner, the absence of all friction, had impressed on him the familiar thought that happiness was so passing in this world; it was evanescent. His uneasiness continued even now. Their happiness could not last. Nothing could last. Christmas Day itself was a day in which one's joy was interrupted by a saddening sense of how time passes, how another year has gone out of the life of everyone on the face of the earth. On Christmas Day a Catholic would often think of the long past of the Church, of the centuries that had rolled over the world since Christ was born in a manger. All the people who had lived since then, the families, the hundreds and hundreds of Christmas Days that had come and gone, the Christmas masses, thoughts of these would come to one's mind. One would see life as a place of sorrow and death. Yes, happiness was a transient bit of warmth in a cold and raging world. He was often uneasy when he was happy.

"I ate so much I can't even talk or think," Danny said.

"Well, Christmas only comes once a year, Dan. We ate our fill, too. Mama cooked a goose."

Walking over here with presents for everyone, he had thought of how all over Chicago today, all over America, all over the world, families had sat down to eat big meals. Many of them had been happy. The food itself made people happy, forgetful. And he had asked himself if there shouldn't be more to life than this? One of the highest peaks of happiness was to have a family gathered together around a family table, the food spread out for everyone to eat as much as he could, and everyone feeling love for one another. This was happiness. Uncle Al, Uncle Ned didn't want much more. Suppose they were rich, could they eat more than they had? Would butlers, cooks, a big house, an expensive table, really make them any happier? For years Uncle Al had worked hard, traveling and living in lonely hotel rooms to keep together the home, to have days such as today. There should be more to life. But what more could there be?

"How are things at the express company, Bill?"

"Dan, nothing ever changes at the express company. It's always the same," Bill answered, lighting a cigarette.

"Well," Danny began, but he didn't continue. He forgot what he wanted to say in a fog of vague thoughts and reflections. His mind was suddenly dull. He heard his stomach quietly rumble. "Well," he began, again forgetting what he wanted to say.

"Yes, we had a good Christmas, but am I glad that the holiday rush is over! Hell, Dan, some of them cold nights I didn't get into the garage until nine and nine-thirty, and I would have to be back on the truck at seven the next morning. Of course, I made my overtime, but am I glad it's over."

Bill worked hard, harder than he did. Physical labor was harder than study. And yet most people could do physical labor and few could discipline themselves to study. Even most students at school couldn't concentrate on a book for long. Often he watched them in the library. After a few minutes, a half hour, they would look up, whisper to one another, go out for a smoke. Was physical labor harder than study? If you had the muscles, you could lift a box. But muscles couldn't create understanding, could they?

"Dennis was worked to the bone, too. He was coming in dog tired every night. He was given a special wagon under Dutch Mueller," Bill said, tapping cigarette ashes into a tray beside him.

Danny licked his upper lip reflectively. When he had left home, they had been sitting around content, talking idly, hopeful about next year. Little Margaret had gone off to a movie. He'd go back home and read soon. The day would slip by, one of the best Christmas Days they had ever had.

He should have gone to Communion today. He would next Sunday.

"Eddie Collins is coming to the end of his string, isn't he, Dan?"

"I guess he must be slowing up. Next season I'll have to see a game or two. I haven't seen a game since I got out of high school."

"I don't see many any more, but I never miss a box score. Well, we saw our fill of ball games when we were kids, didn't we, Dan?"

Danny nodded.

"I wish those days were back again," Bill added.

They were happy now only in nostalgic retrospect, only because one eliminated the unhappiness from one's revery. He didn't really wish for the past to return. His eyes were on the future. But he had a future. Bill didn't. Bill would go on, working on the wagons at the express company. Uncle Al and Uncle Ned, did they have a future? Aunt Margaret was too old to marry. What future did she have? Or Mother?

He glanced around the parlor. It was clean. It looked respectable. The kids didn't have to feel ashamed now if they brought friends home. He was proud. He was partly responsible for this. He was glad he was able to give Mama half of his pay every month. But he felt almost like a stranger with his own family.

"Yes, Dan, we had good times when we were kids," Bill said.

Lizz came in. She wore a neat black dress with an apron over it.

"You look nice, Ma," Danny said.

"Oh, I dressed up for Christmas for my children," she said, sitting down.

"Will Dennis be back soon?" Danny asked.

"He went out with his friends."

"Dan, don't let her kid you. He has a girl."

"I'll bet he has a flapper," Danny said, winking at Bill.

"Don't you dare say that!" Lizz jumped up. "Don't you dare! If I find my son Dennis chasing after girls, I'll have a word or two for those girls. Son!" She pointed dramatically at Danny. "Son, stay away from the girls. All they want is to get a fellow to spend his money on them to give them a good time."

"Ma, we were only kiddin' you," Bill said, seeing that his mother was really disturbed.

Lizz's face beamed with joy.

"Oh, let me tell you—I was down to see the O'Reilleys last week," Lizz said.

She went on talking, and Danny and Bill only half listened to her. She stopped. She sat in the parlor, her face saddened. Danny observed her expression. He wondered—did Mama realize that her children were growing away from her, didn't need her?

"Let me make you boys some tea," Lizz said eagerly, getting up to go to the kitchen.

III

"My parents don't understand. They seem to think that books and knowledge are some secret vice like masturbation," Jim Gogarty said, sitting in the parlor with Danny.

Jim had just told him how his parents always nagged him

because he went to the University of Chicago. He was better off than Jim. Everyone in the family was proud of him for working his way through school. No one at home ever called the U. and A.P.A. place. So often in the past he had envied others because of their homes. Hadn't he been wrong? Who could have had a happier Christmas Day than he had at home today?

"There's nothing more to say about it," Jim sighed as if to complete his gripes about home.

"Everything comes out in the wash," Danny said, at a loss for any other comment.

"Dan, I wanted to ask you—have you given any thought to the question of which political party we ought to join?"

"No, I haven't—why?" Danny asked, surprised by the question.

"I have. After all, it doesn't make sense for us to be Democrats just because our parents were, does it?"

Danny shook his head negatively.

"The Democrats have had only two Presidents since the Civil War, and I think they're going to lose out here in Chicago in the next mayoralty elections. It might be a mistake for us to become Democrats. There's no use in starting your career by backing a losing horse, is there?"

"Sometimes, Jim, I think I'm becoming a socialist," Danny said.

Jim reflected for a moment, and Danny waited to hear what he would say, anxious to know Jim's opinion.

"I've thought about it, too. Many of the things the socialists want are right. There's no denying that. If socialism could only be achieved, I'd be for it. But is it practical to be a socialist? You can't get anywhere in American politics if you're a socialist, and if you can't get anywhere, how can you do any good?"

Danny paused a moment before answering.

"Politics will change. And, Jim, think of this—all over America, in colleges and universities, the idea of applying scientific method in political science is being taught for the first time. Students like ourselves, we're going to go into politics. We'll have new ideas, new standards. In twenty or twenty-five years, when our generation grows into maturity, politics will be different from what it is now. There won't be any room for the boss, the ward heeler, the politician like my cousin, Alderman Paddy Slattery."

"That's too optimistic. Prejudices can't be rooted out so easily."

"Why can't they?"

"It's just not human nature."

Danny scratched his head. Was what he said merely impractical idealism? He didn't want to be impractical.

Uncle Al came back from a walk and, seeing Jim, wished him a Merry Christmas. After taking his coat off, he joined them.

"Well, well, well, how are the two mental aristocrats tonight?" Uncle Al asked jovially, taking a chair.

Danny regretted Uncle Al's intrusion. He'd rather talk alone with Jim.

"Jim, let me ask you this—have you studied Napoleon yet?" Uncle Al asked.

Jim nodded.

"You know, he was one of those fellows who suffered from the chronic disease of cranium giganticus. Jim, that's highbrow for a swelled head," Uncle Al said, showing a modest pride in his language; Danny perceived that Uncle Al had guided the conversation to this subject in order to spring this wisecrack that he already had heard so many times.

"Napoleon was one of those fellows who thought he could conquer the world. The smart psychologists call that schizophrenia, delusions of grandeur."

"That doesn't explain Napoleon," Danny said. "He had to establish his continental system in order to defeat England. He was pushed into it by the economic and political situation in which he found himself."

"He had a swelled head just like the Kaiser. All these conquerors who make wars are the same."

"The war wasn't made by any one man. It was the product of economic rivalries," Danny answered.

"What the hell kind of bunco is that?" Uncle Al asked.

"It's economic rivalries that cause war," Danny began in an expository tone.

"Some of those professors of yours must be suffering from cranium giganticus themselves," Uncle Al interrupted.

Danny was disappointed. Uncle Al hadn't studied history as much as he had; Uncle Al didn't know as much history as his professors, and yet he was making wisecracks instead of discussing the questions he raised.

"Well, I have to go home," Jim said.

"Stay a while, Jim," Uncle Al urged.

"I'd like to, but I can't. If I could, I know I'd learn a lot by discussing things with Dan and you, Mr. O'Flaherty. I can see that you've read and thought a lot," Jim said, speaking very formally.

"I try to study and to arrive at my own views on affairs. I'm sorry you can't stay. But come again. We're always glad to see you."

Danny went to the door with Jim and talked for a moment. He found Uncle Al in the back parlor, beaming, with a book opened on the table.

"Your friend is a very fine and cultured young man, Dan."

Danny flopped in the chair opposite his uncle. He wondered what he'd read now.

"Coming back from my walk, Dan, I thought of a good suggestion for you, one that will always aid you in slipping one over on the wiseacres. It's this—develop your diction so that you can always put the fine Italian twist in your words."

"What's that?" Danny asked spiritlessly.

"I mean always to find the right word, the *mot juste*, as the French say," Uncle Al said, mispronouncing the two French words. "The French were birds for finding the *mot juste*."

Danny was bored. The uneasiness which he had felt all day disturbed him now. He wanted to be alone to think or read. Uncle Al didn't seem to sense that he didn't want to talk.

"And there's a passage here I marked in Lord Chesterfield that contains some profitable suggestions for you. Here, I'll read it to you."

Uncle Al picked up the opened book from the table and read monotonously.

"*The art of pleasing is a very necessary one; but a very difficult one to acquire. It can hardly be reduced to rules; and your own good sense and observation will teach you more of it than I can.*"

Uncle Al looked at Danny, his face eager for agreement. Danny said nothing.

"And listen to this: *Of all things, banish the egotism out of your conversation.* You know, Dan, to many fellows conversation is nothing but expostulation of the egotism of their own self. That is what Lord Chesterfield meant. Never do that. Always discuss ideas and manners; and cultivate the art of pleasing by conversation."

Why was he in such a mood? Was it because he hadn't received Communion this morning? He absolutely didn't want to talk.

"Let me see the book," Danny said, reaching across the table for it.

Uncle Al handed it to him with pleasure.

"That book is a great classic, Dan."

Danny skimmed through the pages. Uncle Al sat back reading the latest issue of the *Blue Book*.

Uncle Ned came home from a movie and called in hello to them. They continued to read without answering him. Uncle Ned put away his clothes and came into the back parlor, rolling up his shirt sleeves, a frown on his face.

"For cripes sake, look at the two of them. The house could be on fire and the two of them would have their nose in a book."

"Oh, hello, Ned."

"You two are the damnedest bookworms I ever saw."

"Sport and I were having a quiet, intellectual evening. Don't you believe that one should learn the best that man has thought and said in the past?" Uncle Al said.

"What book did you get that out of?" Uncle Ned asked.

"Matthew Arnold," Danny said.

"Who the hell was he? Some guy who died a couple of centuries ago and was dead from the neck up anyway?"

"Ned, haven't you ever read Matthew Arnold?" Uncle Al asked.

"Do I sound like I read Matthew Arnold?"

"Ned, he was the great *obiter dicta* of his day," Uncle Al said.

"And what the hell is that?"

"That's mental aristocrat for arbiter elegantiarum."

"One of these days that lingo of yours is going to choke you, Al."

"Ned, where in hell did you get all your crack-brained prejudices?" Uncle Al asked.

Uncle Ned picked up the volume of Lord Chesterfield's letters from the table and looked at it.

"What scatter-brained professor robbed the dictionary to write this book?" he asked.

"That's Lord Chesterfield," Al said proudly.

Uncle Ned glanced through the book.

"Hmm, so you got a book written by some guy who lived in the eighteenth century. What the hell do you want to be wasting your money buying this junk for?"

"Ned, that's a book you ought to read."

"What for?"

"Lord Chesterfield was a man of breeding, of manners; I tell you his sense of manners was so refined that the neologism Chesterfieldian was coined from his name."

"I thought he was the guy who put out cigarettes," Ned laughed.

Uncle Al's face turned almost purple.

"That's cheap," Uncle Al said.

"What the hell's cheap about it?"

"That's a great book. I bought it for Dan so he could learn manners, become a refined gentleman."

"Cripes, I never had to read a book to learn manners."

"It wouldn't hurt you to."

"What the hell do you mean now? Because I won't waste my time hunched over a long book written by some pig-tailed lord in knee pants, I have no manners?"

"I didn't say that."

"I don't know what the hell you did say."

"That's because you never listen to anyone."

"A fat chance I have of doing anything else but listen when you get started."

"Why, you goddamn fathead," Al said, jumping out of his chair.

Danny trembled, afraid they might come to blows. Uncle Al had a mean temper.

"Don't call me a goddamned fathead," Uncle Ned shouted.

"You give me a pain in the ass," Uncle Al yelled at Ned, rushing out of the room.

"Don't think that the long-whiskered words you spring on me give me a pain any place else," Ned replied heatedly.

"Why, goddamn it!" Uncle Al cursed in the hallway.

Aunt Margaret suddenly appeared in the room.

"Can't you let me sleep?" she yelled.

Uncle Al started to answer her, but she shouted:

"I slaved over a hot stove cooking for the two of you today, and this is the gratitude I get. This is the payment I get from you goddamned mollycoddles after all I've done, all my sacrifices."

"But, Peg—" Uncle Al began.

"Don't talk to me. Why don't the two of you get the hell out of the house? For Christ sake, forget books and go get a woman," she yelled.

She rushed out and cursed as she went down the hallway back to her room.

Uncle Al and Uncle Ned faced each other impotently. Their eyes dropped. They stood shy and abashed, like boys caught in a mischievous act, and were so shamefaced that they could do nothing but look down at the floor. Danny was equally embarrassed. He remembered, with pain, so many fights and quarrels in their home. Often it was just such flare-ups as this that sent his aunt off drinking. Now she was screaming at his grandmother in the kitchen. The happiness of their Christmas had only been a calm before a storm.

"Well, do something," Ned told Al.

"What can I do? Jesus Christ!"

Al rushed out to his sister.

"Did you ever see the beat of it, Dan?" Uncle Ned asked, his voice gentle, distressed.

Danny shook his head in shame.

"Cripes, my own sister cursing like a truck driver on Christmas night," Ned said; he went to the front bedroom and closed the door.

"Al O'Flaherty, you can take an express train straight to Hell," Aunt Margaret yelled from the kitchen.

IV

Danny was in his bedroom sprawled out on his bed, reading. The quiet of the apartment was menacing. His door was closed. Uncle Ned and Aunt Margaret were in their bedrooms behind closed doors. All of them were alone in the world, shut in behind these closed doors, isolated behind the doors and walls of their own minds. All of them were unhappy, except Mother, who was sleeping. The apprehension he had felt all day had been like a premonition that a family scrap was coming, that the contentment at the dinner table and at supper was a mere illusion. And hadn't it been that? He twisted about on the bed nervously. No, it hadn't been an illusion. It had been real, but not lasting.

The pain of scenes like this one tonight returned to him from the past. He brooded over them, his eyes fixed on the wall. In this apartment, in the one at Fifty-seventh and Indiana, in every place they had lived since he could remember, there had been scenes like this, fights, squabbles. He saw his own home as different from almost every other in the city of Chicago. But that couldn't be so. Every family had its fights. Every family had its skeletons in the closet. He shouldn't be sentimental or bitter; he shouldn't overemphasize the meaning of these scenes.

When Aunt Peg had told his uncles to get a woman, he must have blushed to the ears. Sex was always beneath the surface of his mind, a cause of shame, a subject that embarrassed him whenever it was mentioned in the presence of his family. They must all think of sex in connection with him. They must remember their own youths. He closed his book and pushed it aside. He closed his eyes and thought of naked girls. Last summer, why hadn't he had the crust to say yes to one of the whores who'd solicited him? Why didn't he have the nerve now to go and get one and end this damned strain of recurring desires?

By an effort of will he read again. But Lord Chesterfield bored him. Lord Chesterfield had written all these dull letters to his son, and what the hell had become of the son? Who had ever heard of him? What had he ever been, done, achieved? He stopped reading. Inner distress, sadness about the whole world, turned every thought into gloom. Why should he feel this way at twenty-one? He was weak, lacking in character because he let himself become a prey to these thoughts instead of concentrating on a book. His mind was always wandering, wandering like an empty canoe down a lonely river. Yes, his mind was a canoe drifting down the sad river of life. The black clouds overhead were warnings of the rain of death. He had been sad almost all of his life. He had lived filled with one shame and one fear after another. Why? He had never been confident that he belonged. But you didn't just belong in the world and have it accept you. You had to force it to accept you. And he had his chance to force the world to give him a place. He ought to see himself as the Happy Warrior marching against the world, full of the joy and lust of combat, gay and daring in his youth.

He was afraid.

And now Christmas Day had come and gone. One more day had slipped into the oppressive past, the oppressive past of all mankind.

He stared at the wall. He fell asleep.

v

Danny lay in bed. He had awakened this morning aware that a change had taken place in him. It had seemed as if the moment he had opened his eyes and his head had cleared of sleep that there was a difference in him. He wasn't the same person he had been when he went to sleep last night. Painfully, he had understood that his whole attitude toward Uncle Al had changed. He hadn't wanted to accept this realization, but he had known that it was true, known it so intimately that he didn't have to express it to himself in words. It had been coming for some time, and the discussion with Jim Gogarty last night, the quarrel with Uncle Ned and his aunt, the thoughts he had had alone in his room, these had not been the cause of his change but only the end of an emotional process that had been going on half consciously in him for a long time.

How could he express his new attitude toward his uncle? He was sorry for Uncle Al. He pitied him. He no longer feared him. He didn't depend on him. He could think for himself in opposition to his uncle. He had escaped from his uncle's influence. Yesterday at mass he had realized he was growing away from the life of the neighborhood. With the family, he had seen himself more or less a stranger looking on at them. New attitudes had been quietly developing in him and they now were making themselves felt. Just as a tree grows, so had these new attitudes grown in him. He had hardly thought out these new attitudes, but he had known all the time that they were growing. That night in the hotel room after the Illinois-Chicago football game he had known. Then his uncle had seemed a sad and lonely figure. Yes, that night had been a very important one in his development.

For Uncle Al had always regarded him as a son. When he'd been a boy, he'd dreamed of the time when he'd be a young man, and he and his uncle would be like father and son. He was certain that this had been his uncle's dream, too. They would have interests and ideas in common. He would be a student, and they'd discuss his studies. They'd go out together, go to mass together on Sunday, see ball games. They never went out together. He and Uncle Al talked about books, ideas. But how? Look at the discussion with Jim last night. Only the externals of the dream had come true. The psychological changes in him had destroyed the dream forever. It made him unhappy to accept this fact. But yet, even in his unhappiness, he knew he had gained a new freedom. He knew now that all these years he had been ignorantly groping and trying to stand on his own feet. And now he was doing it. His relationship with his uncle, with his family, was a casualty of his own development.

He fixed his eyes on the bedroom ceiling and wondered— did Uncle Al sense that their relationship was altered so radically? The question frightened him.

He wished he could pray, pray that Uncle Al didn't sense anything. But what could prayers do?

He'd get up now. He had stayed in bed until Uncle Al had left the house. He hadn't wanted to face him. He'd feared he might reveal his new attitude. And lying here in bed, hearing his uncle and grandmother talking in the kitchen, he had realized that his uncle was physically so small. It was singular that even though he'd grown so much taller than his uncle, he hadn't observed how small his uncle was. Of course, stature and height didn't mean smallness in character, or anything like that. But still, how had it happened that he had been so unaware of his uncle's size? This awareness had come only with emotional and psychological changes.

Was he fair to his uncle? Uncle Al had bravely kept the home together for years. He had worked hard. He had kept his worries to himself. He'd practically never complained. Uncle Al still kept up the house, allowing him to give money to Mama and use the rest for himself and for school except for a kind of token of ten dollars a month he gave Mother. Was he fair? This question had nothing to do with fairness, no more than love did. You could be fair in your actions, but you couldn't change your deepest feelings and needs on the ground that they were unfair to someone else. When you did, you merely pretended to yourself.

Suddenly he jumped out of bed. He was hungry. He washed and dressed in a hurry and went out to breakfast. Mother gave him a cup of coffee, and put on eggs and bacon. He watched her. Her hair was turning gray fast now. She was fading. Uncle Al was growing into middle age. He was young. As he was developing, they were all growing older.

He ate heartily.

Yes, Mother was fading. Changes went on in the mind and in the emotions, and changes went on in the mortal flesh of everyone. All the uneasiness he felt yesterday, all the distress and sorrow he felt last night returned to him.

Little Margaret, tall and thin, walked slowly toward Sixty-third Street. She was going to see the new Patsy Gilbride picture at the Tivoli. He was so wonderful. She never missed one of his pictures. She wished she were in the theater already, watching the picture begin. But soon she would be.

She would have to walk home because she only had enough money for the show. If she were working, she could go to a movie on a Sunday afternoon, and then afterward have hot chocolate and ride back home on the elevated train. Gee, she didn't see why she should go on pretending that she was going to high school. She had not gone to school for two weeks now. She didn't like high school. She didn't like the nosey nuns who were always worrying about the girls using powder or seeing boys. She didn't like having no money, never being able to buy herself any clothes, never having spending money for movies and sodas and hot chocolate. Lots of girls she knew had never graduated from grammar school. They were working and bought themselves clothes and hats, and they got along, didn't they? Aunt Peg had never gone to high school, and she had a good job.

Gee, if Aunt Peg could get her a job at the hotel! She didn't want to be a waitress, but why couldn't she be a cashier? She would make a hundred dollars a month, maybe, and she could buy clothes and things for herself, be independent. If she worked for herself, she wouldn't have to ask anyone for money. She was tired of never having any money. She wasn't going to go to school. She was going to get a job. She'd tell Aunt Peg tonight and let Aunt Peg tell Uncle Al. If Aunt Peg said it was all right, Uncle Al wouldn't object. Aunt Peg wouldn't let him.

If she could get a job as a cashier, she might meet someone as rich and as good-looking as Patsy Gilbride. Didn't Aunt Peg meet that Mr. Robinson while she was working as a cashier? Aunt Peg still telephoned hotels to see if he was registered, and he never was. She never heard from him. She was sorry for Aunt Peg. Aunt Peg must really love Mr. Robinson. Well, she would never let a man do that to her, not even if he seemed as wonderful as Patsy Gilbride. Gosh, from seeing him in movies she felt almost as if she knew him as well as she did her own brothers. And she had read in a moving picture magazine that he made five thousand dollars a week. To think that there was that much money in the world.

As soon as she got a job she was going to save her money and buy some spring clothes. Tonight she'd talk to Aunt Peg. She'd say she wouldn't go to school, and she meant it. They couldn't make her. It was wasting money. She didn't need to go to school in order to get along.

She turned the corner of South Park Avenue and walked on along Sixty-third Street. Her feet were tired, and she had to go all of the way to Cottage Grove, and then there would be the long walk home. She could try to have someone in an automobile pick her up and give her a ride, but she was afraid to. It was dangerous to do that. Soon she would be earning her own money, and then everything would be different.

Chapter Fifteen

I

Now, after more than six months at school, he was making his first new friend. Walter Broda, the broad-shouldered and powerfully built Pole who sat near him in his Poli. Sci. class, faced Danny across a table in the Coffee Shop. Whenever he'd come here before, he'd been alone. He'd envied others who had friends to talk to. Now he had someone to talk to.

"I can't understand why I only got a B for the reading report on Beard. I let Mike Mooney borrow my paper. He copied it, and he got an A."

"The system of grading papers on campus is a mystery. And as you no doubt have learned, a mystery is something that cannot be understood by a mortal mind," Broda said dryly.

Danny smiled, but the Pole's face remained expressionless.

"So you know Mooney?" Broda asked.

"Yes. He's a nice fellow, but he isn't very smart."

"I never had the pleasure of making his acquaintance although I am sure it would be a pleasure. When he answers a question in our class, I would not say that he reveals any singular intelligence. But then, he is a football player, and that is something so rare at this University that I believe the anthropologists will study the local football players as if they were aboriginals. Yes, football players are very rare at this citadel of cerebration," Broda said, continuing in his dry tone.

Danny liked Walter Broda. He liked his sense of humor. But he couldn't make him out.

"What are you majoring in?" Danny asked.

"Philosophy."

"I plan to take some philosophy courses."

"You're a freshman, aren't you, O'Neill?"

"Yes, aren't you?"

"No, I have advanced to the position of sophomore."

Broda didn't continue the conversation. Danny was at a loss for something to say. Through the window he saw a group of students pass lazily away from the Reynolds Club. Students here walked differently, more slowly, more poised than did many people away from campus. The University was a world set apart. When could he spend all of his time here? Perhaps Uncle Al would make more money soon and he could quit work.

"Did you ever read *God Loves the Irish* by Desmond?" Danny asked.

"No, no, I am sorry to say I do not have the time to read all of the contemporary classics. I regret it, but I don't always have the time."

"I don't think it's a classic. I didn't agree with it. There's too much feeling that one race or another is set apart. I agree with Burns that *a man's a man for a' that*," Danny said.

"No, I think that there is evidence to believe that Providence has a special concern for people who inhabit islands. The English live on an island, and you have no doubt learned already that they are born with a special genius for governing, especially for governing other people. And then, Irish friends of mine have always given me absolute assurance that the Irish are the most civilized race on earth."

Enjoying Broda's talk, Danny was puzzled by it.

"Tell me, O'Neill, have you ever read any of Joseph Conrad?"

"I read *Lord Jim*. I liked it. He has a wonderful style. Isn't he supposed to be one of the greatest living writers?"

"I think he is. Yes, yes, he's a truly remarkable writer," Broda answered, becoming really enthusiastic. "He is broad in his compassion, and his irony is deep and human. Yes, yes, I find him very remarkable. I have read *Lord Jim* three times."

"I want to read more of Conrad."

"I think you should. Even his first novel, *Almayer's Folly*, is a great book."

"I thought *Lord Jim* was a swell study of fear and cowardice."

"If you will permit me, I'd say rather that it is a study in the irony of fate. Fate is Conrad's theme, and he shows how it acts on men like some ironical god."

When Danny had read *Lord Jim*, he had formed many tentative impressions. Now, when he had someone to talk to about these impressions, he couldn't remember them. He had nothing to say about the novel. He had to train his memory.

"O'Neill, I was thinking—do you think your friend Mooney is intelligent enough to be a cop?"

"He's got the name. That's all a cop needs. A cop is a person who must come from an island that is green."

"Yes, that seems so. I often wonder how countries like Germany and Italy solve the problem of the police power. Do they import Irishmen?"

"What about Poland?"

"Poland is not a country. It is a platonic republic. Yes, yes, Poland is the purest democracy in the world. It permits in its parliament not only politicians, but also rogues, priests, bishops, army captains, and, I believe, even the Holy Ghost. Under the circumstances, it is clear that Poland does not even have a police problem. Poland is so democratic that all men are free. Crimes in Poland are impossible by definition."

Danny laughed.

"Have you ever been in Poland?"

"No, unfortunately I have never had the opportunity. But I have heard the glories of Poland described to me all of my life. I am convinced that God created the Garden of Eden in Poland."

Broda was stimulating. Yes, here was a friend he really would be glad to have. Reluctantly he looked at his watch and saw that he had to leave in order to get to work.

They shook hands outside of the Coffee Shop, and Danny hurried away, carrying his stuffed briefcase.

Thinking of his talk with Broda, he realized that they had told each other nothing of a personal nature. He hadn't found out anything about the Pole. And yet he already regarded him as a friend.

II

"Hi, Big Boy," Stall said genially as Danny strolled into the station.

"Anything new, Cavalry Sergeant?" Danny answered.

Stall, a wiry, bow-legged fellow with hair standing up on his head like needles, handed Danny a new bulletin.

"What the hell's this one? Have they got an efficiency expert now to help us waste time, or is it advice on how to sell oil?"

"Read it. You go to college," Stall kidded.

"Well, another plan hatched in the main office. We'll get more personal attention from our boss this way when there is a Supervisor for every ten stations. You see, Cavalry Sergeant, the company has our interest at heart," Danny said, flinging the bulletin on the desk.

"Our new supervisor is named Brown. Know anything about him?"

"No, and, say, he has an uncommon name, hasn't he? He must be a Turk or an Armenian."

"Can your dumb jokes! I want to get out of here. I promised my wife I'd get home early and take care of the kid."

"The joys of double wretchedness."

"Don't let anybody kid you about marriage. I horsed around. I know the ropes. A guy's better off married. You're settled, you save dough, and you get it regular."

Danny changed his clothes and put on his overalls in the lavatory.

"Hey, student, do me a favor today, will you?" Stall called in to him.

"I will if it doesn't cost me any money."

"Well, find out how it feels to bend your elbow doin' some cleanin' here. You're leaving it all to me. I worked all day, and the damn place here still isn't clean."

"Oh, that—sure I will. I felt lousy yesterday, too lousy to breathe."

"Well, kid yourself into thinking that them pumps outside are some janes and you're feelin' 'em up. You'll have a good time then."

"But I'll be depriving you of a pleasure."

"Listen, Gaston, for Christ sake, clean the pumps, will you?"

"Sure," Danny said, emerging in his work outfit. "Are we short today, or didn't you check up?"

"The audit's all made. We're nine cents over."

"That's a shortage."

"O.K., Jesse James."

The armored money wagon drove in. Stall got the receipt book, took the locked money bag out of the safe, and went out with it. He came back and put his receipt on the spindle.

"Say, Charlie on the money wagon is a swell guy. He's always having tough luck, too, poor bastard. Another one of his kids is sick."

"I like him. He's a decent guy, but I don't fancy his sense of humor. Every time I give him the dough, he asks me— 'When you getting operated on, College?' I answer, 'What for?' He says, 'To take the lead out of your pants.' "

"Your jokes are no better."

"No, I really like him. What a lousy job he's got, sitting cooped up inside that goddamned battle wagon, taking in bags of money through a hole. I'm glad I don't have to do that."

"You mean you're glad you don't have to work, don't you?" Stall corrected.

"You better get home now. The kid needs some diapers washed. And, listen, don't worry. I'll keep the flag of Upton flying here."

"And I won't know about it. Say, once I leave here in the

afternoon, I forget about this station until I open it the next mornin'."

"I do better than that. I forget it twenty-four hours a day," Danny said.

"I know that," Stall groaned.

Stall left. Danny sat at the desk, looking out the window and at the carburetor factory on the opposite side of Twenty-fifth Street. A fleet of trucks rumbled by on Wabash Avenue. This station was small, easier to keep clean than the one on Michigan Avenue. He wondered how old Sperling was. The old codger had been so sore at him for asking to be transferred that he wouldn't speak. That was all past. The company kept after them to sell five-gallon cans of oil. Well, he knew how to sell the five-gallon cans and coupon books, too. All it took was a little arithmetic. Regularly, they put through as sold a coupon book in their daily audit. They'd just take ten dollars out of the petty cash fund for the cost. They made up some of the money on the pumps, and every few days they put through the coupons as cash to straighten out their shortage. It was a clever stunt and helped them build up a record. And whenever they had a good day in bulk oil sales, they'd dump a five-gallon can of oil in the bulk oil tanks and list it as sold. Five-gallon cans were cheaper than five gallons of bulk oil sold at two bits a quart. So they sold the oil from the can as bulk, made a few pennies for supper or to fix up a shortage, and were credited with being go-getters who sold cans of oil. This juggling was a good idea of his, all for the record.

He stared at the Wayne pumps. He had to clean them today. Yes, they were filthy.

A chap like Broda could sit all day in the library and study. He was glad he'd had the talk with Broda today. They'd have to have talks often. He was fed up with working his way through school. He hadn't any real kick, though. He really got all the time he needed for study. But the more you read, the more you learned how ignorant you were. Every time he read a book, he learned of ten or twenty books he hadn't read and ought to. Now, instead of reading he'd have to shine the damned pumps.

Lazily, he got a rag, soaked it with kerosene, and went out to the pumps. He cleaned them lackadaisically. He didn't like the feel of rags soaked in kerosene.

Some day he might become a Senator, and he'd look back on these days with pride, the days when he had worked himself up the hard way. Was it such a hard way? It was harder than having an old man who gave you the money for college. Imagine himself Senator Daniel O'Neill, making a speech like La Follette against the vested interests, or, better yet, conducting a filibuster to keep the country out of another war of steel and gold.

He went on cleaning the pumps, imagining himself making historic speeches in the United States Senate.

III

Danny laid his fountain pen on the desk and apprehensively watched a tall, fleshy young man get out of the Ford coupé parked at the side of the station. He guessed that it was Brown. A boss driving in unexpectedly was always a cause of anxiety, a warning to be on guard.

"O'Neill, I'm Brown, your new Supervisor."

"Yes, sir," Danny said, rising, disturbed by the curtness of the stranger's voice.

"You're on duty now. What is a book doing on your desk?"

"I was studying, Mr. Brown."

"Mr. North has said time and time again that you fellows aren't allowed to read on duty."

"Yes, sir, but he gave me special permission to study when there was no business and as long as everything is going all right at the station."

Brown took out a notebook from his pocket and scribbled in it.

Danny knew he was not going to get along with Brown.

Brown snooped around the station. Danny serviced a customer, frightened, but assuring himself that he needn't worry since he had permission to study. If he couldn't read and study on this job, it would be intolerable. It was a break for him that Stall had done so much cleaning this morning. And he was glad he'd shined the pumps this afternoon.

"You average four or five hundred gallons of gas a day, don't you?" Brown asked when Danny came back inside the station.

"Yes, about that."

"You have plenty of time to keep this station looking immaculate." Brown made another note. "I want this station kept cleaner. And you ought to be doing more business, too."

"The other day we received a letter of congratulation from Mr. North for having gone over our gas quota in November. Stall and I have increased the sale of canned goods and coupon books, too."

"Keep that up."

"Yes, sir, we will."

Brown had turned his back while Danny was speaking. He went out of the station. Danny watched the car drive out.

Glum, he fixed his eyes vacantly on the dark and quiet corner. He had just about lost all his illusions concerning success in business. He no longer wanted to rise in the Upton ranks. He wanted something else in life, free of business and all Babbittry. And to think of it, only a year ago he had taken the writings of Arthur Brisbane and Dr. Frank Crane seriously. He wanted freedom, complete freedom. When you worked for someone else you didn't own your time. You sold not only service, your body, and your mind—you also sold time. And he didn't have time to sell. No salary, no wages were sufficient compensation for your time. When would he be the master of his own time? And besides all this, he had to say sir to bastards like Brown.

Maybe after he took some composition courses he could become a writer and win his freedom with his pen. No, he couldn't count on that.

He sat down and carefully read the decision of Chief Justice Marshall in the case of *Madison versus Marbury*. How could there be a government of laws rather than of men? Men administered the laws. And they acted according to their economic interests. Behind their economic interests there was force; it was called the police power. In this world there was force and money. Where did he fit in, in this scheme? In Poli. Sci. he was studying the theory of democratic government. At work was there any democracy? Could there be any democracy in business? The Upton Oil and Refining Company was a hierarchy. It was a pyramid. And he was one of those at the base of this pyramid. There was a contradiction between this system and a democratic system of laws based on justice.

Bewildered, disillusioned, he studied the next selection in his book.

IV

Danny looked up from his book. It had begun to snow. He hoped there wouldn't be a storm. If there were, he'd have a lot of shoveling to do around here tomorrow. The corner was desolate. The carburetor factory across the street loomed like a mysterious hulk without definiteness of outline. Flakes of snow caught in the glare from the overhead Upton sign near the sidewalk seemed like flying insects. A young Negro passed, whistling a tune and rapping his heels on the sidewalk. A truck rumbled by on Wabash Avenue; it was probably a beer truck. If it were not for his study and his thoughts, this corner would be a very lonely one. But loneliness was not in stones and sights; it was in the emotions.

Mason, a stocky policeman, came toward the station.

"Hi," Danny greeted him as he came inside.

"Hello, O'Neill. How are you tonight?"

"Oh, all right, how's yourself?"

"This block is like a coffin at night. Poundin' the beat around here is like walkin' inside of a coffin with the lid closed down on you."

"Yeh, it's dull all right."

"How's the book this evenin'?"

"I still got to plug away at study."

"Well, kid, don't let me interfere. I'll just sit there in the can out of sight and give my dogs a rest."

Mason unbuttoned his coat and used the lavatory as a sitting room.

"I heard there was a stabbing around here last night," Danny said.

"It wasn't much. One nigger found another with his girl, and just thought he'd get some good carvin' practice in on juicy black meat. Nothin' serious."

Danny leaned back in his chair.

"I wish they'd take me off this beat. Just like I said, it's like bein' inside of a coffin. Now, if I was only down a few blocks on Twenty-second Street. It's excitin' there."

"There's a big whorehouse on Twenty-second Street. It's Al Capone's, isn't it?"

"I don't know whose it is, but it's there all right."

Danny resented Mason's presence because the cop prevented him from studying. He guessed that he couldn't do any more work now until he closed up and got home. Mason lit a cigarette. Danny was uneasy. Smoking on the premises was against the rules. Suppose a spotter went by? Brown would see to it that spotters came around. He was sure Brown was that kind of boss. He still rankled from Brown's visit this afternoon. But, hell, Mason was the Law, the police power. You couldn't treat the Law the same as anyone else, could you?

"Jiggers, there's two sergeants," Danny said.

Mason hastily closed the door. Danny watched two fat sergeants pass.

"They're gone," he called.

"Are you sure?" Mason asked, worried, when he opened the lavatory door.

"Yes."

"It's the Mayor. He's a reformer. He's got them out watching us. Well, I'm just waitin' for the elections to vote against him. He's always got someone on our tail." Mason paused to muster up more contempt. "Well, what can you expect from a reformer?"

Wasn't the Mayor trying to eliminate graft and corruption, to give the citizens of Chicago a more efficient and honest government? The taxpayers were putting up Mason's salary. Mason stalled. He was helping Mason to get out of doing his duty. He sympathized with the mayor. But then, didn't he himself stall? Problems like these were totally different when you discussed them in generalities and when you saw them concretely, in terms of your own personal experience. Most men who worked for a living stalled.

Danny shrugged his shoulders.

He didn't give a damn if Mason shirked or not. But why didn't Mason find another sitting room so that he could study? The cop's very presence distracted him. Well, it was a quarter after eight already. He didn't have much longer to go.

He swung around in his chair. Mason was sitting there, gun in hand. Danny was frightened.

"Don't worry, O'Neill. I'm holding my gat ready here, just in case some lug comes in and tries to do a job. You know, if we catch one of these bums pullin' a histin' job on a station, we get a reward, and it's bigger if we plug the rat. Friend of mine out on Western Avenue, he caught one of them punk bums the other night histin' a station; and plugged him right through the brain. Well, that's sweet for him. I was just thinkin', if a rat comes in here, I'll catch him. You just do what he says, but be sure to get out of the way so I can let him have it."

Danny shuddered. He remembered how Nolan might have killed him last summer except for Studs Lonigan. To die because of such an accident would be utterly stupid.

"I've never yet been stuck up."

"You never can tell. A station on a lonely corner like this one, it's mighty invitin' to some young punk with a gun."

A car drove in.

"If that's one, I'll get the bastard," Mason said as Danny rushed out to the pump island, terror-stricken.

It was a gasoline customer.

"I was all set," Mason said in disappointment when Danny returned.

Danny plumped into his chair. If there was a holdup and a shooting, he'd have to get out of the way. He wished Mason would leave, but he couldn't tell him to go. He'd rather take his chances in a holdup without protection than to be in the center of a shooting match. If there were a holdup, he might be a hero and have his picture in the papers. He'd rather not take the chance, especially when it was over insured money that didn't belong to him.

"Yes, some of us get the breaks, and some of us don't. Maybe life wouldn't be so interestin' if everybody got all sevens and elevens. I suppose somebody's got to roll the deuces, too."

"Yeh, that's the way it is, Mason."

Mason standing in the can with a gun in hand was not his idea of too much comfort. Danny tried to conceal his nervousness. He eyed the clock, wishing for nine o'clock.

"Well, it's a long, long night," Mason said.

Danny yawned. He wanted to study, and the cop was still wanting to chew the fat. Mason yawned. The clock ticked away monotonously. How different his life was in the morning at school from the afternoon and evening at the station. How different it was talking to Broda from what it was talking to Mason.

XVI

Bill O'Neill was tired. The weather had turned very cold, and he had been driving a big five-ton truck all day in the freezing winds, getting in and out, helping load it with heavy crates and barrels. He wished he had a different route, one in which he didn't have to pick up so many factories that shipped such large pieces. But he couldn't complain. He had a steady job, with seniority. He had nothing to worry about. Still, he wished the winter were over. Winter was cruel, a grueling grind, and he always looked forward hopefully to spring and summer.

His back ached. He sniffed from a cold. His mind was dull. He needed a bath, but he was too weary to lift his aching limbs, climb into the tub, and clean up. He'd have gone to a movie tonight if he hadn't felt so rotten. He ought to lay off a few days, but he didn't want to lose the pay. Mama was such a bad manager, they were still in debt. There were still two of the kids in grammar school. They needed so damned much.

Restless, he didn't know what to do with himself. He took a copy of the 1926 edition of Who's Who In Baseball *and read about the lifetime batting and pitching averages of big-league baseball players.*

Chapter Sixteen

I

Danny O'Neill saw himself walking through the dim shadows in Saint Patrick's Church, that seemed so small although it was a large cathedral. He stopped at a pillar and gazed at the faraway altar which stood a few feet in front of him. The marble altar was half hidden by shadows. There was something strange about the altar, but he didn't know what it was. Something was missing. Something was different.

What has happened? he asked himself, standing by a pillar.

He had come to church to gain understanding. He would walk out of here knowing, knowing Eureka. What had been done to the altar? Shadows moved over it like spirits. If the shadows would talk now, they would tell him Eureka and he would know. The silent shadows swept back and forth across the altar. Something had happened.

He walked slowly toward the altar that was so far away and yet so close to him, but he could not reach the altar. At the altar he would know that which no other man knew. He must reach it. The altar faced him, so near, and yet so far away, and he walked toward it and he could not reach it. He would kneel down and the silent shadows would talk to him.

He bent his fingers in a fit of terror. He stared with wide eyes above the altar.

The altar light had gone out. It hung above the altar with no flame. The flame of Jesus Christ was quenched. Christ was in the tabernacle behind the golden door on the center of the altar and no flame paid him honor, no fire announced his living presence.

He gazed at the darkened altar.

Who had blown out the light of knowledge of God? Who

211

had blown out the flame of the candle of eternal honor to God?

Sacrilege! Sacrilege! Sacrilege!

Blessed be Sacrilege!

Blessed be its eternal name!

Blessed be its eternal shame!

Holy Sacrilege pray for us!

Holy Sacrilege spare us!

Holy Sacrilege pray for us!

Pray for us now and for never ever never namemen.

He heard singing. He turned and saw the empty choir. He heard voices, the voices of school children from Saint Patrick's singing like angels.

Tantum Ergo

The sad Latin words faded out.

The voices were silent.

The angels of Heaven were silent. Heaven above was draped in black.

The tabernacle was covered with a purple cloth. Why was the light out? It was not Good Friday, and the altar light was out.

Who had blown it out?

Danny O'Neill.

I have committed the sin against the Holy Ghost, he told himself.

He rose. He went toward the altar that he could not reach.

Blessed be darkness!

Blessed be its unholy nothing!

Blessed, blessed, blessed blackness!

He gazed at the dome, seeing uncertain figures traced in the red and purple stained glass. When he had been a boy, Saint Patrick's Church had had no dome, and now it had a dome of many-colored stained glass. Purple glass, purple, color of Christ's agony on the cross. Christ had died for him who had blown out the light of Christ in all the world, and here he stood in sin.

Get down on your knees, for the fool crieth out in his folly, voice spoke unto to him from the stained-glass dome.

And I stand in my folly.

The silent shadows drifted across the dome of glass like ouds hiding the sun. Could the sun shine when Danny O'Neill id blown out the altar light?

I fled him down the nights . . .

A woebegone man in a velvet jacket with scraggly hair fled ist Danny, and the silent shadows pursued him. Danny atched the fleeing man. Who was he? He stared at Danny, s face pale and twisted in agony like the face of Christ on the oss.

Who are you? Danny asked.

The man fled. Danny followed him. Around and around the iurch they ran. The man fled by the altar of the Blessed Vir- n Mary, turned back to the rear, passed the stations of the oss, and climbed up into the choir. Danny, with one leap, nded in the choir. The man was gone.

The man chased Danny around and around the church and sappeared, and Danny sat in a pew.

A huge hound slowly, steadily, followed the woebegone an with the scraggly beard. Danny knew. It was Francis hompson. The Hound of Heaven majestically followed the et. He wanted to talk to Francis Thompson. He could not se from the pew. Francis Thompson climbed the pillar near m. The Hound walked up the pillar, and Francis Thompson d down the other side, and down, down came the Hound of eaven.

All things betray . . .

The Hound of Heaven was chasing Danny O'Neill's be- ayal. Francis Thompson collapsed at the foot of the altar. he Hound of Heaven stood at his right. Danny knew that he ould march up and kneel beside the poet. He could not move. he church grew darker. The silent shadows swept over it.

Danny grew tense, his whole being contracting with fear. He pressed his elbows to his sides and gazed transfixed as the darkness crushed slowly, relentlessly, down upon the church, and there was no altar light burning, and there was no contentment in the world and in the church, and the darkness came slowly down, crushing out all joy and all faith, and he was to blame, he was bringing down the darkness slowly and forever, darkness without end, darkness without end, blessed, blessed unblessed be the unholy sacrilegious darkness of Danny O'Neill, and Francis Thompson stood beckoning to him and he did not move and the darkness came down slowly right over his head and forever, forever darkness without end—

—and the alarm clock jarred him awake. He yawned. He rubbed his heavy-lidded eyes. Streaks of gray came in through his opened window. He wished he could sleep all morning.

There is no God.

Unwilled, the thought came to him from the dream he had already forgotten.

There is no God.

He got out of bed and pulled on the light. He looked around his disordered room. He saw no change in it from last night. His clothes lay in a heap on a chair. His small desk was cluttered with books and papers.

There is no God.

He could tell himself this calmly, without fear, and nothing happened, nothing would happen to him. He need fear no punishment.

God was not even dead. God had never been. God was nonexistent from always in the past to always in the future. And on this cold March Saturday morning in the year 1926 he had awakened with knowledge of the non-existence of God.

"There is no God," he told his room. He added: "There is no Santa Claus."

He washed and dressed and went to the kitchen.

II

The elevated train was filled with sleepy-faced stolid workmen. Did they all believe in God? What would they say if he told them of his atheism?

He squeezed around in his seat to look out the window. The sky was streaked with pink and red. Soon the sun would be up. The dawn of a new day was breaking all over the world, the world that had not seemed to change since yesterday morning. For him, it was a first day, almost like the first day of the world. Out there, above the buildings, he could see the grayish vastness of the empty universe. And here he was, on an elevated train, hanging by his heels on a second-rate planet which was spinning dizzily in this empty universe. He had the illusion that he was gazing upward at the lifeless nothingness of the solar system. He might really be looking down into it. But it didn't matter whether he was looking up or down.

"Forty-seventh Street," the conductor called.

More workmen crowded into the car. The knees of a thin old man rubbed Danny's legs.

The world was nothing by itself. Man in it was everything. A happy thought, a thought of freedom. When priests and believers railed that the atheist was unhappy, miserable, they knew not what they were talking about. When they threatened the non-believer with the terrors of eternity, they were telling fairy tales, scarcely worthy of belief by children. Lies, lies, and he was free of lies. With one clear thought he had swept contradiction upon contradiction from his life. And that was the means to free himself. He was free of lies now. He was happier than if he had been in love.

He nervously waited for the train to reach Twenty-sixth Street. He wanted to be outside, in the air.

III

He hummed a tune as he opened up the station. He put the cans out in a display on the little rectangle of sidewalk in front.

He got the red, five-gallon bucket and tested the pumps, pouring back the gasoline through a funnel into the tanks. The pumps were throwing the right measure. He was all set for the day's work. It was sharp out, but getting warmer. He could smell spring in the air. In the spring a young man's fancy turned to thoughts of atheism.

Confidently, he told himself he had lifted his head. He was saturated with confidence. He was standing straight and sturdy on his own feet, prepared to depend on himself and on his own efforts. That was the real problem man faced. He was going to live the only life he would ever know, free of superstition and of all the fears it had bred.

A truck rumbled into the station. The first customer on the first day of a new life for Danny O'Neill.

IV

A cold wind swept Washington Park. Danny and Jim Gogarty strolled across the hard ground. Not one other human being was in sight.

Danny sensed that Jim had something on his mind. Jim had called for him and had suggested this walk so that they could talk. He wanted to tell Jim that he was an atheist, but he was hesitant. What would Jim say?

"It's cold now, isn't it?" Jim said.

"Yes," Danny answered thoughtfully.

"So you like Broda," Jim said.

"He's a brilliant fellow, and I like his sense of humor."

"I can't make him out."

He wanted to see Broda next week and talk to him about religion.

"Dan, I've been doing a lot of thinking about how we've been fooled."

"So have I."

"A lot of things we were told as kids aren't true."

"What?" Danny asked excitedly.

Should he tell Jim now?

"Well, religion, for one thing," Jim said.

"Jim, I'm an atheist."

"I guess I am, too."

Far from being shocked, Jim was with him. Relieved, encouraged, he saw that he was not alone. There were others. He looked back to the west. Over the line of bare trees he could see the tops of the apartment buildings on South Park Avenue. Dull third-floor windows. A dull sky. Those buildings bounded his neighborhood. That neighborhood was a world. He denied that world. Between him and that world there was now a line that could not be crossed. That world and its God had become his enemy.

"What are you thinking of, Dan?"

"Jim, I was looking at the buildings on South Park Avenue. I was thinking—the neighborhood. It's a different world from ours. We have nothing left in common."

"You know, when I go to mass on Sunday, I feel like a stranger."

"I'm never going to mass again."

"What are you going to tell your folks?"

"I'm not going."

"But, Dan, you'll hurt them."

"They hurt me. God hurt me. I'll tell them there is no God."

"But it'll take everything they have away from them, Dan."

"We all have to face the truth. They have to know it."

"That's not practical. Dan, they're ignorant. If they have no God, what have they got? We, we're different. We're young. Oh, hell, Dan, I don't know what to do."

"We can't give in, Jim."

They walked on in silence. Danny felt a bond between him and Jim. They were breaking with the same kind of past. Their silence was stronger than any words they could utter.

They gazed at the gray lagoon. The scene was desolate.

"I can't hurt my parents, Dan."

v

"Well, how's the impeccable scholar this morning?" Uncle Al asked as Danny joined him at the kitchen table for breakfast.

"Oh, pretty good," Danny answered, tense.

"Dan, come on to ten o'clock mass at Crucifixion with me."

"I'm not going to mass."

"What's that?" his uncle asked, puzzled.

"I'm not going to mass. There is no God," Danny bitterly proclaimed.

"What?"

"I'm an atheist," he said defiantly.

"What the hell are you telling me?" Uncle Al shouted, almost jumping out of his chair.

The die was cast. There could be no retreat. No concessions could be granted.

"What in the name of God is he saying? Al, sure, and bless me, he's a pagan, a heathen."

"Dan, what's the idea?" Uncle Al asked, trying to be persuasive.

Uncle Ned came out into the kitchen, wearing his faded purple bathrobe.

"Well, they're at it again, swinging broadswords of words at each other," he said.

"Ned, Ned, he's a heathen," Mrs. O'Flaherty cried.

"What's that, Mud?"

"Ned, he tells me there is no God," Uncle Al said, hurt, his voice weary.

Uncle Ned glared at Danny. Now he must not flinch.

"I knew that some goddamn crap was going on," Uncle Ned said.

"Well, prove there is a God to me," Danny said.

"You're drinking a cup of coffee, aren't you?" Uncle Ned asked.

"What's that got to do with it?" Danny asked.

"After all the education you've had, I ask you—can you

answer a simple question? Are you drinking a cup of coffee?"

"Yes."

"Do you believe that it is coffee?"

"Sure."

"Then why do you ask me to prove to you that God is God?"

"Because I can't see Him. I can't find any evidence to prove He exists."

"Is that the crap you're learning?" Uncle Ned asked.

"Give him hell, Ned, give him hell," Mrs. O'Flaherty urged.

"How do you know that China is China?" Uncle Al asked.

"Because there is evidence. Men have been there and they've described it. The United States government has diplomats and marines there. There are missionaries there. We get tea and rice from China. We know there are people there, because we have seen Chinese laundrymen we know come from China."

"Ned, don't tell me he's becoming a Chinaman," Mrs. O'Flaherty said.

"But you didn't see it," Ned insisted.

"I don't have to, to know that China is a real part of the earth."

"Then why do you have to see God?"

"God isn't a country. God isn't something we know we can prove to exist. We have to take the proof of God's existence on faith, without evidence."

"Ye of little faith," Uncle Ned sneered.

"Ned! Ned! Al! Al! It's that Connaught beggar man, Gogarty. Oh, wait till I get me hands on that Connaught beggar!" Mrs. O'Flaherty yelled.

"The brainiest men in this world, priests, the Pope, men who have devoted their whole lifetime, their trained minds, to theology and metaphysics—they have told us that there is a God," Uncle Al cut in.

"And who are you to set yourself up against them?" Uncle Ned added.

"Because somebody tells me something, I don't have to be-

lieve it. I don't care who says it—there is no God," Danny
answered, his voice strained, taut.

"Not even an agnostic says that. An agnostic says he doesn't
know."

Danny looked at Uncle Al.

"If there is a God, it can be proved. Well, what proof is
there?"

"Look at the sky. Doesn't that prove there's a God?"

"No."

"What does it prove?"

"That it's the sky."

"Who made it?"

"I don't know. It probably just was."

"And so that's what you're paying over three hundred dollars a year to learn."

"It's worth it, even if that's all I do learn."

Danny noticed that Uncle Al sat slumped, weary. Suddenly
sympathy for his uncle tempted him to give in. No! No,
never! He felt like a louse. But he couldn't yield.

"You mean to tell me that you can look at the beauty and
the harmony in this world and say there is no God?" Uncle
Ned asked.

"Yes, I can."

"You goddamned little fool! You goddamned whelp!"
Uncle Ned yelled.

Danny trembled. He feared his uncle was going to take a
poke at him. Well, he must keep his head. He must.

"You can't win an argument by calling me names," Danny
replied.

"Dan, why don't you go see a priest? Talk to a clever, brainy
Jesuit. He'll set you right," Uncle Al said.

"I've set myself right."

"So you know it all?" Uncle Ned jeered.

"Dan, you could still go to mass. Perhaps if you go to mass,
you'll change your mind. The mass can work miracles of faith,
you know. Dan, come on to mass with me. Even if you don't

believe, it won't hurt you any to go to mass," Uncle Al pleaded.

"Yes, go on to mass," Uncle Ned urged.

"You don't go to mass," Danny replied.

"What's that got to do with it?" Uncle Ned asked.

"Then why do you ask me to?"

"The world, the beauty of the world, is my church, God's world."

"Dan, suppose you found a watch on a desert island?" Uncle Al asked.

"I'd say it was a watch. Somebody made it. A watchmaker. But that's only proof that there are watchmakers in the world."

"See, he's so smart he won't even listen," Uncle Ned said.

"I'm not alone in that."

"Don't get fresh."

"I'm not fresh."

"Dan, come to mass as a favor to me."

"I can't."

"Why?" Uncle Al asked helplessly.

"Because I don't believe."

Danny finished his coffee and got up.

"Dan?" Uncle Al called plaintively.

"Let him go, Al. He'll get over it. It's only a half-baked idea. He's read too many books. He'll outgrow it all when he's a little older and gets a little sense."

Danny left the room.

"Jesus, Mary, and Joseph! Me grandson runs with the tinkers and the heathens!"

VI

Aimless streets. Familiar, aimless streets that he walked on this chilled but sunny Sunday morning. The world was aimless. The universe was connected by aimless paths of motion. He had to find, create his own aims in this world.

Was this enough?

He crossed Garfield Boulevard and drifted on along South Park Avenue toward Fifty-first Street.

People passed him on the sidewalk, and he was unaware of them. Atheism created a feeling of springtime in himself. It was a new beginning.

How weak his faith had really been all these years! How powerless had the influence of the Church been in his own life in the face of simple logic and intelligence! How meaningless had been the influence of the nuns who had taught him in grammar school, the priests who had been his high-school teachers! How painless it was to lose your faith! There was no regret. No sense of loss. The only pain he had felt was a sympathetic one for his uncle. Would he ever forget the expression of injury, misery, on Uncle Al's face when he'd finally refused to go to mass and had walked out of the apartment? Something had been knocked out of Uncle Al. He'd struck him a blow, and he'd done this just at the time when Uncle Al was upset by business worries. He had been cruel. But what alternative did he have? He was forced either to corrupt himself with lies, hypocrisy, or else to hurt others. No, he had not fully reasoned the problem out in these terms. He had acted more than he had thought. What he had done this morning had not been to give expression to a fully matured thought as much as it had been to take a drastic action forced by nervous compulsion.

He strolled on, his gait rolling, ungainly.

The bridge between himself and a rotten world was going up in fire. He was untouched by its flames. But it didn't hurt him. It hurt others. But what else could he do? He had done right. He could not accept responsibility for almost two thousand years of superstition. If Uncle Al believed in two thousand years of superstition, did he have to? What you believe in was life or death to you. If he went on believing in lies and superstition, why, then, others after him would.

And yet that beaten, hurt look on Uncle Al's face almost destroyed his self-confidence. If you trampled on a person's superstition, you hurt them more than if you insulted their character. It was grimly funny and very sad to realize that you could hurt someone by telling him that what did not exist just did not exist. When you were a kid, and you found out that there was no Santa Claus, a grownup person would tell you not to take it too hard. But if you told many grownup people not to believe in their Santa Claus, they did take it too hard.

He turned around and wandered back along South Park Avenue.

He kicked a piece of ice that lay on the sidewalk.

Excitement boiled up within him. He could smell the coming spring in the Sunday morning air. And he knew that spring was in his mind.

XVII

"Did you hear about O'Neill?" Studs Lonigan asked Tommy Doyle in front of the poolroom.

"No, what's he doin' now?"

"He's an atheist."

"I always knew he had some screws loose."

"Imagine the crust of that guy! Why, I knew him when he was nothing but a goddamn punk."

"If his old man was alive, he'd get his ears knocked off. His old man was a great guy. He didn't take nobody's crap. He wouldn't let this kid run around loose, full of that kind of B.S."

"It just goes to show what can happen to a guy when he reads too many books."

Chapter Seventeen

I

Therefore, I say there is no God

Danny walked off the stage at Mandel Hall, realizing that his speech had been a verbal bombshell thrown into the Public Speaking class. He sat by himself in the front row of the large theater. Professor Wolcott, a stocky man with graying hair, took his time coming down the aisle to stand in front of the stage. Danny waited, anxious for comments, hoping to be praised.

"Mr. O'Neill," Professor Wolcott began. "Yes, first of all, Mr. O'Neill, I'd like to remark that in a speech one of the important questions is that of content. We can't divorce content from manner, style, delivery, gesticulation." The professor paused again. "Content should be suited to the audience. In an audience like this class, where there are various kinds of faiths represented, a controversial subject such as yours is not the wisest or the most tactful one to select for a four-minute speech."

He could ignore such criticisms. Wolcott's ideas were those of an old fossil, an Episcopalian.

"Your content, your thought, is almost uniformly of a high order. It's serious, well thought out, stimulating. I know, of course, that you were serious today. You've given thought to the ideas you expressed. You were passionate, and your tone was one of conviction. But nevertheless, your topic was inappropriate for this course."

"If somebody disagrees with me, they can refute my argument. If I told the truth, it can't be inappropriate unless the truth is not appropriate," Danny defended himself.

225

"I can rebut him," Francis Xavier Murphy announced from the last row.

Danny's lips curled with contempt. A Catholic club luminary.

"I think we can find many more suitable subjects for debate, Mr. Murphy."

"But if he isn't answered, he might have left heresies in the minds of the class. I can't let heresies pass unanswered."

"Don't worry, he hasn't," several voices called out wearily.

He was alone in this class, against twenty-three believers and dullards. He was proud to be so isolated.

"In your delivery, Mr. O'Neill, you still show some faults, although the intensity, the passion, the conviction of your thought partially overcomes these faults. Still, your delivery is far from perfect. You are nervous and you hop around when you speak. You keep jerking your knees and swinging your shoulders. You never stand still on the platform. In public speaking, control of the body is very important, and that is one of the lessons you must learn. I'd advise you to rehearse your speeches before a mirror and watch your body; practice controlling it. And then, gestures. Your gestures are not always positive, emphatic, decisive. And pacing. You sometimes talk too fast. Your mind races ahead of your words and a flood of ideas come out too rapidly for the audience to understand and assimilate what you are driving at. Watch these faults."

Professor Wolcott glanced about, deciding on whom to call next.

"Miss Gilman."

A pert young thing stamped to the stage, her buttocks wiggling.

"My subject is *A Picnic at the Sand Dunes*," she announced coquettishly.

Danny slumped in his seat. An appropriate subject for a talk. This was higher education, he reflected with bitter irony. He didn't listen to Miss Gilman.

II

Unsure of himself, Danny sat with Francis Xavier Murphy and Jim Gogarty in the Coffee Shop. He hadn't wanted this meeting, but Murphy had buttonholed him after class and insisted on a discussion. If he'd refused, it would have looked as if he were afraid to accept the enemy's challenge. He knew he was no match for Murphy in disputation, so he'd brought Jim Gogarty along for support. He'd tried to get Broda, too, but he hadn't been able to. He had to stand up to Murphy. He felt separated from Murphy by more than beliefs. Murphy was a snob. He wanted to be a social boy as well as a campus intellectual, and now in his junior year he was still trying in every possible way to get bid to a frat. Last quarter he had taken Jim Gogarty aside and warned Jim not to associate so much with Jewish students because that lowered one's social standing. Why had Murphy demanded this talk? Was it to show off, or did Murphy really want to bring him back to the Church and save his soul?

"But," Jim asked, "isn't it much simpler to accept Pascal's wager than to let ourselves get involved in abstruse theological questions that great minds have debated for centuries without coming to any agreement? Even if we don't know for sure, isn't it better to accept the wager, and live as if we believed in God. Then if God exists, we'll be saved when we die, and if He doesn't, what will we have lost?"

"That would make salvation the stakes in a moral crap game," Danny said ironically.

After their talks since that Saturday afternoon in Washington Park last March, was Jim deserting him?

"Oh, Gogarty, I'm surprised at you. A Catholic can't accept Pascal's wager. It admits of the possibility of doubt. You can't doubt the truth of revelation," Murphy said impatiently.

"But, Francis, I don't think you understand me . . ."

"Jim," Danny interrupted, "if you accept Pascal's wager, you say that there might not be a God, and if that's so, then you don't need to believe in God in order to live a good life. Then God isn't necessary."

"Dan, after all, isn't it what we do that counts? This way, we won't hurt anybody in life and we'll live decently. Isn't that what counts?"

"Then an atheist could live a moral life with as much chance of salvation as a good Catholic. How can you talk that way, Gogarty?"

Jim was letting Murphy get the impression that he was a Catholic. He would have to argue it out alone with Murphy. Doubt of his own doubt crept up on him. Couldn't he be wrong? No!

"Without God moral codes are relative," Danny said.

"But we don't know what's true, do we?" Jim defended himself.

"Yes, we do," Murphy asserted cockily.

"You do. I don't," Danny taunted.

"You don't want to, you mean. O'Neill, I'm ashamed of you. Why, these people over here will only laugh at you behind your back. They'll have contempt for you. You're an unconscious pawn of the enemies of the Church. You've let the Devil get hold of you."

"I suppose I ought to be exorcised," Danny countered, grinning.

"But we're not getting anywhere," Jim said.

"Even the very way man thinks, proves God."

"Prove that!" Danny exclaimed, realizing that his best defense would be to keep asking questions, to make Murphy prove everything he said.

"All right. We know that we are, that we live, and that we understand, don't we?" Murphy began. "We accept ourselves, we accept our faculties and attributes as facts. Otherwise we'd be deluded. So—which of these excels—to exist, to live, or to understand?"

"I don't see what you're driving at, Francis."

"It's clear that understanding is superior merely to existing and living."

"Doesn't that raise the old question—is it better to be a cow and chew your cud in contentment, or to be Socrates and suffer because you can think and feel?" Jim asked.

"Oh, Gogarty, let Protestants be sentimental with their humanitarianism. Truth doesn't hurt us. It frees us from evil, brings us closer to God. Saint Augustine taught that to mankind centuries ago."

Why didn't Jim talk back to Murphy?

"To understand means to excel over that which merely is, exists, and lives. Why? A stone is, an animal is, and it lives, but so does man. Man has that much in common with a stone and an animal. But man is superior to both because he also understands."

"No, men are just different from stones and animals," Danny said.

"Well, Dan, admit it for the sake of argument so that Francis can make his point."

"All right," Danny acknowledged grudgingly.

"When we say that we understand, what do we mean? We have five senses, and with these we are in contact with the world. We see with our eyes. When our eyes see a color, blue, do our eyes tell us that we have seen blue? Obviously not. Our eyes do the seeing, and our understanding tells us what it is we see. Our senses, then, are merely the servants of understanding. They only receive sensations. Sensations aren't ideas. They are the means whereby we test true ideas with correspondences to their appearances in the world."

Danny and Jim followed Murphy, bewildered. Where was Murphy's trap, Danny asked himself.

"Our understanding is a sixth sense, an interior sense."

"When a dog sees a cat, doesn't it know it sees a cat?" Danny interrupted.

"Yes, animals possess this interior sense. But they can't know

the meaning of what they see. A dog can't write the history
of cats, telling why it hates cats."

"Neither could I," Danny flippantly interrupted.

"O'Neill, don't judge the capacities of human understanding by your own limitations."

"Now, let's not be personal," Jim cautioned.

"I'm not personal. This is a serious question. We have seen
that man is superior to all else in God's creation, to objects and
animals. We have seen that man understands, and that the
senses can't be the seat of understanding. We see that we have
a sixth, or an interior, sense. But what is this? What is the understanding? Just as the senses are the servants of the senses,
so is the understanding the servant of something—reason."

"Therefore God exists," Danny said sarcastically.

"You can try to answer me, O'Neill, when I'm finished. We
know that the world is orderly. Science tells us that. There
must be cause and effect. Something cannot happen without a
cause. We can't understand unless our understanding has
a cause. Reason is that cause. Thus, reason stands above understanding. But man is an imperfect creature who reasons im-
perfectly. After all, something perfect cannot come from
something imperfect. All else beside man is lower than he is.
He excels everything else in creation. If reason came from
something lower than man, then the more imperfect would be
the cause of the less imperfect, but that's absurd. Reason must
come from some source higher than man, some source more
perfect. This is logically necessary. And reason is a faculty that
belongs to being, not to non-being."

Danny and Jim were still bewildered.

"If reason were an attribute of non-being, stones could
reason. But we know that is ridiculous. And if reason didn't
come from some source excelling man, then we would have
an effect without a cause. That's ridiculous, too, because then
we'd have a world without order. Therefore there is a higher
source. That higher source is God—Just a minute, O'Neill—

and so, when we reason, we seek to approach more closely to the light of God. We go toward our sun."

How could he answer this argument? He was nervous.

"It's our nature to do this. And so it's our nature to seek God. The very way we think, then, proves that there is a God."

Murphy gloated at Danny triumphantly. Danny waited a moment, hoping that now Jim would answer Murphy. Jim scratched his head, puzzled.

"All right, refute me, O'Neill."

"I don't have to."

"But, Dan, that's not an answer to what Francis says. You have to admit that."

"That's a fine way to answer logic. Is that what you call science, running away when you're licked?" Murphy asked.

"There's nothing for me to refute. You begin by believing in the existence of God and then look for proofs. You merely rationalize. I don't know what's higher and lower. You impose a hierarchy of things that excel so you can say that the highest faculty is reason and that means there must be a God. Man's an animal. He is what he is, and functions the way he does. I don't know why. Nobody does."

"O'Neill, you're not only licked, you're damned unless you see the light of reason. Come to your senses, fellow, before it's too late."

"You Catholics always end up with the same threat. Believe or you're damned. Well, I'm not going to be threatened. If you're right, and I don't agree with you, what kind of a God is it who's going to damn me forever because I'm honest enough to refuse to believe something that I can't honestly accept?"

"Don't confuse honesty with pride. And don't play so lightly with the idea of God's justice. God's justice is a terrible thing, O'Neill. You'll pay a terrible price for your obstinacy."

"And then when I'm damned, those who are saved will get pleasure watching me suffer," Danny said bitterly.

"Danny, you can't say that. After all, no matter what else

you say of the Church, it is humane. And it wouldn't be humane to take pleasure in the suffering and tortures of others," Jim said.

"That's what the Church says."

"No, Gogarty, that's true. Saint Thomas Aquinas tells us that the saved will derive pleasure from the sight of the damned in Hell."

"You can believe in that kind of religion if you want to," Danny said.

"I've done my duty, O'Neill," Murphy said.

Danny left, saying good-by to Jim but not to Murphy.

Crossing the campus, his anger cooled. He had defended himself badly. But he was right. Why must the existence of God be proved by such rigmarole as Murphy's? If you proved you existed by saying that you felt, you saw, and you thought, why didn't God just let all men see Him? Then no one but a lunatic would deny God. But God didn't do that. And if you didn't believe in the unprovable God, your inflammable soul would burn forever. He wanted none of this. You had to take a knife and cut it out. Murphy believed because he wanted to. Well, he would deny. He walked on, absolutely convinced that all the arguments of the Church, all the reasonings of the medieval schoolmen, all the books of Saint Augustine and the other saints could not shake him in his denial.

He thought of Jim Gogarty. Jim had deserted him.

XVIII

It was one o'clock. Brown was sleepy, but he felt that he couldn't go home. He had driven around to all of his stations, and he didn't like the way things were going. The men at the new greasing palace on Michigan Boulevard had to be cleaned out. They weren't watching their p's and q's closely enough. He had driven in there at eleven-fifteen and caught Devlin gassing with a girl on the telephone instead of attending to business. Rostand, the manager, had been sitting on his can. Attendants couldn't be trusted. What might they not be doing when no one was watching them? And if anything went wrong, it was his responsibility, not theirs. If there was a complaint, to whom did North come? To him.

He parked the car across the street from the new greasing station and sat, hunched over the wheel. Nothing was doing. The station was quiet. Rostand was standing by the window, Devlin was cleaning up the greasing pits. Well, the bawling out he'd given them had had some effect. But he'd have to keep tabs on them to see if they would go on hitting the ball. He stepped on the starter and made a final tour of all of the stations under his supervision in order to be sure they had been locked up, that no implements or tools had been left outside, and that the tool sheds were locked. Worn out, his nerves on edge, he got home at two-fifteen, and had a bitter quarrel with his wife.

Chapter Eighteen

I

Danny pulled up several blades of grass and chewed them. When he'd been a kid and had spent so much time playing baseball in Washington Park, he used to chew grass. That was such a long time off now. Distance wasn't only measured in time. Distance was measured, also, in ideas, in intellectual growth, in the changes in your own mind. And think of how he had changed during this long school year. Last summer was only about a year off in time. How many years ago was it in ideas?

He spat out the grass and watched several co-eds pass in the distance. He was sitting in the grass near Harper's, one of a group of students. Alternately he'd listen to them, and then his thoughts would stray. It was only in moments like this, when he was fully relaxed, that he was able to tell how really tired he was. He was all done in. But then the end was in sight. The final exams would be held next week, and after that he would be able to enjoy his well-earned summer vacation. By now he was able to take exams in his stride. He studied day by day all quarter and then, when he walked into the room to take the exam, he was prepared and confident. He ought to finish the year with an A-minus average. He had stood the test of the University, stood it well. Still, he didn't feel himself to be the equal of the students with whom he was talking: Carter, short and stocky, a friend of Broda's, whom he thought so brilliant; Broda, with his sharp wit; Solon, a tall, thin, rather handsome and serious Jewish student; and Gardiner, moon-faced, a fanatic advocate of the theory of the single tax. Gardiner and Carter were arguing now about Henry George. He ought to listen because he could learn something. He ought to contribute something to the argument, but he didn't know what to say. Anything he could say could be said better by Carter. He looked off across the campus. It was such a fine, cool morning. He chewed more grass, gazing off moodily.

"But, Tom, how are you going to get the single tax across? Can you get it passed as a law, say, by the City Council?" Jim Gogarty asked.

"Even John Dewey recognizes the importance of Henry George as a thinker. And I see new faces at every one of our meetings. We're gaining. We had twenty-eight people at our meeting last week," Gardiner said.

"I don't think you can get it across, and if you can't put an idea over, doesn't it fail to meet the pragmatic test?" Jim continued.

"Hell, how could you expect to get the single tax theory passed by the City Council? Nearly all the aldermen are building contractors, aren't they?" Danny said.

"O'Neill, I'm afraid you're becoming cynical," Broda said.

"That's a reflection of your influence, I suppose," Solon said to Broda, laughing.

"My dear chap, far from being cynical, I am filled with endless wonder when I contemplate the spectacle of knowledge afforded me on this campus."

"But, fellows, speaking seriously, don't you think we are getting a liberal education here? I think I am," Jim said.

How about himself? He was learning, but learning had only unsettled him, and he didn't know how and why he was learning, nor what he believed any more. You couldn't merely say that you believed in truth and in intelligence. What truth? Intelligence to what end? He could spend a whole summer trying to answer these questions.

"There's a lot of talk about a liberal education," Danny said, "but the whole emphasis is really on how everyone is going to get ahead."

"The University has some of the advantages of a college, and all of those of a country club," Carter said.

"Say, did the president raise any more money this last week? I get dizzy trying to keep track of the millions that have been given here of late. Hasn't any meat packer or pork butcher or bootlegger given the University any money of late?" Broda asked.

"Oh, there must have been at least a few millions tossed in for some endowment or other," Solon said.

"That's nothing. A few millions in endowments—why, that's chicken feed," Carter said.

"Every little penny counts," Broda said.

"Say, there goes Walker. Any day now he will publish his n-dimensional price curve and save civilization," Broda said, nodding in the direction of a passing professor.

"No, he won't," Solon said.

"Why, what happened?" Broda asked with simulated curiosity.

"He's balked because he doesn't know algebra. He's looking for some senior who knows algebra to work out his equations. If you know any senior who can do algebra, send him to Walker. Walker will get him a fellowship in economics," Carter said.

"I'm waiting for that price curve."

"Broda, why don't you take more courses in economics and rail about it less?" Solon asked.

"Think of it, with all the courses given by the Department of Economics, there isn't one on Henry George," Gardiner said.

Was he getting a liberal education? He recalled the writings of Newman, Arnold, Huxley. He still wondered which of them had been right. He was learning, learning facts, learning how to get A's on term papers and in examinations—but was he thinking, finding his way to what he wanted? At times he felt he was studying so much, taking so many notes, was plugging away like a grind so that he didn't have time to think.

Yes, he felt now and then as if he were stuffing himself, and
as if some day he would wake up with indigestion and revolt
against the whole procedure. No, he wouldn't. Having gotten
this far, having proved himself, he would never give up.

"There goes a genius," Solon remarked as a callow, red-
faced young man walked by them.

"Who is he?" Broda asked.

"His name is Hawkins. He wrote a doctor's thesis on Wordsworth, Milton, and Tennyson and proved that Wordsworth
was the greatest of these poets because he wrote the largest
number of iambic pentameter lines," Solon said.

"That's nothing, I know a girl who's writing a thesis on
how to save time in dishwashing," Carter said.

"If you want to meet with real nonsense." Broda said, "you
should take a course in Education. Do you know, a friend of
mine was in one of the Ed. courses, and he was asked this question—If you are teaching and the janitor is off, ill, on a cold
day, is it beneath the dignity of a teacher to make the fire in
the little red schoolhouse?"

"I don't believe it," Jim said.

"What would you do, O'Neill?" Carter asked.

"Hell, I'd tell the kids to go home," Danny said.

"Carter, do you know this chap Murphy?" Jim asked.

"You mean the secretary of the Catholic Club?"

"Yes."

"He used to try to buttonhole me to prove that there is a
God. I avoid him whenever I can."

"Outside of being a damned fool, he's not a bad chap,"
Solon said.

"If he doesn't settle his war with the evil ideas of John
Dewey, he's going to become a mental case. He thinks Dewey
ruined the University. I didn't see the point of arguing with
him. I pointed out that belief, not fact, is the basis of all the
scholastic arguments on the existence of God, and that you can
be logical about anything in the world as long as you accept
your premises and follow from them. So he told me my mind

was corrupted and that I lived like an animal," Carter said, smiling. "I told him that God had ceased to be a really important problem in philosophy. He answered that I was pathetic."

"I have run-ins with him all the time. He takes Wolcott's course with me. Yesterday he said I was a faded carbon copy of a devil's advocate. So I said he was a jackdaw of Rheims. We get along in a very Irish way," Danny said.

"Broda, what do you think of that?" Solon asked, nodding at an attractive co-ed who was passing near them.

"Broda is above such interests," Carter said.

"I wouldn't throw her out of bed," Danny said.

"Tell me, Carter, before I answer your question, what does she think about the special theory of relativity?" Broda answered.

"What interests me is how she'd apply relativity to morals."

"Ask her," Solon said.

"You ask her and give me a full report on it," Carter said.

Danny looked after her. He wanted a girl.

"With what she has, who'd care what was in her brain?" he said.

"Maybe Gardiner could get her to read Henry George," Solon said.

"Henry George has pointed out the way. Nobody can deny that. He shows that the ills of society are the result of private appropriation of the unearned increment . . ."

"Our question is what increment will result if Broda and I take her out," Carter interrupted.

They laughed, but Danny observed that they were all rather embarrassed by these references to sex. Suddenly he felt superior to them. He had drunk, gone out on dates, lost his virginity. But, hell, what miserable pride this was. Again Danny gazed off across the grass. Yes, he was unsettled, but the perspectives of the mind were endless. The future offered so much possibility of knowing, understanding. Study was the greatest adventure in the world. He felt suddenly that he could be happy all of his life as a student here at the U. He looked at his watch. Reluctantly, he got up, said so-long, and left. They'd all eat together and have the afternoon to talk or study, and he would be at the gas station, pumping away. And maybe that bastard Brown would come around again today to ride him.

He walked on.

II

The quarter had ended today. The school year was finished, and he had come through it with flying colors. He might get three A's this quarter, and he'd close the full year with an A— average. Depleted, but filled with a deep and quiet contentment and self-satisfaction, Danny reported for work.

"You missed the shooting," Stall announced excitedly.

"So Brown was around bellyaching again?"

"Listen, I'm still shaking in my boots. I never want to see what I saw again, no, sir, not as long as I live. Say, I'll be having nightmares for weeks."

"What happened?" Danny asked, his curiosity roused.

"Charlie, the money-wagon man, got killed, right here. Jesus, I just cleaned up the blood off the floor."

Danny stared at Stall, unbelieving.

"I just about puked. I'm goin' home now and get drunk."

"What happened?" Danny insisted.

"That flat-foot Mason was in here, in the can. Well, Charlie gets out of the money wagon today to use the can. You know, he was always a kidder. Well, he comes in, kiddin', and he says to me: 'Stick 'em up.' And the goddamned flat-foot, he's in the can there, and before I know what the hell has happened, he busts out shootin'. He shoots twice, and Charlie goes down, stone dead. Christ, look at my hands. They're still shaking."

The news was a shock. It did not register in Danny's mind immediately. Then he turned pale, imagining Charlie dead on the station floor.

He shook his head.

"Christ, would you think such a thing could have happened?" Stall asked.

"The goddamned fool!" Danny exploded.

He was alive. Charlie was dead. Why should the accident concern him? He was sorry. It shouldn't have been. And it could have happened when he was on duty. He could have been shot. His sympathy for Charlie deepened. Everyone's life hung on a frail thread of circumstances. The only life he would ever know could be ended without warning just as quickly, as senselessly. Poor Charlie! Life was so often stupid, utterly stupid. Life was unfair.

"I've been knockin' on wood since it happened. I could have been killed myself. The noise almost floored me. I was by the safe, and before I knew what it was all about, the dumb flatfoot pulls the trigger, and Charlie's on the floor. Then Mason stands with his mouth hangin' open and the gun in his hand. 'What the hell did I do?' he asks."

Danny shook his head from side to side. What was there to say?

"Of course Mason didn't mean to do it. He just wanted to uphold the law and collect a reward, that's all. But the goddamned flatfooted fool."

"Mason gives me the creeps here at night. He sits in the can there, with his gun out, telling me that I don't need to worry."

"Charlie was a decent guy, a decent guy. He was a kidder and a practical joker. Well, poor Charlie, this is one practical joke that sure was no joke. And, you know, he's got a wife and two kids, too."

"It's too bad," Danny said, realizing the banality of his remark.

They faced each other, speechless and appalled.

III

"I don't understand it, O'Neill. A fellow who could be as brilliant as you," Brown said.

Danny didn't answer. Just after Stall had left, he'd sat

down, thinking of Charlie, and Brown had bobbed up like bad news. The bastard had a new trick, too. He put on a clean white glove and ran his hand over the shelves to snoop for dust. How could you work for a boss like that?

Brown gazed suspiciously at Danny.

"What's the matter with you, O'Neill?" he asked in an injured tone of voice.

"Nothing."

"Why do I have to keep coming around here nearly every day to check up on you? Why can't I trust you?"

"You can trust me," Danny said defensively, his voice tense.

"All of you attendants are alike. I have to be after you night and day. You never clean up. This place should be spotless, and look at it."

"It's clean. Stall did a lot of work this morning, and I was just going to do the rest of what is necessary when you came in."

"Clean? Do you know what it means for a station to be clean? Listen, I was an attendant. I know what I'm talking about. I would have been ashamed of myself to let my station get the way this is."

Danny repressed his impulse to tell Brown what he thought of him. But he wouldn't be able to do this much longer. He couldn't take this constant riding.

"O'Neill, this can't go on. You're not playing fair with me. You're not being loyal to the company. What's the matter with you?"

"Nothing's the matter with me. I do my work. I can't do everything at once. I can't let the customers wait while I dust the shelves, can I?"

"You have plenty of time. Don't give me that. I'm no dummy. Just because you go to college, don't think you're too smart for me. I'm on to you."

"But if you want to sell oil, you have to take more time, talking to your customers, giving them sales arguments. And today, in particular, everything got upset because the money man was shot here."

"Don't use that as an excuse. I'm not interested in your excuses. I want things done. I'm responsible to Mr. North for your conduct. If there are complaints, I am the one who is told about them. I have to take the blame for what you do."

"Are there any complaints about me?" Danny asked, trying to hide his apprehension.

"I get it in the neck for you fellows. I have to be after you night and day. It's too much for me. O'Neill, jack up, or else you can find something else to do. You've given me trouble enough."

"What trouble did I give you?"

"Don't play that innocent game on me, O'Neill. It won't work."

"I don't know why you're always riding me, Mr. Brown."

"You know damned well why I ask you to be more co-operative. Do you want your job?"

"Yes, sir."

"Then prove it. This is my last warning. Keep this station cleaner."

Brown stalked out. Danny stood in the center of the station, cursing Brown. He watched his boss's Ford disappear. Now he'd have to watch his step. Brown would see to it that spotters were put on his tail. His days as an attendant might be numbered. He sat down. Well, the school year was over. But what about next year? He was confident that he was among the twenty freshmen with the highest grades at the U; he'd probably win a freshman honor scholarship. He wouldn't have a tuition problem next year. If he lost out, he'd get something. Hell, he was too damned worn out to worry.

He could do more cleaning up around here, too, now that his summer vacation from school had started.

It was too bad about Charlie.

Instead of doing any cleaning, he took out a book of selections from English poetry. He read aloud. A plump, seedy-looking man with a cheap bulging suitcase entered the station without Danny being aware of it.

"Good afternoon, nice sunny day, isn't it?"

Danny looked up, surprised, and saw the man open the suitcase on the floor. Another damned salesman. Didn't they ever try to sell their junk to anyone other than attendants? What did they think gas-station men were—dopes?

"I don't want any ties."

"Here, look at this one," the salesman said, holding up a shoddy tie with a pattern of red and blue squares.

"I said I don't need any ties."

"Socks, underwear? I have some real bargains, and goods of the same quality that would cost you twice as much in a Loop department store."

"Listen, I'm busy," Danny barked.

"Let me show you some of my socks, only ten cents a pair."

"For the last time, I'm busy."

Danny turned back to his book. The salesman didn't bulge. His presence made Danny nervous.

"I don't want any clothes. I don't want any ties, B.V.D.'s, or any goddamn thing else," Danny said.

"You don't have to get sore."

"Well, I'm busy. Quit bothering me. Get the hell out of here before I throw you out!" Danny shouted, jumping to his feet.

The salesman stared at Danny like a whipped and broken man.

Danny felt sorry for him. He watched the man close his grip and tag off, a pathetic figure.

He was sorry he had lost his head. The poor guy was merely trying to make a living. Did he like it when customers yelled at him and cursed him for his persistence in trying to sell them oil? He could have eased the poor fellow out. He was worn out from the long hard grind at school, and that was why he'd lost his temper. And then the news about Charlie was an invitation to reflections on death, your own death.

He wished he were off today and lying in the grass in Washington Park, doing nothing, thinking of nothing.

A car drove in. Danny slipped his book in a desk drawer and went out to it.

A well-dressed man got out of a new Chevrolet and held up five fingers. When Danny spoke to him, the man's face remained blank. He still held up five fingers. The customer was a deaf mute.

He pumped in the five gallons.

He pointed at the hood. The deaf mute didn't understand him. Danny pointed again. The deaf mute didn't respond.

Danny motioned for the man to come into the station.

Inside, he wrote on scratch paper:

Do you need any oil?

No, the man wrote.

How many miles have you gone since you had your crankcase drained?

I don't know.

Is it more than five hundred miles?

I can't read your writing.

Is it more than five hundred miles since you drained the crankcase?

Maybe yes and maybe no.

You ought to drain your crankcase every five hundred miles. It keeps your motor good, no grit in the oil. You save money and your motor that way. Gives car longer life.

All right, drain it.

If you want to save money, I can save you some.

How?

I can sell you the oil cheaper.

How?

Oil costs 25c a quart. You need six quarts. That's $1.50. You can buy a five-gallon can of oil for $3.95. You save a dollar and five cents.

What will I do with the can?

Keep it. When you need another drain, take it to any Upton Station. We sell the best oil on the market, and give you best service.

All right.

And you ought to flush your motor out with flushing oil. It only costs forty cents. It cleans the motor, takes out all dirt, grit.

All right.

Do you need grease in your transmission? Our grease is superb.

Please drain my car, and don't sell me the station.

Yes, sir. I only thought if you needed grease, I could do the whole job for you.

All right, give me a shot of grease.

Yes, sir. Drive over to the crankcase pit on the side of the driveway.

Danny picked up a wrench and started to drain the car. He was proud of his salesmanship. He'd have to find a way of letting Brown and North know about it.

IV

After eating supper, Danny carted the plates back to the restaurant across the street. He dashed back to the station. It was twilight. The corner was quiet. There had been a brief rain, and the June air still was fragrant with its odors. The sidewalks were drying. Danny began to pace back and forth on the driveway. All afternoon he had felt a mounting nervousness and tension within him. He was at loose ends. Had the accidental killing of Charlie today caused this? No, for, after all, he had hardly known the poor devil. The long months of study were really ended. He'd had hardly any relaxation in all this time. Just think, he had seen only one movie in nine months, and had had no dates. Poetry had been his only relaxation. Day after day he had stuck to the grind. And think of how he had changed intellectually.

> *Grow old along with me,*
> *The best is yet to be.*

He recited Browning without paying heed to the meaning of the lines. He continued pacing.

You got to see your mama every night,
Or you can't see mama at all.
You got to kiss your mama, treat her right . . .

This vacation he wanted to get himself a mama. He'd treat her right. What about one of the factory girls who worked across the street? Some of them were beauties. He'd watched them pass tonight, wanting to fondle them.

By the old Moulmein pagoda, looking eastward to the sea . . .

Mandalay brought memories of Beatrice. This time last year he had been in love with her. He had not even thought of her for months.

He stopped to fill an empty water bucket by the side of the station.

Three drains this afternoon. Brown couldn't get his job if he kept on selling oil. He'd clean out the pit with kerosene in the morning. No he wouldn't have to work every night as he had during the school year.

My heart aches and a drowsy numbness . . .

He continued walking back and forth.

The whole summer was before him, spread out like a green field. He had earned rest and relaxation. This last year seemed so long, and yet it had passed so swiftly. And during it he had left all gods dead behind him.

He stopped by the pump island and watched a troop of ten Negro children pass. They wore ragged hand-me-down clothes. A pig-tailed black girl of about ten lagged behind the rest to pull up her torn and dirty white stockings. She ran to catch up with her companions. Eleven-year-old Andy Morgan, who was on probation from the Juvenile Court, gave her a shove, and she cursed him. His father was a ditch digger who came around with an old red can to buy a few pennies' worth of kerosene. Few of the Negroes around here could afford electricity. The father always seemed tired, weary, and one night he'd said that this was no world for a black man to be born into. What chances had the Negro? What chances had these kids? They ran down Wabash, screaming as they disappeared. Here was a flash of the sad poetry of the street. His mood changed. He had learned a lot about how the Negro lived since he'd worked at this station, and he had lost all race prejudices. In Public Speaking two weeks ago he'd created an uproar in class by speaking on the Negro problem, attacking the white man for exploiting the Negro and demanding that the city build decent homes for the Negro, free. He'd been proud of himself that morning, attacking the prejudices of everyone in class. Murphy had called him a radical. Well, he guessed he was. He closed his eyes and thought of the Negro kids in this neighborhood, and of the worn-out old Negro men and women. He thought of Crabbe's poem about the old gypsy, and quoted aloud.

> Last in the group, the worn-out grandsire sits
> Neglected, lost, and living but by fits;
> Useless, despised, his worthless labours done,
> And half protected by the vicious son,
> Who half supports him; he with heavy glance
> Views the young ruffians who round him dance;
> And by the sadness of his face appears
> To trace the progress of their future years—
> Through what strange course of misery, vice, deceit
> Must wildly wander each unpractised cheat!
> What shame and grief, what punishment and pain,
> Sport of fierce passions, must each child sustain—
> Ere they like him approach their latter end
> Without a home, a comfort, or a friend!

These lines told a story he saw from this station every day. Yes, they told him the story of the Negroes in this neighborhood.

The telephone rang, and he answered it anxiously. It was a wrong number. He sat down to read, but he became restless again. He couldn't concentrate. He stood outside.

. . . on a darkling plain . . .
Where ignorant armies clash by night

He paced back and forth. He was wound tightly and felt as if he were going to explode.

But he was free, free on this young night of the young June of 1926.

I will arise and go now, and go to Innisfree
And a small cabin build there . . .

v

He turned the key in the time lock at about nine-fifteen and, carrying his book, walked slowly along Wabash Avenue, past the old houses where the Negroes lived. It was a wonderful night. He had walked himself into a state of lethargy on the driveway. He had thought again of the brutal accident which took Charlie's life in the station today and of how free and happy he was. And this had led him to thoughts of the coldness, the cruelty, the injustice in the world. Suddenly, it seemed ironical and unfeeling that he should be joyous merely because he had been released from school.

How could he take it easy this summer? No, he wouldn't. He would go on working, studying, preparing himself. He had to study about Russia. Just as they had lied to him about everything else, he was now sure that he had been told lies about Russia, about Lenin and Trotsky. Christy the Greek waiter on Fifty-eighth Street had told him that Russia was the hope of the future. Recently he'd read Henry George, too, and while he didn't agree with the idea of the Single Tax, he had been moved by the first part of *Progress and Poverty*, with its description of poverty and misery. History was a tale told about those who had profited from the efforts, the sufferings, the deprivations of thousands who were dead, the nameless dead. And Papa, too, he belonged with the nameless dead. This life was one of suffering, and then, of nothingness. The graveyards of the world, all the Potter's Fields were filled with the rotting bones of the nameless dead.

And yet he had been happy today.

He walked slowly, sadly toward Twenty-sixth Street. Why had his mood changed so drastically? His feeling of freedom had collapsed. What could be done? He wanted to know. You had to do something. His generation had to do something. This last year had taught him that life wasn't good. It was cruel and stupid. Tonight he had drifted into these thoughts. Why should the young, those who owned the future as he did, go on acquiescing in stupidity?

He stopped and looked at the sky. So blue, so vast. It was full of shining stars. The sheer extravagance of the stars struck him with wonder. God was supposed to be in the sky, beyond the stars, sitting in Heaven. If God were there, God was looking down on the world of misery that He had created.

Tears came to his eyes. He shook his fist at the sky.

Goddamn you, God! he said to himself in anger.

There was no God on whom to blame the misery of the world.

Goddamn you, you non-existent God! he flung to the star-filled sky.

These same stars now shone on the grave where his father's bones had rotted. They shone on the graves of all the nameless and unrewarded. The poor devil Charlie, he had now earned such a grave.

He walked slowly on. He hated life. He despised it. He had been thrown into this Godless, purposeless world, for what? To die, another nameless sufferer? No, never, never would he let that happen to him. He would fight this world. From this minute forth he declared war on this world. Again he shook his fist at the heavens. Again the tears came to his eyes.

He wiped his eyes. He turned the corner of Twenty-sixth and Wabash Avenue to go to the elevated train.

This summer before him wasn't a green field over which he could wander. It was a time during which he must go on without sparing himself.

SECTION FOUR

1926-1927

Dr. Pearson was a tall young man with a fleshy face. He had thick, weak lips, a long, pointed nose, small and shifty dark eyes, silver-rimmed spectacles, and a shock of coarse, black, straight hair. He wore a loud tweed suit. He stood poised in front of the large class in Cobb Hall. Danny, sitting near the window, watched him, intently absorbed, filled with admiration for the young instructor.

"Now I'll analyze the political situation in present-day Germany." Dr. Pearson said in an over-cultivated voice.

Danny wrote a heading in his notebook: Pol. Situation Germany Today.

"The Weimar Republic is now stabilized. It appears to be in no danger either from the right or from the left. On the extreme left we have the Communists, the lunatic fringe. On the extreme right, there is another lunatic fringe. The extreme right is very weak. One of its representative parties is the National Socialist Party, led by a man named Hitler, Adolf Hitler. He organized one comic opera putsch in Munich, and he spent a little time in jail, cooling his impetuous heels and reflecting, no doubt, on the grandeur and misery of political frustration. In order to understand the extreme right in Germany, it is necessary to read the works of the famous psychoanalysts such as Dr. Sigmund Freud and Dr. Jung."

Danny asked himself how psychoanalysis applied to politics?

"You have in the extreme right of Germany a frustrated ego, a condition of mind, of psychoneurosis which amounts to the frustration of the libido. The extreme right has no program worthy of the name. For instance, the program of this Herr

253

Hitler is a hodge-podge, a mish-mash. It promises something to everybody and nothing to anybody. Mr. Hitler is a man who hates the world. He dislikes the Jews; he blusters against the chain stores; he hates France; he hates everything. He leads a small band of followers, equally lunatic, to whom almost no one pays any attention."

Danny jotted down in his notebook: Ext. right. Not imp.

Dr. Pearson continued his lecture. Danny took notes on it.

Chapter Nineteen

I

"Look what the little divils did," Pat Whelan said; he was a tall, sunken-cheeked, bony Irishman.

Danny saw that the telephone had been ripped off the station wall. It was a narrow, red-bricked Upton station at Thirty-fifth and Morgan.

"What did they do, break the window?" Danny asked.

"The side one. Wolfert, the repair man, is after coming and putting in a new glass."

"Did they get anything else?"

Danny studied the wall as if he were interested, and then shook his head from side to side.

"You were a dollar short this morning."

"I'll make it up," Danny said.

"It's all right now. I checked up already."

He was lucky in the partners he'd been teamed up with. He'd never had one dishonest partner.

"Say, Pat, I told you about that bastard, Brown, who used to be my supervisor. Well, I dropped in to see Rostand at the greasing palace on Michigan last night and he told me Brown went out of his head the other night. He was taken to the hospital in a straitjacket."

"What's that you're after saying, man?"

"He took his responsibility so damned seriously that it got him."

"Ah, life's too short to worry."

"I feel sorry for him. But I had to go to North and ask to get transferred. I'd have gone nuts myself if I hadn't. On Twenty-fifth Street he used to come to see me every day and raise hell."

A fleet of trucks passed on Thirty-fifth Street and the station windowpanes vibrated.

"Here's your book," Whelan said, handing Danny a copy of *Mr. Gilhooley,* by Liam O'Flaherty.

"Did you like it?"

"And don't I know the streets and sights he describes? It took me thoughts back to Dublin. For six months, wasn't I a cop along Grafton Street meself?"

"I want to go to Ireland some day."

"Often I do be thinking that here I am, sitting in a peaceful gasoline station in America instead of being out in the hills and the bogs on the run. The sights I've seen would make your hair stand on end. But the Black and Tans are gone now. I struck me blow for Ireland, and I'm glad to be out of it."

Whelan had to take care of a customer, and Danny changed into his overalls. Whelan cleaned up and left.

What should he do?

This work was a boring routine. He'd started at it in March, 1925, and it was now November, 1926. He'd have to go on at it for several more years. But why complain? Wasn't he in a spot to be envied? He had an honor scholarship, and expected to win another one. He only worked from one to eight, and he was off every other Sunday. This station didn't do too much business. He had all the time he needed for study. And for some reason or other there wasn't a time lock on the door here. Some nights he closed up early and went home or to a show. But he was bored, bored to death with this damned gas station.

A dull day. Across the street an ugly factory. This whole area was an industrial scab on the city. They'd called it Central Manufacturing District at the express company. The express company was part of another world now.

A rattle-trap Buick pulled into the station.

"For Christ sake!" Danny said, seeing Jack Kennedy, who used to hang around the corner of Sixty-third and Stony Island.

"Hello, oil man, oil me up. I want some gas on the finger," Jack said.

"I'll give you five gallons. The public can pay for it."

"O'Neill, is there an honest attendant in the city? You know, if Diogenes knew about you bastards, he'd have committed hara-kiri."

Danny gave Jack five gallons.

"I heard you were selling cars and doing good."

"The agency I worked with sold so many cars that we sold ourselves out of business. The more we sold, the more the manufacturer made us take. He raised our quota so high we just went on the fritz. My boss went bankrupt selling cars."

Danny laughed.

"How's Marty Mulligan?"

"He's a salesman. He drives around in a Nation car with a cigar in his mouth and uses part of his pay to buy stock in the company. Yes, Marty's a man of affairs. We all call him Babbitt now."

He leaned on the side of the car and couldn't think of anything to say to Jack.

"Heard anything about Ed Lanson?" Jack asked.

"He went to sea."

"That dame who hara-kiried herself for him, Ellen Rogers, she was neat stuff. Why the hell should she have walked out in the lake over any guy?"

"I don't know."

"Some of the boys were sore at Lanson for it. I don't see how he was responsible. They all get dames and drop them. Well, her old man hushed it up, kept it out of the papers."

"Yeh, it's about a year ago, isn't it, since she drowned herself," Danny said.

"Time flies, my lad. And here I am wasting time. I could be licking Dopey's pants right now in a game of bridge. By the way, Dopey had a job for two weeks in September, and he's still bragging about it. Thanks for the petrol, O'Neill."

Kennedy drove off. Danny kicked a stone. What should he study first? Ethics, Sociology, or Poli. Sci.? Even study was becoming routine now.

A Ford coupé drove in. Mickelson, his new Supervisor, got out, carrying a briefcase. He was a lanky, quiet man with blond hair.

"Hello, O'Neill."

"Hello, Mike."

They went inside the station.

"Everything all right?"

"Yes, you heard about the telephone being stolen?"

Mickelson nodded. He opened his briefcase and handed Danny a folder. Danny skimmed through it. It was an announcement outlining a plan for company employees to buy Upton stock.

"We're giving you fellows a chance to buy stock, as you see from that folder," Mickelson said.

"Yes."

"It's an opportunity we're offering everyone. I'm taking stock myself. After all, it isn't the same working for Upton and working for just any firm. The oil business is the business of the future."

Mickelson was delivering a set spiel without enthusiasm. It was part of his job to do this.

"You have a chance to put something away for a rainy day and become a joint owner of the company. Over a period of time you can lay a little nest egg for yourself. And for every dollar you invest in this plan, the company gives you twenty cents more in stock. For every hundred dollars you invest in this stock, you really get one hundred and twenty dollars. As soon as you sign up, you own your first share, and then whatever amount you plan to invest is taken pro rata from your salary check. Most of the men are signing up and taking advantage of this opportunity."

"I wish I could, but I can't afford to. I have to save money for my tuition, and of course I have to help out at home. I couldn't afford it."

"That's too bad; it's an opportunity."

Mickelson closed his briefcase.

"No shortages?" he asked.

"No, we're running all right."

"The auditor is covering my stations this week."

A hint. Mickelson was the decentest boss he'd ever had.

"Well, so long, O'Neill."

Danny said so long and walked out to the Ford with Mickelson. Why should he own stock? *The sickness of an acquisitive society*. If he bought stock he'd become part of this sickness.

He went across the street with a can to buy coffee and drank it in the station, restless, bored.

II

A fine, cold rain was falling, and the corner was dark and gloomy. Danny glanced up from a copy of *Beyond Good and Evil*. He'd begun to feel that he himself was beyond good and evil, and that was why he'd decided to write a term paper on Nietzsche. He was almost dizzy from Nietzsche's phrases. Now he understood why Ed Lanson used to talk about Nietzsche. Here was a great thinker. His words were like iron. They intensified his restlessness, nourished his dissatisfaction. They spurred his protest against the dull and almost meaningless life he was leading.

He quoted lines he had memorized from *Thus Spake Zarathustra*:

Now razeth my hammer ruthlessly against its prison. From the stone fly the fragments: what's that to me?

Oh, to destroy the walls of his prison. He wanted a hammer. He needed weapons with which to fight this world. He needed weapons. He was in a state of war with the world, but he was without armor. He fondled the book. Here was a weapon. He looked out at the dreary corner.

The motley whirl of the senses . . .

This was life. This was what he, what all men, must be subjected to.

The motley whirl of the senses . . .

Yes, he was beyond good and evil now, and he would rise
above this motley whirl. Today in his Ethics class he'd defended
immoralism. Some of the students had laughed at him as if he
were crazy. Let them laugh! Should we judge conduct ethical
or unethical in terms of motivations or because of consequences?
Kant or John Stuart Mill? Nietzsche was right—Kant had
taken the backstairs into theology. Last summer he'd started
reading *The Critique of Pure Reason,* but he'd burst a blood
vessel in his right eye on the small print and he'd had to stop
all reading for three weeks. Kant said that all knowledge begins with experience but does not arise out of experience. Where
did it arise? He'd break no more blood vessels in his eyes on
Immanuel Kant. What should he do with himself?

He remembered that in grammar school Sister Magdalen
had said to him:

Danny O'Neill, you have the germ of destruction in you.

Had she been clairvoyant? He wanted to destroy worlds. His
spirit was free, but his body was in a prison at Thirty-fifth and
Morgan. He stood by the door of the narrow station, seething
with resentment.

III

Danny got off the streetcar under the Thirty-fifth Street
elevated station. His face was drawn, and his lips were tight.
He crossed the street, determined, and heedless of the rain.

Thirty-fifth Street was a dreary, sordid street. From somewhere he heard a raucous jazz band. Nondescript-looking Negroes passed.

He turned toward Michigan.

"Want some love, honey?" a prostitute asked in a coarse
voice.

"Yes," he gasped, trembling, without will.

"Come on, dearie."

He followed her as if he were an automaton. She was a hawk-
nosed, plump woman whose small suspicious eyes were set in an

oval face. Her lips were thick, smeared with rouge. She wore an old blue coat with a moth-eaten, imitation fur collar. She led him into an entranceway next to a flower store, and they went up a rickety, unswept stairway. She opened a door in a dimly lit hallway and turned on the electric light. Danny entered. He wanted to run out. He stood rooted, his hands shaking.

He saw a large, sagging bed on which were soiled sheets. He sniffed. The odor of the room was musty. The blue wallpaper was torn and spotted. There were three chairs, upholstered in faded imitation tapestry. A large, cracked white bowl stood in a corner near the bulky, ornate and scratched dresser.

"Give me two dollars, honey," she said, after throwing her coat on a chair; she wore a dirty gingham dress.

He took out his wallet and handed her the money.

"Honey, don't you want to have a real good time? If you give me an extra dollar, I'll really give you love."

Danny handed her another dollar.

She pressed herself close to him and wriggled. Danny was revolted as he had never been before in his whole life.

"Honey, make it five. Come on, dearie, be a sport," she pleaded, clinging to him.

He handed her two more dollars.

His head swirled. He stood as if transfixed, hypnotized. He feared looking at her. She went out with the bowl, and he waited, without will power telling himself to leave.

She returned with the bowl and studied him, curiously.

"You haven't had much experience, have you?" she said.

He was speechless. His throat was parched. His lips seemed feverish.

"Well, dearie, it's never too late to learn."

IV

Riding home on the elevated train, Danny was shaky. He tried to convince himself that he was beyond good and evil. But it wasn't good and evil that was involved; it was aesthetics. He felt soiled.

He looked out the window. A thick mist filled the air. He wished he could disappear, dissolve himself into that gray autumn mist.

Why not forget this little episode?

Man was the victim of his needs. A glandular discharge had been a physical release for him. Irony: the contrast between need and expectation on the one hand, and a person's shabby fulfillment on the other. *The motley whirl of the senses* on Thirty-fifth Street: cost, five dollars.

He opened his copy of *Beyond Good and Evil*. He couldn't read.

His anger with life mounted as he left the train. He walked home, feeling how dreary this walk was, how dull and familiar, how stale, flat, and commonplace. He smelled autumn in the air. He thought of autumn as the season of decay, of turning leaves, of the world dying and being buried in a winter's coffin of snow. And if winter comes, can spring be far behind? But what springs were there to be in the life of a disillusioned young man?

Human, all too human, he kept repeating to himself.

XX

Al O'Flaherty thought of money as he rode downtown on the elevated train. He remembered how, years ago, when he had first gone on the road and had started to make more money, he'd handled it easily, freely, with a bewildered pride in seeing it pass through his hands. A liberal expense account had given him the feel and power of money. He'd bought clothes, he'd moved his family into steam heat, taken restful vacations. Often he had been amazed by the power of money. He would go into a shoe store, talk to the owner or buyer, and sell him shoes. That meant so much money for him. It came in a check, which he took to the bank and cashed, receiving green bills which he stuffed into his wallet. At times money had seemed so easy to get. What was money? If he had gone to college and studied economics, he would understand more of the philosophy of money. The Romans said that it was the root of all evil. Often it seemed as if the Romans had hit the nail on the head. But wasn't money also the root of all good?

He had put money into stock in the factory and now he was in danger of never seeing that money again. It was a crying shame that this should happen to him. He prayed and he sent out wishes to the Spirit of Good in the universe so that he wouldn't lose his money. If he did—if the factory failed—what would he do? He ought to be able to land another connection, but after all these years he dreaded even having to look for one.

If some people didn't live by the philosophy of the hog and want all the business for themselves, he wouldn't be in this position of danger. The big shoe factories made enough, didn't

263

they? Why did they want to hog it all? They refused to apply
the golden rule in business. They didn't believe in letting the
other fellow have some good things, too.

Harassed, groping to penetrate the mysterious philosophy of
money, Al entered the Potter Hotel. He gained confidence
when he crossed the showy lobby. He went downstairs to the
barber shop. It was a large room, gilded and ornate. A Negro
in a white jacket took his coat and led him to a chair. He saw
the shiny chromium, the subdued lights, the rows of bottles
and tonics, the well-dressed men sitting and waiting for their
treatments. His turn came. He got a haircut, a shampoo, a
shave, a shoe shine, and a manicure. Hot towels were laid on his
face. He was spoken to with respect. He floated in a dream, assured that there could be no disaster, no failure in the world
when you could afford to buy such service in a barber shop that
was fit for a king. No kings of old, no Sun King—what was
French for it, roi soleil?—had had better service and attention
than this. He finished off at the table of a pert and pretty mani-
curist, with whom he joshed in a gentlemanly manner. No
rough stuff.

He rode upstairs to his hired sample room, his confidence
restored, his worries taken out of him with the aid of a mani-
curist, towels, clippers, tonics, and lotions. He spread out his
samples, beautiful and expensive lady's shoes, and, sucking on
a good cigar, waited for the first buyer of the day.

Chapter Twenty

I

Danny was glad Ed Lanson had returned to Chicago after having been at sea. He'd come into the station, jaunty as ever, surprising Danny.

"Even though we haven't had a chance yet to discuss and exchange ideas, Dan," Ed said, "I can see how much you've changed for the better. You've made remarkable progress, and I approve of the program you've followed. In fact, I envy you. I wish I had the will power to do what you're doing."

Danny was pleased by the compliment. He smiled deprecatingly.

Ed sat comfortably in the lone station chair, and Danny was perched on an oil barrel.

"It'll take me hours to describe what happened to me. I've had more experiences, more ups and downs in the year or so that I was away, than most people would have in three lifetimes. Yes, Dan, I've lived like a Lanson."

Danny envied Ed his daring, his adventures, his bravery. He knew no one who lived as Ed did. His own life paled into a series of commonplaces when it was contrasted with Ed's.

"Well, tell me what you've seen and done," Danny said.

"I don't even know where to begin," Ed said, smiling charmingly.

Yes, it was the same old Ed. And he looked swell, lean and lithe, and in tiptop condition. He was a good-looking, well-built fellow, all right, but even more than his physique, his personality always made itself felt.

"I suppose I was condemned all over town because of Ellen Rogers," Ed said.

265

"No, I didn't hear much said. I don't see the old bunch much any more, and I hardly ever go around Fifty-eighth Street."

"I know a lot of guys have made snotty cracks about me. If they do to my face, they'll talk another language," Ed said; he frowned.

"I never felt that you were to be blamed."

"I knew you wouldn't, Dan. You're true blue. But a lot of bastards shot their traps off. They prated the hypocrisy of society only to mask their own despicable envy. The mealy-mouthed hypocrites, they're envious because a girl didn't commit suicide over them."

Not answering, Danny realized that there was at least a grain of truth in what Ed said.

"Is it all right if I smoke?"

"It's against the rules, but rules are made to be broken."

"I can see that you have changed, grown up, Dan," Ed said, lighting a cigarette. "Yes, and it makes me proud of my old buddy. But there's an unpleasant interruption outside."

Danny saw a car by the pump island and ran out. He waited on the customer in a hurry, not bothering to try to sell him any oil. Then he leaned against the wall, facing Ed.

"I enjoyed the few letters you wrote. I hardly ever wrote to anyone in Chicago because I wanted to blot this goddamned place out of my mind."

"What made you come back?"

"A lot of bastards in this town probably thought I didn't have the guts to. I returned to show them that old Hellfire wasn't afraid to face what they'd miscalled the music."

It didn't sound like a good motive for returning.

"But, Dan—I wasn't responsible for Ellen. Christ, what could I do? I was tired of her always asking me—'Do you love me?' I'll never love a girl the way I loved her. And I would have come back to her. But I had to think, think and mull things out, and she started playing Pinkerton detective and cops and robbers on me. She gave me no alternative but not to see her. So I went away. How did I know that the very day I was leaving she'd drown herself? Women are generally insincere in their emotions. Well, Ellen was a real free spirit, after all. You know what Nietzsche said—a person who commits suicide is an optimist—he seeks to better his condition."

Danny put a shovelful of coal in the stove.

"Christ, you can't imagine how broken up I was when I heard the news. Some dicks came to see me, as if I were guilty of a crime. One of them got snotty, and I told him, 'Listen, I'll answer questions, but don't think you can pull any third degree on me.' He said that he ought to poke me. I told him to take his star off, come outside and try it."

Ed didn't seem to know fear.

"I settled down in Cleveland and had my own little room. I was reading and making notes for a book. I blotted out memories of Ellen. And then a dumb dame named Mary fell for me. She pestered me so much that I had to leave. I went south and toured the South as a traveling salesman. When I got fed up, I shipped out."

"What did you think of London?"

"I was there for a few hours."

"Did you see Westminster Abbey?"

"No, I meant to, and to see the galleries, but I was with some shipmates, and we made a round of the pubs. When I landed back in Galveston, I blew my pay. I took my last dollar and staked it in a gambling joint, and ran it up to three hundred. I blew most of that with a whore I picked up in a can house, and then I made three hundred more. I spent most of that. Now I'm going to settle down here, get a little job, read and study, and live a quiet, simple life. I've had all the adventures and excitement I ever want to have. The world has never been able to tame Hellfire, so I'll tame myself."

Danny went out to another customer.

"Dan, I think my return calls for a celebration. Let's get two dates and a bottle and go out after you close up here."

"It's pretty late to get dates now, isn't it?"

"It's never too late for Lanson. Where's your telephone book?"

II

"Ed, I understand this place has taken most of the business that used to go to the Palm Tree Inn," Danny said.

"It sure is pretty," Anna Sheehan said.

"Gosh, no one ever goes to the Palm Tree Inn any more," Mary Catherine Boyle said.

"When I think of the pubs of Liverpool, I'd say this is a swell joint," Ed Lanson said.

The two couples sat close to the spacious dance floor in the Neapolitan Room of the Westgate Hotel on Stony Island Avenue. It was a large, glassy place with imitation marble pillars.

Danny pushed his glass of ginger ale toward Ed. Ed took a bottle from his hip pocket and poured gin into Danny's and his own glass. They took a drink.

"Tell us more about your trip and your adventures, Ed," Mary Catherine Boyle urged.

"No adventure in my whole life is as exciting as this one tonight," Ed answered gaily.

"What do you mean?" Mary Catherine asked.

"Going out with Mary Catherine Boyle on a date."

"Same old Ed. You haven't changed at all," Anna Sheehan said.

Danny laughed. Ed was outshining him. He smothered his envy. Mary Catherine was more of a knockout than ever. He didn't like her. She was prettier than Anna Sheehan, but Anna was the best he'd been able to get at the last minute. Anna seemed much the same as she'd been when he'd taken her to a frat party over three years ago. To be exact, it had been June, 1923. Her face and breasts were more full now. She was a nice girl and must be still a virgin; dancing with her, he didn't even try to shimmy. This date was an anti-climax. He wanted to go out with different kinds of girls, girls who didn't worry about their virginity, or else who were intelligent.

He sat back in his chair and took another drink. He didn't feel nervous now. He was under no compulsion to have to talk, to try and make an impression on the girls. During the last dance with Anna, he hadn't even said a word. But what kind of a jackass was he, thinking seriously about books and problems when he danced?

"After I left Toledo, I went to Washington. But that burg wasn't hot enough to hold me. Instead of working for the government, I want the government to work for me. So I passed on south."

"Did you like the girls in the South, Ed?" Anna asked.

"I like all girls. It's congenital with me."

"All girls?" asked Mary Catherine.

"But to different degrees," he said to her meaningfully.

"It must be fun to travel," Anna Sheehan exclaimed wistfully.

"Some day I'm going to travel," Danny said, taking another drink.

Travels, adventures to talk about, experiences that made one seem a romantic personality. All those things that went to make up what was called personality—all these were lacking in him. Well, forget it. He was walking down a different street. You couldn't change places with anyone else. Still, he wanted to have a good time tonight. And he wasn't having one. There was no good talk, no prospect of necking and sex. He was wasting time in polite, banal talk and boring dances.

"Dan, this is a celebration, and there you sit as if you were carrying the burdens of the world on your shoulders," Ed said.

The orchestra began to play.

"There's the music. Ahoy," Ed said, rising.

III

Danny suddenly felt wonderful. Gin was a miracle.

"What are you beaming about now? A little while ago, Dan, you looked glum and philosophical. Now your face is abeam with smiles," Ed said.

"I was thinking."

"About what?"

"I was thinking of our fellow human beings in this ballroom, or Neapolitan Room, or whatever you call it."

"What about them?"

"Well, are they enjoying themselves, or is a lot of the talk and the laughter here forced, artificial?"

"I imagine they must be having a good time," Mary Catherine said.

"Yes, of course. This is a nice place, the music is good," Anna said.

"There's a dame over there smoking," Danny said.

"Some of my friends smoke in private, but never in public," Mary Catherine said.

"You're a Saint Paul girl," Danny said.

Mary Catherine answered him with a disdainful look.

"Here's a question, Ed, that I can't answer. Is it the school or the girls? Because, I tell you, it can give some very fancy and highfalutin' ideas to the daughter of a man who, after all, is only a coal dealer, a paving contractor, or a ward committee-man."

Ed laughed.

"But what's wrong with being the daughter of a coal dealer?" asked Mary Catherine.

"How about another drink?" Danny asked.

Ed reached for the glasses and poured in more gin.

"Yes, why do girls with names like O'Donnell and Muldoon —whose fathers sell coal—when they go to Saint Paul's, why do they fail to discover the difference between themselves and a duchess?"

"What do you call them, Dan—lace-curtain Irish?"

"Yes. From stove heat to a radiator in ten years, or the career of Bridget the Princess."

"That's a card," Ed said.

"I don't think it's funny," Mary Catherine said.

"Dan, the slightest whim of these girls is our command. It isn't funny," Ed said.

"Correct," Danny added, drinking.

Ed whispered to Mary Catherine and her eyes lit up. Ed leaned back and lit a cigarette.

"Say, something just occurred to me," Danny announced.

"What?" Ed asked.

"It takes all kinds of people to make a world, doesn't it?"

"It does, all right," Anna Sheehan said, taking Danny's remark very seriously.

"Yes, it does," Ed said, winking at Danny.

"And what in the name of Jehovah would we do, Ed, if we did not have a coal dealer, not to mention the coal dealer's daughter? Why, we'd freeze at night. The coal dealer performs a service to society. What does he do? He sells coal to them that has the price. After all, a coal dealer's daughter can think that her daddy is a great boon to American civilization. He keeps the nation warm in winter."

"Goodness, do we have to go on talking about things like this?" Mary Catherine looked at Danny with hatred. Ed kicked him under the table.

The orchestra was playing *The Song of Love*. Colored lights played on the dancers. The song touched old sentiments in Danny. Suddenly he was moody. In his befogged mind the understanding of the present struggled with the hopes and sentiments of his recent past.

He took another drink.

"Goodness, you drink a lot. You didn't use to, did you, Danny?" asked Anna Sheehan.

"Ed, tell me more about your travels," Mary Catherine coaxed flirtatiously.

IV

"You talk so well," Mary Catherine exclaimed enthusiastically, after Ed had finished describing how he had thrown a plate of stew at the cook on the freighter bound for England.

Danny knew he was getting drunk. He ought to stop, stop before he made a damned fool of himself. Ed was holding his liquor a little better. Danny gulped down a shot of straight gin.

"I think there may be some excitement here any minute," Ed said.

"Why?" asked Mary Catherine.

"At the next table there is some clerk or soda jerker who's been gawking at me in a way I don't like," Ed said, raising his voice.

A young man at the next table turned and looked sharply at Ed.

"What did you say, Bud?"

"You heard me."

The girls were too frightened to speak. Ed went to the next table. Danny staggered after him.

"Now, what do you want to do? I warn you, talk fast, because I'm a bad listener," Ed said, towering over the young man, his fists cocked and ready for action.

"Ed, is he tough?" Danny said drunkenly.

"We'll find out," Ed said.

"Listen, I'm out for a good time. I just overheard some of your conversation, and I was interested. Here, fellow, have a drink on me, my name is Digges."

The young man stood up and held out his hand.

"Well, if that is your disposition, my name is Lanson."

They shook hands.

"And this is Miss Smiley."

They shook hands.

"Won't you join our little party?" Lanson asked.

"Surely."

v

Danny didn't like Digges, didn't like the guy's looks. Well, the guy had shown peaceable intentions, and what the hell, it was a little party, and he'd take another drink.

"Say, I got a wonderful idea, a very wonderful idea," Danny said, his voice thick.

"What is it?" asked Digges.

"I have the most wonderful idea I ever had."

"What is it, Dan?" Ed asked.

"My idea is this. Now, listen, everybody. I have the wonderful idea that I'll have another drink."

Ed laughed artificially, as if in kindness to Danny. No one else laughed.

Digges poured drinks from his bottle for the three of them.

"How about me?" asked Miss Smiley.

"Of course, my dear," said Digges, pouring her a drink.

"What was your idea, Dan?" Ed asked.

"What—oh," Danny struggled to remember. "I forgot," he mumbled soddenly.

Mary Catherine looked at him, disgusted.

"I have to go home," Anna said, distressed.

VI

"I don't want to go home," Danny said after Digges had deposited Miss Smiley and the three of them sat in a cab.

"The night's young," Ed said.

"I know a good can house," Digges said.

"All right, give the cabby the address," Ed said.

Digges gave an address in the 4700 block on Michigan.

"Hey, we need something. Tell him to stop at a drugstore," Danny said, his head slightly cleared.

"It's too late. All the drugstores are closed," Digges said.

"What the hell, tell him to find one," Danny said.

"Say, buddy, see if you can find a drugstore on the way," Ed said.

The driver could find no drugstore. He stopped before a two-story brick house.

"How much is it?" Ed asked.

"Four bucks," the driver said.

Ed jumped out of the cab. Danny was climbing out slowly. His feet wouldn't move normally.

"Listen, buddy, you're not hauling around a bunch of greenhorns. This time you tried to rim the wrong fellow."

"Pay up and shut up," the driver said.

"Don't tell me to shut up. Get out of that cab, goddamn you!" Ed said.

Digges had walked toward the steps. Danny stood near Ed, befuddled.

The driver leaned down and picked up a crank handle.

"Drop that and get out of the cab! I'm gonna send you home with a mouthful of teeth in your hand," Ed said.

"Listen, I'm crippled," the driver said, showing a withered left hand.

"That's no excuse for trying to gyp me. How much did you say the bill was?"

"Two bucks."

"That's different," Ed said.

He paid. The cab drove off. Ed looked after it.

"Jesus, you're always ready to fight, aren't you?" Digges said.

"The person who tries to gyp me or tells me to shut my trap hasn't been born," Ed said.

"Well, here we are," Digges said.

"Looks like a nice family residence," Danny mumbled.

They saw reddish lights through a shaded parlor window. Digges led them up the steps and rang the bell.

Why hadn't they found a drugstore? Danny asked himself. Well, hell with it.

A slit in the door was pulled aside, and then the door was opened by a light-skinned Negro in his thirties.

"Hello, remember me?" Digges asked.

"Yes, yes, come right in."

They went in. The Negro led them into a dimly lit parlor. There were lamps on the tables. The rug was purplish in color and soft. The chairs were comfortable. Two pretty Negro girls sat on a large divan.

"I only have one girl left. This here one, she's a-goin' home now," the Negro said, pointing to a thin mulatto girl; the other was smaller, plump, and wore a chemise.

The Negro looked at Ed, as if recognizing him.

"Why, Ed, where have you been?"

"Oh, away," Ed said noncommittally.

Digges and Danny gaped in curiosity, not knowing what to make of the scene.

"Say, boy, I sure am glad to see you." The Negro turned to the others. "Why, Ed, here, I haven't seen the old bastard in two years. We stuck up a bakery together, remember, Ed?"

Danny was wide-eyed. Suddenly he told himself, silently, pronouncing his words to himself with drunken slowness.

This is sociology field work.

"I stuck up a joint recently, and I had to take a lam. I was hiding out in Minneapolis. But I risked it to come back here. Nothing like the old home town, you know," Ed said.

"So you're in hiding?"

"Yes, but I wanted to have some fun."

"Well, have a drink." The Negro turned to the thin girl and spoke as if to a servant. "Get drinks for my friend and his pals."

The skinny girl obeyed. Danny sat near the plump prostitute.

"Tell me about yourself?" he asked.

She looked at him blankly.

"I want to know. How did you get into this business? You see, I'm a student of sociology, and I'm going to be a writer. Tell me about yourself," he said, still speaking drunkenly.

"You see, I'm in a better business now," the Negro said to Ed.

"Yes, I'm a student of sociology," Danny repeated.

The skinny prostitute came back with drinks and handed them around. Then she left.

Danny drank the whisky and made a face.

"Suppose I start off the jolly fun?" Digges said, rising.

"Sure, sure," the Negro said.

The plump prostitute got up, bored, and casually led him out of the room.

"Say, how about another drink?" Danny asked.

"Boy, don't you want to save what you got until afterward?"

"Hell, both of us can have a few drinks and still go strong," Ed said.

"I'll get it for you," the Negro said, getting up and going to the back.

Ed put his index finger to his lips as a signal to Danny. Danny gazed about the room. The Negro returned with drinks.

They raised glasses.

"Better times," Ed said.

"You know, I was saying, I, I, I . . ." Danny began; he leaned back on the divan. Ed and the Negro continued talking. Danny's mind whirled.

Digges reappeared, grinning.

"Go ahead," Ed said to Danny. He staggered into the hallway.

"You know, I'm student of sociology," Danny said, meeting the prostitute in the hallway.

"Boy, isn't you too drunk for this business?" she asked, looking at him in pity.

"Huh?"

"Maybe you would like to come back when you is sober."

"Huh?" Danny exclaimed, taking her arm.

VII

Danny staggered beside Ed on Forty-seventh Street as the dawn slowly broke.

"I never saw the shine before. It was a case of mistaken identity, but I got a kick out of stringing the shine along," Ed said, chuckling.

"Funny," Danny said thickly.

"He wasn't pulling the string on us, because we didn't have enough dough, and he trusted us. That's the most amusing aspect of our experience—his giving us credit. And it's a five-buck house, too. That bastard Digges ran off to let us hold the bag. I should have poked him when I first met him."

Danny yawned.

"I wanna cab," Danny muttered.

"Christ, we're not holding enough."

A milk wagon passed, the horse's hooves and the wheels echoing on the street. Danny gaped at it, transfixed.

They went on. Ed began to sing.

I'm drunk, drunk, Danny told himself.

"Lanson, I'm drunk."

"You'll sober up in the morning."

"Don't care if I ever . . ."

Danny halted, swaying in the center of the sidewalk.

"Here's how much I care," he yelled defiantly.

Lumbering, he punched a slab of brick wall beside a store window. His knuckles bled. He felt no pain.

Ed led him gently along.

"I don't, don't . . ." he droned drunkenly.

Ed took him into a dingy restaurant. Three Negroes sat at the counter. Ed bathed Danny's hand in the lavatory. Then he got black coffee for him and took him home.

VIII

"What's the matter with the gas business?" Carter asked.

He and Broda had spotted Danny sitting in the Reynolds Club and had come over to talk with him.

"I took the day off. I was drunk last night. Hell, I was so drunk that I came to school this morning plastered. I fell asleep in Wallingford's sociology class. Toward the end of the hour, when I woke up, Wallingford said that he knew more about baseball than anybody in the class. So I called him on it, and we had a contest, asking each other questions. I won it. He couldn't name the batting order of the Boston Red Sox in 1912," Danny said.

"It goes to prove the usefulness of all knowledge," Carter joshed.

Carter and Broda dropped into chairs beside him, and Broda filled his pipe.

"I went on a tear last night," Danny said enthusiastically.

"A real jag, huh?" Carter asked.

"I ended up in a Negro whorehouse discussing sociology with one of the girls."

"Is that all you did?" Carter asked.

"Hell, no," Danny boasted.

"Didn't I ever tell you my definition of a sociologist, O'Neill?" Broda asked.

"No, what?"

"A sociologist is a person who spends fifty thousand dollars of endowed money in order to find out where a whorehouse is."

"I only spent the cab fare. And do you know, we got credit, too. We didn't have enough dough, so the pimp trusted us. I owe for my adventures in sociology. Christ, what a time I had!"

He was bragging about having had a hell of a good time, but actually he'd been so soddenly drunk that he hadn't known what he was doing. He had gotten up this morning feeling rather ashamed of himself. If you started feeling guilt and shame, you would end up in a vicious circle in which you would keep feeling endlessly remorseful. Hell, wasn't he beyond good and evil?

"Yes, the wages of sin is a headache," he said.

"The wages of sin, or of sociology?" asked Broda.

"I was telling you, Walter, I read *Science and the Modern World*," Carter said.

Danny listened, still thinking of how he had tried to create the impression that he was really wild. Carter wasn't interested. After all, why should he expect fellows as intelligent as

Carter or Broda to pin medals on him because he'd gotten stewed and had accidentally strayed into a can house?

"What did you think of it?" Broda asked.

"You know, whenever you read anything by a brilliant man, you're forced to respect him and what he's doing, even when you can't agree with him. That's the way I felt about Whitehead."

"I confess I couldn't get excited over his chapters about God as a principle of concretion in the event," Broda said.

"Neither did I. He's creating a new cosmology, and what the hell, it's too late in the history of thought for metaphysical cosmologies."

This was a long way from the whorehouse on Michigan Avenue. Listening to this conversation was a sharp change from listening to Ed and the pimp last night.

"Have you read Whitehead's *Science and the Modern World*, O'Neill?" Carter asked.

"No, I haven't. I will some day."

"It's a damned interesting book, and he's full of stimulating ideas. As a matter of fact, you have to admire his ingenuity in trying to prove that there's a God."

"What happened to your hand there?" Broda asked, pointing to Danny's bruised knuckles.

Vaguely, dimly, he remembered punching a brick wall. He didn't want to brag about such a foolish action.

"I don't know how the hell I got that. I woke up with it this morning."

"Was the fight you were in a sociological experiment, too?" Broda asked.

"I just raised hell."

"He's going to put it all down on three by five index cards as field work for Wallingford," Carter said.

"I ought to," Danny said, realizing again how he was merely bragging.

"I wanted to tell you more about Whitehead," Carter said.

"Say, let's talk about him in the Coffee Shop. I'm making myself gradually feel human by drinking coffee," Danny said.

"All right," Broda said.

They rose to go into the Coffee Shop across the corridor. He didn't feel ashamed so much over his escapade of last night as he did over his boasting of it now. Without having said much, Carter and Broda had made him feel foolish. They hadn't entered into the spirit of this vainglory. And, after all, was last night what he wanted? Or was it this, a life of ideas, discussion, serious study?

Oh, hell, he had a headache and a hangover, and he was too dull now to follow what Carter had to say about Whitehead.

"Say, did you hear the story about Koll?" Danny asked when they were seated in the Coffee Shop.

"He was the handsomest football captain in the Big Ten last season, but that didn't win any football games," Broda said.

"I was taking a course with him last quarter in Social Control. The prof kept looking at him curiously, and about the second week of the course he asked him: 'Mr. Koll, haven't you taken this course before?' Koll scratched his head and answered: 'Have I?' It turned out that he had."

They laughed. Danny's head ached. Carter discussed Whitehead.

"Mother, Bill has a girl," Lizz whispered.

"You don't say?" Mrs. O'Flaherty clucked.

Lizz shook her head affirmatively.

"Ah, they're only babies. Fifty is the time for a man to get married."

"Mother, if he marries her, what am I going to do? It would set such a bad example for Dennis, and why, he's only a boy."

"Not my grandson. If my grandson looks at a girl, I'll tan his hide."

"He's a good boy."

"Indeed he is. Who do you think raised him?"

"He's my son."

"He's my grandson."

"Saturday night, you should have seen my Bill, dressing himself up. She lives on the West Side. And, Mother, he didn't get home until all hours. Why, it was two o'clock."

"Sure, and you ran off and got married yourself."

"Say, Mother, didn't you? You were married when you were sixteen."

"But I married a good man."

"Did ever a finer man than my Jim walk this earth?" Lizz asked.

"He was a good man, Lord have mercy on his soul. Lizz, if your Bill won't toe the mark, make him. He's too young to be chasing after the chippies. Me grandson, Daniel, wouldn't be doing that, the innocent boy that he is."

Chapter Twenty-one

This was a damned fool idea. The pimp didn't know who they were. He had the chance of a snowball in Hell of finding them and making them pay him. But Ed had insisted that he do this.

Danny rang the bell of the two-story brick house on Michigan Avenue. He was thrilled.

"Hello," Danny said casually when the Negro opened the door.

"Oh, hello, hello there, boy, how you feeling?"

"Pretty good."

"Come on in."

"No, I can't. I've got to hurry. I came to pay you the ten bucks Ed and I owe you," Danny said, taking the money out of his pocket and handing it over.

"Thank you, boy, thank you. How's my buddy, Ed?"

"He's hiding out. He told me to tell you that as soon as it's safe, he'll come around."

"Tell him he's always welcome. He can hide out here if he wants to. He's two hundred per cent with me. Come in a minute. Have a drink. I'm sorry I haven't any girls here, but I can telephone for one."

"No, I have to hurry."

They shook hands.

"Come back and see me. And tell Ed I have a little idea I want to discuss with him."

"I will."

Danny sauntered off, enjoying the romance of association with the underworld. But this was the strangest coincidence he'd ever met with. He couldn't understand it. Ed planned to see this through. Christ, Ed might let himself in for some real stick-up work. Ed could get into serious trouble, and he might be caught in the web, too. Circumstances so often trapped one. He had to watch his step, or else he could ruin his life. But, hell, Ed was daring and adventurous. He couldn't back out of something like this and show a yellow streak.

Disturbed and perplexed, Danny boarded a streetcar to go to work. How dull work and school now seemed.

II

The restaurant next door to the Chicago Public Health Institute was empty.

"According to folklore, son, you've become a man now," Ed Lanson remarked genially.

Danny grinned ironically.

"When I woke up this morning, I knew that I had it. It didn't worry me. I accepted it casually and I went to school as usual."

"Christ, I'd like to get that pimp in my power. My only form of punishment would be to massage his prostate gland five or six times a day."

"I told you it was a dumb idea to pay him."

"It tickled me. The whole experience is amazing. Imagine it, Lanson being taken for a common, ordinary stick-up man."

"Ed, you're not going back there, are you?"

Ed leaned back and lit a cigarette.

"I haven't held a conference with myself to decide that."

"It's foolish to."

"Folly to the world," Ed said, smiling as if at a private joke, "is Hellfire's arena of action."

Danny smiled, trying to conceal his worry. He had started living dangerously, and he must not draw back now out of fear.

"Yes, I can see the depth of your change, Dan. If anything like this had happened to you two or three years ago, you

wouldn't have accepted it like a stoic. You've taken it in stride
just as if you were an old experienced veteran like myself. Yes,
I can see that you have freed yourself of the fetters of society."

The fact was that he had taken the damned bug casually, and
in stride. Not completely, though. He'd almost cracked upstairs in the Institute when the doctor had drawn blood for a
Wassermann. He had to forget this until he got the report.
And he had to face the music with a careless smile, just as Ed did.

Ed smashed his left fist into the palm of his right hand, and
frowned menacingly.

"I'm going back there and throw arsenic in that whore's
face," Ed said in anger.

"But, Ed, what the hell, it isn't worth the risk."

"Risk?" Ed exclaimed, smiling contemptuously.

"What the hell, she was merely working in the line of duty,
that's all. In this case it isn't worth the candle."

Ed leaned on the table, a brooding expression on his face.
Danny waited anxiously for him to talk.

"Would a philosopher seek such vengeance?" Ed asked with
a choked laugh.

Danny's face broke into a wide smile of relief.

They had more coffee.

"I took a week off work. I limp a bit, so I thought I'd better
take it easy."

"We can roam, and go to the library. I've had my fill of excitement. I'm going to do some studying now, not mere casual
reading, but truly serious study."

III

The danger of his infecting anyone in the house was in-
finitesimally small, especially since the Wassermann had turned
out negative. But he couldn't take any chance.

Clad in his wet pajamas, he sweated in the steamy bathroom
with the door locked. He was almost dizzy from the heat. Boiling hot water gushed into the tub. Perspiration poured down
his face, and he kept mopping it with a towel and wiping his

glasses. The mirror over the sink was coated with gray steam. Well, he had to do this.

This disease was disgusting, unesthetic. And look at the trouble and waste of time it caused. He had to go to the C.P.H. for irrigation treatments almost every day. These were irritating, leaving him with the uncomfortable sensation of a filled bladder. And argyrol stained. He had to hide his medicine so that they wouldn't find out about him. Every time he took a bath he had to stay in here like this and steam out the bathtub. The damned bugs could only live away from body heat for twenty minutes, he'd been told. He was confident his precautions would kill any of them in the tub.

If his folks had different attitudes, were broadminded like Ed's mother, he could tell them. But he couldn't do it. They had trouble enough as it was. And it would almost kill Mother. He couldn't hurt her. She might not be with them much longer. He ought to be more considerate of her, pay more attention to her, read her the papers, tell her about school. He would from now on. The trouble was that he never had enough time.

He dashed his hand in the water, pulled the chain connected with the stopper, and quickly dried his hand. Not much burn. He waited impatiently for the water to gurgle out. He must have baked off two or three pounds. He was dopey.

Life, biology, was disgusting. Romantic love, poetry, was a delusion, a lie that was murdered day in and day out by a host of facts about human physiology. The history of man was much more a history of bugs and biology than it was of sentiments.

The water was out. He opened the door and went to his bedroom, hoping no one would go in the bathroom until some of the steam had disappeared.

He closed his bedroom door and sprawled out on the bed with a book, planning to read himself to sleep. Lethargic reveries flowed through his mind, distracting his attention. He grew nostalgic for the naive days of his boyhood when love had been an almost religious worship of Roslyn Hayes. He fell asleep. The light burned overhead.

IV

It was exciting to get mail at the General Delivery window in the post office. He envied Ed, who stood beside him, reading a letter with an amused smile on his face. To be without an address was to be free. Some day . . .

"Read it," Ed said, handing Danny the letter.

Dearest Ed;—

Gee but it was great to hear from you just when I thought you had completely forgotten me and were mad at me because I haven't sent you the $40 I owe you. Ed Dearest I wouldn't think of not paying you and as soon as I get on my feet and get some clothes I will. That's a promise and Peaches keeps her promises.

I bought a new dress that I wish you could see. It is very pretty & I still owe $10 on it but I bought it through a friend of mine so I owe her the money and not any store.

Ed I miss you. I still realize how much I miss you walking in the park and I miss our long talks that seemed to be a part of me. I have lots of boy friends but nearly all of them ask for my sexual favors & I don't want to give them and they disgust me and if they don't stop asking and pawing I'm going to drop them one & all. I'm through with that. I wonder at my own thoughts & I try to analyze my mind & I only phrase this—

Our mind is a house with many rooms & many doors. We store memories in these hidden rooms behind the locked doors. Memories that are alive, but sleeping. When we waken the memories of hate or fear or envy they live again & set about their old poisoning. When we wake the memories of Love, courage or beauty they smile & shed a lonely light upon our souls.

All this, Ed, sounds too stereotyped and a little foolish but I can't phrase my thoughts better. Perhaps some day I will

*when I find the unknown but I wonder what the unknown
will be like when I find it.*

*I am reading Arrowsmith & like it. I work in a tea room
and since I have to work it is as good as any job I can get & I
won't go back to my old life, Ed, not after my talks with you
& what you did to save me. Honest, Ed, I miss you & I'm going
to send you that $40 as soon as I get on my feet.*

Just
Peaches

Danny handed the letter back to Ed.

"She's sweet and decent, isn't she?" Ed asked.

"Yes," Danny said, touched, thinking there was something
pathetically ridiculous in the poor girl's efforts to think.

"Peaches was a whore I picked up in Cleveland. I loaned her
the money to get out of a house and saw her a number of times.
She fell in love with me. I talked to her about herself and about
life, and I gave her courage, poor thing, to make a new start.
I set her straight. That letter is no crap. Of course, she got
boring, but it was amusing."

Ed put the letter in his pocket, lit a cigarette, and they left
the post office.

"When she talks about memory, she expresses naïvely the
theory of memory that Saint Augustine expounded in his *Confessions*," Danny said.

"I'll tell her that when I write her. Ah, Peaches, all of the
Peaches of the world," Ed exclaimed. "But let's go back to the
Public Library."

He whistled a gay tune. Ed was always so full of buoyant
spirits. Danny wished he had as happy a disposition.

V

It was late. Ed and Danny crossed a rocky patch in Grant
Park after standing by the breakwater for a long time. The
wind whipped the bottoms of their overcoats from behind.

"I like a snarling lake," Ed said. "A storm at sea gives me the exhilarating feeling that I'm contesting with a foeman worthy of my steel," Ed said.

Their difference in temperament revealed itself in everything they did together. By the lake, Ed had laughed exultantly as the waves sprayed his face. He had silently watched the angry waters, recalling poems by Joyce and Matthew Arnold, brooding about time, telling himself over and over again that the lake was insensate, trying to imagine himself as a sad *unyielding Atlas* sustaining himself and his ideals alone in an alien world.

They came out on Michigan Avenue. Cars shot by. The sidewalks were almost deserted.

"Let's walk," Danny said.

"Here, let me take your briefcase for a while; you've lugged it around all day," Ed suggested.

"No, that's all right."

"Here, give it to me," Ed said, carrying it.

They strode north, each absorbed in thought.

At Randolph Street they turned west, past the darkened Public Library.

"I fancy the streets at night. I despise crowds, mobs."

"Sometimes they confuse me. I'm absentminded and walk along thinking of something, and I bump into people," Danny said.

A cop passed them. A few couples drifted by. An elevated train roared overhead.

"The moving picture theaters are morgues for morons. I like them dark," Ed said, pointing to the Chicago Theater on his right as they crossed State Street.

They walked on, and turned down Dearborn Street. The buildings loomed shapelessly on either side.

"You finished your Nietzsche term paper, didn't you?" Ed asked.

"Yeh."

"I'm anxious to read it."

They walked around and around the Loop, scarcely talking.

"Well, adios, see you for the irrigation treatment at our club tomorrow," Ed said, shaking hands firmly with Danny by the steps of the Randolph and Wells Street elevated station at three o'clock.

"Yes, and I hope I get promoted from irrigation soon," Danny said.

They parted. Danny rode home, feeling calm.

VI

They left the reading room of the Crerar Library and went to the elevator.

"Say, you fellows are smart. I want to ask you a question," the dark-haired elevator operator said to them.

"Yes," Ed said.

"What do you think of life?"

"That's an interesting problem," Ed answered with a twinkle in his eyes. "I've thought it over many times and I've reached this conclusion. Life is complicated, and everyone has his ups and his downs."

"Say, that's just about what I think," the elevator operator said, easing his car onto the ground floor and opening the door.

They waved to him and went to a Raklios Restaurant for coffee, laughing.

"I've been speculating about time, and I have to thrash the problem out," Ed said at a table.

Danny waited for him to continue and tried to collect his thoughts.

"Does time exist, or is it an illusion, an *as if*?" Ed posed.

"Kant says it's a mode of preception."

"I was studying Bergson. He shows us that time by the clock is an artificial conception."

"Time does pass."

"Does it, or do we have an illusion that it does?"

"According to Nietzsche, there must be time, or else there couldn't be eternal recurrence," Danny said.

Danny finished his coffee.

"And I'm wasting time. I got to get back to the library," he
said.

"Danny, you have too damned much conscience. You feel
you always have to be reading. After all, discussion, thrashing
things out, is just as important a part of one's education as
reading."

Danny grinned sheepishly.

"If there were no clocks, how would we know that time
passes? By the sun—but the sun isn't a clock. It doesn't register time. Yes, this is a question we ought to try and solve. But
let's have some more *café*," Ed said.

They went to the counter.

VII

Ed's coffee cup was filled with ashes. Christy, the wall-eyed
waiter, looked approvingly at the two of them, and then he
went to the back to get the orders for Studs Lonigan and
Tommy Doyle, who sat at the counter.

"Dan, I don't think you understand the full gist of Nietzsche. Your paper is well written, and you deserved an A for
it. Its organization is good, and it shows that you have the
capacity for serious thought. But I don't like the suggestions
of humanitarianism in it. You criticize Nietzsche for his disapproval of the French Revolution. Dan, I don't like to see you
backsliding now, not now after the way you've stubbornly
mulled and bulled your way through to free your soul."

"But, Ed, I sort of tried," Danny began haltingly . . .
"well, I tried to lift my head. If I can succeed a little, everybody can. That's why I criticized Nietzsche on this point."

"Dan, you've got too much pity."

"Hey, O'Neill, for Christ sake, shut up. We don't want to
hear your atheistic crap around here," Tommy Doyle sneered.

Danny winced. He was shocked into the feelings of the past
when he'd been a punk kid in short pants and fellows like
Tommy had been older than he, tougher.

Ed jumped to his feet.

"O'Neill and I are talking. Anybody who doesn't like it can stick cotton in their ears. If you want us to shut up, shut us up! If you want us to get out, throw us out! That goes for anybody around this corner."

"Boys," Christy interrupted.

"What the hell, Lanson, Doyle was only kidding," Studs conciliated.

Danny felt protected. If it came to a fight, he would pitch in. But Ed wouldn't need any help.

"Ed, I didn't mean anything. What the hell do I care what you fellows say," Tommy said.

"What I said stands," Ed declared loudly.

He sat down.

"Now, Dan, let's go on. . . ."

VIII

"I didn't go for treatment today. I foolishly lost my last five bucks last night in a crap game, so I didn't have the wherewithal. I was going to put the bee on Father, but he seemed grouchy, so I didn't," Ed said, having coffee and a sandwich with Danny at the filling station.

"That's too bad. What about work?"

"That's a problem. I suppose I shall be forced to abdicate my freedom for a while and indulge in the indignity of working."

"Tough," Danny kidded.

"Yes, it's tough tiddy," Ed smiled.

"Did you eat?" Danny asked.

"No, how about you?"

"I was just going to run across the street for some grub."

"I'll do it."

"Here," Danny said, pulling the roll of cash out of his overall pocket. "We'll let my esteemed employers pay for our dinner. Get me two ham sandwiches and coffee, and whatever you want."

"What'll I put the coffee in?"

"I'll wash out the pail," Danny said, and he went to the lavatory to wash out the tin pail.

Whistling, Ed went across the street and returned with the food.

"When do you get paid?" Ed asked.

Danny didn't mind lending Ed money, but after all, he was giving his time for his wages. Ed could work, too. He didn't like the idea of lending money to be lost in gambling.

"Are you holding?"

"No, not much."

"I expect to have some money Saturday. Could you spare a ten? I'm out of medicine and don't want to give up treatments. The bugs we picked up so casually are obstinate. They like me even better than the girls do."

"Well, gee, I haven't got ten now."

"What about the cash you took in today, and your petty cash fund?" Ed asked.

"Ten would be too much. The petty cash fund is only twenty-five bucks, and we're expecting the auditor any day."

"It's too risky to take a chance?"

"I'll risk this much and make it up on the pumps in the morning."

He peeled off five from his roll of company funds and handed it to Ed.

"Thanks, Dan, you're a real friend."

"I'm taking an advanced composition course under Professor Saxon. At least I hope I am. To get admitted I have to submit a piece of writing, and if he approves I'll be admitted. I hear that in such courses you are free to write what you want. I'll get a chance to write a lot, and maybe see if I am able to hope to be a writer."

"Good, what are you going to write about in this essay?"

"I'm going to write about the last war, the war of steel and gold."

"Is that a good subject?"

"Well, I think it is better to take something like that than it is to risk a story. I don't know if I have enough experience or imagination to write stories."

"That's wise. I think your talents lie more in the critical line. I don't mean to be critical, you know, because I think you've got something, but after all, to be a writer, you have to have experiences, many of them."

"I don't know what to say. All I know is that more and more I keep thinking to myself that I want to be a writer."

"I always would reason this way. I want to be a writer—therefore, I will be a writer. I am a writer, even if my writings remain in my head, in embryo."

Danny wished he had such self-confidence. He believed that Ed would achieve things in the world. Ed would surpass him.

"I feel that I have a destiny," Ed said.

"Well, I don't know. After all, isn't that a metaphysical idea, assuming—well, assuming, that there is some guiding purpose in the universe—and isn't that—well, a substitute for God?"

"No. My destiny is to be myself. I think I have the ability to do anything that I want to do. So far, I've done everything I ever wanted to do. If I wanted to make a girl, I made her. If I wanted a job, I got one. If I said I was going to travel some place, I did."

Danny's face clouded.

"Danny, you have to have more faith in yourself. Shyness, lack of self-confidence is worse than virginity."

Danny nodded thoughtfully.

"Well, it all comes out in the wash. In the end we sink or we swim," Danny commented.

"I wonder where you and I will be fifteen years from now. It's an interesting speculation, isn't it?"

"Yes. Of course, where we'll be depends on what we do now, every day."

"Yes, perhaps, but there are different temperaments. I believe in inspiration. I work and think by fits and starts. That's my temperament. Yours seems different. You are stubborn, and you stick to something like a bulldog. Dan, I admire you for it. I wish I had more of that in my nature. But I am flighty, temperamental, impulsive, and maybe it's not the best of personal equipment, but it's me, really *me*."

Danny knew that he enjoyed contemplating the image of himself as a romantic figure, but every time he played that role a fiasco resulted. God, what had his life been but a series of fiascos? He was not an inspiring—not even an admirable—figure. He was a plodding drudge, and for him genius would have to be one hundred per cent perspiration. What would he become? What would be Ed's future?

"Whatever happens, Dan, I'm sure that you and I will always be friends."

"Yes," Danny affirmed sincerely, and deeply moved.

"Dan, is there any lingering Catholicism, any priestliness left in your nature?"

"Hell, why should I let the world I've rejected judge me? I have no confessions to make. The world gave me nothing, and it makes me fight to have a decent career, and it not only wants to tell me what to do, where to work—it wants my mind. I'd say it wants my soul if I believed in a soul. Well, no matter what happens, I won't give that. I want to take Saxon's course because I want to write. If I can write, I can be free."

"Danny, you were hurt by something, weren't you?"

"I don't know. I just suddenly woke up one day angry. That's all. I suddenly got sore. I got a goddamned grudge in my heart. Don't you have a grudge?" Danny asked.

"No, I wouldn't say I have. I have contempt, contempt for man, for most men and, above all, contempt for women. Most people are putty. A few of us, you and I, Dan, each in our ways, we are different, although, of course, we take different means of expressing ourselves. As I said, I am impulsive. Really, I want to be *me*, to find the real *me* behind all the artificial *me's*, and to live that *me*. You want to write. I live and want my life to be like a book."

"Here's a customer. I'll begin making up that five of yours on him," Danny said, going outside.

XXII

Margaret O'Flaherty left the Shrifton Hotel in tears. It wasn't her fault. She hadn't done wrong. She wasn't a thief. She was an honest woman. All that she'd done was to borrow money from her cash drawer for home, and then she'd felt so good that she'd gone to a party with Dora Hilton and Cynthia Gray, and they had gotten her to take a drink. She hadn't meant to go on a drunk and spend the money. And she hadn't found a friend in the world who would loan her the money to return it to the cash drawer. They would have gotten their money back. Everybody had deserted her. The last time she'd needed money, she'd gone to Father Gilhooley, and he had been kind and good, and she would repay him if it were the last thing on earth she did. She'd telephoned every important hotel in town trying to locate Lorry Robinson, but he wasn't registered. She'd written him letters. He'd never answered them. She'd humiliated herself by trying to borrow money from the waiters and the bus boys. She'd gone to her old friend, Myrtle Peck. Myrtle was rich. Would she lift a finger? Would anyone lift a finger?

It wasn't her fault. She had committed no crime. All that she'd done was to borrow some money. She'd meant to pay it back. The auditor had caught her by surprise. Now she was fired. Here she was, a fine experienced business woman, with her life ruined. She had nothing to look forward to. Did her mollycoddle brothers think she was going to stay home and wash their pots and pans?

She wandered on, nervous and distressed. The world was against her. She had never had anything but work and misery.

She had always worked conscientiously. What good had it done her? Now, for this one mistake, she was penalized.

What should she do? Al was in danger of losing his money. Mother was old. Who would take care of the home? What would she do?

She felt like throwing herself into the lake. They could drag the lake for her body and then fish her out. She didn't care. That girl Brother knew, who had gone with his friend Ed Lanson—what was her name? Rogers?—that poor girl had drowned herself. She ought to end it all. But she couldn't even do that. Mother, the boys, her nephews and nieces needed her. Oh, she was trapped, the most unhappy woman in all Chicago.

What should she do?

Wearily, she walked the streets of the Loop, crying. Strangers stared at her as if she were a curiosity.

Chapter Twenty-two

I

Oblivious of the chatter, the flirtations, the noise, Danny stood aloof from the crowd of students in front of Cobb Hall, rereading the penciled comments the famous Professor Paul Morris Saxon had written on his composition, *A Vision of the Last War.*

Dear Mr. O'Neill:—

The outstanding quality of your style in this is EASE. No one (certainly not I) can say whether you will ever think clearly enough, or invent dramatically enough, to satisfy editors or publishers, and to reach a public, but without doubt you are qualified to work in Eng. 210.

P. M. Saxon

This was both encouragement and a rebuff. He was puzzled by it. But he had been admitted to the course, and that was most important. Now he had his chance. Professor Saxon had said in class that they could all write as much as they wanted to, on any subject they pleased, and at whatever length they felt impelled to write. A minimum of a paper a week was required to get a passing grade, but if you wanted to write more, you could, and it would be read. Some applicants to the course hadn't been accepted. He had been. But what had Professor Saxon meant by not knowing whether or not the paper proved anything about being able to think clearly enough or to invent dramatically? That was disturbing, because he feared it might be true. He might never acquire such talents.

He had checked up on Professor Saxon during the war. Professor Saxon had written pro-war poems. Did this condition the remarks, did it condition Professor Saxon's coldness this morning when he'd returned the essay? Had he struck at Mr. Saxon's jugular vein? After all, on campus, and all over America, there were many tired radicals, men who wanted to forget what they had done and written during the years of 1914–1918. His generation criticized and condemned the writers and professors who had supported the war. But he and his generation had not really suffered because of the war. They had been too young to fight, even too young to understand. He and others of his generation were indignant after the fact, resentful for the dead, not for themselves. The war had never touched them. In fact, Papa had been promoted because of the war. Uncle Al had sold more shoes and made money, too. The war hadn't hurt his family. Why was he indignant? Why should he be critical of Professor Saxon and others because they had been for the war? Why should he admire George Bernard Shaw, Debs, Ramsay MacDonald, Randolph Bourne, Bertrand Russell, Lenin and Trotsky, for having been against it? But hadn't the war only prepared the ground for the next World War? And then wouldn't he have to march off to be a soldier, to die for steel and gold? And hadn't all the talk of making the world safe for democracy only led to this period of normalcy, to Harding and Coolidge and Andy Mellon? And didn't they represent part of what he was against? He had written this vitriolic essay out of feeling. But he was right. And more important, he had expressed his own emotions.

His eyes fell on A. Lincoln Jones, who was talking with a co-ed. His lips curled in contempt.

He put his manuscript in his briefcase and walked off. Classes were over for the day. He had an hour in which to do nothing, and he wanted to walk and think. It was chilly and sunless, but not too cold. Dirty snow was banked alongside of the campus walks. The Gothic buildings rose in the quadrangles like brooding spirits of stone. He saw Mike Mooney in the distance, and he turned his eyes in another direction contemptuously. Girls passed him and he scarcely saw them.

Hatless students, letter men keeping their overcoats open to reveal their athletic honors, professors with briefcases—all walked by him.

The papers were full of lurid stories about flaming youth, jazz-age youth, expressing a postwar reaction. Well, he was part of the generation of flaming youth. He'd even tried to be a flaming youth, but he had to confess to himself that his had been a miserable flame. He was paying the penalty for his flames—a dose. But then that promised to clear up. He'd graduated from irrigation and was receiving injections. He was going to be cured. His flaming youth had merely been occasional moments of drunken stupefaction. It was irrelevant to the war. Yet the war angered him. Why had so many young men like himself been maimed and killed? Why had there been so much suffering? Yes, in so far as reaction against the war was concerned, it was not a personal grudge, but he felt it deeply. And now the war was history. He had his own war. He wanted to fight all society—church and state, business and commerce, home and Fifty-eighth Street. Nietzsche had written that in a peaceful period a militant man warred with himself. Didn't that apply to him?

He turned at the circle in the center of the campus and walked back slowly.

He wanted to write what he felt. This was his sword. And here was his chance. But wasn't he presumptuous? Mr. Saxon's comment had really been a rebuke. He strolled on, disheartened. No, he couldn't allow himself to be disheartened now. He had his chance. All one could ask for was a chance.

Danny O'Neill, can you never learn to think clearly and invent dramatically? This was not a question to stew about. This was a problem. This was a challenge. He set his chin. Yes, this day, January 9, 1927, was the day when he, Danny O'Neill, had finally discovered the weapons he would wield. Now he was setting out in earnest to be a writer. For good or for ill, he would go on. For good or for ill, this was the aim in his life. He halted by the snow-banked walk of the campus which led away from the circle toward Cobb Hall. What a dismal day. A black, low sky. Clouds that seemed to have been smeared with dust. Students passing him, heedless of him. The world heedless of him, not knowing who he was, what he was, and not caring. The purposeless, the godless world, a gigantic machine that had thrown man, descendant of an ape, willy-nilly into life, to build all his empty dreams, to strive and suffer, above all to suffer in a bloody century that had succeeded other bloody centuries. But he had snatched a purpose out of this world. He seethed with emotional excitement. His throat choked. Tears almost came to his eyes. He was moved to the depths of his being. No power on this earth would stop him from writing. Perhaps he would be a failure. Succeed or fail, he had found his arms now, and he would use them. This was a vow. A vow to whom? A vow which Danny O'Neill, knowing no gods, made to Danny O'Neill.

He suddenly relaxed. He felt empty, exhausted by his own emotions, as if he were a mere shell. He left the campus to walk home. He thought again of his past. It was a comedy. He was a comedy, a comedy suddenly turned serious. He quoted Rabelais to himself:

Draw the curtain: the comedy is ended.

II

Danny knocked on the door in Classics.

"Come in," Professor Saxon's voice boomed cheerfully.

Danny entered, and the professor looked up from his desk. On either side of the office there were cluttered bookshelves and on the desk magazines and manuscripts were piled in disorder. Professor Saxon was a large, near-sighted man with graying hair, ruddy cheeks, and a pudgy face which at times seemed babyish and at other times resembled that of a bulldog.

"Can I talk with you, Mr. Saxon?"

"Yes, yes, of course, Dan," the professor said, ashes from his cigarette dropping onto his gray suit. "Take a chair and wait just a second while I look through the rest of my mail."

Danny sat down beside the desk. Professor Saxon lit a cigarette from the butt of the one he was finishing, and continued to read.

Danny was not sure he should have come here to talk with Professor Saxon. Professor Saxon couldn't solve his problems for him. He might be intruding, and he might even seem like an exhibitionist. Now, as the last week of the winter quarter was coming to an end, he knew that he had really found himself in Mr. Saxon's course. Professor Saxon was the first teacher he had had here at the U who had truly inspired him; he had been encouraged to go on writing, and Professor Saxon had left an impression on him that he thought would be indelible for the rest of his life.

"Well, Dan, shoot," Professor Saxon said, putting his letter down and facing Danny.

"I quit my job at the gas station."

Professor Saxon raised his bushy brows a moment, jerked the cigarette from his mouth, inhaled, put the cigarette back.

"I don't know what I can do about getting you another job. I'll try, but I can't promise. I don't think I can get anything for you on *The Questioner*. You've had no experience. It's not easy to become a journalist. It took me eighteen years to land my job on *The Questioner*," Professor Saxon said rather coldly.

"I don't want a job."

"I don't understand what you want, Dan," Professor Saxon said, annoyed.

"It's not that I want anything. I don't. I've decided that I'm going to become a writer or nothing."

"There's nothing I can do for you. I can't give you any letters to publishers, if that's what you want, or help you with magazines. I don't think your work is publishable—yet."

"The magazines return my stuff with formal rejection slips."

"Is it typed?"

"No. I have a typewriter, but I can't type well enough, and anyway I've had to do most of my writing at the gas station."

"Do you expect busy editors to read your illegible scrawls?"

He knew that he had no right to expect them to do it.

"Do you know, I'll never forgive you for what you did to me this quarter," Professor Saxon said, casually brushing cigarette ashes off his suit.

"What?" Danny asked in a strained voice.

"You turned in something like sixty thousand words, written in pencil on yellow paper. I read every word of it. At times it swept me along so that I couldn't lay it down. Some of your stories and sketches almost ruined my digestion. But what you did to my soul is nothing to what you've done to my eyesight. I went to see the oculist yesterday. Thanks to my conscientiousness in reading every word of your stuff, I'll have to get new glasses."

"Gee, I'm sorry. I didn't mean to do that. But you told us to write as much as we liked about any subject that interested us," Danny answered apologetically and defensively.

"How was I to know that I would get such an avalanche from you?"

"I like to write."

"Why did you come to see me here? Do you want me to tell you what I think your chances of being published are?"

"I don't think much of my chances. I merely wanted to talk."

"I can't give you any advice. There's nothing I can tell you that I haven't already in class. I don't know if you will ever be a writer. Your work is powerful. You're one of the most promising students I've ever had."

Then Professor Saxon did think he had a chance. And he was not a fool in doing what he had.

"But I honestly don't believe that the work you've submitted to me is good enough to warrant your putting all your eggs in one basket. It might be years, if ever, before you'll be able to support yourself writing."

"If you want to be a writer, you can't compromise. I don't want to be a writer with the idea of making money. I've learned and read enough to know that a writer has to make a choice—

his aim has to be to try and say something or else to make money."

"Oh, for God's sake, O'Neill, don't be so romantic," Professor Saxon said angrily, lighting another cigarette.

Tactlessly, he had happened to strike Professor Saxon's sore point. Professor Saxon had told his classes how he had wanted to write but had compromised in his youth, had then given it up in order to get married and support a family.

"You want me to be honest with you, I assume, or else you wouldn't have come here to talk?"

Danny nodded.

"Frankly, I don't think you'll get anywhere unless you realize that all of humanity doesn't live in the gutter. You've almost swamped me for ten weeks now with stories and sketches about whores and pimps, stealing in gas stations, drunken women, unhappy homes, beggars, poor workingmen, miserly immigrants, ignorant, superstitious, prejudiced Irish Catholics. There never has been a glimmer of joy, of hope in your stuff. There's no relief. You write one greasy slab of life after another. The public won't take that. Editors won't buy it."

"I try to put down what I've seen, what I feel."

"You want to be a realist. But is it realism to say that all life is unhappy? Isn't there balance? Isn't there a contrast of joy to sorrow? It seems to me that the true realist is the one who tells us there is good and bad in life, that happiness and unhappiness balance one another. Your writing is too mordant. You're too bitter. You know your material, but you go at it with two feet, kicking and punching. Your irony is always overstressed. Unless you change your tone, I don't think the public will ever bother to read you, even though you learn the technique of writing."

"I didn't make unhappiness. I didn't invent Chicago. I'm only trying to describe Chicago as I know it."

"Oh, come on now, Dan, I know that there's a seamy side to life, but I've lived in Chicago much longer than you have. There's goodness and hope in the world, too."

"To make the world better, don't you have to make people know what it's like, make people know what they're like?"

"But, my boy, you're not doing that—you're giving a one-sided and distorted picture."

He'd had the same argument with Professor Saxon in class until most of the students had become so bored that they had almost cried for mercy. Was there really any use in continuing it here?

"I think I've read enough for almost thirty years now to have some sense of public taste, and it seems to me that the reaction against the pretty-pretty has gone just about as far as it can. Tastes always sway back and forth from romanticism to realism. After Dreiser and Anderson and Sinclair Lewis, after Joyce, I can't see where there can be any further development along the line of realism. And I think the public has had its fill of it, too. Dan, if you keep on as you are, you're going to find yourself in an impasse. I honestly couldn't advise you to sacrifice your work, your livelihood to do that. I don't think you have to, either. Why can't you go on writing in your spare time, work in the gas station and continue with your plan to be a lawyer? Or else, if you don't want to do that, plan to earn your living as a teacher? You have a good head. You can succeed in some line." Professor Saxon suddenly changed the tone of his voice. He spoke with feeling and, Danny suspected, even with a touch of bitterness. "Writing is a cruel profession. If you stake your life on the hope of being a writer and fail, you can ruin your whole life."

Professor Saxon nervously lit a cigarette.

"Most lives are ruined. One might as well ruin one's life in one's own way," Danny said.

"Well, it's your life, not mine," Professor Saxon answered with irritation.

Danny was aware that Professor Saxon wanted to terminate the interview. He sat rooted in his chair, not understanding why he didn't leave.

"I guess I'll have to go on and write in the teeth of a hundred and twenty million walking prejudices that look like human beings," Danny said bitterly.

"Stuff and nonsense, O'Neill."

"Well, I hope you don't consider my visit an intrusion," Danny said.

"Not at all. But I'm rushed this morning. I have to finish my mail and hurry downtown to the office to do my column for *The Questioner*. I wish I could give you advice, but there's nothing more for me to say."

"Thank you, Mr. Saxon, and I'm grateful for the way you've read my stuff. I really got a lot out of your course."

"See you in class, Dan."

Danny left.

Don't put all your eggs in one basket. And suppose the eggs in the other baskets are rotten. Thoughtful, he rode downstairs and came out into the sunshine.

III

"Hello," a girl called to him as he came out of Classics.

"Oh, hello," Danny answered, seeing Marion Willingham, the daughter of a highly respected professor in the Department of Political Science.

He had spoken to her several times during this quarter, but he'd never gotten a chance to get to know her. Here was a fortunate chance meeting. She was intelligent and lovely, fresh and virginal in appearance, with light brown unbobbed hair, blue eyes, and rosy cheeks. She needed no makeup. He liked everything about her, her soft voice, her dignified walk, her friendly smile, her gay laugh, her sophistication.

"You remember those little stories Saxon read in class?" she asked.

"Yes, I liked them."

They were sketches, written with grace, conveying a sense of campus, of atmosphere, of vague yearnings. He liked them, but he thought them slight.

"I sent them to Mencken, and he wrote me a very nice and

encouraging letter. He says they're good, but he can't use them in *The American Mercury*. He wants me to send him more of my writings."

"That's good," Danny said.

She was different from the girls he used to know. She was a beautiful girl of talent, a serious person.

He walked slowly away from Classics with her, and she greeted a number of students who passed them.

Couldn't he and Marion build a life and a career together? They could both write, travel, live like two artists perhaps in Paris. Since she wanted to write herself, wouldn't she understand poverty? He might lead the conversation around so that he could tell her of his decision, his plans.

"I've met Mencken, through my father. He's a perfect gentleman," she said.

She knew professors, writers, met them on terms of equality. Her life must be full. Couldn't she help to make his life more full?

"He's a perfect gentleman," she repeated casually. "I missed Saxon's course today. Did anything interesting happen?" she added.

"No, he read another story of Mr. Gilbert's about unrequited love," Danny said, and she smiled.

He had to go down now for a treatment. If she knew that, what would she think of him? Suppose he was cured and able to marry her, would she want to marry him if she knew how he had gotten a dose? He hardly knew her, and he was poor and unknown, yet here he was, thinking of marrying her. What attractiveness could she see in him?

A sallow, homely girl with freckles passed, saying hello to Marion.

"That's Angela Malloy. She's supposed to be a genius. Saxon said she writes beautifully. I don't like her, do you?"

"I don't know her. Somebody mentioned her name, and I've seen her around. She's homely as sin."

"That's mean. She can't help it."

"No, her looks are an act of providence," he said, checking an impulse to add a compliment about Marion's looks because of sudden shyness.

You didn't pull a line on an intelligent girl.

How soon would he be cured? Ed had graduated to silver nitrate treatment and ought to be released from the club soon. He was getting to that stage. God, treatments were a bore. And he had to get cured now. He'd not have much money to pay for many treatments. What a damned fool he'd been, quitting his job, taking this chance. No, he was right!

"Let's go and have a bite at the Coffee Shop," he suggested, concealing his elation.

Proud, he accompanied her to the Coffee Shop, and they found a vacant table near the window. Several students said hello to her.

"So you didn't have another argument with Saxon in class this morning?" she asked.

He shook his head no.

She seemed to be singularly aloof from him. He had to find a way of approaching her before he could really talk seriously. He wanted to. He wanted to talk to someone. The interview he'd just had with Saxon seemed to him now to have been pointless. Perhaps here was the girl who could give him the intellectual companionship for which he really hungered. With a girl such as Marion, couldn't he harmonize instinct and reason, live a decent life? She could help him in his work, too, inspire, encourage him.

He cursed his poverty.

They gave their orders to a student waitress.

"I was going downtown to the Art Institute. I wonder—would you like to come along?" he asked; he'd forego today's treatment.

"Gee, I would, but I can't. Some other time," she said, implying that he could hope for a date in the future.

"Do you like painting?" he asked.

"I adore it. Who are your favorite painters?"

"I like Cezanne. When I look at his pictures I see something aloof, lonely, removed. His pictures are wonderful. There's a kind of sadness in them. They are removed from man, and yet they are full of emotion. He was a great painter. And then there's a Titian nude in the Art Institute."

"I don't like Cezanne."

"Why?" he asked, disappointed.

"He's cold."

She offered him a cigarette. He took it and lit it, his first cigarette since he'd tried to smoke once when he'd been a kid living on Prairie Avenue, years and years ago.

He smoked carefully so as not to become ill.

"You don't believe in romance, do you?" she asked.

"Try me," he replied flippantly. Perhaps that question was an opening.

"I mean in writing. You don't believe in romance in writing."

"Do you mean sentimental writing?"

"I don't exactly mean that. I mean in writing so that a story has aspiration, so that it lifts you up. Whenever Saxon reads one of your stories, it's always, oh, it's always cold and terribly unpleasant. There's never any aspiration in it."

"You have to accept and understand and come to terms with what is in the world, and out of that you gain a sense of what life can be. It can be lovely, but to make it so, you've got to criticize it."

"There's nothing spiritual in your stories. All of your stories are about uncivilized people. I think a writer ought to write about civilized people, civilized life. Isn't that what's most important?"

Civilization was an attainment. His hopes of knowing her had been idle. There was a dividing line between them. What had been natural to her all her life was something he had to win. He had not won it.

While he sought to formulate his thoughts carefully, Pete joined them. Lean and tall, he was a long-haired Greek student wearing tortoise-shelled glasses and a shiny blue suit.

"Pete, do you know Tom O'Neill?" Marion said condescendingly.

"Yes, we met. You're a young writer, aren't you, O'Neill?" Pete said.

Had the *Tom* been deliberate or accidental?

Jim Gogarty had brought Pete and him together here in the Coffee Shop for a few minutes, and Pete had rattled off names like Freud and Nietzsche, but had not made one concrete or intelligent statement about anything.

"Marion, did I ever tell you? You have a soul," Pete said.

"Pete, you're so original," she bantered.

"Why don't you and I get together? There's only one kind of girl I like. An American girl with a soul."

"What is America?" she asked, and Danny became convinced that her air of condescension had been carefully cultivated; she was the same with Pete as with him. He wasn't jealous of the Greek.

"Don't you know what America is?" Pete asked.

"A nation of frustrated baseball players, delicatessen-store princesses, snobs and go-getters," Danny cut in sarcastically.

"Oh, you just like to be bitter in order to shock," she said, dismissing him.

He smothered his resentment. Why, precisely, should she want to insult him?

"America is a wonderful country. The land of opportunity. A good American is anybody who makes money. I'm going to be a good American," Pete said, talking rapidly.

"Are you serious, Pete?" she asked, suddenly perplexed.

"I'm always serious. Say, I have a new place, a studio at Fifty-seventh and Stony Island. Come on and see the bohemians. I'll make you Turkish coffee."

"I'm sorry, but some other time. There's Bill Bergson over there and I have to see him."

She excused herself and, taking her check, went to another table.

"I'd like to make her, Irishman," Pete said.

Danny didn't answer. He felt a little foolish. He couldn't even think of making any girl. He had to live in this damned forced continence.

"Come and see me some time. I'll give you a Greek supper. Greek food's wonderful," Pete said.

"All right."

He got up to go. He might as well get the treatment over with.

IV

Riding home on the bus, Danny got off at Forty-third and Michigan. He stopped in a drugstore and then walked north. He stopped in front of the old station and looked in. Sperling wasn't on duty. He thought of stopping in and talking to the attendant, but why should he? He had freed himself from this world. Why talk of pulling the pumps, crankcase drains, bosses, and the rest of it? He had had all of that he ever wanted in this world.

"Hello," a high-yellow girl said, stopping by him.

"Hello."

"Looking for something?" she asked insinuatingly.

"Not any more," he said, firmly taking her arm. "You look nice."

"Ah can make mahself look nicer for three bucks," she said.

"Well, where at?"

"You turn down Forty-second Street and come along. When you get to Prairie, just follow me."

"But wait a minute, sister."

"You don't want to wait when you gets a chance with me, white boy. Ah promise to be good."

"Yes, but you got to take a chance with me."

"In my business, honey, you always takes chances."

"I got a dose."

"Where did you get it?" she asked, walking along Forty-second Street with him.

"A nice girl, just like you, almost the same color."

"Is it bad?"

"No, it's almost cured."

"Well . . ." she said.

"If you want to take a chance, I've just bought some . . ."

"Come on," she said.

She stopped suddenly at the alley cutting between Michigan and Prairie.

"Let me feel your pockets. I don't want to take no chance with anyone having a gun and burglarizing me."

"Don't worry."

"Ah just take no chances," she said, feeling his back pockets and his coat pockets to see whether or not he had a gun.

"That's a book," he said. "I'm no burglar."

"Ah didn't think you was. Only ah take no chances. You looks all right to me. Ah know you is one of the first to tell me you has a dose. Most fellows will just not say a word and don't care what they do to a girl."

They entered a respectable-looking apartment building on Prairie Avenue. The hall was clean and the mail boxes were polished to a shine. She led him into a front bedroom on the first-floor flat. He smelled cheap perfume and saw silk lingerie lying on a chair. A pink coverlet was spread over the poster bed. Toilet articles were neatly arranged on the dresser.

"Ah'll give you a bargain. Two times for five bucks," she said.

"Here's five, and once is enough."

She took the five and locked it in a dresser drawer.

v

Was he going to spend his whole life being a damned fool? What was the source of folly in his nature? Riding home on the bus, he'd suddenly, without thought, gotten off and found a prostitute. He'd given her his last five dollars and now he had to walk home.

Sin was so casual. A young man sowing his wild oats was a miserable spectacle. In the library tonight he had struggled through some of Baudelaire's poetry with a dictionary, and now he remembered a line that had impressed him:

Eldorado banal de tous les vieux garçons.

It described the world of vice, sin, and evil. Yet he had gotten what he wanted, relaxation. He had pitied himself in the library and on the bus. Today Ed had been released from the club, cured. He had begun to feel that he would never be cured, that he would carry those bugs with him all his life. He had asked himself what was the use of anything. Despair had motivated him tonight. He had quit work to become his own master, even though it meant poverty. And this was the way he had exerted his self-mastery.

He stopped in front of the two-story building where he had become infected. A middle-aged man walked up the steps and rang the bell. Danny walked on. Another adventurer in this banal Eldorado. He pitied the poor fellow. Today over coffee he and Ed had argued heatedly about Dreiser and Cabell, and Ed had said that Dreiser was a bad influence on him. Ed had accused him of having too much pity for mankind and had said the reason was that he pitied himself. Was it true? If true, was it wrong? Shouldn't all mankind be pitied? Laughter, scorn, irony—weren't these emotions of self-defense, defense mechanisms, blinders one put on to avoid looking at oneself and into one's nature, the way a hurt person licked his wounds?

He turned the corner at Fifty-first Street and strolled eastward. He lit a cigarette. He had smoked a few cigarettes after having taken one from Marion in the Coffee Shop. Smoking was the one influence that Marion Willingham had had upon him. It was the one contribution she had made to his life. She was the briefest romance in his life, he reflected ironically.

He was now in familiar territory. The streets he would walk from here to home were populated with ghosts, ghosts of himself. He had still to free himself from these ghosts. He was not yet free. His escape was not complete. Would it ever be? In this neighborhood he had been hurt. Would he carry the scars of this injury all through his life?

He threw away his cigarette and nervously lit another. He strolled on, sick with himself, despising himself.

Tomorrow he was going to start working on his first novel.

XXIII

Al sat alone in the dark parlor.

The blow had come. The factory had gone into bankruptcy. He had lost his life savings and here he was in middle age, with nothing, not even a job. He had no one in whom to confide, nothing but misery at home. Peg was asleep now. He had come home, crushed by his losses, to learn that she had been drunk for a week. Tomorrow he had to leave here, leave a drunken sister and an old mother, and look for work. He had to write letters, obtain interviews, tacitly admitting that at the age of fifty-three he had failed.

He had always been attentive to business. He had constantly tried to improve himself, to be different, to become a cultured man of breeding. He had always plugged. He'd never believed in waiting and letting the buyer come to you. He had sold thousands and thousands of dollars' worth of shoes. He had saved what money he could while carrying the heavy burdens of the home on his shoulders. So here he was with little left to show for his years of work. All that he now had was a few public utility bonds and his life insurance. Tomorrow he had to make a new beginning.

And he had to keep together the home.

Dan was out. He'd quit his job and seemed to be running around too much. He often felt that Dan was drifting away from him.

Dan hadn't turned out to be just what he had hoped, but still the boy was getting an education, proving himself to be scholarly. He was deeply disappointed in Dan, hurt by his conduct, afraid that he was going to ruin his chances of a success-

314

ful future. Dan never wanted to talk much, unless it was to argue. He had lost his religion. He was running around with this fourflusher, young Lanson, who had driven a sweet girl to suicide.

God! He rose and reached his arms upward in entreaty to God. God, give them all happiness. God, abide by him now in this hour of trial.

He knelt down and his prayers came from the depths of his heart. He blessed himself and rose.

This was a period of ill luck. But it wouldn't last. Tomorrow he would begin to build anew.

He relaxed. He began to dream of a future of success and happiness.

Margaret suddenly began shrieking curses. Tense, licking his lips in anger and despair, he ran out to quiet her.

Chapter Twenty-three

I

The gloomy forebodings about the future of the family which he had felt so often now seemed to be coming true. The sadness which filled the home humbled him. He was conscience-stricken because of his many neglectful actions toward the family, because of the arguments he'd had with his uncle, and because of the anger he had expressed against their ideas and their religion. He was humbled. His anger turned from his own folks to the world. Uncle Al and Uncle Ned were talking in low voices in the front bedroom, discussing what Uncle Al should do about a job. After several disappointments, Uncle Al had received several offers, but Danny knew on what terms. Uncle Al never discussed his business affairs at home, except quietly with Uncle Ned.

Aunt Margaret had sobered up after having been drunk for four days. But she was nervous, moody, miserable. For over an hour she paced the hall, wringing her hands, smoking one cigarette after another. Now she was cooking supper, and Mother was puttering around, more or less helping her. He had watched Mother this afternoon. She was thin, wrinkled, almost totally gray. She moped around the house, and slept a lot.

Yes, the home was going to hell. The worn parlor carpet was a symbol of its whole spiritual state. So was the scratched victrola which Uncle Al proudly had bought years ago as a Christmas present for Mother. He had been a boy, seven years old, and he'd been ill with an upset stomach that Christmas. That had been in 1911. Even back that many years they had not been happy. In those days Aunt Margaret had drunk; she drank now. Uncle Al had been nervous, sharp-tempered; he still was. Did people ever really change? Could you change them?

He'd heard the low murmur of voices from the bedroom.

He looked out of the window, restless. Tonight, he was going to the wake of Mary O'Reilley, Pa's first cousin. Why was he going? He knew. Curiosity.

He sat down again. He must not allow the misery in their home to trap and weaken him. That, he must always remember.

He thought of Uncle Al. Uncle Al had placed all his faith in the system into which he had been born. Uncle Al had been a go-getter, and he had had faith in America, faith in this economic system of buying and selling, expanding markets, faith in its homilies of success and money. But it had betrayed him.

He had no faith. That was one reason why he had quit his job. He couldn't work unless he had faith in what he was doing. And he could have faith in nothing but rebellion. He was trapped himself. He now had to sponge off his uncle. He'd have to get a new job. If things weren't going so badly, if it weren't for Mother, he'd leave home. Yes, he was trapped.

He slowly walked back and forth across the parlor. Little Margaret came into the room.

"Why did Aunt Margaret lose her job? Did she get caught with her cash drawer empty?"

"Yes. And, you know she borrowed the money. She went up to see Father Gilhooley, and oh, my God, what she didn't say. She's putting you through college, and me through high school, and she's helping Mama. And she said Uncle Al lost all his money. She gave him an awful story, and he loaned her five hundred dollars."

"He gave it to her?" Danny asked, amazed.

"Oh, Aunt Peg can talk anybody out of money when she needs it. God, she owes hundreds of dollars to the bell-boys, the waiters, and the manager of the Shrifton."

"She should have been Ponzi's wife."

"Gosh, I hope she stays sober. You know, this last time she

borrowed money hand over fist. She hired a hotel room and took me down and, gee, the meals she bought me! But then she got her girl friends and all kinds of funny people and they yelled and drank. I was afraid. She went to almost all of the neighbors around here and borrowed or tried to borrow money from them."

"She tried to get a dollar from Ed Lanson the other night here," Danny said.

"Gosh, I'm ashamed to show myself in the neighborhood."

"It's none of their business."

"But it's a scandal."

Uncle Al and Uncle Ned came out of the bedroom. Little Margaret and Danny stopped talking. Danny saw that Uncle Al was getting gray around the temples.

"How's school, Dan?" Uncle Al asked.

"Oh, I'm getting along."

"Professor Saxon liked your compositions, didn't he?"

"Yes."

"You must develop a beautiful, elegant style in writing. You ought to study Christopher Morley's style. He's an elegant modern stylist," Uncle Al said.

"Why don't you help your aunt with dinner?" Uncle Ned said to Little Margaret.

She went out to the kitchen.

Uncle Al nervously followed her.

"Dan, I got a little money the other day. I got a new job and it looks good. Here, don't tell anyone I gave you this," Uncle Ned said, slipping Danny a folded bill.

"Why, thanks," Danny said, touched and almost speechless.

"Everything's going to be fine and dandy from now on."

Uncle Ned went out to the kitchen. Danny was so moved that tears came to his eyes.

II

Sitting in a corner, Danny glanced about the white-walled sun parlor at Joe O'Reilley's. The room was crowded and filled with cigar smoke. Most of the men were sleek and well-fed; they exuded an air of prosperity and comfort.

Dennis Gorman came in, shook hands all around, and found a chair beside Danny. He didn't recognize Danny at first.

"Hello, Mr. Gorman."

"Oh, hello, hello, Dan, how are you? I'm glad to see you," Dennis Gorman said, shaking hands with Danny. "How's your mother?"

"She's well. She'll be here later on tonight."

"It's sad, yes, sad. She was a fine woman."

Danny nodded.

"You're running for judge, I hear," Danny said.

"Yes. I think the outcome is a certainty."

"I'm glad to hear that," Danny said, merely to be making talk.

"Yes, we have a coalition ticket, and the only opposition is an independent one of no consequence."

Danny nodded.

"Excuse me," Dennis Gorman said, rising and finding another chair.

He talked with a pot-bellied man. Danny watched Joe O'Reilley at the doorway. Joe was white-haired, dignified, handsome. He had a soft face.

"The other day I was talking to Judge O'Hara," Dennis Gorman said to the pot-bellied man oratorically. "Judge O'Hara was wondering why the Irish are the most intelligent voters. He couldn't seem to find the answer, and he informed me that he had often pondered about this question. I explained that the Irish are not afraid to ask questions. The Irish in back-of-the-yards will ask questions. The voters in the richer districts, where there are more intelligent, more educated people, are ashamed to ask questions. If they do, why that might establish the presumption that they do not already know the answers. So they don't question. The good book, you know, says: *Ask and ye shall receive.*"

Tommy O'Reilley passed out cigars. He held the box in front

of Danny, but said nothing. Danny shook his head. Tommy passed on. Danny grinned. He didn't even resent the cut.

"In France during the war the buck private feared his sergeant more than he feared his God," a priest at Danny's right explained to a fat man, and they both laughed.

Dennis Gorman drew the priest off to a corner.

"I was talking with the boss," a mousy man with a gray mustache said on Danny's left. "He was telling me that everything is fixed up in connection with the coalition ticket for the judicial elections next year. He was saying that it's the best ticket worked out in years. He's going to have two Polacks, one Bohemian, three Germans, two Jews, a New England Yankee, an Episcopalian, two Italians and the rest Irishmen."

They laughed.

A stiff man with an iron-gray mustache sat down beside Danny.

"She was a fine, noble woman," he said.

"Yes, she was," Danny answered.

"It's too bad," the man said.

Danny nodded.

"Are you related to Joe O'Reilley?" the man asked.

"Yes, I'm his cousin."

"What's your name?"

"O'Neill."

"I'm General Wallach."

They shook hands.

"A fine man, a fine, upstanding man—they don't make men out of better stuff than Joe O'Reilley."

Danny nodded.

"I was just talking with him about preparedness. Since the war, the politicians and the pacifists have been allowed to interfere. Joe agrees with me, and he was saying that we have to have a big army and navy, the biggest in the world."

"But won't the next war be different? Won't poison gas, airplanes, tanks, new weapons make it different? And won't the navy be less important than new inventions?" Danny asked.

"I was in the last war. That's nonsense, my boy."

"Well, of course, I don't know. I don't know anything about military affairs."

"A shame. Our young men grow up without military training. My God, the job we had putting them in shape for the war—it was a job. And now the reds and pinks and pacifists are talking all of the time about reduction of armaments. The only way to keep peace is for us to be so strong that nobody will dare fight for fear of us."

Across the room his cousin Tommy O'Reilley said: "In politics, you have to play the game."

Dennis Gorman was next to Tommy, and he was speaking approvingly to Tommy, but Danny missed what he said.

A bald-headed man joined the conversation, saying:

"Christians shouldn't argue about politics. They have to combine against the unbelievers."

A thin, weazened old fellow in a corner told a big-jowled man: "Yes, the blacks are getting in on the South Side, ruining real estate values. They've ruined Grand Boulevard already. It's fierce. Bill, I tell you, it's fierce. A shame. A crying shame. We shouldn't allow it. It's the damned Jews. The Jew, he sells to the nigger. So what can you do? Look at the fine home Joe O'Reilley had on Grand Boulevard. He had to sell it. Why? Because the Jews sold to the boogies."

"Yes, it's a shame."

"I don't know why we can't send them some place—send them back to Africa."

"Yes, it's a shame," Bill said.

Danny slumped in his chair. No one here was interested in him. He didn't want these men to be interested in him.

A dapper young man stood near the window, talking to a lad who looked as though he had been pressed out of a university fraternity; he puffed on a huge cigar and lamented.

"I had four divorce cases, four cases, and I lost the fee on every one of them because the people went back together."

"Those things happen," the lad who looked like a fraternity man said.

"Of course, it's good. After all, where would we be without the home? Only I didn't like the idea of losing my cases. After all, lawyers must live, Al."

Joe O'Reilley passed out cigars.

"Oh, hello," Joe said.

"Hello, Mr. O'Reilley," Danny said.

"I heard you were going to school and studying law," Joe said.

"I'd planned to, but I changed my mind."

"Well, there's not such a big future for lawyers any more. We have too many of them. If I was a young man again, I'd study engineering. But here, have a cigar."

"No, thanks."

Danny lit a cigarette. He was bored and resentful. Here was success, here was the world he had once wanted to become a part of. He saw in these aging men a picture of what he could have been, what he had once aspired to become. He became proud of himself because of his revolt. He thought of Uncle Al and these men and saw his uncle in a new light. In his way, hadn't Uncle Al aspired to rise above this, to be different from these men? And these men were well off. Uncle Al was a failure. He got up and left in mounting anger, deliberately passing Joe O'Reilley without saying good-by. It was fitting that he should meet these men at a wake. They were all dead, dead in their souls, dead in spirit. And they were the men who helped ruin Chicago. Yes, he was damned proud of himself for having renounced everything which these men stood for and lived by.

III

He had cut classes today and was working at home this morning. He planned to do more work at home so as to be with Mother. He wouldn't have her for long. He had been too neglectful of her. They all had. In all these years not one of them had ever taught her to write. But, yes, they had all tried, and she hadn't learned easily, so they'd all given up.

The front door opened, and his grandmother hurried out to the kitchen, her wrinkled face lit up with joy.

"Son, this is a wonderful country."

"You liked voting?" he answered.

"I was the cock of the walk. It was Mrs. O'Flaherty this, and Mrs. O'Flaherty that. That Gogarty boy and Tommy Doyle, they took me by the arm and led me downstairs to the basement, and there were the men at a long table with the books before them. And do you know what? They had me name and address down in one of the books and they were waiting for me."

Danny smiled.

"Ah, they treated me like a queen. Sure, and there was nothing like this in the old country. Son, there's no place like America."

"What else did they say to you?"

"Ah, the man at the desk with the big book looks for me name, and then he says, 'Mrs. O'Flaherty, are you a citizen?' 'What?' says I, 'What in the devil is that?' And then Jim Gogarty, he speaks up for me, and isn't he the smart one? He says, says he, 'Mrs. O'Flaherty is a citizen by act of Congress.' And the man gave me the ballot, he called it, and sure, you should see the size of it, and Jim Gogarty, he goes into the place behind the curtain with me, and he shows me what to do. He says, says he, 'Mrs. O'Flaherty, you make a cross here.' And so that's what I did, and they were all so pleased. Sure, and I had the time of me life votin', and I says to them, says I, 'Why in the name of God didn't you have me votin' before this?' Oh, but they treated me with respect. Sure, and don't I want to go back to vote again this afternoon, so one of the men said he'd come for me in a car and let me vote some other place. This afternoon I'm going to put me new hat on and wear me false teeth when they take me to vote. Son, how many times can you vote?"

"As often as you like."

"Ah, they're such nice men."

"Here, Mother, let me get you a cup of coffee."

IV

Jim wore a Dever badge on his coat lapel. He had a stack of pamphlets on the piano stool beside him.

"But, Dan, it won't hurt you. What difference does it make? Sometime you might want to have a little favor done. Hell, if you do it, you can help get your uncle's taxes reduced."

"I won't do it."

"After all, Dever is better than Thompson—he's more honest, isn't he?"

"What the hell do I care?"

"Suppose every intelligent person took your attitude, what would happen?"

"It's a filthy business."

"Why did you register?"

"I made a mistake."

"But, Dan, you should consider it your duty to vote, particularly when it's a case of putting an honest mayor back in office."

"If I vote it means that I approve of something that I hate. By voting I would give my consent to this damned system. Jim, there's no use in discussing it. I won't do it, and that's all."

"Dan, do it as a favor to me. The boys were all denouncing you. They said, 'See what he is? See what the A.P.A. University has done to him?' So I defended you. I said they didn't understand you, and I guaranteed I'd bring you to the polls. If I succeed, it'll help me. After all, I have to get on in politics, and it'll be a help to me. It'll prove that I'm a good worker."

"I haven't anything more to say."

"You won't do it, even as a favor to me?"

"No!"

Jim picked up the pamphlets that had dropped from his hand, and slowly got to his feet as Mrs. O'Flaherty came into the parlor.

"Mrs. O'Flaherty, we appreciate what you've done very much," Jim said.

Danny walked out of the parlor, disgusted.

v

"Let's see the circus," Danny said, lighting a cigarette with Ed in front of the library.

"Why go to watch the little greedy half-dead yell like idiots? They insult the very idea of human dignity."

"Let's see it."

From two blocks away on Randolph Street they heard the roar of a crowd celebrating the election.

"Dinny Gorman's a judge now."

"Can you use him?"

"Oh, he'll give me a reference if I try to get a job. But men like that wouldn't be where they are if they could be used."

They walked two blocks on Randolph Street. As they approached the mob, the noise swelled. A milling crowd filled the street. Scraps of paper were falling like snow from the City Hall and the Sherman Hotel.

"Well, my grandmother helped elect Dinny. She voted twice," Danny said.

"That's a card. There's your democracy for you."

Danny didn't answer. He hated this system as much as Ed, but he couldn't agree with the idea of a world ruled by Nietzschean supermen. If they discussed their differences now, they'd only rake over the same ground that they'd already covered. Ed talked better than he did. Ed would win the argument, but it would be a meaningless verbal victory.

They crossed the street and edged by shouting men, many of them drunk, and took positions by the Sherman Hotel. They watched, smiling ironically.

"See that drunken fat man," Danny said, pointing to a man of over two hundred pounds who was being shoved around as he tried to blow a little tin horn.

"He threw away his hammer and got a horn," Ed commented.

"Idiocy dances on his jowls."

"That's a good phrase."

Five nondescript drunks wobbled by in parade formation with brooms slung over their shoulders.

"Help keep the City clean," the first of the group bellowed.

"Of Democrats," a little old man behind him cried out.

"Big Bill Thompson said we should get brooms, so we got 'em," the third parader yelled in Danny's face.

"They got the brooms to sweep King George out of Chicago," Danny said.

"I enjoy Thompson. I enjoy mountebanks," Ed said.

"Where's Dever now? Where's Dever now?" a woman screamed; her hat was askew; her hair was falling over her forehead.

"Mencken should see this," Ed said.

"A wonderful sight for someone like Daumier or Toulouse-Lautrec," Danny said.

The woman snatched a cowbell from a middle-aged man and rang it.

The roar became more deafening. The crowd was increasing, and people kept milling around like cattle.

"Look at them—weaving a web of idiotic frenzy," Danny sneered.

"Look at that drunken little runt in the blue suit," Ed said.

Danny saw a little man who had his hands cupped to his mouth as he bellowed.

"He's John Dub, the dumb Americano who slaves in an office and goes home to beat up his wife and kids," Ed said.

A drunken woman came out of the hotel and began singing:

America, first, last and always . . .

She fell on her face.

A fleet of Yellow taxicabs nosed slowly through the crowd,

their open cut-outs barking like machine-guns. Danny put his hand to his ears until the cab turned down La Salle Street.

The Yellow taxicabs returned.

"Let's go before I tee off on one of these idiots," Ed said.

They brushed through the crowd and left the scene.

"Chicago is saved from all decency," Danny said with bitterness.

"You're too serious, Dan. If you want to be a writer you'll have to learn how to observe the lunacy of the human race with equanimity," Ed said.

Danny gritted his teeth. He was depressed. He couldn't agree with Ed. The world had to be changed. It wasn't enough to observe and laugh.

VI

It was late. The lights were on in the parlor. Danny wondered if anything were wrong as he climbed the steps.

"That you, Dan?" Uncle Al said sadly as Danny opened the door.

He heard Aunt Margaret sobbing. God, what was it now?

"Come here, you!" Uncle Ned shouted from the parlor.

He went into the parlor. Uncle Al sat with his head in his hands. Aunt Margaret was sobbing. Uncle Ned was solemn.

"Where the hell were you? What the hell were you doing out so late?"

"I was at the library, and I watched the election crowds. It's none of your business what I do!"

"You damned pup, out late like this. Do you know what's happened?"

"Dan, Mother is in the hospital," Uncle Al said quietly.

"My poor, poor, dear, dollie," Aunt Margaret sobbed.

"What happened?" Danny asked, stricken with fear.

"She fell on the steps coming home this afternoon. She went out to vote. She broke her hip," Uncle Al told him.

"My poor, dear Mother," Aunt Margaret sobbed.

Danny dropped in a chair and said nothing.

VII

He tried to smile cheerfully. In bed, Mother seemed so small, so shriveled. He noticed the wrinkles in her neck and the sagging skin.

"Son, are you getting enough to eat?" she asked.

"Yes, Mother."

She wore a red jacket and a lace nightcap. Her face was hawklike. A broken hip was not fatal. She would live. But she'd be a cripple. He tried to hope that she wouldn't be crippled for life. For life? How old was she? She didn't know. Was she eighty? If not, she was approaching it.

"Do you like it here, Mother?"

"Indeed I don't."

"Aren't they treating you well?"

"They never come when I call."

She jammed the bell, ringing it steadily. A pretty nurse rushed in. Pretty nurses in their uniform always were so attractive.

"Yes, Mrs. O'Flaherty, what do you want? Are you all right?"

"What's your name again, dear?"

"Miss Good."

"This is me grandson."

Danny and Miss Good acknowledged the introductions.

"He's a scholar. But don't be looking at him. If he passes an eye at you, I'll jump out of bed and horsewhip you."

Danny and the nurse smiled at each other.

"Do you want anything, Mrs. O'Flaherty?"

"If I did, I wouldn't get it, not in this left-handed hell-hole."

"Oh, Mrs. O'Flaherty, we always come running when you ring for us."

"Be about your business. I want to talk to me grandson."

Danny winked at Miss Good. She left, smiling.

Mother was restive because she was confined, but she was

well cared for. The nurse had answered her ring immediately. A damned pretty nurse, too.

"A woman died in the room next door last night. She had what they call gallstones. She was a heathen. They had no priest for her."

Death. Death had written its signature on her yellowing, shriveling skin. No prayers to be said to preserve her life. Nothing to be done. The signature was there. How long? How long? The signature of death—that most ominous signature in all of the world. Even the weariest river. . . . Standing on an earth which was made from death. Death and life, an endless cycle. The eternal spring had come again, promising life, but not for Mother. But a broken hip wasn't fatal.

"Son, you're too thin."

"I'm all right. Don't worry about me."

"Son, there's a nurse here that does be carrying on with a doctor. It's a disgrace."

"How do you know that?"

"Don't I have me two ears? Son, I'm a wise old head. Me night nurse comes from Galway. I told her that where I come from we always said that Galway people are sheep stealers."

"What did she say?"

"The truth hurts. But she's a nice girl. She sends her mother in Ireland ten dollars a month."

Danny looked at his watch.

"I've got to go to a class now, Mother. I'll come back tomorrow."

He kissed her good-by.

"Your grandmother is a darling. Everybody in the hospital is crazy about her. She's cross, but we like her because she is," Miss Good said to him in the hallway.

Danny smiled.

"But she'll give it to me good if I talk to you."

He watched the nurse go off. Pretty.

Outside. Spring sunshine. Spring and life and youth. The signature of death in yellowed, shriveled skin. What was there to make out of life? Suffering and sadness reduced one to a feeling of humility and impotent anger.

He crossed the Midway bound for a class in Public Finance.

XXIV

Margaret O'Flaherty sat on her bed and put down her newspaper. She was pensive.

She was overwhelmed by a sense of guilt. She remembered incidents of her last drunk, attempts she had made to borrow money from total strangers, mean and bitter things she'd said to her brothers. She winced. She was sorry to the depths of her being. She had not meant to get drunk. But she had been so upset over Mother, so worried about expenses. She had taken a drink hoping it would make her feel better.

Was it in her blood?

No! And now she had learned her lesson. She would never touch another drop of liquor, never as long as she lived. She knew her strength. She had been weak, but she would no longer be weak. Her life was ruined, and she was one of the unhappiest women on earth, but she would bear her misfortune, carry her cross like a martyr.

Her resolution calmed her conscience for a few moments. But then she remembered herself drunk in a speakeasy, screaming and shouting, and she cried, trying to escape from her own sense of shame.

She smoked a cigarette. She looked at her hands. They shook. But she would never again touch a drop. She was through now. If her life was one destined to be miserable, she would carry her sorrow and misery. God would repay her for doing this. God would punish all those who had made her suffer, who had helped to ruin her poor life.

She got ready to go to see her mother in the hospital.

Chapter Twenty-four

I

Danny took a sip from his glass of gin and ginger ale, lit a cigarette, and looked around. The party was being held in a barnlike studio on the near North Side. It was jammed. The walls of the studio were daubed with shrill colors and hung with modernistic pictures. Over in a corner he saw Ed talking to some girl. He'd have to find a girl. He was eager, elated. This party was just what he needed. Yesterday he had been pronounced cured at the club. A celebration was definitely on the agenda. Ed had taken him to the party. Ed knew the host, a weazened little fellow named Nick Fields, who had some kind of inspector's job for the city. He knew that something wonderful was going to happen to him. He was going to have a wonderful time. He'd get a little tight, but he wouldn't pass out. And he'd certainly pick up some girl in this crowd. Here were his kind of people, Bohemians, free spirits, people interested in art and literature, in living according to their convictions. Like him, they would scorn money and all the gods of success. They wanted life to be beautiful. They wanted to be themselves, to express themselves. Yes, here he was in his element. Invigorated, feeling as if he were walking on air, he took another sip from his glass, and moved about.

The conversation rose to a roar. People milled about. Girls were laughing. A Negro was singing. Danny went from group to group, seeking an unattached girl. Yes, he wanted a Bohemian girl, one who was free, intelligent, serious, gay, and pretty.

II

Danny appraised the sallow girl who stood coughing in front of a cubist painting. No, she wouldn't do.

She gulped down a shot of gin. She coughed.

"That's nothing to worry about. Just consumption."

"Perhaps you'd better stop drinking," he said.

He noticed her more closely. She was like a wraith. No color in her face. Sunken eyes. Bright, carmine lips, too much paint.

"Say, who are you, a boy scout?"

"No, not at all, it isn't my business."

"You're damned right. Do you know what I got?—a lung that collapsed like a balloon with no gas."

She took some X-ray photographs out of her pocketbook and handed them to him.

"Here, look at it. That's my collapsed lung."

She gulped more raw gin.

III

Nick Fields stood in a corner. He held a glass of gin in one hand and a cigarette and long ivory holder in the other.

"Or take Ben Hecht—a savage barbarian trying to get along without a loin cloth," Nick said.

"You take him," a fat woman said.

"What'll I do with him? Annabelle, you bovine imitation of a female, your genders are complicated."

"Nick, a cow is more productive than a worm."

"Now we're getting down to real polite conversation," a skinny fellow with a beard said.

"Tell us about Jesus, Nick," Annabelle sneered.

"Listen, you go to the Sour Apple and pay a half a buck and see my little dramatic masterpiece, *A Traveling Salesman in Judea*," he answered.

"Hell hath no despair like a wilted lingam," Annabelle said. They laughed.

IV

A tall, frowsy girl slouched near a huge canvas of drab gray and smoky brown planes that was titled *Metropolis,* and talked to a quiet, dark-haired young man.

"Are you circumcized?" she asked.

"Honey, that's what I call a strictly private question."

"Why don't you answer me?"

"I'm no exhibitionist," he said.

"I've never seen a circumcized guy."

"I couldn't—here."

"Modern plumbing is a great invention," she said.

She led him to the bathroom.

V

"Cezanne's so grim," a pale, effeminate blond boy told a stout girl.

"Yes, he has perfectly synthesized form and color."

"I like Whistler."

"He's literary, second rate."

"Have you ever been to New York?"

"Yes, many times."

Danny was wistfully envious.

New York! Dreiser had gone there. Anderson. Other writers from Chicago. Would he ever get there? And beyond New York—Paris.

"Do you know a picture there by Boeklin, *The Island of the Dead?* It's a brownish gold island, with two large cliffs and a harbor, leading in between them banked by trees that are more desiccated than death. A lone figure drifts into the harbor in a row boat. The picture has such balance of sensuousness and color, and it's so profound philosophically."

"Literary," the girl said.

"Oh, it moves me," the boy said.

"You should see Leger, Picasso, Braque. They're not literary. They are form. Pure form. Form in pure pattern."

Danny went over to Ed, who had the bottle they'd bought.

VI

"What have you written?" a sharp-faced girl in a red blouse asked an unshaven young fellow who was drunk.

"I can't prostitute my art for money. My writing is home, locked in my little garret."

"Well, lose the key."

"Do you like the poetry of Harold Hersey?" the boy asked Danny.

"I never heard of it."

"The greatest poet of Bohemia."

"What about me?"

Danny looked at the intruder, a man with a beaked nose, sandy hair and decayed teeth, who held a corncob pipe in his hand.

"Who are you?"

"I am Hugo Bromberg."

Hugo Bromberg belonged to the Chicago school of writers which included Ben Hecht, Bodenheim, Sandburg, and Anderson. Danny admired his books, especially his poetry.

"If I could write like you . . ." the drunken young man began.

Bromberg stuck his pipe between his yellowed teeth and stared sardonically.

"I've read your books, Mr. Bromberg," Danny began.

"Who are you?"

"Oh, I'm just a college student . . ."

Bromberg made a dash for a girl.

Danny looked after him. Bromberg was the first well-known writer he'd ever met personally and talked with.

VII

"This is quite a party," Danny said to the thin, short woman he was dancing with in the center of the crowded floor.

"Who are you?"

"Myself."

"Who are you? What do you do?"

"Me, I am."

"Do you write, paint, sculp, make cabinets?"

"I go to school."

"Oh, a college boy."

"Is there anything wrong with that?"

"No. Just classification."

"Who are you?" Danny asked her.

"A gypsy."

"I like gypsies."

"Yeh."

He pressed against her.

"Listen, son, I'm twice your age. For ten years I've been waiting for some male to spring a new line when he tries to make me. I guess there's nothing new under the sun."

She left him. Bewilderment turned into anger. He had the word *bitch* on the tip of his tongue. He laughed.

He glanced around for another free female.

VIII

Nick Fields stood outside the bathroom door with a watch in his hand.

"They've been in there thirty minutes," he told the crowd gathered around him.

The crowd laughed.

IX

"Joe, I'm still collecting money for my abortion," a girl said.

"Hell, darling, I'm broke."

"I haven't much time left. I got to get the money."

"Can't you work?"

"Oh, I'm tired of being a waitress."

"Well, here's five more to the kitty."

"Thanks. Now, I only need fifteen bucks."

X

Hugo Bromberg stood in the center of the room. Lights were out and candles burned on a table near him. He closed his eyes, held his head back, and recited one of his poems in a lisping voice. He came to a part referring to a baseball pitcher throwing a ball. He made a gesture to pitch a ball, and fell on his face, drunk. Several fellows rushed him to the bathroom and doused his face in cold water.

XI

"Your name is Georgia?" Danny asked.

She was bovine of face, wide-hipped, and dressed shabbily.

"Yes. I know Ed. He said I should see you and go out with you," she said.

"Well, why not?"

"Why not?" she repeated.

He put his arm around her and kissed her.

"Let's wait," she told Danny.

XII

A nervous, middle-aged man drew Ed into a corner.

"I've seen you before. Let's leave this noisy din of vulgar people. Come home with me and we'll talk. I have some music I want to play for you, music that makes one think of soaring eagles," the man said.

"I can't tonight. Can't we make it some other time?"

"What is all this rout? Debauchery of those who love the mire. I can tell by your eyes, the curl of your lips, that you were not made for this."

"Some other time we'll listen to the music."

He slipped Ed a poem. Ed read it alone. He found Danny.

"A fairy tried to make me. He gave me this. I'm an eagle, you see," Ed said.

XIII

"Where do you live?" Danny asked Georgia.

"No place."

"How's that?"

"Oh, forget it. Curiosity killed the cat. Can you get me another drink?"

"Come on, I'll try to," Danny said.

He took her hand and led her through the crowd.

XIV

An effeminate young man rolled on the floor screaming.

"Take them away! Take them away! They're filthy! They ooze."

A crowd watched him.

"I'm dying. They're choking me. The snakes!"

"Singular that he should see snakes in his delusions," Nick Fields said.

The effeminate young man was carried off by three others.

XV

A middle-aged man, pale, almost deathlike, lay on a couch.

"What happened to Toby?" someone asked.

"Marijuana again. He's been like that for twelve hours," a girl said.

"The sleep of the just. He won't have to look for work tomorrow," a fellow said.

"Tomorrow's Sunday," a girl said.

"Toby only looks for work on Sunday because he knows he won't find it."

XVI

"Your mouth is too tight. Relax," a drunken woman told Danny.

"I am relaxed," Danny said.

"Look at your mouth. It's tight. It's tense. Listen, tell me, what's your complex?" she asked.

"You."

"I'm old enough to be your mother," she said.

"That's it. I have a mother complex."

She grabbed another young man.

"He has a mother complex, what's yours?"

XVII

"Did you see the pretty pictures of my collapsed lung yet?" the consumptive girl asked a man.

"For Christ's sake, Tamara, haven't you died yet?"

"When I die, do you want to be my pallbearer?"

"You've asked fifty lugs already to be your pallbearers."

"Why not?"

"You only have six pallbearers."

"Why?"

"Custom."

"You don't believe me. You don't believe my lung collapsed, do you?"

"I've got troubles enough of my own, Tamara."

"Here, let me show you my X-rays. I never paid for them."

XVIII

"What does he do?" a man asked, pointing to a tall, Lincolnesque man.

"He paints."

"Pictures?" someone else asked.

"No, he's a modernistic house painter."

"That big fellow over there, his name's Lieb. He used to be a housebreaker."

"What's he now?"

"I don't know."

"And there's an old Wobbly."

"Yes, a lot of interesting people here. There's no place like Bohemia, is there?"

"I just love it," a sweet young thing said.

XIX

"How's the soap-boxing, Mendel?"

"Hell, the bums in Bughouse Square don't appreciate ideas. I only collected a couple of bucks the last time I spoke there. I gave my best speech, too—art as the spiritual life of man. I'm fed up. I'll have to give it up. Humanity doesn't want to be educated."

"Why don't you marry a girl with jack?"

"Christ, I wish I could."

XX

"So, Grace, you're a virgin?" Hugo Bromberg asked a sweet, teen-aged girl who sat beside him.

"Please don't put your arm around me. It's not nice."

"Nice? Do you know what's nice?"

"What?"

"Pagan love. Fauns sporting and gracefully gamboling like Greeks on a patch of grass which throws out nets to catch the fragile gold of spring sunlight and to break it into jewels of color."

"My, my, my goodness."

"Let me teach you to be a pagan."

"But I'm a Catholic."

"Ah, but let me teach you to be a pagan, a child of Eros."

"I can't. I have a friend."

"Friend? What is that to Hugo Bromberg?"

"Are you Mr. Bromberg?"

"I am Hugo Bromberg."

"I'm writing a paper on you for my English course."

"You are? I am honored." His hand slid on her leg. She moved over on the couch. "Now you must let me teach you the pagan meaning of my poetry."

"Oh, I wish I had a notebook with me."

"Come—it is night out. Spring nights give me my greatest inspiration. You can walk with me by the lake."

"I can't. I have to go home now."

XXI

"We'll go now," Danny said, holding Georgia's hand.

"All right."

"I'll get Ed and Bill."

He kissed her.

"Camera," someone called.

XXII

Five men picked up Bromberg bodily and threw him down the stairs. They threw his coat, hat, and pipe after him. He stood with drunken dignity at the bottom of the stairs.

"Tonight I'll write a poem. *The Poet Among the Atoms,*" he said with lisping seriousness.

He staggered out.

XXIII

Danny staggered beside Ed. The two girls walked ahead of them.

"Hurry up," said Clarissa, Ed's pickup.

"Conference," Ed called to her. He said to Danny, "Dan, I know a hotel we can take them to. We don't need baggage."

"Can we get in?"

"Hell, yes. It's done all the time. How much are you holding?"

"I got ten bucks. I collected yesterday from that girl who hired me to write a term paper on Whitman. And I lined up two old women to tutor in Political Science, two bucks an hour. So I'm well fixed."

"I hit Father for five. This hotel is over on Cass Street."

Ed whistled for the girls. They waited. Clarissa was more

attractive than Georgia. Georgia was nice enough for the night, though.

"Now, Clarissa and I are going to register as Mr. and Mrs. Schopenhauer because, you know, Schopenhauer was a misogynist."

"What's our name, Georgia?" Danny asked.

"Search me."

"We'll be Mr. and Mrs. Baudelaire," Danny said.

The girls had decided that they wanted to eat before going to the hotel. They went into a restaurant. Ed finished his coffee and sandwich and began to sing.

"Hey, shut up," a big fellow yelled at Ed.

"Make me," Ed challenged.

"Oh, ignore him," Clarissa said.

"We're having a good time, Ed, the hell with the monkey," Danny said, hoping that a fight could be avoided.

"Come on outside," the big fellow said.

Ed rushed out. Danny followed, afraid.

Ed and the big fellow squared off and started slugging. A crowd collected and cheered them on. A lad of about Danny's size took a poke at Ed from behind. Danny went at him, slugging. Ed knocked the big fellow down. Danny bored in, and his glasses were knocked off. Danny's adversary swung low but missed. Danny grappled, and clamped a head lock on his opponent. Ed punched the fellow while Danny held his head. The big fellow got up and said:

"Let's forget the fight."

"Come on, fight! I don't want to debate," Danny said.

"You do, do you?" the big fellow said.

"I'm settling with you," Ed said, mashing the big fellow's nose with a left hook.

The two fellows ran off. Ed and Danny left with the girls.

"Where are my glasses?" Danny asked.

They returned and found Danny's glasses broken in two pieces.

"I'm tired," Georgia said.

"That was wonderful, Ed darling," Clarissa said.

"Hang around with me, baby, and you'll see lots of wonderful things."

"Well, Hellfire, we worked in form tonight," Danny said.

Now he was glad of the fight. He had proven himself. Georgia ought to be proud of him, too. He took her arm.

"Gee, I'm sleepy," she said.

"Well, Mr. and Mrs. Baudelaire, here's our hitching post," Ed said, leading the way into the hotel.

Danny followed, nervous. The sleepy-faced clerk took their money, gave the bellboy keys, and they went up in the elevator.

XXIV

Danny awoke with a headache. Georgia was sleeping beside him. In sleep, her broad face looked stupid. He saw their clothes thrown on a chair and the floor. He glanced back at Georgia in disgust. His disgust turned to pity.

He couldn't sleep, and he lay in bed with his eyes closed, thinking, asking himself what he really wanted, and what was really going to become of him?

XXV

Miss Good brought dinner on a tray into Mrs. O'Flaherty's room. She sat, with her foot weighted, frowning.

"You're all dressed up. You look so pretty, Mrs. O'Flaherty," *Miss Good said.*

"Indeed I don't."

"You'll be walking again. Don't you worry."

"Ah, I'm no good any more. And what's all this? Tell me, in the name of God, what's this?"

"Why, that's your dinner. Aren't you hungry?"

"The food here isn't fit for a dog."

"Why, Mrs. O'Flaherty, we thought we were giving you such a nice dinner."

"So you did? Ah, me grandson once had a dog by the name of Liberty. Sure, and I wouldn't have given him the trash you feed me."

"Oh, Mrs. O'Flaherty, you're just cross today."

"Indeed, I'm always cross."

"Here, now, let me put you up and you eat this chicken soup while it's warm."

The nurse turned the handle to lift the back of the bed.

"Take this back and give it to some tinker. I won't eat it."

"But you have to. You want to build up your strength, don't you?"

"I'm a lady."

"Of course you're a lady."

"Well, I'm not the one to be eating food fit for the tinkers."

"You eat your food," *the nurse scolded.*

"I won't be having you tell me what to do."

344

He sat down to drink his coffee.

American life was changing. Homes were changing. Society was changing. And Mother, product of such a different world from this, Mother was fading away in a hospital.

Well, if you live long enough, you'll die of cancer. Gloomy thought. And he was too young to be gloomy.

He finished his coffee and got his other pair of glasses from the dresser drawer. He had a headache from having been without glasses for a few hours. He sat down in the parlor and read the newspaper.

A gang murder.

Boring news.

Briand makes a speech. No more war. By 1935 the skies of Italy will be black with planes. Thus Spake Mussolini. War? So hard to imagine. When would it come? The lineup now seemed Russia, Germany, Italy, versus the old allies. How old would he be when there was another war? Briand, Briand-Kellogg Pact, Locarno Pact, League of Nations—who respected Woodrow Wilson now?

The news. Death from bootleg liquor. He yawned and put aside the paper. How many trees had been felled to make this Sunday morning paper?

Uncle Ned in the bathroom. Aunt Margaret asleep. Uncle Al at mass. Mother fading in the hospital.

What did he want?

II

Aunt Margaret was a wonderful cook. Danny ate heartily.

"I took a walk over toward the lake this morning. There's a lot of fine homes over there. I was thinking that, God willing, and we have some luck, we could buy one of those homes. We'd have plenty of room then, and a porch for Mother to sit on in the sunshine. Golly, it would be fine," Al said.

"We'll have such a home some day," Ned said.

This was sad. Pathetic.

Danny remembered reading somewhere that Spinoza had

once said something to the effect—not to weep nor laugh, but to understand.

"If things could keep getting better for us and this California job works out, in a year or two we'll all take a summer off, buy a yacht and sail on the ocean. We'd see Ireland. We could take Mother back to Ireland and see where she was born. You know, Ned, I've always wanted to kiss the Blarney Stone. Some day we'll go in our own yacht. Ireland must be wonderful to see. The old Celtic crosses. Dan, do you know anything about Celtic crosses?"

"No."

"We'd see the ruins . . ."

"A lot of stones falling down. Cripes, suppose you were visiting them and a stone fell on your head? Nuts," Ned said.

He watched Aunt Margaret, brooding. A storm was brewing now.

He had to remain calm. That was all you could do when she was getting ready to go off the handle. Coming now. Coming. Uncle Al and Uncle Ned were so wrapped up in their dream that they didn't sense it coming.

"After we go to Ireland, we'll go to Rome, sailing on the blue Mediterranean. Golly, it must be a lovely sea," Uncle Al said.

When would he be able to travel?

"In Rome we'll see Saint Peter's, and the Pope . . ."

Aunt Margaret frowned.

"And we can leave our yacht in the Adriatic and go to see old Vienna and the blue Danube."

"It would be fine, Al. We could get a line, too, on how they make shoes over there. But cripes, I'll bet they can't touch us."

"We'll see the old castles where the knights of old and their ladies lived."

"Listen, nix, nix on the ruins."

"But they're beautiful. And after we see Vienna, we'll sail to Greece."

"Hell, I've seen enough Greeks in restaurants right here."

Aunt Margaret nervously rolled and unrolled her napkin.

"And then we'll go to Constantinople."

"The hell we will. I don't want to see any Turks. Hell, they all keep harems. They never take a bath, and talk about Allah all day."

"But, Ned, we can visit there and see how they live."

"I won't. I won't go to Constantinople. Why in the name of God do I want to look at a bunch of Turks with whiskers walking in alleys?"

"But don't you want to see old Constantinople? It was once the metropolis of the Roman Empire."

"Yes, and they were warriors, too, and what the devil do I care about the Roman Empire? I'm telling you I won't do it."

"For Christ sake!" Al said angrily. "You can at least be open-minded enough to go and see what Constantinople is like."

Aunt Margaret flung her napkin on the table and shouted:

"Will you two shut up! I'll scream if you don't."

"I'm sorry, Peg. We were just talking."

"We can't hardly pay the expenses here, and they're sailing around the world in a yacht like a millionaire. You're no good. You ruined my life. You're driving me crazy."

She screamed. She ran into her room and sobbed. Al ran after her.

"Get the hell out of here. Don't I even have any privacy in my own room?" she yelled.

III

Once, years ago, he'd gone with Aunt Peg to a hospital on a Sunday to see Bill, who had broken his leg. Years ago. Now Mother was in the hospital.

"Mother, you look like a spring chicken," Ned said.

"Oh, Dollie, as soon as you come home I'll take such good care of you. You won't have to lift a finger," Margaret cooed.

"And what will I do with meself then?" the old lady asked.

"You're feeling better, aren't you, Mud?" Ned asked.

"Indeed I'm not. The pain in me hip was a fright last night."

"It'll go away. You'll be dancing before you know it," Ned told her.

Mrs. O'Flaherty looked off out of the window at a green tree which sparkled in the sun. Danny watched her. She was melancholy.

"Mother, I cooked the loveliest dinner today. It would have melted in your mouth."

"Yes, Mother, we had a fine dinner today," Al said.

"Sure, I do be worrying what you are eating."

"Don't you worry, Mud. We're all right," Ned said.

Suddenly, oppressive memories came over him. The past of their home seemed like an almost crushing weight.

"I'm only going to wear red," Mrs. O'Flaherty said.

"Of course you are. You'll look like a stylish doll, Mud," Ned said.

"Doctor McDonald came by this morning. I told him that he was no good. Here I am, lying here day after day, and he can't make me get up and give me the good use of me limbs."

"Mother, the bones take time to knit," Margaret said.

"I told him he wasn't fit to be doctor to horses."

"He understands Mother," Margaret told her brothers.

"Ah, he's a good sort. His son is going to be a doctor. So I said: 'Doctor, me grandson is going to write poems.' That's what I told him."

"You'll be home soon now, Mother," Al said.

"If I don't, I'll tear the hospital down."

"But, Mother, you're so popular here, everybody here likes you," Margaret said.

"And why shouldn't I be? Don't I tell them what's what? Wait till I tell you about the old lady in the room across the hall, the poor thing. It would tear your heart out. She has the cancer just like me poor Tom had it, and the poor thing, she's cryin' and moanin' all through the livelong night. I tell you, it would break your heart," Mrs. O'Flaherty said.

"Mud, forget it. Let's be jolly. This is the Lord's day," Ned said.

"I asked the nurse what's it that ails the poor woman, and she told me. It's the cancer. The poor thing."

Ned winced.

"And her daughter comes to her every day. Her daughter is so big and strapping. She's married to a man who sells stamps. Sure, and behold, there's people in the world that collects stamps after they have been used. Do you know, he makes a good living at it? And he comes of an evening to see the poor woman. Ah, the poor old woman, she makes me heart bleed."

Ned went outside, his hands shaking.

Why was Uncle Ned so fearful about any reference to death, illness, unhappiness?

The old lady looked off again. No one spoke. No one of them looked at another.

IV

Bob, his younger brother, came over to see him when he got back from the hospital. Bob was growing like a reed. He wore glasses and was supposed to show some physical resemblance to Danny.

"I got kicked out of school."

"Why?"

"It isn't my fault. Father Dennis kicked me out on my ear."

"He never liked me, and I never liked him."

"He didn't like me. But oh, gee, I don't know. I suppose he thought he was doing right."

"What happened?"

"Oh, I was in class. Well, sometimes, you know, we all make wisecracks, kids talk in class. The kid behind me was talking, and Father Dennis yelled at me. He said, 'O'Neill, this is the last time I'm warning you! Close your trap!' So I said to him, 'I'm not talking.' He told me I was contradicting him. I said I wasn't so why should I be blamed for something I didn't do? He went on with the French lesson, and this kid kept jabbering away. So he bawled me out again. I asked him what for? He told me I knew what for. I said I didn't. I was called a liar. I said I

wasn't a liar. He tossed me out of the room. The next day, when
I came in class, he told me to get out. I asked him what for. He
told me I knew what for. I said I didn't. I had to see him after
school, because he's Prefect of Discipline instead of Flaming
Michael now, and he told me I had to apologize before him in
front of the class before I could be re-admitted to school."

"You didn't apologize?"

"I don't see why I should. I didn't do anything wrong. So
I got kicked out of school. Mama went to see him, and he told
her I was a liar and a sneak and all sorts of things. So now I'm
in a hole. It's getting near the end of the school year, and if I
don't get in some school quick, I'll lose the year. Mama is seeing
Joe O'Reilley tonight and asking him to get me in Christian
Brothers right away without my losing the year."

"If we had a lot of dough you wouldn't have been kicked out
of Mary Our Mother," Danny said.

"I guess so. Sometimes, oh, I don't know. Many things aren't
fair in life. Why should I be kicked out of school like this? He
just didn't like me saying I didn't do what I didn't do."

"I'm glad to hear it, Bob."

"You don't think I did wrong?"

"Hell, no."

Uncle Al came in at this moment.

"Say, what the hell is this goddamned business, your getting
kicked out of school, talking back to the priest?"

Bob looked at his uncle, afraid.

"Listen, when I talk to you, answer me."

"I only stood up for my rights."

"Why, you goddamned little fool, aren't you ashamed of
yourself?"

"No, he isn't."

"What the hell are you talking about?" Uncle Al asked
Danny.

"You bossed me around. You're not going to boss him
around. He's right. The priest is wrong," Danny shouted.

"Jesus Christ!" Uncle Al said.

Danny's heart was palpitating. He was so excited that he was on the verge of tears because of his tension and anger.

Uncle Al went into the front bedroom and talked with Uncle Ned.

"Since he's been running around with those long-haired bums, you can't talk to him. Let him make his own bed. He'll come to his senses sometime. Cripes, I saw something he had written. Nothing but thighs, and breasts. Cripes," Uncle Ned said loudly.

Uncle Al closed the door.

"Let them jabber. Tell me, Bob, what do you want to be when you grow up?"

"I don't know. I want to read, and I like science."

Danny went to the bookshelf and got a copy of *The Origin of Species*, which he'd bought before he'd quit his job at Upton.

"You ought to read this."

"I heard about Darwin."

"You read it. You ought to start reading now. I didn't when I was your age, and have to make up for it now."

"Gee, I will."

"Let's take a walk."

He and Bob went out and found an empty bench in Washington Park.

"Bob, I want to tell you something. Nobody told me. You've reached the age where you are interested in girls."

He looked sidewise at his brother. The boy was embarrassed.

"There isn't anything wrong with it. But you have to know how to take care of yourself. If you have anything to do with girls, you have to know how to take care of yourself. You go to a drugstore and ask for a prophylactic, so you don't get any diseases. Don't forget that."

"I won't."

"Well, that's that."

They sat watching people stroll by. Georgia and last night suddenly seemed to be part of the remote past.

"Come over and see me about four tomorrow afternoon, and I'll teach you a few things about football," Danny said.

"Gee, thanks, Dan."

v

Danny sat on a bench in Washington Park with his brother Bob.

He ought to be in better condition. Bob had beaten him two sets of tennis, six to two, and Bob had shown more strength than he had when they'd wrestled, and in their football practice.

What a fine tiredness this was, the tiredness of physical exertion, the tiredness of feeling a certain sense of skill, control, even power in your body. Even though he wasn't in the best condition, he still had some power left in his body, in his shoulders.

"Bob, learning to be an athlete is, among other things, learning to have control over your body."

"What do you mean?"

"To control your muscles, your body. In athletics your body is a weapon, an instrument."

"I think I see what you mean."

"There's something else I want to tell you about football. Most high school coaches work on the idea that their players are dumb, and they try to teach them how to do things in a routine way. And most of the players are dumb. I don't mean that they don't read books. I mean that many of them are dumb in football. In football, you think, too—you think in a flash. You more or less think with your feet and your shoulders, your muscles, your thighs, your hips."

"How can you think like that?"

"All I mean is this—I don't care what you call it. You're running with the ball. A tackler comes at you. You change your stride, side-step, sway your hips. All these things, you do them on the spur of the moment. But besides that, study the game, and when you play study the way the other fellows play. In high-school football particularly, most things are done according to routine. Well, shift the routine on them. We had some plays in which I, as end, was drawn back, and a halfback was out on the end in an unbalanced line. I was supposed to go through the line. Well, that play would never work. I'd always watch the end on our unbalanced side of the line. Whenever he was drawn in. So sometimes I'd just run around end. Nobody would be there to stop me. That is an example of what I mean."

"I see your point."

"Often I'd dream about coming games. I'd dream of the glory, imagining myself making big runs, being the hero. But sometimes I had more sense. I would think of what to do, what to pull, how to plan so that I would have a trick in store if it could be pulled. Don't waste your time dreaming about how you will be the hero. When you think about football, think about it practically. But let's get going again. I'm rested. Let me see how you can charge."

They got up. Danny felt good. He was nostalgic for his high-school football days. Yes, he felt good, clean, having a work-out like this with his kid brother.

VI

"Brother, are you going to write poetry? Oh, I read the loveliest poem in the paper by Edgar Guest. I meant to cut it out and show it to you. It will give you such inspiration," Aunt Margaret said at the supper table.

"I saw a fellow today," Uncle Ned said. "He was down on his luck. He had a store and lost it. He was telling me how he read *Nautilus Magazine,* and how New Thought carried him through. He would not let himself say, 'I'm licked.' He said he wasn't licked. And, by God, you should see the store he has now, with a happy wife, two children, and a dandy automobile."

"Fine, fine, I'm glad to hear stories like that," Al said.

"Oh, the world is good, and God is good," Aunt Margaret said.

All this that he had heard and heard *ad nauseam.* Pray for

something. Wish for something. The world was sick. Oh, for a
knife to cut out sickness, the sickness of vain dreams, vain hopes.

"Well, you certainly are sociable," Uncle Ned said to him.

"I was eating."

"Don't you criticize Little Brother. He's going to be a poet
like Edgar Guest, aren't you, Little Brother?" his aunt said, almost cooing at him.

"Like hell I am," he said.

Keep your temper, he warned himself.

"That's certainly an example of politeness," Uncle Ned said,
sarcastically.

"Why, Little Brother!"

"What's wrong with Edgar Guest?" Uncle Al asked.

Danny sulked.

"He's too highbrow to answer anybody unless it's some
bum he hangs out with," Uncle Ned sneered.

"I don't want to talk about writing," Danny said.

Aunt Margaret began to cry.

"All I ever did was slave for him, take care of him, and now
he insults me. Oh, his black ingratitude!" she sobbed.

Danny felt rotten. He hadn't meant to lose his temper and
hurt his aunt's feelings.

"After all I've done for him, and this is my repayment. Oh,
I'm a fool."

She went to her room in tears.

"Now you're satisfied, you fathead," Uncle Ned said.

"Why, you goddamn little fool," Uncle Al said.

"Don't call me a goddamn fool," Danny said, getting up to
leave the table.

Uncle Al licked his lips, rushed at Danny, and smashed him
with a left to the chest. He felt a sharp pain in the heart. He
looked down at his uncle, and he kept his temper.

"Now you're acting crazy," Uncle Ned said to Uncle Al.

"Listen, you shut up!" Uncle Al said.

"Don't tell me to shut up."

He went to his room. Against his will, he cried. He put on

his hat and left. He went over to his mother's, but happened in on a quarrel about a party his kid sister Catherine had given last Saturday night. The kids had necked in the bedroom and Bill was up in the air. As he left to meet Georgia on a date, Bob said that, thanks to Joe O'Reilley, he'd been admitted to Christian Brothers' School.

VII

A squirrel darted across the path and disappeared into the bushes.

And down the long and silent street,
The dawn, with silver-sandalled feet,
Crept like a frightened girl.

He quoted these lines to himself several times.

He looked into Georgia's eyes. Nothing in them, no expressiveness. A cold and placid face. Her hair was disarranged. Her tan skirt was rumpled. He felt rumpled, disheveled himself, disheveled in clothes, in body, in mind. They had slept in the park on this bench.

And down the long and silent street. The dawn. A girl with silver-sandalled feet. Poetry did and did not reflect reality. It reflected the aspirations you wanted to tear out of the guts of reality. It was the phoenix which rose from the ashes of disillusionment. And that was why there was such a sad and terrible cry in all great poetry.

The chorus of the birds in the park. The smell of the leaves and the grass fresh with dew. The warm sunlight. Every dawn was a slow awakening of a maiden from a dream. Every dawn was the birth of a beauty in this world that covered the feelingless mechanisms of nature with the loveliest of dresses, just as a girl with a bruised body, with an abdomen scarred from operations and childbirths, with varicose veins and flabby breasts, could perfume herself and put on a long and flowing gown to cover these imperfections.

He slouched on the bench beside Georgia. She was a drab

girl, a poor thing. But she had been good to him. She had given him forgetfulness of home, himself, everything.

He wanted to talk with her about his feelings. But what would be the use?

"Tired?" he asked.

"Uh huh," she muttered. "We had a night of it, didn't we?" she said in tones of intimacy.

"Yes," he said.

He looked off.

Little drops of dew hung precariously on the leaves of the shrubbery.

He pulled her over to him and kissed her.

"You never told me where you come from?"

"Oh, what the hell difference does it matter?"

"None."

"I was born here. I ran away from home. I hate my old lady. She's an old bitch. I hope I never see her again. I don't like to talk about it."

"Don't. It's a nice morning."

"Yes, it is."

He looked off again. The sun was spearing the grass, and he tried to see in the field of grass the wealth of surface life that the impressionist painters had seen in it. If he were a painter, to paint a picture of the park alive after the dawn, the two of them here on the bench. Somehow, in their posture, their rumpled clothes, their faces, he would suggest weariness and disappointment. The background would shine with the beauty of the world at dawn. This contrast to be stated, not in words, but in forms and colors. The grass, the play of the sunlight on it, this should be broken, done in the impressionist manner. The formless background, the isolation of glittering colors in spots, these would suggest the insubstantiality of man's grasp of what is called beauty. But he was not a painter.

"Got any money for breakfast, Danny?"

"I got a dollar."

"Let's eat."

They arranged their clothing and strolled hand-in-hand toward a Cottage Grove exit to the park.

"Doesn't it smell wonderfully here?" he said.

"Pancakes will smell better."

VIII

Ned carried Mrs. O'Flaherty upstairs.

There was a new couch in the parlor for her to lie on, and near it stood the wheel chair.

"Mother, I cleaned everything up. I wanted you to come home to a clean house," Aunt Margaret said, after Ned set his mother on the new couch.

Mrs. O'Flaherty peered around the parlor. Her face broke. She cried like a baby, her features seeming to lose all shape. Aunt Margaret wiped away a tear.

"Come now, Mud, you're home with us. Soon you'll be as spry as a spring chicken," Ned said.

"I'll never walk again. Ah, that this should happen to me in the latter end of me days."

"Mother," Danny said; he didn't know what else to say.

"Mud, you can sit at the window and look out at the park. The park is beautiful now. You'll see the sunshine and the trees, the people walking, and before you know it you'll be on your feet."

"Mother, I'm going to build you up, cook you the finest foods. Tonight I'm boiling such a tender chicken for you."

"And look—in the name of God, why do I have to have that contraption?" she said, pointing to the wheel chair.

The bell rang. Lizz came in, still wearing mourning for her dead husband.

"Where's my mother?" she cried.

"Ah, is that you, Lizz?"

"Mother, I'm making a novena for you," Lizz said.

"That's the idea, Lizz," Uncle Al said.

"Lizz, doesn't Mother look like a doll?" Aunt Margaret said.

"There's my son," Lizz said, embracing Danny.

"Son," Mrs. O'Flaherty said, jealously.

"Yes, Mother," he answered, freeing himself from his mother.

"Are you all right?"

"Yes, Mother."

"I'll make you a cup of tea, Mother," Aunt Margaret said.

"Put me in that contraption," Mrs. O'Flaherty said, pointing to the wheel chair.

Ned gently lifted her in the wheel chair.

"Now, what in the name of God do I do?"

"See, Mother, you turn the wheel, and it goes," Ned said. She looked at him, blank.

"Ah, the devil made this contraption," she said.

Ned demonstrated how the wheel chair should be manipulated.

"Push me, Son."

Danny pushed the chair slowly forward.

"Let me see me house. Let me see what you been doing to it while I was laying in that left-handed hospital," she said.

Danny pushed her out to the kitchen.

"Mother, the tea will be ready in a minute," Aunt Margaret said.

The others came out to the kitchen.

"Push me in me room," she said.

Danny pushed her to the door of her little room and then he eased the wheel chair into it.

Again she cried like a baby.

XXVI

Notebook

D. O'Neill

"How much there is in the world I do not want." Socrates.

I want to see Russia succeed. But to build a structure in the face of such opposition, fight and plan and work and scheme and sacrifice in a country, unorganized, undeveloped, ignorant, that is a spectacle for the artist to contemplate. That is something great in this lousy world.

The cold, glittering loveliness of winter snow, remembered in the springtime.

Capitalism must decay before Russia can become dominant in Europe. All this disillusionment in the world, will it lead to the decay that makes Russia dominant?

Cardinal Newman says that religion as a mere sentiment is to him a mere mockery, a dream. But what the hell else is religion? A sentiment founded on delusion. And there is nothing in the world that mocks man but himself. And often man is so stupid that he doesn't know that he is mocking himself.

Stephen Crane. The Red Badge of Courage. "These men were born to drill and die." What was my generation born to do—sell bonds—drink itself to hell? Oh, what the hell.

When is the war coming? After the next war America will rule the world unless Russia does. I look at myself and laugh, one born of a generation to rule the world. Write a story about this some time.

Read new writer named Ernest Hemingway.

In Brothers Karamazov Mitya is ashamed when he is arrested because he has dirty feet.

361

Chapter Twenty-six

I

Soon! Soon!

Me daughter, Louise, me beautiful, virgin daughter Louise wouldn't be out with Tom in Calvary Cemetery if the type-writer hadn't given her the consumption. And there he is at that machine that comes from the mouth of Hell itself.

Soon! Soon!

Ah, Tom, it's many a year since you are gone, sleeping out there alone, and it's the fine man that you were sitting on top of your wagon with the horses, and me grandson will be giving himself the consumption with that typewriter, machine of the Devil.

Look at the little children playing in the park, the little angels. Was there ever a prettier little one than me grandson with his long curls, and didn't I keep him spotless, and when I sent him to school, didn't he wear a clean shirt every day? And there was me mother with me inside of her, and she was screaming and yelling, and the pain was twisting her guts and she was screaming and yelling and there I was coming out, with the candle on the table and I well remember it just as I remember the day I was born. I remember me mother lying on the bed, and she screaming and yelling, bringing me in sin and perdition into this world.

Soon!

Me poor Tom, your Mary that could run swift as the wind and sang you the songs that day of the Mullingar Fair is coming to you.

And they do be telling me that I'll be up and walking about, spry as a chicken. Ah, but the wool is soft on their eyes. Ah, they think me a fool, and it's no fool I am, a poor old woman at the latter end of me days with no strength left in me bones.

Soon it will be.

"Son, she's still out gabbin'."

"Aunt Margaret just went to the store. She'll be right back, Mother."

"You must be hungry, you poor boy."

"I'm all right. How are you feeling today, Mother?"

"I'm well. I'm well, Son."

She looked out the window.

And I swan but there is that poor Mrs. Doyle next door, she that buried her poor husband, ah, the poor thing she can hardly walk, the poor woman with her feet ailing her. And there's the old man that had the stroke like Jim O'Neill, with his daughter pushing him in his chair. The poor man. Dying on his feet there in the wheel chair. Well, may the Lord God take care of his poor soul.

"Son, I see poor Mrs. Doyle. Ah, the poor woman she can hardly walk with her ailin' legs. She walks like a poor old woman with hardly the breath of life in her."

"Yes, Mother."

They died like flies in the year of the big famine, and there was me father telling me mother, the Brennans aren't fit to shake the hand of the Devil himself. And their old Aunt Elly Brennan that lived to be a hundred and two, a hundred and two, taking the soup in the year of the big famine. Me mother looked out and she said to me father there goes Potcheen Gannon and me father said to me mother, there goes Potcheen Gannon with his arse sticking out of his pants, and lo and behold his arse was sticking out of his pants, and me father said it's balmy the man is, I tell you it's balmy he is. Poor Potcheen Gannon, he must be over a hundred years old now, a hundred years. And me son, Al, was after asking me last night, Mother did you ever see the fairies in the old country? And what the hell would I be doing seeing the fairies? The gentlemen would be out after the fox on their fine horses and they wearing their boots, and such fine gentlemen they were, and me father would say to me mother, the curse of God be on them that's taking ours from us, and then the redcoats came for Tom's brother and he in church, and in they came and out he went by the other door, and he came out to America, and weren't they fighting over the niggers in America, and they had the draft and me Tom's brother didn't want to go in the draft and he went out to Australia. It's the fine rich man he must be today with a fine head of horses of his own. Neither sight nor light was heard of him since he went out to Australia.

The nigger is coming to wash tomorrow and Peg is always giving her the best food in the house, me son's butter and eggs. The nigger washerwoman, she's a good woman, but she can't be eating me son's food. Not while I'm alive, indeed she won't.

Mrs. O'Flaherty turned the wheel chair around.

"Do you want me to take you to the bathroom, Mother?"

"No, Son. I'm just going to go out to the back."

She wheeled slowly out to her room and opened the top drawer of her dresser. Seeing the eggs and the plate of butter which she had hidden there, she smiled triumphantly. Her son's butter, the best that money could buy. Let the nigger washerwoman eat the help's butter.

She looked up at a picture of Christ as a young man, which hung over her dresser.

The poor man. They made him drink vinegar and gall, and they drove the nails in his hands, and when he died, there was darkness, and on the third day he rose again. The poor man.

Soon!

She wheeled herself back to the parlor window.

Me grandson is traipsin' about and highlifin' with that Lanson. I say that that Lanson is worse than a married man. And didn't I spot him for what he is the first day I set light of him? There goes Tommy Doyle, and me son Ned had me out the other day, wheeling me for the air, and I said, I said, Tommy Doyle, I'll give you twenty-five cents, twenty-five cents if you'll beat up that Ed Lanson. And he said, he said, Mrs. O'Flaherty I can't, he's too good a fighter. Ah, let me have the use of me limbs and I'll fix him, indeed I will.

"Son, the doorbell's ringing. It must be your aunt. Run down and help her, the poor thing, she's carrying those heavy bundles."

Danny went to the door.

Ah, Jesus, Mary, and Joseph, another bill collector, and you can't get blood out of a turnip, and all day the bill collectors are streaming to the door, streaming to the door, and how in the name of God is a man going to get blood out of a turnip? Me poor son Al, carrying those heavy grips to pay all the bills. The poor hard-working boy, he's a good son.

"That was the collector on the wheel chair. He said we hadn't paid him for two weeks. He's coming back tomorrow."

"Tell him to take it and give it to the Devil himself."

Last Sunday at dinner, there they were fighting away and sure I couldn't make head or tail of what they were saying. Me grandson was at it with me son Ned, and me son Al at it with me grandson Bob, and there they were at it for all they were worth and so I put me two cents in to keep them fighting away. And then I told me grandson, I told him, Son, I'm only fooling, and sure it's the fun of it I like. So I kept them at it for all they were worth.

What in the name of God is keeping her out so long and she just going to buy the victuals? It's no fool I am and don't I know that she was up and getting money from Father Gilhooley, that walking saint of the earth, and she telling him the gab she tells everyone, and sure where is she going to get the money to pay him back? Wait till I tell Lizz that Father Gilhooley wrote her a letter this morning asking for his money, wait till I tell Lizz. Lizz will be scandalized. Father Gilhooley's a good man, sure, the earth isn't good enough for him. That I should live to see such a day when me own daughter would be borrowing money from a priest. Glory be to God, what's the world coming to?

And didn't I piss in me bed yesterday, and Peg, didn't she say, Mother let me know when you want to go to the bathroom, and didn't I say to her, didn't I, a mouse came in and knocked the pan over. Devil a mouse there was. I wasn't born yesterday and I'm smarter than they think I am. I didn't go to school but I met the scholars.

"Son, there's the man that takes out the dogs. He takes them out every afternoon, just like a clock. There he goes with the two dogs."

"I don't know who he is."

"There he goes."

Lo and behold, when I was a girl running the bush in the old country I did hear tell of stories and stories of America. And didn't the people say how rich it was and there was money to be had in America, and some there were that did hear tell that the streets were paved with gold in New York. They were killing and fighting in the old country, and they're killing and fighting in America. And look at me now, here in America, an old woman in the latter end of me days. It's a queer world, indeed it is. All of them are going straight to the Devil himself. Ah, Tom, it was a black day, a black day when we came out to America. Didn't I know that there'd be no luck when I sailed away on a Friday?

Soon!

A queer world it was indeed, and sure the women nowadays wear skirts up to their knees and sure they take off every stitch they have and stand in their pelt to take a bath and they have no shame. And the girls nowadays here in America, they all want to be seen in their pelt, and don't they walk down the street shaking their arse at every man that passes them by. And there I was, a wisp of a girl, and me Tom, he says to me, Mary, it won't hurt you. I was the pretty thing then, indeed I was, and look at me now, wasting away with no strength in me bones and one foot already in the grave.

"Son, take me to the bathroom."

Danny wheeled her to the bathroom door in the hall. He

picked her up. She felt so light; she must weigh less than a hundred pounds. She clung to him. He set her down on the toilet seat.

He waited outside.

"All right, Son," she called.

He went in. Somehow he felt that he was committing an indignity against his grandmother. He picked her up and gently set her down in her wheel chair. He pushed her back to the window and returned to his typewriter. He wanted to finish this book before she died. If he did and it were published, he'd dedicate it to her. But she couldn't read.

What was she thinking of by the window? What went on in her mind?

Mother!

"Son, I think me hip is knitting. Get me out of this chair."

He lifted her out of the chair and held her up.

"Now, watch me walk."

She would have fallen if he hadn't held her. Sadly, he lifted her back into the wheel chair.

She gazed out the window.

Soon!

I wonder is it lonely in the grave? There you are in a box, and they close it down over you, and throw dirt on top of it. They give you six feet of earth, six feet of earth.

"Son, is your mother coming to see me today?"

"Yes, she said she'd be over this afternoon."

Me Lizz, me darling Lizz, the poor woman with all of those children, and one coming after the other, just wait till I tell her about Peg and Father Gilhooley. The poor woman having all those children, and when I had me own first one, weren't the pains tearing at me back, and there was Tom at me bed, and what in the name of God was he doing in the room with the woman? Ah, didn't I chase him out. And me first-born is out with Tom, and his headstone is sinking into the ground. We christened him, the little angel, and he died, and what Christian name did we give him? And here I am forgetting the name of me own son, John, the little darling, he's happy in heaven with Tom and Louise and all of his own flesh and blood. And will I be having a headstone over me? Why in the name of God would I be wanting a headstone? You could buy a hundred bars of soap, a hundred bars of soap, with the money that a headstone would cost.

Why doesn't me daughter Lizz come over and tell me what's what and what's going on?

Soon!

There I was all alone, and the boat going out of Queenstown harbor, and sure didn't I get down on me knees and pray to me God when the boat was rolling and tossing and rolling and tossing, and I was seven weeks coming out, seven weeks. What in the name of God do they mean when they say, Mother will you ever go back? So they think I'm a greenhorn, do they? I'll greenhorn them. Greenhorn them, I will. Blessed Mother of God, sure Ireland's a poor country. And there was I, all in white, and Father Kilbride in Brooklyn married Tom and meself, and we went out to Green Bay, and then we came to Chicago, and here I am an old woman, good for nothing, and I'll well be out of this world. All that I ask is for me bones to rest in peace.

Soon I'll be with me Tom, and I'll be bending me knees to God Himself and saying Ga Lob Jesu Christi and sure I don't know what in the name of God it means, and there I'll be on me knees before God, the good man. And why should He be wanting to send me to Hell? Ah, Hell wouldn't hold me. And if I ever get me hands on Satan himself, the Black Demon causing all this fighting and sinning and killing in the world, if I ever get me hands on him, I'll chase him out of Hell itself, I will.

Me daughter Peg is wearing her hands to the bone caring for me and bathing and washing me, and cooking and caring for me and emptying me pots, the poor girl, she could be out earning good money, and it's a queer world, ah, black was the Friday I went out of Queenstown harbor. And there I was with me sister of a Saturday going to the post office and giving her a dollar of me wages, and she giving it to the man, and it going all the way across the ocean to me mother, Lord have mercy on her. And there was Tom and meself in Green Bay, Wisconsin, and the letter came and sure, we couldn't read nary a word of it, and we went to Pat McGann, and he took the letter and he read it off just like that, and Pat McGann, Lord have mercy on his soul, he turns and he says, he says, Mary, your mother has passed away, and there I was in Green Bay, Wisconsin, not knowing if me father had the money to give her a decent burial. Well do I remember the wake of poor Mickey O'Gara, and the men drinking, and the women crying, Timmy O'Shea rolling on the floor drunk as the lord. Ah, well do I remember it, and me just a girl. Ah, I was the pretty thing then, and look at me now. 'Tis a poor country, and why in the name of the Sacred Heart would I be wanting to go back, when Tom, poor man, he paid fifty hard-earned dollars to buy a little plot of burying ground out in Calvary Cemetery. Poor Kevin Macnamara, the poor man, he died a pauper of the drink and his father stood in the doorway and said to me mother, he said, he came into the world with nothing, and there he has gone out of the world with all he came in with. Now riddle me that, will you?

Soon!

There's no strength in me old bones and no power left in these old limbs. They take me out in me wheel chair and they push me around, and I do see the old men with death in their eyes. Nobody fools me. I won't be long here, and it's long, long I'll be under the earth with Tom and me dead children. And sure wouldn't I be giving me right arm to be seeing the steeple of Athlone in the sunshine, ah, but it was beautiful and wasn't it tall? Indeed it was. Sure, what use am I to anyone, a burden and the world will be well rid of me.

Soon!

When I'm dead and gone, who will there be to watch after me grandson, and him an innocent boy? I raised him, and sure it's the poet and scholar he'll be. And don't I know it? Sure, and don't I know that they'll be saying what a fine man he is, and it's poems he'll write, and sure in the west and in the east and in the north and in the south, sure, won't the men be saying such fine things about me grandson? Don't I know it? Me old bones are tired and I'm going, and then who will there be to keep me grandson toeing the mark? Who will there be to wash his clothes and mend his socks and cook his meals? Ah, he needs his poor old grandmother. There he is at the machine, and the boy doesn't have to work in overalls at the gas station any more. And there was the day I walked into the station and I said to the man in the dirty overalls, do you know me grandson, Daniel O'Neill, he works in the station like you, and the poor man, he didn't know what I was talking about.

She wiped away a tear.

Me grandson, he's my son. Doesn't he call me Mother? Sure, if I didn't have him, wouldn't I lay down in the night and wouldn't I not wake up in the morning? What's kept me alive, with me family raised all these years, but me grandson? And when I'm gone, who can protect him from the chippies but me? Don't I know that he runs with the chippies, and what does he be doing staying out all night, and didn't he almost die when he was with the priests in school, and don't I know they took him to the hospital drunk as a lord? I'm no scholar but I met the scholars. And sure, me grandson is like me Tom, and the blood is hot in him, and sure, didn't I keep Tom on the straight road? And who will keep me Danny toeing the mark? The strength is gone out of me bones. Here I am, and they take care of me just like I took care of them, and they carry me around like a baby, and sure, I'm going to a home with six foot of earth over me. And who will take care of me grandson?

Ah, I'm going to me husband. Tom, your Mary is coming to you.

Glory be to God, there goes Mrs. Canavan.

The bell rang.

Danny answered it, letting in his aunt and taking some of the bundles from her.

"You were so good to stay with Dollie, Brother. Brother, I was in the drugstore and I heard some boys talking about you. I didn't let on who I was, and I said to them, 'I know Daniel O'Neill, he's the finest boy I know. He's a writer.' How's Dollie?"

"Mother's all right. She's been sitting by the window."

Danny helped Aunt Margaret put away the groceries. They went into the parlor. Mrs. O'Flaherty was asleep in her wheel chair.

XXVII

Al sat in the lobby of the Potter Hotel, thinking, thinking.
He had been forced to sell one of his public utility bonds in
order to meet the expenses of Mother's accident. Well, thank
the Lord that he had had the bonds. Bad luck came in batches.
It never rains but it pours. There was wisdom, sometimes a
saddening wisdom, too, in many old sayings. It never rains but
it pours.

Thank the Lord that Mother was still with them. Perhaps
being confined in a wheel chair would preserve her longer. She
would expend less energy.

His new boss was a piker. Wouldn't let him have a sample
room. Having to work for a piker didn't give him more pres-
tige in the shoe world, either. His products were paper, and
they didn't sell. He had nothing with which to compete with
rivals handling good lines.

He had to keep his eye open for something better.

There was a proposition for him and Ned to go in with a
fellow named Corcoran on their own, selling nuns' shoes. This
would mean no more traveling. He was tired of traveling, and
he would be near Mother. Peg was wonderful now. She'd risen
to the occasion, and she was better than any nurse. She took
care of poor Mother so tenderly, as if she were a baby.

If he went in with Corcoran, it would take every cent he
had left. Could they make it go on a shoestring? How could he
dare take the risk? If he went into business, he didn't want to be
a piker.

What should he do?

"Why, if it isn't Al O'Flaherty. Hello, Al, how are you, how
are you, how's business?"

372

"*Well, bless me, if it isn't good old friend Tom Stout. How's business?*"

"*Hell, I'm selling shoes faster than they can make them. How are you doing, Al?*"

"*Good, good. Yes, good.*"

"*Glad to hear it, glad to hear it. And the brother?*"

"*Good.*"

"*Come upstairs to my sample room. I want to show you my line, Al. I have some real birds.*"

Al went with Tom Stout to the elevator.

Chapter Twenty-seven

I

Danny walked across the campus toward the Reynolds Club. He was fed up with himself.

He'd quit his job to be free for serious work.

Item: he was frittering away his time and wasting his energy tutoring two dumb old-maid school teachers in comparative governments, and hiring himself out to write book reports and term papers for rich students who were too dumb or too lazy to write their own.

Item: he had fallen so far behind in his own classes that he wouldn't get good enough grades to clinch an honor scholarship for his junior year.

Problem? He had to find work.

Possibility: he wouldn't be able to get as good a job as the one with Upton.

Where was he going?

Nowhere.

An incorrect answer.

Correct answer: he was going to Hell on wheels.

He was a Bohemian now. A Bohemian was a free person. Rot.

Item: a Bohemian had to think about money all the time. Bohemianism made failure a positive value, failure in work, in living, in social and human relationships.

Conclusion: he was not a mere damned fool: he was a god-damned fool.

He met Broda, Jim Gogarty, and Carter for lunch at the noisy and crowded Commons. Contrasting Carter with Ed Lanson, he realized Ed would never do anything. He'd never write, never think out any problems. Knowledge to Ed was

374

something to be shown off like a flashy diamond pin. When Ed now talked of books and ideas, he didn't take him seriously. He wasn't seeing so much of Ed. Ed had found a meal ticket in Clarissa, and they were living together as man and wife on the North Side. Ed was promising to write a novel like *Ulysses* based on Ellen Rogers and the other girls he'd known. It would never be written. But would he himself ever write?

He had to do something drastic with himself.

"I just learned something amusing—did you know that in Germany the secret police were once put on Kant's tail, watching him as a person suspected of being dangerous to things that be?" Carter remarked.

"I don't understand that," Jim said.

"Haven't I always said that intelligence is a social evil, and that stupidity is the most powerful social force in history?" Broda said ironically.

"That's too cynical," Jim told the Pole.

"Any great thinker or writer seems sooner or later to become a dangerous influence and the object of police supervision," Carter said.

"The police won't need to waste much time supervising the master minds on this faculty," Broda said.

"Times have changed, though. Now isn't everybody pretty free to say what they like?" Jim said.

"Not if their names are Sacco and Vanzetti," Danny said.

"They might be saved," Jim said.

"And what about the last war? An effort was even made to arrest a pacifist named Thomas Paine," Danny cut in bitterly.

"But people have learned since then," Jim said.

"Oscar Wilde was persecuted, arrested, jailed," Danny said.

"But that was for moral turpitude," Jim said.

"Still, he was a poet, and he was arrested," Danny said.

"Well, is the artist above laws?" asked Jim.

"Why shouldn't he make his own laws? The lawyers make their own laws—for us," Danny said.

"That's going too far. Should the artist be allowed to commit murder?" asked Carter.

"No, that's a privilege that society reserves for itself," Broda said.

"These days, people aren't slaughtered in battle. They are merely destroyed in the peaceful warfare of competition," Danny said.

"But, Danny, why should the artist be superior to everybody else?" Jim asked.

"Because he earns it," Danny said.

The greatest achievement in the world was to earn for yourself the right to say—*I am an artist.*

"What place has the artist in society unless he becomes a whore? Humanity doesn't want to be told what it's like, and it spits at the artist who does it. Look at what they did and said about Whitman. Tolstoy was once too immoral to be sent through the United States mails. *Ulysses* was burned by the postal authorities. What the hell are you talking about, Jim?" Danny asked.

"Those are only mild instances, my dear chaps," Broda said. "Dostoevsky was put before a firing squad. Other Russian writers were driven mad."

"Chernishevsky went mad," Carter said.

"Even in beautiful Victorian England, look what happened. Nineteenth-century English literature begins with the persecution of Shelley, Byron, and Keats, and it ends with Swinburne going mad, Ruskin going mad, Rossetti going mad, and Wilde going to the hoosegow. Of course, these men were not first rate, except for Shelley and Keats, but their persecutors weren't even tenth rate," Broda said.

"But this is America," Jim said.

"What the hell is going to happen to America?" Danny asked.

"Rimbaud might have the correct idea. He gave up poetry before he was twenty-one," Broda said.

"Of course, the artist as rebel is not an eternal figure. It is no law of society that at all times such must be the fate of the artist," Carter cut in rather pedantically. "The *philosophes* in eighteenth-century France, for instance, they were confident, self-assured men. They were rebels against the aristocracy, but they had the middle class behind them. It's in the nineteenth century when bourgeois culture becomes a crushing weight on the artist, and he becomes a rebel against all society."

"But look at how successful and well liked Dreiser, Lewis, and Sherwood Anderson are in America," Jim said.

"Dreiser had a hard road," Danny said.

"I suspect that Dreiser's success was an accident, and I have no great confidence for the future," Broda said. "Dreiser and Lewis cause great perturbations among the old maids of both sexes who belong to the faculty here."

"What's the answer?" Jim asked.

"There are no answers but one—never to stop fighting," Danny said, with a bitterness out of keeping with the tone of their talk.

"O'Neill, what do you think of *Ulysses*?" Broda asked.

"It's a masterpiece. And didn't you like that wonderful scene where Joyce describes himself as a young man, refusing to pray when his mother was dying?" Danny said.

"But was that kind?" Jim asked.

"What has kindness got to do with conviction?" Danny retorted.

"Would you pray to please your grandmother if she were dying?" Jim asked.

"No. I would do anything else for her. But I won't bend my knees."

"Unless some real principle is involved, it seems to me that it's unnecessary, even cruel, to do such things. What is the use of riding roughshod over a father or a mother, and pretending that you are doing it for a principle? After all, doesn't one act on principles in order to make the world better? Any effort to make the world better must be a product of imagination, sympathy, kindness," Carter said.

"But, goddamn it, suppose it is a case of their hurting you or you hurting them?" Danny asked.

"This revolt of youth of today is really too unfeeling," Carter said. "It's full of folly, destructive of emotions, even of nerves and bodies. I'm no Puritan myself but, honestly, I think Puritanism is better than meaningless immoralism, than this lower-middle-class Sanineism that you find in some people of our age. What's the use of it?"

"Sanine wasn't unintelligent," Danny said.

"Well, I think he was. He was utopianism standing on its head and melodramatically stewing in a miserable imitation of Nietzscheanism," Carter said.

"Don't you like Nietzsche?" Danny asked.

"He's full of contradictions. The big thing in Nietzsche's life was Bonaparte. But Nietzsche denied everything that made Bonaparte. To him, Bonaparte was devoid of historic past, a comet flashing out of nowhere. That's not historical. Bonaparte was a child of the Revolution, and a bourgeois emperor, and he would have been nothing without the democratic movement in the first days of the Revolution. He was a great man, but there were other great men, too, in the French Revolution—Robespierre and Saint-Just. Well, Nietzsche hated democracy, and he falsely correlated any popular movement with Christianity. He argued that the great man, the superman, stands above the masses of the people. I don't accept that. Simple people will one day show that they have their will, too. I don't believe in supermen. I believe in people. I believe in giving them the will that Nietzsche reserves for his superman," Carter said.

"But you've go to take a hammer—that's what Nietzsche taught me, although I agree with most of what you say," Danny said.

"Nietzsche's idea," Carter went on, "was that of a moral

élite of supermen who would be ruthless, but honest with themselves. It seems to me that this is different, even though I don't agree with it, from the present vogue of Nietzscheanism, of hooliganism and Sanineism. A lot of this carousing and drinking that some guys do, and then try to justify philosophically—what the hell, you don't need a philosophy to get drunk and to go to bed with a dame. Do it. But why justify that by a cosmic principle? And that's the meaning of the vogue of Nietzscheanism today. You're not doing anything singular by raising some hell and sowing wild oats. Empty-headed frivolous fraternity snobs on campus do that. Every weekend they whore, they drink, they pass out, and they don't have to have a philosophical justification for it. If you're seriously interested in art and ideas, and do that and blame it on your art, you're perverting something that can be noble," Carter said.

"Danny, I think that Carter has got something," Jim said.

"Oh, what the hell," Danny said.

"You don't have to drink up the whole Atlantic Ocean to know that it's salty," Carter said.

"What do you mean?" Jim asked.

"You don't have to knock the hell out of yourself, make a bum out of yourself, because you don't like the world and the rule of the middle class. In fact, if you have talent, ideas, promise of being a fine writer, or an independent and courageous thinker, why the middle class would be more pleased if you'd become a bum, wasting your youth and health in carousing like a gang of Babbitts at a convention."

Danny asked himself—after all, was he just a bum and a hooligan pretending to have a philosophy? It was too easy calmly to dissect yourself, or a generation. In revolt you sometimes exploded all over the place. And yet, no, you couldn't rationalize with yourself. Where was he going? Where?

"We're getting too damned serious—let me tell you about the latest story of a mental case they found on campus," Carter said.

II

"Have you ever had any experience?" asked Kelly Malloy, the fat city editor of *The Chicago Questioner*.

Danny's confidence dropped. He wouldn't get the job.

"No, sir, I haven't, but I think I can do the work. I took a course with Professor Saxon, and he thought very well of my writing."

"You did, huh? The professor's a fine fellow, fine fellow. Well, O'Neill, I'll take a chance on you. You know, we only pay space rates. We like to get stories of the boys and girls on campus, you know, and if you can dig up anything about the girls and professors, that's right down our alley."

"Yes, sir."

"I'll introduce you to Bill Judson at the city desk. He'll tell you what to do," Malloy said, rising.

III

Danny O'Neill walked along Madison Street telling himself that he was a newspaperman. No, not quite, for he was merely a campus reporter. Malloy himself had begun his newspaper career as a campus reporter. Yes, he was a newspaperman, and he carried a press card in his wallet.

After lunch with the boys today, he'd met Pete by chance. Pete had told him of this opening, and he'd come downtown immediately and asked for this job. His outlook on himself and the world had changed radically when he'd walked out of the city room of the *Questioner*. He was no bum with a philosophy now. He had a position. He could walk around campus feeling cocky and confident, asking questions, prying into anything that interested him. He could use his card to walk through fire lines, get into shows, bust into police stations for information about crimes. His card was not only an open sesame, but it was a mark of status. He was somebody. He could work himself up the ladder. A newspaper career offered good training for writing. It permitted you to see all aspects of life. He'd work at this. He'd do feature stories about campus, about the streets, pieces along the line of Ben Hecht's *A Thousand and One Afternoons in Chicago*. What he wrote would be printed and paid for. He might get scoops. His future was promising. Here was a shortcut to literary success.

He stopped in a Thompson restaurant for coffee and gazed around at those at the other one-armed tables. A restaurant could be a feature story. Who were the men sitting around here? What dreams did they have? He could describe their faces. A man on his right had a nose like a strawberry. He was thinking of something. His lips were pressed together tightly. His eyes were sad. You could see emotions expressing themselves in the little changes of his countenance. In fact, the faces of people on streets and sidewalks were like a moving picture, an endless series of suggestive little stories. Something was going on inside of them every minute. They walked along the streets, thinking, sorrowing, hoping, dreaming, filled with themselves and their problems. He did the same. Sometimes he would walk along brooding or thinking, and he'd suddenly notice that a stranger had been watching him. He would slink off, as if ashamed of having exposed his consciousness to strangers. Others were the same. He would watch people now with a professional eye.

He would be a newspaperman.

He read his name on the yellow press card with pride.

IV

"Hell, you could let me have some of the releases in advance," Danny complained to Bobby Wallace, the Director of Public Relations for the University.

They were in Wallace's office, and Danny held a sheaf of publicity releases, mimeographed in purple ink.

"You dig up your own news. Our job isn't to give you news. We have a boy and can send our releases down to the papers ourselves. We don't have to bother with you."

"I asked you to do me a favor. I only work space rates, and

some of the releases you send down like this one announcing
a lecture by John Dewey, you could have let me turn in."

"Sorry, O'Neill. I can't change my policy for you."

Danny looked at him angrily.

"You don't have to get sore. I don't mean anything personal."

"I'm not sore."

Danny walked out of his office.

"So long."

"So long," Danny called.

V

"City Desk."

"Just a minute, please."

Danny waited in the phone booth outside the barber shop
in the Reynolds Club basement.

"Judson, City Desk."

"O'Neill. Anything for me?"

"Wait a minute. . . . Yes, Kelly wants some more leg pictures for Sunday."

"I'll fix it up. I got some more funny stories."

"Good, I'll give you a rewrite man."

Danny waited.

"O'Neill, Wallace, shoot."

He got Bobby Wallace's brother. This gave zest to his
triumph.

"Mike Mooney, captain elect of next year's football team, is
an expense to the University."

Wallace laughed through the phone.

"He's taking a geology course. They pass rocks around for
the students to examine, and Mike doesn't know what to make
of the rocks. So he tosses them out the window. The Geology
Department has lost all its stones and is in a dither. Dr. Shafton
is organizing a field expedition for Geology students to hunt
for his rocks on campus."

"Jesus, O'Neill, cut it out, will you?"

"Kelly told me to give him funny stories. He likes 'em."

"All right, what else?"

"There are rumors that one of the prominent frat men has pilfered the funds of Blackfriars."

"I know all about it. My brother came down here and quashed that."

"One more. The class of 1899 contributed funds for a lamp-post on campus. The University held the dough all these years, but now it's finally put the post up."

"Is that straight?"

"Well, there's a new lamppost over near Harper's, and it says gift of the class of 1899."

"All right, I'll write these up."

"Give me Carson now. I need a photographer!"

VI

"Brother, I'm so glad you came home for dinner," Aunt Margaret said.

"Like your dinner, Mud?" Ned asked.

"Mother, poor thing, she hardly eats enough to keep a sparrow alive. Now, Mother, this is such a tender chicken."

"Say, Mud eats like a horse," Ned said, winking at Margaret.

The telephone rang. Al answered it.

"Dan, it's for you."

He went to the phone.

"O'Neill, Questioner, Cappel, night city editor speaking. Listen, there's supposed to have been a holdup in a delicatessen store at Fifty-fifth and Harper. Can you shoot over and see if there's any story?"

"All right."

Danny hung up the phone, eager, excited. He was getting assignments off campus, regular news stories instead of leg pictures. Last week he'd covered two protest meetings of citizens on tax assessments, and his stories had been used, and they'd sent him to interview a dame who had been decorated by Mussolini. She'd told him how wonderful Mussolini was, so he'd told Judson that she was a publicity hound and killed the story. He was learning the ropes and getting along.

"I got to dash off on a story," Danny told them in the dining room.

"Hell, you're hardly ever home for dinner, and now you rush off again like a bat out of hell. Haven't you any interest in your home?" Uncle Ned asked.

"I got to go on a story."

He called the Yellow Cab. Then he sat down and gulped chicken while he waited.

"Ah, it's left-handed jobs he's always getting."

The bell rang. He was off. Riding through Washington Park in the cab, he thrilled with a sense of power and position. Yes, some day he'd be a newspaperman. He strutted into the Hyde Park police station, flashed his press card, and asked about the holdup. The sergeant knew nothing about it. He hung around the station, his hat pushed back on his head, and a cigarette in his mouth, waiting to learn if a report on the alleged holdup came in. He phoned Cappel to say that there was nothing doing on the report, and then took a cab home. One of the gratifications of his job was the expense account.

VII

"Judson wants pictures of the annual seniors' mustache race," Danny told Bobby Wallace.

"Nothing doing."

"They want the pictures."

"I said nothing doing. Listen, tell Kelly Malloy he's not running this University. We have been getting too damned much undignified publicity. I was talking with the assistant to the President this morning, and he hit the ceiling. This cheap publicity has got to stop. This is an institution of learning, O'Neill."

"I used to think it was—once," Danny said.

Danny left the Publicity office, phoned *The Questioner* for a photographer. Then he dug up Mike Mooney, A. Lincoln

Jones, and two co-eds with shapely legs. He had the pictures taken and phoned in a story.

This was another notch in his belt. Wallace would pay plenty for holding back on that Dewey lecture and other innocuous stories. Wallace wasn't going to lick him.

VIII

"I told you, O'Neill, that you couldn't take pictures of the mustache race," Wallace fumed.

"I didn't take the pictures. A photographer did," Danny answered with a twinkle in his eye.

"Goddamn it, don't lie to me. You pulled this dirty trick on me. Every goddamn day you're up to something. You're making the University look ridiculous."

"What do you want me to do about it?" Danny asked.

"Cut it out!"

"You wouldn't give me any stories."

"I haven't got time to bother with you. We don't need you. You're just a cheap little amateur reporter on space rates. For Christ's sake, quit playing that you're a newspaperman. I was in the business before you were born. You're not going to get away with anything on me."

"I'm not working for you," Danny said, turning to leave the office.

"Just a minute, O'Neill. I'm not finished with you."

"I'm finished."

"Wait a minute, wait a minute, you're a student here. I got something to tell you. Here, look at this goddamn clipping. Professor of Anthropology gives free haircuts in class. I checked up on this one. It was a request made in class by Dr. Colwell in order to get hair samples for a scientific experiment."

"I merely turned in the facts."

"Listen, do you want to get thrown out of the University? Do you know that Mr. Quick, chairman of the board of trustees, is raising hell about the kind of publicity we're getting? I'm telling you, cut it out! Quit making the University look ridiculous or else you're going to get tossed out of school on your ear!"

"I just turned the story in."

"Well, watch your step if you want to stay in school. I'm not going to tell you again."

"You don't want to throw me out of school, now, Bobby."

"Don't kibitz with me."

"I got a good record, you know, scholastically. I have to make a living, don't I? I'm working my way through school, you know—and the University throws me out—on the charge of making it look ridiculous. That wouldn't be a decent thing to do, would it?"

"I'll be decent with you when you're decent. I'm sick and tired of this goddamned game you're playing."

"I have to turn in some stories."

"Why don't you do a story about Dr. Conkwell in physics?"

"He's the one, isn't he, who says that because an atom doesn't know which way it'll jump, there's a God?"

"You're too damned flippant. You're going to get in trouble."

"Any news?"

"Yes. There's a three-legged duck in a kosher meat market on Fifty-fifth Street, near Kimbark. Write it up."

Danny left Wallace's office, triumphant. He had Wallace half licked already. Even Morton G. Quick, the stockyards capitalist, was up in arms because of what he was doing.

He went to the phone booth and turned in a story about a three-legged duck in a kosher meat market at Fifty-fifth and Kimbark, adding that the University was trying to get the duck for experimental purposes, and that it was competing with Northwestern University, which also wanted the duck.

IX

Danny sauntered into *The Maroon* office.

"You're a hell of a guy, these stories you're turning in about the U. Ain't you got no school spirit?" asked Art Knight, the editor.

"What's new?"

"I wouldn't tell you if I knew."

"Who's going to be elected next year as editor? Or is the finagling still going on?"

"What, you want to print that, too, in *The Questioner*?"

"Hell, no. The readers of *The Questioner* don't give a damn about that. They want to see the legs of co-eds."

"Who doesn't?"

"Who's getting the editorial plums next year?"

"It's not a plum. It's hard work. You know that."

"Yeh, pocketing the receipts."

"We built up the paper, got ads, made it interesting, didn't we? Shouldn't we have a right to the profits?"

Danny picked up a copy of the day's issue and said sarcastically:

"Here, page one—Constance Cargill to lead Military Ball. Dekes Give Smoker. Harry Haggin Jackson gives talk on football and ideals. Interesting? Listen, *The Maroon* isn't merely dull. It's ferociously dull."

"O'Neill, I haven't got anything for tomorrow's Open Forum column. Write me a column, will you?"

Danny sat down and wrote off an attack on the Campus Dramatic Club, describing its members as tea drinkers and demanding that colored students be admitted to the club and permitted to act in the plays. He handed it to Art Knight.

"You are looking for trouble, aren't you?" Art asked after reading the piece.

x

Danny walked across campus toward Harper's as the sun was setting. He was fed up, disgusted with the work he was doing as a campus reporter. He wasn't doing his own writing. He wasn't studying. He was selling out. Was this worth the damned twenty or twenty-five dollars a week he earned?

He made a routine call to the office. He was told to cover a lecture a Baptist minister was delivering on modern youth. Again he was being robbed of time for study. He phoned for a Yellow Cab.

Waiting in front of Harper's for his cab, he gazed across the Midway. He had to quit this job. He still was not free.

Mrs. Gogarty stopped Lizz O'Neill after ten o'clock mass.
"*You're Mrs. O'Neill?*"

"*Yes, I'm Mrs. O'Neill,*" *Lizz said, on guard.*

"*Your son, Daniel, has been a bad influence on my son.
Your son is without religion, and he has taken my son away
from me. He is a bad influence. I wish you'd be telling him not
to be seeing my son.*"

"*Oh, but no, no, my son Daniel is a good boy. Why, he almost studied to be a priest. He is the finest boy. Why, he comes
home and pours his wages out to me on the table. All of my
children are decent boys and girls, I'll have you know.*"

"*I'm a mother and my only son is always seeing your son at
that heathen university.*"

"*If he sees my Daniel, he couldn't be seeing a finer and a
more decent boy.*"

"*The Lord himself doesn't know what these bad companions
may be doing to my boy, and after I slaved and sweated to
raise him a decent Christian young man.*"

"*I'm a Christian, and I'm the mother of six living and nine
dead, and I'll have you know that I raised my children to be
decent boys and girls.*"

"*I wish your son would stay away from my Jim.*"

Lizz raised her nose.

"*We O'Neills, Mrs. Gogarty, we're choosy people.*"

Lizz walked off, her head high.

389

Chapter Twenty-eight

I

Danny wrote at the little desk in his bedroom. He had laid his emptied coffee cup on the window sill beside him. The apartment was quiet. He was absorbed in the words he scribbled on sheet after sheet of paper. The best way to keep working on his book was to get up early and do his thousand words a day immediately. Coffee woke him up. He resented the necessity of having to get much sleep. It wasted your time.

He tiptoed out into the kitchen and poured himself another cup of coffee. By the time the rest of the family woke up, he'd have his day's work on the novel finished.

Mother ought to be awake by now. Let her sleep. Usually she slept so badly. Four times in the last ten days she had awakened the house, crying. She couldn't sleep. She was afraid in the dark. What did she think of alone at night?

He carried his cup of coffee back to his room.

Last night he'd stayed home, read her the newspapers, and he had tried again to teach her how to write her name.

She'd talked, too, about Ireland. If he could only remember her conversations, but he always forgot them.

He lit a cigarette and sipped his coffee. He tiptoed to the bedroom, looked in. She lay still. He tiptoed back and resumed work.

It was strange that Mother was sleeping so late.

II

Aunt Margaret screamed. Uncle Al ran out to her in his B.V.D.'s. Uncle Ned followed him. Danny hurried to the kitchen. He didn't need to be told what happened.

390

With her eyes open, Mother lay dead on the bed.

"Ned, get a looking glass, quick."

"Call a doctor," Ned said.

"Ned, quick, for Christ sake, a looking glass!"

"I'm getting it."

"My poor Dollie. What'll I do? What'll I do?" Aunt Margaret sobbed at the kitchen table.

Last night he had kissed her good night. At dinner she had worn her red jacket, and she was sprightlier than she had been in several weeks.

Uncle Al carefully wiped off the looking glass. He put it to Mother's lips. He examined it anxiously.

"Yes, she's passed away," Uncle Al said.

"What'll I do?" Margaret sobbed.

Danny stood in the kitchen, bewildered, feeling impotent.

Mother is dead!

Uncle Al realized that he was in his B.V.D.'s.

"Peg, I beg your pardon," he said shyly, ashamed.

He skipped down the hall.

"Peg, don't cry. It must be the will of God," Uncle Ned said.

"Aunt Margaret . . ." Danny consoled.

No words could give any consolation.

Mother is dead!

Mother is dead!

Uncle Ned went into the room with him. He closed her eyes and drew a sheet over her corpse.

Uncle Al returned to the kitchen, wearing trousers and slippers.

"She had the grace of a happy death," he said.

"Yes, she passed away like in a dream," Uncle Ned said.

"I want my Mother. I want my Mother back," Aunt Margaret said.

"Let's kneel down and pray," Uncle Al said, looking at Danny, distressed.

Danny knelt down with them. He blessed himself, and pretended to pray.

Hail Mary, full of grace . . .

Mother!
Mother is dead!
No thoughts, no prayers. Not even surprise.

Blessed art thou, among women and blessed is the fruit . . . .

Good-by, Mother!
Words she cannot hear. Prayers she cannot hear. Nothing could do her good or harm. Yes, quietly, as in a dream, she had passed away, softly, as in a dream, she that was something became nothingness.

Mother, I was going to dedicate my book to you.

Uncle Al rose.

Margaret sobbed on Danny's shoulders.

"Peg, that's the brave, brave, brave girl," Uncle Al consoled.

"Oh, Brother!"

"Yes, Aunt Peg, I know."

"Peg, let me give you a cup of coffee," Uncle Ned said.

"I want my darling dollie mother back," she sobbed.

They sat her around the kitchen table.

Danny returned to his room. He sat on his bed, motionless, gazing about, dull-eyed.

Mother gone.

Papa had died.

The sorrows of death remained, remained in the hearts of the living. In the presence of death the living felt guilty.

He understood now why people did what he could not do, what he could never do—pray.

Now he would sit here and try to be like a stone. Nature and biology had asserted themselves in an unequal fight put up by an illiterate old peasant woman. Nature had won. Her heart had just worn out. A worn-out heart had stopped beating. In the night, in silence and darkness, alone in her little room, she had lain, and slowly, slowly a feeble heart had grown more feeble, more feeble, like a watch gradually stopping, tick tick, tick tick more slowly, and then, silently as in a dream, silently, alone, without agony, without a cry, a feeble heart had ceased to beat.

Oh, Mother, oh, Papa, oh, we ungrateful living! This life which he had been so spendthrift of, how precious it was.

He heard his uncles trying to calm Aunt Margaret.

It was unmanly to cry.

Tears came to his eyes.

He lay on the bed and sobbed.

Mother!

Mother!

Mother!

SECTION FIVE

1927

XXIX

"*Say, who the hell is that kid with the goggles?*" *asked Joe Willis, star reporter on* The Questioner.

"*Oh, that's O'Neill; he's the campus man out at the University,*" *said Wallace, the rewrite man.*

"*What is he, a student of journalism?*"

"*He's an intellectual.*"

"*Yeh, I always see him struttin' in here as if he owned the paper. And he's always carrying a book. What the hell kind of a newspaperman runs around with a book under his arm?*"

Willis watched Danny get up from a typewriter and bring some copy to Judson.

"*I don't like the way he walks around here. Why, he acts like he's a newspaperman. Is that the best we're getting these days?*"

"*Hell, he's just got a pissy-assed job on space rates, sniffing co-eds to get their pictures, that's all,*" *Wallace said.*

"*You wouldn't think it to watch him.*"

Danny passed them, nodding casually to Wallace.

"*Hey, what's your name?*"

"*O'Neill. What's yours?*"

"*Oh, I'm just Joe.*"

Danny lit a cigarette.

"*Say, you like newspaper work?*"

"*Oh, it's all right.*"

"*It's kind of boring, not intellectual enough, huh, O'Neill?*" *Joe asked.*

"*That's a relative question. Different people have different capacities to be bored. Well, I'm glad I met you, Joe.*"

Danny went off and left the office. He knew that it was Willis, the star reporter, with whom he had talked. What the hell, the days were gone when he would act like an acolyte, or with respect for a man's mere position or his prominence in this world. He knew now where he could learn, from whom, and what he wanted to learn.

He rode down in the elevator and walked along West Madison Street. It was sunny. He'd go see Georgia if she hadn't left town. Well, he'd stroll around and look at the crowds.

Chapter Twenty-nine

Al O'Flaherty finished packing his grip.

"You ought to like California," Ned said.

"It's the only part of the country I've never seen."

"Are you taking the Chief?"

"This piker I work for is too damned cheap to let me take an extra-fare train."

"Don't let him bull you."

"Al, here's your handkerchiefs; I ironed them for you," Margaret said, coming into the bed room.

"Thanks, thanks, Peg. You're wonderful, Peg," Al said, putting the handkerchiefs into the suitcase.

"I'll take care of Ned and Dan while you're gone."

"Yes, Al, everything will be fine here. Don't worry."

Al sighed.

The bell rang. Danny went to the door. It was his mother. She wore mourning. He kissed her.

"I came to say good-by to Al."

"Thanks, Lizz, thanks."

"How are you, Lizz?" Ned asked.

"Oh, I don't know. My legs are bothering me. I don't feel well."

"You have to take care of yourself, Lizz," Ned said.

"Well, Lizz, old girl, you got to keep a stiff upper lip," Al said.

Danny stood in the doorway. He'd noticed that since Mother's death last month there had been a new gentleness in all of them. Mama and Aunt Margaret had been drawn more closely together. They went to church and prayed almost every day. Uncle Ned and Uncle Al were kinder to Mama, and they no longer criticized her. Aunt Margaret was solicitous of all of them. Was the change permanent?

"Well, I have to go," Al said.

He shook hands with Ned, and kissed Lizz and Margaret good-by. They both cried.

"The house is so empty," Aunt Margaret said.

Uncle Al almost broke down. He patted his sisters, kissed them a second time.

He closed his grip and strapped it. Danny picked up the suitcase and lugged it downstairs.

Walking to the Fifty-eighth Street elevated station, he kept changing it from side to side.

Uncle Al used to take taxis to the train.

"Be good to your aunt, Dan."

"Yes, I will."

He wouldn't tell Uncle Al. It was too difficult. He would write and say that he had gone away.

He shook hands with Uncle Al by the station door.

He walked slowly back on Fifty-eighth Street. This might be the last time he would ever walk on this street. This afternoon he was leaving with Ed Lanson to bum to New York. He didn't trust Ed any more, and he would rather go alone. But he had let Ed talk him into it. Ed had some experience of the road, and he had none. But he knew that just as he was breaking with everything else in his life, so would he break with Ed. Their paths would be different ones. This was his last step to freedom. Now he was going, and he would fulfill himself. This was his great adventure. He was confident. He felt himself tempered. Why and how he had become tempered he did not know. But he knew himself. He would not fail.

He looked at the stones, the buildings. These stones belonged to something he had escaped. These stones were the physical aspects of a world in which another Danny O'Neill had lived.

His heart was heavy. He had finally taken off a way of life, a world in itself, as if it were a worn-out suit of clothes. He was making a last break with his past. Nothing remained with him of that past now but scars and wounds, agonies, frustrations, lacerations, sufferings, death. These he would always carry with him, just as he would his own weaknesses and his own follies. But his anger had now cooled to irony; his hatred was not against people, but against a world which destroyed people. And in that world the last compromise had been eradicated. He remembered the night when he had cursed a non-existent God on his way home from the gas station. He recalled the morning last January when he had stood in the center of the campus and vowed that no power on earth would stop him. Then he had been without his weapons. Now he had his weapons. Now he was leaving and he was fully armed. With what weapons he had, he would break a world, or that world would break him. He was prepared for battle.

He turned into the alley that he had known since he was a boy. He pushed by the broken backyard gate, climbed the steps, and went into the kitchen. He looked in Mother's room. Her clothes hung in the closet. A picture of the boy Christ and of the bleeding Sacred Heart were on the wall. Over the bed was her crucifix and holy-water fount. Black rosary beads lay on the old dresser. She was gone. Her sorrows, the sorrows of his father, his people, the sorrows of the past lay on him. His people had not been fulfilled. He had not understood them all these years. He would do no penance now for these; he would do something surpassing penance. There was a loyalty to the dead, a loyalty beyond penance and regret. He would do battle so that others did not remain unfulfilled as he and his family had been. For what he had seen, for what he had been, for what he had learned of these agonies, these failures, these frustrations, these lacerations, there would never be forgiveness in his heart. Everything that created these was his enemy.

He went to the parlor and sat with his mother, Uncle Ned,

and Aunt Margaret, brooding over his plans. Yes, he was the first of his family who could go forth fully armed and ready to fight.

He listened to the summer wind in the trees across the street in Washington Park.

XXX

Heinie Mueller looked at the clerks seated at the telephone board.

"Hell, you punks are no good. Every year you get worse and worse," he said.

"What's the matter, Dutch, aren't the kids hittin' the ball?" asked Casey, Assistant Wagon Dispatcher, who worked with Gas House McGinty on the tractor board.

"They get dumber every year. Christ, I can remember the time when we had good kids on the board, kids like young O'Neill. Hell, he was a crackerjack clerk, and he knew what the score was. He didn't goof around like you punks. He went out and got himself an education. Now he's a newspaperman. Christ, why don't you kids make something out of yourselves," Mueller said.

"So Bones is a newspaperman? Well, I always knew that he'd amount to something," Casey said.

"Yeh, Heinie," Collins called down from the other end of the telephone board, "Bones O'Neill was one of the best kids I ever had."